"You mean to cut down this tree?"

He frowned. "Taking a few of the older trees gives more room for the young ones that get crowded out."

She looked up again. "You may have to move to a new house, Mr. Squirrel."

The animal continued to scold them. Mary grinned at Ash. "He doesn't like that idea. Perhaps you can convince him."

Talking to squirrels wasn't how Ash normally spent his time. "Are you getting tired?"

"Don't say we have to go back. Not yet." There was pleading, but also a hint of panic in her voice.

"We can go a little farther."

"*Wunderbar.* You are my hero." Her beaming smile made his heart catch. He closed his hands tightly around his suspenders to keep from reaching for her hand.

She wasn't what he expected. From her correspondences, he assumed they would get along well together, but this attraction was different. Confusing. How could she make him giddy with a simple smile?

After thirty-five years as a nurse, **Patricia Davids** hung up her stethoscope to become a full-time writer. She enjoys spending her free time visiting her grandchildren, doing some long-overdue yard work and traveling to research her story locations. She resides in Wichita, Kansas. Pat always enjoys hearing from her readers. You can visit her online at patriciadavids.com.

Carrie Lighte lives in Massachusetts next door to a Mennonite farming family, and she frequently spots deer, foxes, fisher cats, coyotes and turkeys in her backyard. Having enjoyed traveling to several Amish communities in the eastern United States, she looks forward to visiting settlements in the western states and in Canada. When she's not reading, writing or researching, Carrie likes to hike, kayak, bake and play word games.

USA TODAY Bestselling Author

PATRICIA DAVIDS

&

CARRIE LIGHTE

Her Amish Match

2 Uplifting Stories

Mistaken for His Amish Bride and
Their Pretend Courtship

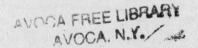

LOVE INSPIRED

INSPIRATIONAL ROMANCE

LOVE INSPIRED®

INSPIRATIONAL ROMANCE

Recycling programs
for this product may
not exist in your area.

ISBN-13: 978-1-335-47602-9

Her Amish Match

Copyright © 2023 by Harlequin Enterprises ULC

Mistaken for His Amish Bride
First published in 2022. This edition published in 2023.
Copyright © 2022 by Patricia MacDonald

Their Pretend Courtship
First published in 2022. This edition published in 2023.
Copyright © 2022 by Carrie Lighte

For questions and comments about the quality of this book, please contact us at CustomerService@Harlequin.com.

Harlequin Enterprises ULC
22 Adelaide St. West, 41st Floor
Toronto, Ontario M5H 4E3, Canada
www.LoveInspired.com

Printed in U.S.A.

CONTENTS

MISTAKEN FOR HIS AMISH BRIDE

Patricia Davids

This book is lovingly dedicated to my father, Clarence Stroda. Rest in peace, Dad.

Beloved, think it not strange concerning the fiery trial which is to try you, as though some strange thing happened unto you: But rejoice, inasmuch as ye are partakers of Christ's sufferings; that, when his glory shall be revealed, ye may be glad also with exceeding joy.
—*1 Peter* 4:12–13

Chapter One

Inside Philadelphia's noisy bus terminal, Mari Kemp clasped both hands to her chest, overjoyed at this unexpected turn of events in her desperate adventure. "You're going to Fort Craig, Maine, too? This is *wunderbar*. Have you been there before? What's it like? Do you have family there?"

She leaned forward eager for any information about the place and her traveling companion.

An *Englisch* friend had driven Mari from her home in the Amish community of Arthur, Illinois, to Champagne to catch a bus during the wee hours of the morning. Mary Kate Brenneman got on in Columbus, Ohio. Mari didn't realize they shared the same destination until they were changing buses during a layover in Philadelphia. Now, waiting for their boarding call in the busy terminal, Mari couldn't have been happier. Mary Kate wasn't exactly the talkative, friendly type, but that didn't deter Mari.

"Tell me everything you can about Fort Craig."

"I haven't been there," Mary Kate said. "I have only

exchanged letters with a young man who lives in the area."

"An Amish fellow? What's his name? What does he say it is like?"

"His name is Asher Fisher. He wrote about his family farm. Potatoes are the main crop in the area. There are many large farms."

Mari struggled to hide her disappointment. "I thought there would be lots of wild forests to explore."

Cornfields surrounded her home in Arthur. Nothing for miles and miles except corn and more corn. Potato fields would be different, at least.

"Mr. Fisher did not mention forests," Mary Kate said.

Mari waited for more information, but Mary Kate wasn't forthcoming. Mari forged ahead. "I'm going to visit my grandmother. Perhaps Mr. Fisher has mentioned Naomi Helmuth. They might belong to the same church district." Did her grandmother still practice the Amish faith?

"There is only one Amish congregation near Fort Craig at a place called New Covenant. I don't recall him mentioning the name Helmuth. I'm getting off the bus near the settlement. It's about three miles from Fort Craig."

It was too much to hope for information about the grandmother Mari had never met. She would simply stick to the plan. She hadn't written to say she was coming. A letter could be returned unopened, as they had all been in the past, but a long-lost granddaughter standing on Naomi Helmuth's doorstep couldn't be ignored. At least that was Mari's hope.

It had shocked her to learn that her father had been

estranged from his mother since before Mari was born.
Mari had assumed her grandparents had both passed
away. When her father died recently, she discovered
letters he had written to his mother over the years all
returned unopened. The last one had been addressed
to her in Fort Craig, Maine, a year ago. That was where
Mari intended to start her search. She hadn't heard of
New Covenant until now.

Her father had been a kind and loving man, raising
Mari alone after her mother died when she was barely
four. She had been incredibly close to her father. Only
God had been more important than family to Raymond
Kemp. Finding out his mother was alive, a fact he'd
never mentioned, was unfathomable to Mari. Something terrible must have happened for him to keep such
a secret from her. She wouldn't rest until she learned
what had driven a wedge between mother and son and
why he hid the truth. The hope of a joyful reception
with her grandmother was slim, but Naomi Helmuth
was the only family Mari had left in the world. She
was the one person who had answers. Mari wouldn't
leave Maine without them. Her father used to say she
was stubborn to a fault. She could be when something
was important.

"Mary Kate? Is that you?"

"Sarah?" Mary Kate's voice trembled with disbelief
as she surged to her feet.

"*Gott* be praised, it is you." A woman squealed with
delight and threw her arms around Mary Kate. She
wore a modest blue print dress with a small black prayer
covering pinned to her hair. Mari assumed she was Old
Order Mennonite, not Amish.

"Sarah, dear, dear, Sarah." The two women clung to

each other, overcome with emotion. After several long moments, Mary Kate recovered her composure and sat down beside Mari again, still holding on to Sarah's hand. "What are you doing here?"

Sarah sank to her knees in front of Mary Kate. "My husband and I are returning from his uncle's funeral. What are you doing here?"

Mary Kate gave a nervous laugh. "I'm on my way to Maine."

"Maine? Whatever for? Don't tell me Edmond is taking you on vacation."

Looking down, Mary Kate shook her head. "Edmond passed away two years ago."

"Dearest, cousin. I'm so sorry."

"*Gott* allowed it," Mary Kate whispered.

"We cannot comprehend His ways," Sarah said.

Mary Kate looked up. "We can't, but He has brought you and I together again. Oh, you don't know how glad I am to see you. It's been what? Ten years."

"Eleven. I can't believe I've run into you here, of all places. You must come meet my children. I have a son and two daughters. They've gone out to the van that is taking us back to Bird-in-Hand. I stopped to get something to drink for on the way. If I hadn't, I would have missed seeing you. *Gott ist goot.* Who is this with you?"

Mari held out her hand. "A complete stranger who happens to be going to Maine on the same bus. I'm Mari Kemp." She prayed her meeting with her grandmother was half as joy filled as the reunion of these two women.

"I'm pleased to meet you. My wits are scattered to the wind. Oh, Mary Kate, we should never have lost touch. I should have tried harder. We were closer than sisters once."

"It wasn't your fault. Edmond forbade it, and he was set in his ways."

"It's not right to speak ill of him, but he caused us both so much pain. I wasn't baptized into the Amish faith when I jumped the fence to marry. Edmond should have allowed us to remain friends. Tell me, why are you going to Maine of all places?"

"To get married."

"You have met someone new and fallen in love. Oh, Mary Kate, I'm so happy for you." Sarah hugged her again.

Mary Kate pulled away from her cousin. "Not exactly. Mr. Fisher and I haven't actually met."

Mari frowned. "I thought you said you were getting married."

"That is my plan. We've been corresponding."

"I don't understand," Sarah said. "You're planning to marry someone you haven't met?"

"I am."

Sarah looked stunned. "Why?"

Mary Kate gripped her hands together. "Things have become too difficult to remain at home. I couldn't stay there any longer. I took a chance and answered an ad placed by a bishop looking for Amish individuals willing to join a new community in northern Maine. He put me in touch with Asher Fisher, a very kind man. We, how do I say it, we connected in our letters. This is my only chance of getting my son back, Sarah."

"What on earth do you mean?"

"I'm ashamed to say after Ed died, I fell to pieces. I could barely function. Our son was only three. Ed's sister and her husband took him in until I could get back on my feet. I saw him often, but the business was in trouble, and it took so much of my time. Ed dreamed our son would run it one day. I thought I needed to save it, but the cost was too high. I was horribly unhappy. I missed Matthew, but I truly thought for a time that he was better off with Ed's sister. To make a long story short, I eventually sold the business. There was a terrible family row over it, and my in-laws refused to relinquish my son. They said the boy needed a father."

"How unfair to you and your child," Sarah declared. "Surely your bishop intervened?"

"He agreed with them. But he said if I married again that would change things."

Sarah clasped Mary Kate's hands. "You poor dear, but is marrying a stranger halfway across the country the answer? Isn't there a man in your community you could turn to?"

Mary Kate looked away. "That wasn't possible."

Mari's heart ached for the young mother. How awful to be kept from her child.

Sighing deeply, Mary Kate gazed at her cousin. "Now that I'm on my way, I'm not sure I'm doing the right thing. Even if it's for the right reason."

The PA system came on to announce Mari's bus was boarding now. She picked up her suitcase. "That's us."

Sarah gripped Mary Kate's hand. "I can't be parted from you so soon."

"We'll write. Give me your address."

"*Nee.* You must come and stay with me. You need time to consider this decision. Mr. Fisher can wait a week or two. I'll buy you another ticket to Maine when you're tired of my company. Please, dear cousin, say you'll stay with me for a little while. I'll help you sort this out."

Mary Kate's eyes filled with tears. "I wish I could, but Asher is meeting this bus."

Mari wanted to help. "I'm going to the same destination. I can deliver a message to Mr. Fisher in person and explain you've been delayed by family matters."

Hope filled Mary Kate's eyes, then quickly faded. "I can't do that to Asher. It wouldn't be fair to stand him up."

Sarah gripped Mary Kate's shoulders. "Mari will make him understand. *Gott* brought us together after all these years for a reason."

Mary Kate bit her lower lip. "I don't know what to do."

The final boarding call for their bus came over the PA system. Mari hooked her black purse over her shoulder and smiled at Mary Kate. "I find it is always best to do what your heart tells you."

Ash Fisher clenched and opened his icy fingers repeatedly as his three brothers inspected him from all angles, smoothed his vest across his chest and brushed imaginary lint from his shoulder. He wasn't exactly sure how he'd gotten himself into this situation.

That wasn't true. One impulsive moment and a stamp had sealed his fate.

Gabe, the oldest, took a step back. "You'll do."

Moses, the youngest Fisher brother, lifted Ash's black hat from the pegs by the door. "You're not nervous, are you?"

"Of course he is," Seth declared. "He's about to meet

the woman he intends to marry for the first time. Who wouldn't be nervous?"

Ash snatched his hat from his little brother's hands. "I'm not nervous. I'm on my way to meet a woman who has been kind enough to correspond with me for the past three months and has simply agreed to visit for a few weeks."

He jammed his hat on his head. "That's it. She's coming for a visit and nothing else."

If only that were the whole truth.

Those around him smothered their chuckles. He glanced up at his brim and turned his hat the right way around.

Gabe and Seth exchanged knowing looks as they leaned against each other. They were identical tall blond men who took after their father. Ash and Moses had inherited their mother's dark hair and eyes. Most people assumed Gabe and Seth were twins, but they were actually two parts of the Fisher triplets. Ash was the third.

"He's lying," Seth said.

Gabe nodded. "He's scared to death."

"Being the most sensible of this lot entitles me to a little more respect," Ash said between gritted teeth. His brothers laughed.

"You mean most stodgy," Gabe said. He was the jokester. Seth was the tenderhearted fellow. Moses was the baby brother who liked to mimic Gabe. That left Ash as the practical and meticulous one. Something his brothers seldom appreciated.

"He's the dull one." Seth shook his head sadly. He was normally sympathetic, but he enjoyed teasing Ash as much as the others did.

"Dull as ditchwater," Moses added, making a long face. The others laughed again.

Ash wasn't amused by his brothers' humor this a.m. He stared at the yawning front door standing open to a beautiful spring morning and took a deep breath. There was no going back now. He had to meet the bus.

Only, what if Mary Kate wasn't like he had imagined from her letters? What if they weren't compatible? She could hate Maine. Maybe she would turn around and head home as soon as he opened his mouth to speak and nothing witty came out. Talking to women made him nervous. They all seemed to want things he didn't understand. Would she be the same?

No. He chided himself for his lack of faith in her. Mary Kate was a practical woman. She would see his fine qualities, his head for business, his faith and his steady character. She wasn't expecting a love match. She believed mutual affection could grow over time. Her purpose for this trip was to get to know him.

That certainly had been his original plan. Nothing good ever came of impulsive actions. Why had he posted that last letter?

He glanced at his brothers. Because he was lonely, and he wanted what they had. This was a sensible way to accomplish that.

Seth and Gabe were married. Happily so. The evenings spent with his brothers and their new, loving wives made Ash feel like an outsider, separated from the brothers he had done everything with since the day they were born. He'd never felt that way before. He and his brothers had always been close. Now, inside his family's boisterous home, he was lonely.

At twenty-five, he was ready to start a family. He

ran a finger underneath his tight collar. It was expected. An Amish fellow wasn't complete without a wife and family. He believed that. What he hated was the idea of wasting time looking for the right woman. The local maidens Moses wanted to impress didn't interest Ash. They were young and immature. They had nothing in common with him. Trying to talk to them made his words stick in his throat.

It hadn't been that way when he was writing to Mary Kate. Pouring out his thoughts on paper was easy. She understood. She wasn't happy in her current situation. Neither was he. It seemed fated that they should get together.

He squared his shoulders. This was the right thing to do. He wouldn't let a few minor worries stop him from following through with his plan.

Gabe straightened. "We should stop gabbing, or Ash is going to be late meeting the bride. Are you sure you don't want us to come with you? We can help break the ice."

"I would rather have all my teeth yanked out by a team of horses." Ash forced himself to walk out the door to the waiting black buggy he had carefully washed from top to bottom. The ebony paint and brass fittings gleamed in the early May sunshine. He stopped in his tracks when he saw Frisky harnessed to it.

The lively black mare was a showy high stepper that belonged to Moses. His little brother had only recently purchased the horse for his courting buggy, planning to impress some of the newly arrived young women in the community. Frisky tossed her head and pranced in place, eager to be off.

Furious, Ash turned to Moses. The last thing he

needed was to look like a ridiculous teenager going courting. "I told you to hitch Dottie."

"She seemed a tad lame this morning." Moses hid his mouth with one hand, unable to keep a smirk off his face.

Seth pushed Ash toward the buggy door. "It will take too long to change horses. You don't want to be late. Frisky will make a fine impression. No fellow who drives a horse like her is dull."

Ash's need to be punctual warred with his desire to look respectable and dignified. Punctuality won. He didn't want to leave Mary Kate standing at the bus stop.

"Relax." Seth patted Ash's shoulder. "You'll love wedded bliss as much as we do."

"Will you men leave Ash alone and get in here? There's work to be done," Seth's wife yelled from the kitchen door.

"Coming, Pamela." Seth gave Ash a sheepish grin. "She's bossy, but she's a fine cook and a better kisser." He jogged toward the door.

Gabe stepped close to Ash. "You told Mary Kate that my Esther is deaf, right? I don't want their meeting to be awkward."

Ash shared a reassuring smile with his brother. "I did. She wrote she has been studying sign language. We'll make sure Esther feels included."

Gabe nodded. "I know you will. We look forward to meeting her. Now get going and hurry back. We have two new buggy orders to fill."

"Right." The Fisher family buggy business was expanding steadily, allowing all the sons to live and work on the farm, something that had been in doubt just a year ago.

Ash stepped into the buggy. It would take him twenty-five minutes to reach the bus stop on the other side of New Covenant. He didn't want to be late, but there was no point in being early. He picked up the lines and slapped them gently against the mare's rump. "Frisky, walk on."

Mary Kate had seemed nice in her letters, but there was no guarantee she'd like him in person. The closer he got to his destination, the more he wondered if courting a woman by mail was a sound plan.

When the village of New Covenant came into view, his palms started sweating. He rubbed them on his pant legs. This was ridiculous. He and Mary Kate had corresponded for months. He knew what to expect. She was the perfect woman for him. Sensible, practical, willing to work alongside him and his family. What more could he ask? Still, he kept Frisky to a walk, although she was eager to go faster.

On the other side of New Covenant, the county road sloped a curving half mile toward the main highway. Ash saw the flashing red lights and heard the wail of sirens as he approached the intersection. Police cars were blocking the road. An ambulance was pulling away. There must have been an accident. He stopped his buggy well back from the activity and looked for the bus. He didn't see it.

Should he go down and offer to help? He was debating when he caught sight of a State Police officer walking in his direction. The fellow stopped beside the buggy. "Morning. I'm Officer Melvin Peaks of the Maine State Police. You're one of the Amish folks that live in this area, right?"

"I am. What has happened?"

"There's been a hit-and-run accident. An Amish woman has been injured."

"Is it serious?" It had to be someone he knew. Their community had only two dozen families in total.

"I'm afraid she's badly hurt. We're trying to locate her next of kin."

"Who is she?"

The officer pushed his trooper's hat up with one finger. "She didn't have any identification on her, but she was clutching this."

Officer Peak held out an envelope. "It's addressed to Mary Kate Brenneman of Bounty, Ohio, from Asher Fisher. Do you know either of these people?"

"I'm Asher Fisher." His voice seemed to come from a long way off. He held out his hand for the envelope with his handwriting on it. "Mary Kate was coming to see me."

"Mary Kate, open your eyes. Can you hear me? Mary Kate? Squeeze my fingers if you can hear me."

She only wanted to sink back into the painless oblivion. It hurt too much to listen to the voice. Everything hurt. Even breathing.

"Open your eyes, Mary Kate." The insistent voice belonged to a woman.

Stop talking. Let me go back to sleep. Why do I hurt so much?

"I'm sorry, Mr. Fisher. Perhaps if you spoke to her, she might recognize your voice."

"She's never heard me speak." It was a man who answered. "It's been two days. How long before she wakes up?"

"It's hard to say with an injury like this. Sit with her

for a while and talk to her. Patients can sometimes hear even if they can't respond."

"What should I say?"

Nothing. Go away. A soft beeping sound penetrated the quiet she craved.

Something scraped across the floor. A chair maybe? She heard a heavy sigh.

"I'm sorry I was late, Mary Kate. The bus was early, but I could have been there sooner. I have no excuse. I wasn't there. You were hurt because of me. Please forgive me."

Thankfully, he fell silent. She sank toward the blessed darkness again.

"I'm not one for small talk. I'm sure I mentioned that in my letters. Your letters were nice. I looked forward to them. Nurse, I don't think she hears me."

"You're doing fine. Tell her about your family. She was coming to visit them, right?"

Why was that woman encouraging him? She just wanted silence and sleep.

"My parents are here waiting to meet you."

"Please go away," she croaked, not recognizing her own weak voice but feeling the strain of it.

"Nurse! She spoke."

A hand touched her forehead. "Open your eyes," the woman said again.

She forced her eyes open, but only her left one seemed to work. The light was too bright. She squeezed her eye shut and turned away from the brightness.

"Hello. Welcome back. How are you feeling?" the woman asked.

"Awful." Her throat was parched.

"I'm not surprised. You've been in an accident.

You're in the hospital. I'm Mandy Brown. I'm your nurse."

"You were hit by a car. I'm Asher Fisher. I'm the fellow you were coming to meet."

She cracked her eye open and tried to focus on his face. He was a young man in his mid-twenties. He had on a white shirt with suspenders over his brawny shoulders and dark pants. His brown hair was cut short, but it curled enough that it didn't look austere on him. Dark eyes filled with concern gazed at her. There was nothing familiar about him. "I don't recognize you."

"We've only written to each other. We haven't met in person."

"It's time for your pain medication," the nurse said. "Now that you're awake, I need you to tell me your name and date of birth."

"It's…" *What was her name? Why couldn't she think of it?*

She started to tremble. "I don't know. Why can't I remember my name? What's wrong with me?" She struggled to sit up, but a sharp pain in her chest made her fall back with a moan.

"Your name is Mary Kate Brenneman," Asher said gently. "You're from Bounty, Ohio."

She tried again to focus on his face. She had to believe him. "You know me, right?"

"Mr. Fisher, you should step out," the nurse insisted. "I'm going to get the doctor."

Fear sent her heart pounding faster. "*Nee*, don't go. You know who I am." She wanted to reach for him, but she couldn't move her right arm. Something weighed it down.

"I won't go. I'll stay right here." His voice was calm and reassuring.

Her panic receded. "My name is Mary?"

"Mary Kate Brenneman," he said again.

The nurse injected something into the IV in Mary's arm. "This will help with your pain, Mary Kate. I'm going to inform the doctor you're awake. I'll be right back."

Why didn't her name sound familiar? How could she forget her own name? "I'm Mary Kate Brenneman." If she said it enough, would it feel like it belonged to her? "I'm Mary."

"I've always known you as Mary Kate."

"Can I be plain Mary?" That sounded better somehow.

"All right. You were on your way to stay with my family in New Covenant, Maine when a pickup struck you."

"Maine? That's a long way from Ohio." How could she know that and not remember where she was from?

"It is a long way. You must have been glad to get off the bus."

She didn't remember riding a bus. His face came into focus. She searched it for some shred of familiarity. "You weren't there to meet me."

His expression brightened. "You remember?"

"I heard you say that."

"Oh. I'm sorry I wasn't there, Mary. I should have been."

The door opened and the nurse came back. "The doctor will be in soon. If you want Mr. Fisher to stay, I need your consent to share your medical information. I understand you can't sign this but if you give me your verbal okay that will be enough."

"I guess it's fine." She looked at Ash. He nodded encouragingly.

"Is there anyone we can contact for you? Family? Friends?" the nurse asked.

"I don't know." *Who were they?* She desperately wanted to see a familiar face.

"I'll be back with the doctor shortly." The nurse left the room.

"Would you like a drink of water?" Ash picked up a foam cup from the table beside her bed.

She nodded and took a sip. *"Danki."* She looked at Ash. "Is that right? That means thank you."

"Ja." Ash smiled. "You speak Deitsh—Pennsylvania Dutch the *Englisch* call it."

"I speak Deitsh because I'm Amish." Relief made her light-headed. Or maybe it was the pain medicine. "I'm Amish. I remember that."

"Sell ist goot." He squeezed her fingers.

"You said, 'That is good.' I understand the language but why can't I remember my name or where I'm from?"

"It will come back," he said soothingly.

"Are you sure?"

"If *Gott* wills it. I pray it happens soon."

"I can't seem to move my right arm."

"Because of the cast," Ash said. "Your arm is broken in two places. You have a cracked rib, too."

That explained the pain when she tried to sit up or breathe. Ash gently laid his hand over hers. "You should rest now."

Sleep pulled her toward the darkness. She clutched his hand. "I have so many questions."

"They will keep." His hand slipped from beneath hers.

She missed his touch and struggled to stay awake. "Why was I coming to see you?"

If he replied, she didn't hear.

The welcome darkness wasn't the same this time. Bits and pieces flashed and floated around her. Faces, places. Someone laughing. The sound of weeping. Letters tied together with a ribbon. She struggled to see the flashes more closely, but they drifted away, leaving her alone and frightened in the dark.

Chapter Two

Ash stepped out of Mary Kate's room with a weary sigh. The nurse at the desk beckoned him over. "Dr. Pierre will come speak to you in the waiting room."

He nodded and walked down the hospital corridor to the room at the end of the hall. His parents sat together in one corner.

"How is she?" his mother asked, laying aside her knitting. Ash was glad she was with him. Talitha Fisher had a kind face and a kinder heart.

"She's awake." Should he tell them everything?

"Praise *Gott* for his mercy," Ash's father, Ezekiel, said.

Ash raked a hand through his hair. It was best to share the bad news. "She was awake for a few minutes, but she doesn't know her own name, and she has no memory of her accident or coming to Maine."

"It's called traumatic amnesia." A tall man with a grim expression, graying hair and wearing a white coat stood in the doorway. "It is likely caused by her head injury. I'm Dr. Kevin Pierre."

"She's going to get better, isn't she?" Ash held his breath.

The doctor's grim expression didn't change. "Most episodes of amnesia are temporary, although she might never recall the accident. Her memory may come back the next time she wakes up. Or it may take a few days. She suffered a significant blow to the head."

"What can we do?" Ash's mother asked.

"Have patience. Don't push her to remember. Having familiar sights, sounds and smells may trigger her recall. Let's wait to see how she is when she wakes up again. If you have questions, the staff knows how to contact me. She should do fine."

"*Gott* was watching over her," Ash's mother said. She picked up her knitting. "May I stay with her?"

"Of course, but only two visitors at a time." The doctor left the room.

Ash stopped his mother before she left the waiting room. "She asked to be called Mary, not Mary Kate."

His mother frowned. "Why?"

"I don't know, but if it makes her more comfortable, I don't see the harm."

As Ash's mother went to sit with Mary, Ash took a seat beside his father. "Now what?"

"I'll go home and make sure your brothers are managing."

Ash rubbed his palms on his pant legs. "I should be there, too."

His father shook his head. "*Nee*, you're needed here. I'm sure Mary Kate, Mary, will have questions for you when she wakes. You are the best one to explain her situation."

Ash blew out a breath and leaned back. How could he tell a woman who didn't remember him that she had come a thousand miles expecting to marry him?

* * *

Mary woke to the familiar soft beeping again and realized it was beating in time to the throbbing in her head. Another sound caught her attention. It was a subdued clicking noise. She tried to turn to look for it, but the move made her headache worse. She shifted her body trying to find a more comfortable spot, but there didn't seem to be one.

The clicking stopped. "Are you awake at last?" a woman asked in Deitsh.

"I guess I am." Sleep was so much better than this discomfort, but it was getting harder to recapture. She noticed the blue sky beyond a window at the foot of her bed. It was daytime but what day? What time was it?

A plump middle-aged Amish woman stepped into Mary's view. She wore a maroon dress with a matching apron and a white *kapp*. She smiled, making laugh lines crinkle at the corners of her dark brown eyes. *"Guder mariye."*

"Is it morning? I can't see well. Do I know you?"

"You do not. I'm Talitha Fisher. You met my *sohn* yesterday. Asher. Do you remember?"

He was the one who knew her. His calm voice had made her first terrifying day bearable. Each time she had opened her eyes, he had been there. "He's been exceedingly kind."

"Do you recall anything else?"

"I was in an accident. I'm in a hospital in Maine. My name is Mary Kate Brenneman. I'm Mary," she said softly. It seemed familiar but still not quite right.

"Wunderbar. What do you remember from before?"

Mary hated looking into the blankness where her life should have been. The pounding in her temples sped up as the emptiness of her past pressed in. The void was too big to be faced alone. She needed an anchor, or it would swallow her. Better to focus on something else. Anything. "Where is your son?"

"He stepped out for a minute."

It was getting hard to breathe. Her chest hurt. Her head pounded. "Ash said he would stay with me. I need to see him."

"All right. I'll get him. He's in the waiting room."

"Please hurry."

Why didn't she know who she was? Who were her parents? What was her mother's name? Who could forget her own mother? Was she married? Did she have children? What did she do in Ohio? What had the bus trip been like to get here? Why had she come? There was nothing. No glimmer of an answer, only frightening emptiness.

She needed to get out of this bed. Swinging her legs over the side, she pushed herself upright. It hurt so much to breathe. She took quick shallow breaths. The room spun. She closed her eyes and felt herself falling.

"Whoa. What do you think you're doing?" Strong hands gripped her shoulders and held her close.

Ash. He was the anchor she needed. She leaned her forehead against his chest until the spinning stopped. She drew a deep breath. His shirt smelled of sun-dried linen and shaving soap.

She saw herself taking a blue work shirt off the clothesline and holding it to her face to breathe in the scent. Was it a memory?

It vanished before she could be sure.

"Take it easy," Ash said. "Let me help you lie back." He shifted one arm around her, cradling her head against his shoulder. He slipped his other arm beneath her legs and easily moved her back into bed. She looked up to see his dark eyes brimming with concern. He was wearing a blue shirt today. Her breathing slowed. The pain lessened. "Thank you for staying."

"I said I would." There was an awkward pause as he looked everywhere but at her and rubbed his hands on his pant legs. Finally, he cleared his throat. "Are you okay?"

Her headache had eased. "I'm better now."

"Can I—do something? Can I—get you anything?" He sounded nervous.

"A drink of water."

"Sure." He stepped away from her line of sight. She found she could open her right eye a slit and saw him pouring water from a gray plastic pitcher into a white foam cup. He came back to her bedside and held the straw to her dry, chapped lips. The cold moisture felt wonderful in her mouth and helped soothe her scratchy throat.

"Danki."

He set the cup aside. "Getting up by yourself was not a good idea."

"I won't try it again. I was afraid I might forget you."

A wry smile tipped up the corner of his mouth. "I'm happy you didn't. Have you remembered anything else?"

"Nothing. It's so awful. My life is just gone like it's never been."

The door opened and Dr. Pierre came in, followed by a nurse holding a chart. "Good day, Miss Brenneman. How are you feeling?"

"Worried. My memory is still a blank."

"Don't attempt to force it. It will return on its own."

"You're sure?"

"Very likely. How is your pain level?" He checked her eyes with a small light, listened to her chest and pressed on her tummy. Finally, he straightened. "Nurse, I want her to get up in a chair later." With that, he left the room. The nurse followed him.

Mary looked at Ash. "His bedside manner leaves a lot to be desired. Tell me about myself. How do you know me? Who are my parents? Do I have siblings? Tell me anything. How old am I?"

"All right. Slow down. I know you because we've exchanged letters for several months."

"Like pen pals?"

"*Ja*, like that."

"So we're friends."

"I hope we are. You're twenty-nine. Your parents are deceased. You wrote they died when you were quite young."

"What were their names?"

"Gladys and Peter Hartzler I believe you said in one letter."

"Gladys and Peter." The names meant nothing. "Tell me something else."

"You don't have siblings. You were married. I'm sorry to tell you that your husband died two years ago."

She recoiled. It didn't feel like she had been married, but what did being a wife feel like? "So I'm a widow. What was his name?"

"Edmond Brenneman."

She gripped the blanket and twisted her hand tight in the fold. "I fell in love with Edmond Brenneman and married him." Had she called him Ed or Eddy? How could she forget the man she wed?

"Do I have children?" She braced herself for the answer.

Ash shook his head.

She let out the breath she was holding. That was a good thing. She hadn't forgotten her babies. But she must have loved Edmond. To know she'd forgotten him was almost as painful as forgetting her own life.

Ash cleared his throat. "Do you want to ask me anything else?"

His answers only brought more questions and a deeper sense of loss. "Not right now."

"Okay, I'll be out in the waiting room."

"What? *Nee.* Don't leave. I mean, please stay for a while." She gripped his hand where it rested on the bed rail. He was the only person in the world she had a connection to.

"All right, I'll stay if that's what you want."

He slipped his hand from beneath hers, pulled a chair up to the side of the bed and sat down. Shifting a bit, he rubbed both hands on his pant legs and cleared his throat again.

She wanted to put him at ease. "Tell me something about you."

"Me? There's not much to tell. I'm a dull fellow."

"You're the most exciting man I've met," she quipped.

His eyebrows shot up. "What?"

"I don't know any other men besides you and Dr. Pierre. He's a dull one. He never smiles."

Ash relaxed and grinned. "I'll have to tell my brothers you think I'm exciting and you didn't even see the high-stepping mare I drove to pick you up."

"You have brothers?"

"Three. Gabriel, Seth and Moses. Gabe, Seth and I are triplets. Moses was the Lord's afterthought."

"I don't imagine he likes to hear that. Do you have sisters?"

"Just in-laws. Gabe and Seth married two sisters. Seth's wife is Pamela. Gabe's wife is Esther. She's deaf, and you had planned to learn some sign language before you came. Do you remember any of it?"

"I don't know."

He laid his hand on his chest, then made an *x* with his fingers before making more gestures. "Do you know what I said?"

"None of it looks familiar. What did you say?"

He repeated the signs slowly. "My—name—is—Ash."

"Ash is your nickname?"

"Just about everyone calls me that. Except for Mamm."

"Does she use your middle name when she's upset with you?"

He chuckled. "First middle and last."

"I wish I could remember my mother doing the same. Isn't it strange that I can remember mothers do that, but I can't recall my *mamm* saying it?"

"The doctor said you shouldn't try too hard to remember. It will come back on its own."

"When? I feel like I'm leaning over a huge dark well. I know something is down there, but I can't see it."

"It will happen in *Gott's* time. Until then you have to concentrate on getting better."

"Why did I come here?"

Ash knew she would ask him that. He had already decided on a simplified version of the truth. He thought it best not to mention their possible marriage. It was out of the question until she recovered her memory. The last thing he wanted was for her to feel uncomfortable around him. He would stick with the pen-pal angle because it was true.

"Our community in New Covenant is young. Families only started settling here about four years ago. Our bishop has been seeking more Amish to join us. He was in contact with your bishop who suggested several people who might consider settling here. My family offered to host them, but you were the only one who choose to come. You and I exchanged a few letters so you could gauge what to expect."

Her eyes drifted closed for a moment, then snapped open. "Why did I want to settle in Maine?"

"You wrote that you were looking for opportunities that weren't available in your area. Us not getting many tourists up here appealed to you, too."

"I don't mind the *Englisch*. At least I don't think I mind them."

"We have plenty of *Englisch* neighbors who have welcomed us, but we see few tourists. At least until the Potato Blossom Festival each year."

"You're going to have to explain that." She closed her eyes as her voice grew softer.

"Aroostook County is famous for potatoes. Lots and lots of potatoes grow here."

"I'm not sure if I have forgotten that or if I never knew it." She yawned, then shifted in bed and winced.

He stood up. "You need to get some rest. Have the nurse come get me when you're awake again."

"Don't go. I'm not really sleepy."

"That's why your eyes won't stay open. No arguing, Mary Kate Brenneman," he stated firmly.

She gave him a little half smile. "First, middle and last. I must be in trouble."

"Only if you don't get some rest."

"All right." She sighed deeply and let her head drop back on the pillow.

He headed for the door.

"Ash?"

He stopped and turned around.

"What is your middle name?"

"Ethan."

She closed her eyes again. "Asher Ethan Fisher. I like that. I hope I never have to use all three. Thank you for being my friend."

He smiled. "Sleep well, Mary."

After stepping out, he softly closed the door behind him. He saw Dr. Pierre standing at the nursing station counter and walked toward him. *"Doktah."*

The doctor turned around, looking annoyed at the interruption. "Yes, Mr. Fisher?"

"How long will Mary need to be here?"

"Overall, she's making good progress. Barring any complications, I don't see why she can't convalesce at home. The plan is to discharge her late tomorrow or the day after."

"That soon? What about her memory?"

"As I said, it may take a few days or even a few weeks."

"But it will come back. You're sure?"

"There have been cases where memory loss is permanent, but it's exceedingly rare."

Ash recoiled. "You didn't mention that before."

The doctor's scowl deepened. "I didn't see the point in worrying the patient with a worst-case scenario that is highly unlikely. If there's nothing else, I have rounds to finish." He walked away and went into a nearby room.

Mary was right. Dr. Pierre had a poor bedside manner. Ash continued to the waiting area where his mother was sitting in the corner chair. An *Englisch* gentleman sat watching the television at the other end of the room.

Ash's mother laid her knitting aside. "How is she?"

"Resting now."

"She's very attached to you."

"I think it could be because we've been writing to each other even if she doesn't remember."

"Maybe."

"The doctor said they could discharge her tomorrow or the next day. I imagine she'll want to go home."

"She won't be up to a trip back to Ohio on a bus for weeks. Certainly not alone."

"I thought of that. I know Bishop Schultz has a phone number for her bishop. He can have her family make whatever arrangements work best for them."

"She is welcome to stay with us for as long as she needs. Make sure they know that."

"I will." He pushed out of his chair. "Bishop Schultz should be at his business by now. I'll call him there."

A nurse came into the waiting area. "Mr. Fisher, Miss Brenneman is asking for you."

"I thought she was asleep."

"The police are here to question her. She wants you to be present."

Ash's mother picked up her knitting. "Go on. She

needs you. This must be so frightening for her. I'll call the bishop."

"All right." Ash followed the nurse down the hall.

In Mary's room, he found a uniformed police officer standing on either side of her bed. One of them was a woman. The other one was Officer Melvin Peaks Ash had spoken to at the accident. Mary's face was ashen. He stepped closer in concern. "What is it?"

"They want to know if I deliberately stepped into the path of a pickup truck."

He glanced between the two officers in shock. "Why would you ask her such a thing?"

"We found the vehicle," Officer Peaks said. "The driver and his passenger both say Miss Brenneman walked out in front of them. They claim it looked as if she did it deliberately. A suicide attempt."

"What you're suggesting is forbidden." Ash placed his hand on Mary's shoulder. "She did no such thing."

"But you didn't see the accident, did you?" the female officer asked, making notes.

Ash shook his head. "*Nee*. Mary was already in the ambulance when I arrived. I thought there was a witness."

"When we get conflicting stories, we have to check them out. You don't recall anything from the accident, Miss Brenneman?" Officer Peak asked.

"Nothing before I woke up here."

"Nothing at all? Not how you were feeling? Were you worried or distracted by something?" he prompted.

"I don't remember."

The woman jotted down another note. "We've arrested the driver. He failed to stop and report the accident or call for help. He's facing serious charges even if he wasn't drinking or texting."

Mary shook her head. "It doesn't matter. *Gott* allowed this. I don't want anyone punished. I forgive the driver. Please tell him that."

Her soft-spoken words were what Ash expected. For the Amish, forgiveness always came first.

"It won't be up to you," Officer Peak said.

The female officer finally smiled. "We're sorry this happened. We have your suitcase. It sustained some damage. We'll return the contents as soon as our forensic team has finished with it. We didn't find a purse. Did you have one?"

"I don't know."

Officer Peak looked at Ash. "Would it be unusual for an Amish woman to travel without a purse or wallet?"

Ash nodded. "It would."

"We didn't find one at the scene." The woman closed her notebook.

"It would be a black bag," Mary said.

Ash squeezed her shoulder. "You remember?"

"I don't, but that is what I would buy. I would choose a black purse."

"We'll keep looking for it. Maybe someone picked it up after the accident and hasn't turned it in yet."

The woman handed Mary a business card. "You can reach us at this number if you recall anything at all. Thank you both for your help."

After the police officers left, Mary massaged her throbbing forehead and then gazed at Ash. She had to ask, but she dreaded hearing the answer.

What could have driven her to such desperation? "Do you think there is any truth to the driver's claim?"

"None," Ash stated so firmly that Mary had to believe him.

"Why would they say something like that?" What had they seen that made them think she wanted to end her life?

"Only God can see into the hearts of men. Only He can know the answer." Ash cupped her chin and turned her face toward him. "The woman I have been writing to is much too practical and grounded in her faith to consider such a step."

Ash had a way of banishing her fears. She relaxed. "I wish I could meet her."

He gently tapped her forehead with one finger. "She is right in there and she will come out when you least expect her. Remember what the doctor said?"

"I shouldn't try to force myself to remember. It's hard advice to follow." All she could think about was recalling some shred of her former life.

"And you are not great at following advice."

Puzzled, she tipped her head. "What makes you say that?"

"Your in-laws cautioned you not to undertake such an expensive trip."

A new excitement gripped her. "Of course I have in-laws. I was married. What are their names?"

"Edith and Albert Brenneman."

Her excitement faded. The names meant nothing to her. She concentrated on recalling her mother-in-law's face. They had to have been united in their grief. They would have consoled each other. No image came with the name Edith. "Are we close?"

Ash stepped back and looked at his feet. "I got the impression from your letters that there was some friction between you."

Mary frowned. "What kind of friction?"

"You never said."

No matter what had passed between them they were her family. Family was second only to God in importance. "I appreciate you telling me. I'll do my best to mend our relationship as soon as I can."

"I could be wrong."

"I hope so, but if I wrote to you that things weren't *goot* between us, it must be serious. That's not something I would mention casually. I mean, I don't think I would. Do you believe that's why I wanted to come here?"

"Don't fret about it, Mary."

"You're right. I can't mend what's wrong until I remember it, can I?"

"Exactly. Now, you were going to take a nap before the officers arrived. I suggest you finish it."

"I'm tired, but I'm not sleepy. Tell me more about yourself. What do you do? I'm going to take a wild guess and say you raise potatoes."

He chuckled. "A few."

He had a wonderful smile. His dark eyes sparkled when he was amused. She could see the resemblance between him and his mother.

"My family farms, but we are also wheelwrights and buggy makers. My brother Gabriel runs a leather and harness shop. We all help with it, too, especially the women. Gabe's wife is a talented artist. She sells some of her wildflower paintings through a gallery here in Presque Isle."

Mary frowned. "I thought I was in New Covenant."

"That's the name of our settlement. It is much too small to have a hospital or even a post office. Presque Isle is about thirty minutes away by car."

"So your home isn't nearby? Where have you been staying?"

"In the waiting room."

"Where have you been sleeping?"

"In the waiting room."

That surprised her. "Are there beds?"

"There's a bench that isn't too bad."

He'd been sleeping on a bench because she had insisted that he stay with her. She studied his face and noticed for the first time the signs of fatigue around his eyes. "I'm so sorry, Ash."

"For what?"

"For keeping you away from your home and family. Don't tell me your mother has been sleeping here, too?"

"We have an *Englisch* neighbor who has been driving her back and forth."

At least she hadn't disrupted his family completely. "That's how you got a clean shirt. You don't have to stay here anymore, Ash. I'll be fine now. Go home." She swallowed against the tightness that gripped her throat. Her head began pounding as her heart raced. How could she bear this alone?

"Hey, I'm not going anywhere."

"You have a farm and a business to run. You need your sleep as much as I do. Go home. Take a break." She clenched her fingers into a fist.

"Mary, are you sure?"

"I am." He would never know how difficult it was to say those two words.

There was a knock at the door, and his mother looked in. "Asher, I need to speak with you."

"Mary wants us to go home."

She gave Mary an understanding smile. "Then we must do what she asks. She is a grown woman, not a child that needs looking after."

Mary could see his indecision. Finally, he nodded. "You're right. Did you speak with the bishop?"

Talitha's gaze slide away from Mary. "I did. We should let this young woman rest. I'll tell you what he said on our way home."

Mother and son exchanged a speaking glance. He frowned but turned to Mary with a comforting smile. "I'll see you soon. The hospital has the phone number of our neighbor, Lily Arnett. She will bring us any message and drive me here if I'm needed. Don't worry about bothering us. It's no bother."

"*Danki*, both of you, for all you have done." Her voice started shaking. She stopped talking and turned away. If only they would leave before she began crying. The door closed with a soft click, and she bit down on her bottom lip. There was no reason to be so upset. She had been alone before.

It wasn't a memory. It was a feeling deep in her gut.

Chapter Three

Ash followed his mother to the waiting room. It was empty. He could see she was upset. "What did Bishop Schultz have to say?"

Her frown deepened. She pressed a hand to her chest. "He contacted Mary's bishop the day after her accident."

"I should've known he would." Bishop Schultz would help however he could without being asked. He was a fine man.

"He heard from her family today." Tears welled up in his mother's eyes.

Ash stepped closer. "Mamm, what's wrong?"

"They don't want her back. They're even refusing to help with her medical bills."

He rocked back on his heels. It went against everything the Amish believed. Caring for one another was of paramount importance.

"You can't be serious. Why would they do that?"

"Bishop Schultz is every bit as stunned as we are. She has no other family."

He paced across the room. "I know. She said as much in her letters."

"The bishop spoke to her father-in-law. Asher, her church has shunned her."

He sank onto a chair. "Shunned? For what reason?"

His mother shook her head. "Bishop Schultz doesn't know. Mary Kate's father-in-law wouldn't say anything else."

"Do they understand her condition?"

"Bishop Schultz explained to him about her memory. He said the man was not interested in learning more. He said he would pray for her recovery and hung up. I've never heard of anything like this. It goes against everything our faith stands for to abandon one in such dire need, but the shunning must be the reason."

Ash raked a hand through his hair. "She can hardly repent her transgression if she can't remember what it is. What does the bishop think we should do?"

"He said he must pray about it. To be shunned requires every baptized member of the congregation to agree to it. It is a serious thing. He can't ignore it. He may decide to continue it."

Ash glanced back at Mary Kate's door. "She doesn't need to hear this."

"I agree. We can't tell the poor child that her family won't help her, they don't want her to return and her church has shunned her, but we don't know why. That would be cruel. We must have faith that her memory will return, and she can explain. Was there any hint of this in her letters?"

"She mentioned that there was some friction between herself and her in-laws but nothing else." He couldn't imagine what she had done that would warrant such a drastic step by her church.

"I called Lily Arnett after I spoke to the bishop. She should be here soon to take us home."

"You go ahead. I'm staying."

"Are you sure?"

"I am. She doesn't have anyone." Ash had spent his life surrounded by a loving family. He couldn't imagine facing such a devastating situation alone.

His mother's expression grew concerned. "I will remind you, *sohn*, that you are baptized, and Mary Kate is shunned."

"I can still be a helpful friend."

"That is true. We must pray the bishop decides we can accept her and allow her to join our church. But." She pressed her lips into a tight line.

"But what?"

"Asher, I'm concerned that she didn't share this with you."

"We don't know why. Maybe she intended to tell me in person. Perhaps they have shunned her because she left her own church to join another. A few churches still forbid the practice. Especially if the new group is less conservative."

His mother nodded. "There are too many unknowns in Mary's case. The answers are locked inside her poor, damaged mind."

"She'll get better," he said firmly. "I know she will. In the meantime, I'm responsible for her. She was coming to meet me. If I hadn't dragged my heels leaving home that morning I would have been there when she got off the bus."

"Asher, *Gott* allowed this. We can't know His plan for Mary, but you can't blame yourself."

He could, and he did. "I still feel I must look after her until she can look after herself."

His mother cupped his cheek with her hand. "You are a *goot* boy."

"I had *goot* teachers. I'll be home as soon as I can. Tell those lazy *brudders* of mine to pick up my slack so father doesn't have to do it all."

"They already have. Your *daed* says they are ahead of schedule on the two buggy orders we got last week."

"I hope they're watching the cost of materials. It won't help to rush the work if we are paying more to get it done. Are they keeping good records?" He oversaw the financial side of the family's buggy-building and wheelwright business. His father and brothers were skilled craftsmen, but they sometimes ignored the paperwork that had to be done. He kept the parts inventory stocked, the bills paid and the invoices current. He hated not being there, but he couldn't ignore his responsibility to Mary.

"I'm sure they are. I told Lily I would meet her out front. Are you sure you won't come home for a while?"

"My place is here for now."

"All right. Send word if you need anything or if you change your mind."

After his mother left, Ash told the nurse taking care of Mary where he would be if she needed him, then he went downstairs to find the financial office. Mary would need help to cover the cost of her medical care without a church to take up a collection for her. He had a savings account separate from the business. His father had insisted on that for all his sons. Ash knew he couldn't cover all of Mary's bills, but it would be a start.

He found the woman in the business office familiar with Amish ways and happy to help set up a billing plan for him. She even offered to contact a local charity that provided assistance to the uninsured. He agreed to the help on Mary's behalf. According to her letters, Mary had money of her own, but he had no way of accessing it for her.

He stopped in at the hospital cafeteria next for a quick lunch. He missed his own bed, but he missed his mother's cooking more. The tuna casserole he chose was filling but short on flavor.

Upon his return to the nurses' station, he found Mary's nurse again. "I'm back. I'll be in the waiting room now if she needs me."

"Miss Brenneman became upset after you left. We think she had a panic attack. Dr. Pierre ordered a sedative."

"Is she okay?"

"Yes. She's fine now. She's sleeping. You can go in and sit with her if you like."

"*Danki.* I mean thank you."

"You're welcome."

He pushed open the door slowly and peeked in. The blinds had been drawn. Mary's eyes were closed. He slipped in and sat down beside her.

She looked frail in the dim light and young for her age. He had pictured her as a larger woman from her letters. She'd written about the farm work she did for her in-laws, planting corn and running the harvester alone. The woman in the bed didn't look like she could manage a draft horse team by herself. She was slender and dainty.

The swelling on her face had gone down a little. She was still black-and-blue on her right side, but with her face half turned away he saw how pretty she was for the first time. Her dark brows arched delicately above a small turned-up nose. Her eyelashes rested on her pale cheeks in soft, thick spikes. Her long dark braid flanked the curve of her jaw and the line of her slender neck as it lay over her shoulder and reached past her waist on top of the stark white sheets. He would have to ask what had happened to her *kapp*. She would want her prayer covering when she could get out of bed.

She wore a faint frown as if she was still in pain, even in her sleep. He wanted to smooth the lines away but was afraid his touch might disturb her. He crossed his arms and sat back, content to watch over her as she slept.

The pounding pain in Mary's head came back before she even opened her eyes. She moaned softly, afraid to move and make it worse.

"Shall I get the nurse for you?"

She opened her eyes. Ash sat beside her. A surge of happiness pushed the pain aside. "I thought you had gone home."

"I changed my mind."

"I'm glad."

That was an understatement. She'd never been so glad to see anyone in her life. At least that she could remember. A woman in blue scrubs came in with a tray of food and set it on the bedside table. When she left, Mary watched Ash lift the warming lid and set it aside. "Do you need to sit up higher?"

"I think so." She braced herself for the pain she knew the change in position would elicit as he pushed the button on the bed controller. She clamped her lips together determined not to complain.

He raised the back of her bed slowly. "Is that high enough?"

She nodded and took a shallow breath. It wasn't as bad as she thought it would be. He positioned the table over her lap.

"What made you change your mind?" she asked.

"I was afraid I would miss the hospital cafeteria food."

She stared at the pale chicken over rice and limp green beans. "You're welcome to mine."

"Tempting. But you are the one who needs to get her strength back. Do you take anything in your coffee?"

"Just black." She picked up her fork. "What is this for?"

His perplexed expression was priceless. "Ah, it's called a fork. You eat your food with it."

She started laughing. "I got you with that one."

It took him a second to realize she was teasing him. He grinned and nodded. "You sure did."

Mary took a bite of the green beans. They were as mushy as they looked and bland. She pushed her tray away. "Is your mother still here, too?"

He shook his head. "She went home."

"I'm glad she has some sense. I won't get any rest thinking about you sleeping on a bench in the waiting room tonight." She couldn't get over how sweet he was to someone he had only just met. "Why are you doing this?"

He looked surprised. "You were coming to visit us, and I feel responsible for what happened because I wasn't there to meet you."

"You can't hold yourself to blame." A new thought occurred to her. "Does my family know what happened to me?"

His eyes drifted away from her. "Our Bishop contacted them."

"Are they coming to fetch me?"

"It's a long trip. They have decided that you should stay with my family until you are stronger. Your father-in-law is praying for your speedy recovery."

"I feel if I walked into my home my memory would return, but I guess it's only practical for me to stay awhile. I don't want to be a burden."

He looked back at her and smiled. "I can promise that you won't. My mother would like nothing better than to have you stay with us. The same goes for my sisters-in-law. They were excited to have you stay before the accident. A cast on your arm won't change that."

She turned away from him. "What about an enormous hole where my life should've been?"

"We will do our best to help you recover your memory."

A chill went up her spine. "What if I don't? What if I never remember anything?"

She felt his hand grasp hers. "The doctor says that is highly unlikely."

Gripping his hand tightly, she gazed into his eyes. "But it is possible."

"It is," he admitted reluctantly.

"Then what will I do?"

"Then you will make new memories with me and with my family."

Fear of living with the overwhelming blankness stabbed her through the heart. "I should return to Ohio. My life was there. I need to go back."

"You will when you're strong enough. Until then you are staying with us." His gaze slid away from her.

Why wouldn't he look at her? Something wasn't right.

Two days later, Mary stepped out of the back of Lily Arnett's car to get her first look at the Fisher farmstead. Set back from the highway on a short gravel lane was a two-story white house with a porch across the front and a well-tended flower garden stretching around the side. Across the farmyard stood a red barn trimmed in white. Attached to the side was a smaller building with a separate entrance and a large multipaned window. A sign over the door said Fisher Harness and Leather Goods. All around and stretching up into the hills was a dense forest. The smell of pine scented the fresh air.

She gazed at the woods in awe. "Look at those beautiful trees."

"Don't they have trees in Ohio?" Ash asked.

"I don't remember. Can I go explore?"

"Maybe in a day or two. You've only just left the hospital."

Looking up at him, Mary sighed, then she grinned. "Ever my practical friend."

"I try."

The front door of the house opened. The Fisher

family came out onto the porch. Ash stepped close to Mary's side. She was grateful for his presence. "This is my *daed*, Zeke Fisher, and you know Mamm."

Talitha came down the steps. "Welcome to our home, Mary. I'm sure you must be tired."

"A little," she admitted. This was the longest she'd spent out of bed in almost a week. Her ribs ached from sitting up for the car ride.

"These are my sons. Gabe and his wife, Esther. Seth and his wife, Pamela, and Moses my youngest."

Mary couldn't tell which one was Seth and which one was Gabe as she glanced over their solemn faces. She looked at Ash. "I think you fibbed to me."

"Why would you say that?"

"They don't look like a loud, boisterous bunch." She grinned at his family to take any sting out of her teasing.

Moses cracked a smile. "We can be."

Mary grinned widely. "That's a relief."

"I don't find them loud at all," one of the younger women said with a mischievous glint in her eyes. A smile twitched at the corner of her mouth.

Mary knew she was being teased. She stepped forward and held out her left hand. "You must be Esther. I'm sorry but I seem to have forgotten the sign language I learned."

Esther took her hand in a firm but friendly grip. "We'll teach you all over again."

Mary lifted her cast slightly. "With only one arm?"

"Finger spelling is done with a single hand. It isn't sign language, but I can read it if you can spell it."

"I was an excellent speller in school."

Esther tipped her head slightly. "Were you?"

Mary's bright mood faded. "I don't know why I said that. I can't remember going to school, but I must have. I know how to read."

Talitha took Mary's arm. "You can get better acquainted with us after you've had a rest. Pamela will show you to your room."

Mary nodded and turned to Ash. "My things?"

"I'll bring them in."

The police had delivered the contents of her suitcase in a large cardboard box. The clothes she had been wearing the day of accident were in a plastic bag waiting to be washed.

Mary turned to Lily. "Thank you for driving me here."

"I was happy to do it. If you ever need anything, my place is a short walk through the woods. I'm sure Asher can show you the way."

Pamela came down the steps and hooked her arm through Mary's. "We are so happy you are staying with us."

She led Mary into the house and up the stairs. At the top, a hallway stretched the length of the house. Pamela opened the first door on the left and stepped back to let Mary go in. "I hope this is suitable. You will find the bathroom two doors down on the right."

The room contained two twin beds, both covered with matching bright green-and-white quilts. Pale cream-colored walls were bare except for a wooden rail with pegs to hang clothes on, a calendar with a picture of a snow-covered pine tree and a small mirror over a chest of drawers. A large window with simple white curtains overlooked the flower and vegetable gardens at the rear of the house.

"This is lovely. *Danki.*"

"Goot." Pamela grinned with relief.

"Where do you want these?" Ash asked from the doorway.

"On that bed." She relaxed and pointed.

He put down the box and bag. "Can I do anything else?"

"You have done more than enough for me, Ash. I'm fine."

He smiled with relief. *"Goot.* I've got to get to work in the shop. There's no telling how big a mess my brothers have made of my filing and ordering system."

"Shall I help you unpack?" Pamela asked as she turned down the other bed.

Mary shook her head. "I'll take care of it later."

"That means get out of her hair," Ash said with a wink for Mary.

She grinned. "You know I would never be so rude to anyone but you. Pamela, I need help to put my hair up." She pulled her long braid over her shoulder. "I hate to ask but I can't manage it with one hand."

Pamela pushed Ash out of the room. "I'd be happy to."

When she finished, she pulled down the quilt. "Rest now and we'll see you whenever you feel like coming downstairs."

Mary sank onto the empty bed, but seeing the unpacked box made her get up again. Leaving her work for later didn't seem right. She put her underthings and stockings in the bureau and hung her two good dresses from the pegs, then sat down again. Rubbing her palms on her thighs she looked around. Now what? When she was alone, all she could think about was finding her memory.

There was a knock at the door. Talitha looked in. "I hope I'm not disturbing you."

"Not at all." Mary felt her tension lessen.

"I'm doing a load of laundry and thought I'd ask if you had anything that needed washing."

"My clothes from the day of the accident are in that bag. I'm afraid they're a mess."

"With four sons I am used to messes." Talitha picked up the plastic bag. She turned to Mary with a sympathetic smile. "I know this must seem strange, but keep in mind that you were coming to visit us. We have been expecting you for days. I enjoy having company so never think you are putting me out."

Mary drew a shaky breath. She tried to maintain her usual smile, but her lower lip quivered. "I'm so grateful for all you and your family have done. If it weren't for Ash sitting with me for hours in the hospital, I don't know how I would have made it this far. The truth is I'm scared."

"Of what?"

"What if I don't want to remember because I was a horrible person?" Tears welled up and spilled down her cheeks. She couldn't hold back a sob.

Talitha sat beside Mary and put her arm around her. "Go ahead and cry. I can't imagine what you're going through. Just remember that our Lord is beside you, too. His comfort is the greatest of all."

Mary nodded because she couldn't speak. The dread and fear of not knowing choked her. Ash would drive back the darkness if only he were here.

Ash was in the living room with the family when his mother came downstairs. "How is she?"

"Exhausted. Frightened half out of her mind. She may not remember anything, but I can tell she is a dear, sweet girl. I find it hard to forgive her family for turning their backs on her."

"We don't know the circumstances of her shunning," Zeke said.

Ash's mother planted her hands on her hips. "She has cried herself to sleep. I don't care about the circumstances. We're going to make her feel welcome and treat her as a valued member of our family for as long as she wishes to stay."

Ash saw a smile twitch at the corner of his father's mouth. "I wasn't suggesting otherwise, but the bishop has the final say."

"I'm aware of that," she admitted.

"We must obey the Ordnung," he said sternly.

"Of course. Esther and Pamela, can you take care of lunch?" She signed as she spoke for Esther's benefit.

"What will we do about Mary?" Pamela asked. "The church forbids us to eat at the same table with a shunned person."

"Our table is already crowded with all of us around it. Too crowded to squeeze in one more. We need a bigger table." Ash's mother shot a stern look at her husband.

"I'm going to build a new one soon," he said.

She rolled her eyes. "I've heard that before. We'll seat Mary by herself at a card table so no one accidentally jars her broken arm, and we will adhere to our Ordnung at the same time."

"A *goot* idea." Pamela smiled and followed Esther into the kitchen.

"The buggy won't finish by itself." Ash's father started toward the door. His sons followed.

"Asher, may I speak to you for a moment?" His mother sat on the sofa.

"I should have a look at the books," Ash said. "I've neglected them long enough."

She patted the cushion beside her. Ash grimaced at another delay. "Mamm, I need to get back to work. Those brothers of mine will have made a mess of the paperwork, and I'm days behind on ordering parts."

"This won't take long. You've devoted a lot of time to Mary and she's grateful."

He sat down and propped his elbows on his knees. "So?"

"I'm worried about her. She's in a very frail state."

"I understand that."

"Not just physically. She's lost, alone, worried. This has made her dependent on you."

"I know that, but now that she's here with you, Pamela and Esther I'm sure she'll be fine. The business needs me, too."

"I believe you should let your brothers continue taking over your work in the shop for a few more days so you can devote your time to Mary. Until she is comfortable here. I believe that will help more than anything."

Astonished by her suggestion, he blinked hard. "You want me to spend more time with a woman the bishop may tell us we must shun?" He couldn't deny he was drawn to Mary, but nothing could be the same between them now.

"She came here because you invited her, Ash."

He clapped a hand to his chest. "And I felt responsible for her in the hospital, but now she has you she can turn to."

"All I'm asking is for you to continue your friendship with the poor girl. I'll tell your brothers and your father what I've decided." She patted his knee, rose and walked out leaving Ash's mind reeling. What was she thinking?

Chapter Four

❧

Mary opened her eyes in a strange room. It took a moment to remember she was in Ash's home instead of the hospital. She sat up gingerly and rubbed her temple. Crying always left her with a headache, but she couldn't remember a time when she had wept in the past.

She must have if she had buried a husband. What kind of person could forget that sorrow? What kind of person was she? Looking out over the garden, she saw Talitha hanging out her washing.

The image of holding a sun-dried blue work shirt in her hands flashed into Mary's mind. She held the shirt to her face and breathed in the smell, and she wanted to weep.

She had cried over that shirt. Why? Whose was it? She tried but couldn't recall anything else. The memory was real. She was sure of it. Maybe this meant the doctor was right, and she was recovering. She should tell Ash.

She rushed from the room and went downstairs. Ash and his father sat at a desk in the living room, intent on the papers spread in front of them. Suddenly it seemed foolish to be so excited over taking a piece of clothing off the line. She must have done it hundreds of times.

Ash looked up. "Are you feeling better?"

"I am. *Danki.*" Would it sound foolish to say she recalled holding a shirt?

He tipped his head slightly. "What is it?"

"Nothing. Well, maybe. I think I remembered something."

He jumped to his feet and hurried to her side. "That's *wunderbar.*"

She blushed and looked down. "It isn't much."

"Tell me."

"I took a man's work shirt off the line and held it to my face. I wanted to cry. That's all."

"Who did it belong to?"

She shrugged and looked at him. "I don't know."

"Perhaps it belonged to your husband," he said gently.

"I reckon that's the most likely answer. It was just a flash but I'm sure it is a memory. I said it wasn't much." Feeling foolish, she turned away.

He gripped her hand and bent his face to look into her eyes. "It's a start, Mary."

She liked the way his voice softened when he said her name. It made her feel special and safe.

Ash's father came to stand beside them. "You must be hungry. You slept through lunch."

"I am a little."

"She's been eating like a bird in the hospital," Ash said.

His father smiled at her. "I'm sure there's something for you in the kitchen. Ash, why don't you show her the way."

She shook her head. "Don't let me take you from your work."

"We're done." Ash looked at his father who nodded. "The kitchen is this way."

He led her through a doorway into a spacious, sunny room with a large oak table in the center that had a card table on the end. A row of windows above the sink and counters were open to the breeze. A coffeepot sat on the back of a huge black stove. Ash walked to the ice-box and opened it. "Chicken or ham?"

"Ham. What's the card table for?"

"It's for you. Mamm wanted you to sit where no one will bump your arm," he said in a rush. "It's crowded with all of us at meals. Mamm had been asking for a bigger table for ages, but Daed hasn't gotten around to making one."

"That's thoughtful." Mary took a seat at the little table while he supplied her with a plate, bread, mustard and a plastic container of sliced meat. She built herself a sandwich. It wasn't until she took the first bite that she realized how hungry she was.

He took a seat across from her and watched her intently. She grew nervous under his scrutiny. "What?"

"You have some mustard on the side of your mouth."

"That's because I'm eating like a pig." She wiped her hand over her lips. "Did I get it?"

"Not quite." He reached across the table, curled his fingers under her chin and brushed his thumb gently across the corner of her mouth.

Her breath caught. A wave of heat rushed to her cheeks. She pulled away and rubbed her face with the back of her hand. Glancing at him, she saw a puzzled expression darken his eyes. He raked his fingers through his hair and got up to fix himself a cup of coffee. He leaned against the counter to sip it.

She concentrated on taking smaller bites and tried not to think about the rush of delight his touch triggered. It had been a simple, helpful gesture. He was only being friendly. They knew each other well enough for that. It was her response that was out of proportion. She prayed he hadn't noticed. He took a seat across from her.

When she finished her meal, she picked up her plate and carried it to the sink. She washed and rinsed it, using the time to regain her composure. She turned around with a bright smile. "Now what? Do not say rest because I have spent far too much time doing that already."

He turned toward her and hooked one arm over the back of his chair. "I'm willing to hear a reasonable suggestion."

"Can we take a walk in the woods?"

"A short one."

She raised one eyebrow. "Define short."

"Ten minutes."

"Thirty."

He arched his brow to mimic her. "Fifteen."

"Fifteen with the possibility of five more if I'm not tired?"

He inclined his head slightly. "If you promise you won't overdo it. I don't want to have to carry you back to the house."

It was easy to visualize being held in his arms. She

ruthlessly pushed the image aside before she started blushing. "I will tell you the minute I start to fade."

He got out of his chair, lifted his hat from the row of pegs beside the door and held it open. She scooted through, making sure she didn't touch him. Outside, she surveyed the woodlands that curved around the property. "It is so beautiful here."

"It looks a lot different in the winter."

"Do you get much snow?"

"Six feet or more."

"Feet? The snow piles up higher than my head?" It was hard to believe, but what a wondrous sight it must be.

"Yup. Sometimes higher."

"Oh, I wish I stay here to see that."

He frowned. "Why won't you be here?"

"Because I'm going back to Ohio as soon as the doctor says I'm strong enough to travel. My family must be worried about me. I'll write them tomorrow if someone will help me."

"Of course we will."

When she was at home among familiar people and places her memory would return if it didn't before then. She prayed it would come back soon.

Pushing her worry aside, she glanced around. "What fun the winters must be here. Do you go sledding? You must with such wonderful hills."

"I do lots of shoveling, and I chop tons of wood."

"But surely you go ice skating and take sleigh rides. Do you ski?"

"I don't. Moses like to. There's a path behind the barn that leads up to a meadow with a pretty view from the top. Shall we go there?"

Her arm ached, but she ignored it. She didn't want to miss a minute of being outside in Ash's company. "Lead on."

Ash walked beside Mary without speaking. He was still coming to grips with the sudden jolt of emotion that had blindsided him in the kitchen when he touched her face. His boldness had shocked her. He could tell that much. Determined not to repeat his mistake, he kept his hands clasped around his suspenders so he wouldn't accidentally touch her.

Her comment about going back to Ohio had caught him off guard, too. Should he tell her about her family's decision? He hated keeping it from her but decided to wait.

As they made their way along the path into the deep woods, she gazed about in childlike wonder, asking him the names of the birds that flitted through the canopy overhead. He knew most of them. His brother Gabe was an avid birdwatcher. He had educated everyone in the family on the different birds in the area, whether or not they were interested.

She stopped suddenly. "Oh, look," she whispered, her voice full of awe.

He followed her line of sight and saw a fox. What was so amazing about that? They were plentiful.

"She has two babies with her." She kept her voice low.

"They're called kits," he said in his normal tone. The fox bolted at the sound of his voice.

Mary frowned at him. "You scared them away."

"They won't go far. You might see them another time. We'll have to make certain to lock up the hens and geese at night."

"Do fox do a lot of damage?"

"They're good at keeping the rodent population in check but not everyone believes that. They are hunted around here."

"What a shame. They're pretty."

Mary kept walking but soon stopped to rub the bark of an old oak. "Moss grows thick on the north side of the trees here."

A squirrel took exception to their presence and began scolding from the branches. She looked up at him. "I like your home."

She leaned in to smell the moss and smiled with her eyes closed. "I think this is exactly what I imagined a forest in Maine would be like. A dim, welcoming place full of earthy scents. Quiet in a reverent way, except for the rustling of wildlife and the sound of the wind in the branches. Like *Gott* had just breathed it to life. Did you describe it like that in your letters to me?"

"Nee." He didn't think of the woods as anything special. They were just trees. He never suspected from her letters that Mary had a fanciful imagination.

Stepping back, she smiled shyly. "Am I being silly?"

He thought it best not to answer. "These woods have many practical uses. The forested acres were part of the reason we purchased this property. We heat our house with the logs we cut so we don't have to buy propane. Some of the timber like this big tree will be logged off and sold to the local lumber mill to supplement the income from the farm and our businesses."

Her grin faded as she looked up. "You mean to cut down this tree? Mr. Squirrel will miss his home."

He frowned. "Taking a few of the older trees gives more room for the young ones that get crowded out.

We can earn a small income and still manage the land responsibly. One of our neighbors is a logger. Nathan Weaver. He's Amish, and he'll use his horses. That way we won't have to clear a way for a road."

"I guess that's okay. It is just sad to cut down something so magnificent."

"People need wood for houses and businesses."

"I reckon that's a practical way to look at it."

"Right," he said with relief. There was the realistic Mary he knew from her letters.

She looked up again. "You may have to move to a new house, Mr. Squirrel."

The animal continued to scold them. Mary grinned at Ash. "He doesn't like that idea. Perhaps you can convince him."

Talking to squirrels wasn't how Ash normally spent his time. "Are you getting tired?"

She frowned at him. "Don't say we have to go back. Not yet." There was pleading, but also a hint of panic in her voice.

"We can go a little farther," he said to mollify her.

"*Wunderbar.* You are my hero." Her beaming smile made his heart catch. He closed his hands tightly around his suspenders to keep from reaching for her hand.

She wasn't what he'd expected. From her correspondences, he assumed they would get along well together, but this attraction was different. Confusing. How could she make him giddy with a simple smile? He forced his attention to the path ahead. "Don't overdo it."

The trail led upward into the wooded hills above New Covenant. There were several breaks in the trees with fine views of the distant mountains and the winding river below.

They stopped at one opening in the trees where the valley lay spread out in a checkered patchwork of fields and farms. She smiled at him. "Ash, this is beautiful."

He cocked his head slightly. It was a pretty view. "Esther and Pamela say the clearing beyond those cedar trees is their favorite spot."

"Then I must see it."

He led her around the trees and noticed her steps were slowing. He'd brought her too far. Luckily, there was a place to rest up ahead.

The clearing they reached held the ruins of an old log cabin sitting amid a carpet of pink, lavender, purple and white spires of lupine. His brother Gabe had built a bench where Esther could sit and sketch the flowers.

Mary gasped and stepped out into the meadow with a delighted smile. She held out her good arm and turned in a circle. "They're beautiful. I've never seen anything like it."

Her smile faded as her eyes grew sad. "I say that, but I can't be sure it's true."

He wanted her to smile again. "It's true today."

"You're right." She pressed a hand to her temple and sat on the bench. "Thank you for showing me this. I reckon we should go back, but I don't want to."

"This will be here tomorrow and the next day. You can come again."

"It's not that." She rubbed her shoulder and adjusted her sling.

He sensed her unease and sat beside her. "Why don't you want to go back?"

She averted her gaze. "Everyone will stare at me, much too polite to say anything, but wondering what kind of ninny can't remember her own name."

He brushed the backs of his fingers lightly across the bruise that still marred the side of her face. "*Nee*, they won't. My family will think how blessed you are to have survived such a terrible accident."

When she looked at him, tears glistening in her eyes. "You're very kind, Ash."

"I thought I was the most exciting man you know. Now I'm only kind. It seems I'm slipping in your estimation." He couldn't believe he was teasing her.

She managed a wry smile. "I don't want to puff you up."

"I see. This is you keeping me from becoming prideful, is it?"

"Exactly."

"You're doing a fine job. Let's get you home before Mamm scolds us both for keeping you out too long."

"I didn't mean I thought your family would be unkind."

"I know that."

"When I think about the missing part of my life, I feel empty and scared."

"I can fill in a few things for you. I wish I had kept your letters. They might have helped."

"How did I seem? Was I a cheerful person, or did I worry over things?"

"I got the feeling that you were unhappy with your in-laws."

"Did I write about my friends and the things we did together?"

"You mentioned going to a church social and a frolic. Mostly you wrote about work on your father-in-law's farm. You didn't mention specific friends."

"What did I do for fun?" she asked eagerly.

"I couldn't say."

Her expression dimmed. "Oh, well, that's okay."

"I'm not much help, am I?"

"Of course you are, Ash." Her earnest tone soothed his failure. "Why, if not for you I still wouldn't know my name. You've been loads of help. I've been praying that my memory returns. Maybe I should pray for patience instead."

"Pray for both." He took her hand to help her to her feet.

Mary was prepared for his touch this time. She didn't pull away but allowed her hand to linger in his strong one for a moment longer than necessary. The same surge of awareness flowed through her veins bringing a bewildering happiness. She liked Ash Fisher. Everything about him pleased her. The color of his eyes, the shape of his lips, the strength in his hands. She especially liked the way he always tried to comfort her.

He nodded toward the path. "We should go."

She realized she was staring at him and began walking. Had she felt this way when she was with the husband she couldn't remember? What had he been like? Did Ash remind her of him in some way? Did they act or look alike? Did she still mourn him? Was that why she was attracted to Ash? Her somber thoughts took the joy out of her walk. She shifted her arm again. It was aching dreadfully and so was her side.

"You've gotten quiet," Ash said.

"I'm afraid I overdid it. My arm hurts." Her headache was back, too.

"Do you want to stop and rest?"

"*Nee*, let's keep going. It isn't far now and it's downhill."

He stopped. "I can carry you."

"Oh, *nee*, that won't be necessary." She picked up the pace and moved ahead of him so he couldn't see how flustered his suggestion made her. He might know her, but she barely knew him. She didn't even know if he had a girlfriend.

That thought brought her up short. He stopped beside her. "What?"

"Nothing." She started walking again. There was no way she was going to ask him such a pointed and personal question.

They emerged from the trees a short time later. She stopped at the front door and turned to him with her chin up. "Thank you for accompanying me on a walk. You have a lovely place. I'm going in now. You should return to your work. I've kept you from it long enough."

Was her tone casual enough? Please let him think so.

"Okay." He looked perplexed.

After opening the door, she slipped inside, closed it and leaned against the cool wood. Why hadn't she considered he might be seeing someone before? He had been attentive to her, but he felt guilty about the accident. That was the reason he was so considerate. Imagining it was something else was a mistake. Until she could remember her past life, she had no business thinking about any kind of relationship with Ash. She had no idea what kind of person she was, what troubles might have prompted her to want to move to Maine.

She liked Ash, but she couldn't continue this dependence on him. He had been there in the beginning when she desperately needed someone, but she was better now. Her memory might be missing, but her strength of will wasn't. It had been badly bent under the overwhelming fear of those first few days, but it was time to straighten it out.

She pushed away from the door. What she needed was to be useful. She went in search of her hostess and found her with Pamela and Esther in the kitchen. They all looked at her when she walked in.

Pasting a smile on her face, she advanced into the room. "I need something to do. Put me to work and don't any of you dare tell me to go rest."

There was an awkward silence in the kitchen. Mary met their gazes without flinching. Having only one arm, a cracked rib and a splitting headache would not deter her.

Esther gestured for Mary to sit at the table. "I'm making cupcakes. Why don't you fill these liners with batter while I start on another batch?"

Mary gave her a grateful smile. "I can manage that. How do I say *danki* in sign language?"

Esther brought her fingers to her lips and extended them to Mary. "This is how you say thank you."

Mary repeated the gesture with a smile for the understanding woman, sat down and began working. While she filled the cupcake liners, she found her mind wandering. To Ash and the way he made her feel today. She wanted to spend more time with him, get to know him better and see where this attraction might lead, but that wasn't possible. She had to ignore those feelings.

"Are you finished with these?" Talitha asked pointing to the pan in front of Mary.

Mary looked up. "Sorry. Guess I was lost in thought."

"Something serious by your expression. Can I help?"

"I was thinking I've been a burden to Ash since the accident. He's such a kind man he'd never admit it."

Talitha tipped her head as she regarded Mary. "Asher thinks more highly of you than you realize."

Mary forced herself to smile. "He has proven to be a true friend."

Ash entered the part of the barn his family used for making buggies and wheel repair with a deep sense of relief. He was more than ready to get back to work and forget how confused Mary made him feel. He didn't even get the door closed behind him before Seth rolled out from underneath the half-completed buggy frame. "You sure landed yourself in a pickle, *brudder.*"

Gabe came through the door that connected to his leather shop. "You poor fellow. Your bride-to-be has finally arrived, and she doesn't know you. Is she what you expected?"

Looking at the grins on his brothers' faces made Ash glare at them. "That's hardly a fair question."

"Oh, I reckon you're right," Seth admitted. "How is she feeling?"

"Better physically, but mentally she's having a hard time coming to grips with her situation."

"Can't blame her for that," Gabe said. "What about you?"

"Me? I feel pretty much the same. We aren't exactly strangers. I thought I knew her. We've been corresponding for months but none of that exists for Mary. She certainly isn't like I imagined. We took a walk up into the forest. You have never seen someone so delighted to be among trees. She was even talking to a squirrel. When I mentioned the logging we planned to do in that area, I thought she was going to cry. Her letters made her sound much more down-to-earth. I'm not sure if the difference is because of the accident or if I don't know her as well as I thought I did. Can we just get to work?"

"Such a serious injury is bound to have a profound effect on her," Gabe said.

Ash nodded. "I expect you're right."

Seth stroked his short beard. "We're worried about you, Ash. Gabe and I know you better than anyone. The three of us are all for one and one for all, remember? This sudden rush into a long-distance courtship isn't like you. We're concerned you are doing it for the wrong reason."

"What reason is that?" Ash asked with a degree of caution.

Gabe laid a hand on Ash's shoulder. "We think our marriages have you feeling left out and maybe lonely."

Ash shouldn't be surprised his brothers knew him so well. "Is it wrong to want what the two of you have? A loving wife and a chance to start my own family? There isn't anyone around here for me. I can't leave the business to go shopping for a wife in another community. I've done the numbers. We're finally getting ahead, but one bad potato harvest or someone canceling a buggy order will be enough to undo all our hard work. The move here and this business is our father's dream. We can't fail him. When the bishop suggested I exchange letters with some single Amish women looking to relocate with an eye toward marriage, it seemed like a good solution. And it was."

"Why Mary?" Gabe asked.

Ash shrugged. "She was a widow in an unhappy

situation with her in-laws, looking for a chance to start over. Her letters said she wasn't expecting a love match, but she believed two practical people could work together to form a lasting relationship. She was desperate to start a new life."

"You felt sorry for her," Seth stated.

"A little. She didn't have high expectations, which suited me."

He turned and took a few steps away. "You know how I am around women. I trip over my tongue the second I open my mouth. It just seemed like the easiest way to get what the two of you have. I know you must think this makes me pathetic."

Seth walked up and punched Asher's shoulder. "You've been pathetic since the day you were born. This doesn't change anything."

Ash rubbed his arm. "Leave it to you to make me feel better."

Gabe punched Seth in the shoulder. "Pointing out someone else's faults does not lessen your own. If not for Ash's way with numbers, our businesses would still be in the red."

"True," Seth admitted. "But if Mary is simply looking for a practical fellow to get her away from her unhappy life and provide nothing more than companionship, she isn't the woman for you, Ash. You deserve to find the love of your life. Someone you can't live without."

"Someone who makes you feel like you can't breathe when they're near," Gabe said softly.

Ash saw the concern in his brothers' eyes. What they spoke of was what he wanted. Had he been foolish to think he could settle for less?

Seth sighed. "When her memory returns, you will have to be honest and tell her that you are looking for a love match."

Ash swallowed hard. "There is one problem with that. When Mary regains her memory, she's going to recall I have already asked her to marry me."

Chapter Five

"What?" Gabe's mouth dropped open. "You proposed to Mary?"

"In my last letter to her." If only he hadn't mailed that brief spur-of-the-moment note. Nothing good came from impulsive decisions.

"What was her answer?" Seth demanded.

"I assumed she would tell me when she arrived."

"So you don't know if you're betrothed or not?" Gabe asked.

"Unless she tells me otherwise, I have to assume I am."

Seth lifted his hat and raked his hand through his blond hair. "No wonder you looked so worried the morning you went to meet the bus. I'm sorry I teased you about it. I thought she was coming for a visit to get to know you and the community."

"That was our original plan, but then I sent that last letter."

"What are you going to do now?" Gabe asked.

"I'm sure Mamm told you Mary is shunned." They nodded.

"I have no idea what to do." Ash folded his arms

and looked down. "I pray the bishop gives us an answer quickly."

Gabe took a few steps away then turned around to face Ash. "Bishop Schultz is a wise and kind man. He'll see shunning her accomplishes nothing until we know the full story. Mary's injury is giving her a chance to get to know Asher Fisher without her preconceived notions. You are learning who she is when she isn't a desperately unhappy widow hoping marriage will solve her troubles. She's already seen how compassionate you are. I know you didn't tell her that in a letter."

"Of course not. I wrote about practical everyday things. So did she."

Gabe smiled. "I'm not sure a fellow as practical as you claim to be would have stayed by her bedside day and night. You've known her a few days now. Do you like her?"

Ash wasn't willing to share how Mary affected him. Those feelings were still new and confusing. "She was alone and needs someone to look after her. The whole thing was my fault. I wasn't there to meet her bus."

"She's not alone now," Seth said.

"I'm the one person who knows something about her. I'm her only friend. She depends on me."

His brothers exchanged speaking looks. Gabe drew a deep breath. "I want an honest answer, Ash. Do you feel compelled to befriend Mary because you feel guilty? Or is it because you like her?"

Ash turned away from his brothers. "Does it matter?"

"Does it matter?" Gabe's voice boomed throughout the workshop. Ash flinched.

"*Ja*, it matters a lot," Seth said. "You can't build a lasting relationship based on guilt and pity."

Ash spun to face them. "It's my life. I'll handle it. You both must promise you won't mention any of this to Mary. I don't want her upset."

"Of course we won't," Seth said. "Do Mamm and Daed know about this?"

"That I proposed? *Nee*, I haven't told anyone. They think Mary has come to see if she wants to move here, but they know we've been writing to each other. Mamm may suspect we have formed an attachment. She always has matchmaking on her mind."

Gabe grinned at Seth. "We're proof she knows what she's doing. If she and her cousin Waneta hadn't cooked up a reason to bring Esther and Pamela here for a visit, we'd still be single men."

Seth's eyes narrowed. "Do you think that's what she's doing now?"

Ash frowned. "What do you mean?"

"She told us to keep working without you because Mary wasn't comfortable with you out of her sight. Our mother always makes people feel welcome and happy. If anyone can make Mary comfortable here without a second thought, it's her."

Gabe nodded. "You're right."

Ash shook his head. "*Nee*, Mamm wouldn't do such a thing unless Mary had rejoined the faith."

Gabe held up one hand. "I'm not so sure. She knows fallen-away Amish have come back because of love. *Gott* uses many tools to lead His children to Him."

Seth stroked his beard thoughtfully. "If Mamm is intent on matchmaking, she'll see that you two spend more time together. She has her ways. You and Mary have a connection you felt was serious enough to propose marriage, but you don't really know her. Spending time with her is the only way you can decide if she's the right one or not. If she isn't, she deserves to hear the truth from you."

Ash was tired of talking about it. "Until her memory returns, I'm a helpful friend and nothing more. Now, I need to look at the ledgers. Did either of you do inventory while I was gone?"

Seth shrugged. "Daed was going to, but it's been busy here."

Ash shook his head in disgust. "I knew this would happen."

The outside door opened. Pamela looked in. "Ash, Talitha would like you to change the propane tank in the end table beside the living room sofa. It's not working."

He struggled to contain his annoyance at another delay. "Where is Moses? Why can't he do it?"

"I don't know. Your mother specifically asked for you to take care of it. I'm just the messenger. Mary wants to read a book, but the lamp won't turn on."

"Okay, I'll be right there." Pamela left, and Ash heard snickering behind him. He spun around to see his brothers trying not to laugh.

"I told you Mamm has her ways," Gabe said. "Don't bother hauling a new tank in. I changed that one yesterday and it was working fine."

Ash went out and slammed the workshop door shut on the sound of their guffawing. He paused and drew a calming breath before he entered the house. In the living room, Mary sat on the sofa with her feet up on the ottoman and her broken arm elevated on a stack of pillows. A blue quilt covered her lap.

She looked at him and frowned. "Is something wrong?"

"*Nee.*"

"You look annoyed."

"Sorry. Work stuff. Nothing I should burden you with. What seems to be the trouble?"

"I am. Your *mamm* insisted I rest here and read or something because I refuse to go back to bed. I'm no use in the kitchen with one hand. Pamela and Esther kindly made sure I'm comfy with these pillows and throw. They are determined to spoil me. Talitha tried to light the lamp, but the tank seems to be empty."

He opened the small door on the front of the oak end table to check. He saw right away that the valve had been turned off. "It's not empty. Someone shut the valve."

"I wonder why she didn't see that?"

"I'm afraid to guess." He should tell his mother he didn't need her matchmaking help.

Mary gave him a funny look. "What?"

"Never mind." He twisted it to the On position and stood up. Using the lighter that was always kept on the table, he lit the mantle inside the glass globe. Bright white light flooded the dim corner of the room. "Better?"

"Much." She smiled and picked up her book.

He had work waiting, but he surprised himself by sitting beside her feet on the ottoman. "What are you reading?" The book had a plain blue cover jacket on it.

"Esther gave it to me. She said she really likes this author. I don't think I've read anything by her before, but I'm sure I like love stories."

Ash felt his face growing warm. "Then I will let you get back to it."

She laid the book aside. "*Nee*, I'd rather visit with you. Unless you're busy."

"Nothing that can't wait. Is your arm hurting?"

She grimaced and flexed her fingers. "A bit."

"Are you regretting our hike in the woods?"

"Absolutely not. It was amazing. Much better than cornfields." A small furrow appeared between her eyebrows. "I don't know why I said that."

"I might. You wrote about planting and harvesting corn on your father-in-law's farm in Ohio. You tried to convince him to hire another farmhand to make the job easier, but he wouldn't."

"I worked as a farmhand on my father-in-law's property?" She tipped her head. "I'm trying to visualize that."

"You frequently drove a four-horse hitch for him. That takes a lot of muscle." He glanced at her slender arms and dainty hands.

"I wish I could remember."

"Nothing has occurred to you since this morning?"

"I would say I'm still in the dark, but you just fixed the lamp." She giggled. "That was a poor joke, wasn't it?"

"Not poor, just silly."

Her eyes widened. "If that's the way you're going to be I'm done visiting with you." She lobbed one of her pillows at him.

He caught it and tossed it back. "*Goot.* I have work to do."

She replaced the pillow under her cast. "Don't let me keep you."

He rose and started for the door and saw his mother

watching from the hallway. She gave a knowing smile and went into the kitchen.

"Ash?"

He looked back at Mary.

She brought her fingers to her lips and extended her hand to him. "For fixing the light."

From Esther it felt like the sign for *thank you*. From Mary, it reminded him of someone blowing a kiss. Was she flirting? No, he had to be mistaken, but he was glad his mother hadn't seen it.

"You're welcome." He hurried out the door and escaped into his small office in the workshop. He opened his ledger and stared at the numbers without really seeing them.

Mary loved trees, talked to animals, made silly jokes, threw pillows at a fellow and she might have been flirting. He had been drawn to Mary's serious, down-to-earth nature in her letters. The woman in the house didn't fit what he knew about her, yet she was remarkably appealing. Spending more time with her wouldn't be a hardship. He smiled at the thought.

Then his common sense made him sit up straight. She was shunned. Until the bishop decided whether to support the shunning of another community, Ash couldn't allow his attraction to get out of hand. He could be pleasant and helpful, a friend. Nothing else.

He heard hoofbeats outside his office and rose to look out the window. Otto Gingrich, a young boy from New Covenant, sat on a spotted pony talking to Ash's father and mother. Ash went to see what was up.

Otto wheeled his pony around and trotted away. Ash saw the concerned look his parents shared as he reached them. "What's going on?"

"The bishop sent word," his father said. "He'll be here to speak to Mary in the morning."

Mary struggled to get her *kapp* pinned on straight the next morning. A knock at her door interrupted her efforts. "Come in," she mumbled around the bobby pin in her mouth.

Talitha opened the door. "I came to see if you needed help to dress."

Mary held out the bobby pin. "I've managed everything but my prayer covering."

Talitha took the pin, straightened the *kapp* and secured it in place. "There. Now you look ready to face the day. Have you remembered anything else?"

Mary didn't bother to hide her disappointment. "I haven't."

"Never mind. All in *Gott's* own time. There is someone downstairs who would like to meet you. Bishop Schultz is here."

"I must thank him for letting my family know about me." She expected to meet him at the church service, but she wasn't surprised he had come beforehand. She was an oddity. A woman with no memory. The Fisher family could probably expect to have a steady stream of visitors over the next week.

She chided herself for being cynical. Ash's family hadn't made her feel like a freak. "What is he like?"

"I think you will like him. He's a potato farmer, but he also owns a shed-building business. He makes tiny houses and log cabins now, too. His sermons are sometimes rambling, but he is a fair man, well-liked in our community and respected by our *Englisch* neighbors."

Mary followed Talitha downstairs. The man was

seated on the sofa between Ash and Zeke. They got to their feet when the women came into the room. Ash had a worried expression on his face.

"Mary, this is Elmer Schultz. He is our bishop," Zeke said.

Bishop Schultz was an imposing man who looked be in his late fifties or early sixties. His shaggy gray-and-black beard reached to the middle of his black vest. His gray hair showed the indented impression of his hat around his head. "How are you, Mary?"

She cradled her cast and kept her eyes down. "Improving thanks to the care and kindness of the Fisher family."

"I'm glad to hear that. Please, take a seat."

The straight-backed chair had been set in front of the sofa. A trickle of unease went down her spine. She sat down. Talitha stood behind her.

"I have a few questions for you. Is it your intention to practice the Amish faith here in New Covenant?"

That surprised her. "Of course. I may have forgotten my name but not my faith in *Gott*."

"Do you offer forgiveness to those who have harmed you?"

Was he talking about the driver of the truck that hit her? "Absolutely."

"What if you have knowingly or unknowingly harmed someone?"

Mary grew increasingly puzzled by his questions. "I would seek their forgiveness and try to make amends."

"If you could leave our faith for any reason, would you do that?"

She frowned. "I would not. I have made my vows to *Gott* and the church."

"Do you remember doing so?"

If only she could. "*Nee*, but I was married so I must have been baptized."

He nodded slightly to Zeke. "I'm satisfied."

Facing Mary again, he folded his hands together. "As you have been told, I notified your bishop of the accident, and he informed your family. Your father-in-law called me two days later. This is going to be hard for you to hear."

Her heart started pounding. "Why? What did he say?"

"Albert Brenneman relayed to me that he and his wife do not want you to return to their home."

Mary was sure she'd heard wrong. "They don't want me to come back to Ohio? If they are worried about my health, I'm getting stronger every day. Once the doctor agrees, I'll be able to make the trip."

"That's not their reason."

"They don't want me?" She sank back against her chair in shock.

Glancing at Ash, she saw his gaze focused on the floor. She tried to make sense of what Bishop Schultz was saying. What reason could her in-laws have to abandon her? "It's not my fault that I have forgotten who they are. It's not deliberate. Can you make them understand?"

"They don't wish you to return because you have been shunned by your church."

Mary sprang to her feet. "That's not possible."

"Why do you say that?" the bishop asked gently.

"Because I know what that means. I would never break my vow to the church. What is it they say I have done?" Her gaze shot from Ash to his father, to Talitha standing behind her. "Tell me. What have I done?"

"Your father-in-law would not discuss it. I have written to your bishop asking for clarification. I await his answer."

The room was reeling. She sat down abruptly. "I don't understand. Ash, did you know about this?"

He looked at her then. She read pity in his eyes. "I did."

She pressed her hand to her chest. "Why didn't you tell me?"

"We hoped you would be able to explain when your memory returned," Talitha said.

Mary struggled to recall something that would explain this. "I don't know what I did. I have to repent to be accepted back into my church." She grew cold. A shiver shook her. She looked at Ash. "How can I repent if I don't know my sin?" she shouted.

Drawing a shaky breath, she strove for composure. "I'm sorry."

"You are understandably upset," the bishop said. "To continue your shunning when you have no memory of your offense does not seem right to me. To us. You have left your old church and arrived at a new one. We are all made new in Christ. He paid for our forgiveness with His blood. If it is your wish to join our community, then we welcome you. To become a member of our church requires that all our baptized members vote to accept you. That will happen in time if you are sincere in your desire to remain a member of the Amish faith and follow our Ordnung. I hope you can join us in worship tomorrow. It will be the best way for you to meet our people."

The bishop got to his feet and looked at Ash. "Your courtship may resume if that is still your wish. Knowing that may speed up her acceptance by everyone. I'll leave you to discuss it."

"What courtship?" Mary's gaze flew to Ash. "What is he talking about?"

"I can explain," Ash said calmly.

She got to her feet with her hand pressed to her pounding head. "You and I were courting? I don't understand. You said we'd never met?"

"It was all by mail."

"Why didn't you tell me that? What else haven't you told me?"

"There's no need to be upset," he said calmly.

"How can I not be upset? You deceived me." She rushed out the door leading to the garden. Outside, she glanced around, desperate for somewhere to hide, but there was nowhere.

"Mary, listen to me." Ash had followed her.

She turned to gape at him in shock. "Listen to you? Why should I listen to you? You knew all of this, and you never said a word. I thought I was going to get strong enough to go back to Ohio and my memory would return when I walked into my own house. Now I'm never going to do that. You shouldn't have given me hope. You shouldn't have kept secrets from me." Her voice broke. She pressed her lips together to stop their trembling.

"I'm sorry. We didn't know how to tell you about the shunning. It seemed cruel when you had no memory of what you had done."

"What would drive me to break my vows to my church and turn my back on my family and friends? I need to know, Ash."

"Maybe it's for the best that you can't remember.

You can make a new start here. Begin with a clean slate."

"A blank one, you mean." She tried to swallow the bitterness rising in her throat. God was asking too much of her. Anger at God and at Ash rolled into a stone in her stomach. "The bishop said we could continue our courtship. Is that why I'm here? Am I some kind of mail-order bride for you?"

"Don't be ridiculous."

"Am I wrong? Was marriage the reason I wanted to move to Maine?" Suddenly she realized what must have happened. "Oh, wait. I see now. I could never remarry back home. It would be forbidden to any Amish fellow to wed me. Who suggested I come here? Was it you or was it me?"

"You mentioned something about wanting to see the countryside and I invited you to visit."

The echoes of a conversation filled her mind. "My last chance for a family of my own." Had she heard them or spoken them?

"I'm sure that's not true," he said without conviction in his tone.

It had to be true. "Did we discuss marriage in our letters?"

"You were coming here to see if we would suit each other."

"But there was nothing definite between us." She could see in his face that there was more. "Tell me the truth, Ash. You've kept too many secrets from me. Tell me everything or I will never trust you again."

"I proposed in my last letter. You said you'd give me your answer when you arrived."

"Did I write to you about my shunning?"

"Nee."

"So I lied by omission." Knowing she was capable of deception twisted a band of pain deep inside her mind. "I told your mother I was afraid I didn't want to remember because I might not like the person I was. Turns out that's true."

He stepped close and took her hand. "This has all been a shock. You would have told me everything."

"I won't marry you." She pulled away from him. "I can't marry you. We aren't courting. Not now. Not ever. I'm sure that comes as a great relief to you."

Ash gazed at her determined face and rubbed his hands on his pants. He cared for her more than he was willing to admit to anyone. He had to tread carefully.

He cleared his throat. "Actually, it is a relief. I have regretted my proposal. It was an impulsive action and nothing good comes from decisions like that."

"Oh." Did she sound disappointed or insulted?

Holding up both hands, he added quickly, "Before I met you."

Anger flashed in her eyes. "Clearly after you met me, too, because you failed to mention it on any of the occasions that we were alone together."

This wasn't going the way he wanted it to. "Let's sit down and talk about this like reasonable adults."

She stamped her foot. "I don't want to be reasonable. I want to yell and scream at you."

"I understand. I'm sorry. I truly am." He turned away and crossed to a bench beneath a rose arbor.

She came over but sat as far away from him as she could get. "So talk."

"If you think about it rationally, you will realize why I couldn't tell you about our long-distance courtship."

"Engagement."

He tilted his head in denial. "You never gave me an answer, so we aren't technically engaged."

"You're splitting hairs. I came all this way."

"Okay, you're right. I decided not to mention our relationship because you were confused and frightened enough by your memory loss. I didn't want to add to your discomfort. What could I have said? Hi, you don't know me from Adam, but you're here to marry me. That's a little hard to work into a conversation."

"I guess I can see your point, but I did ask you why I wanted to come to Maine."

"And I told you part of the reason just not all of it."

"So you lied by omission."

"If that's the way you feel, then yes, I did, but I hope you can forgive me. I had your best interest at heart."

"I wish I could say the same about myself. My lie wasn't to protect anyone—it was to gain a new life. If only I could remember why."

"Mary, can you forgive me for not being completely truthful?"

She glared at him for a long moment, then the anger in her eyes faded. "Of course I forgive you, Ash. You have been my rock in a turbulent sea."

He smiled in relief.

"Where does this leave us?" she asked. "What do we do now?"

"I think we've become friends, haven't we?"

Her wry smile proved he had chosen the right words. She nodded. "We have."

"There's no reason we can't continue being friends."

She looked away. "I'm not the kind of person you should be friends with."

Was she right? He was troubled by her shunning. The bishop's decision to overlook it was the right one, but the fact remained that she had deliberately turned her back on her church for some reason.

Despite knowing that, he was drawn to her in a way that baffled him. He couldn't turn away from her.

He bent forward to see her face. "I met Mary Brenneman for the first time when you woke up in the hospital. That woman is the woman I'm friends with. You haven't done anything to change that."

A sad, lost look filled her eyes. "But before."

"This is after. It's where we start. Agreed?" He would do his best to support her.

"It's not like I have other options. No home, no family. No one wants me."

"You have us."

She stared at him for a long moment. He watched some inner struggle going on behind her eyes and wished he could help. Finally, she sighed and gave a hint of a smile. "I'm grateful. I couldn't ask for a better family. I don't have a brother, but if I did, I would want him to be as kind as you."

"Brothers are overrated. You and I are *goot* now, *ja*?"

"*Ja*."

"Then try to appear a little happier."

She rolled her eyes. "This is all I've got. Take it or leave it."

"Then I'll take it." He stood and held out his hand. "Come inside and have some breakfast."

"I don't think I'm hungry."

"That come in and watch me eat. I am starved."

"My life has been turned upside down and all you can think about is food."

"A man has to eat."

Her frown returned. "Will everyone in the community hear about this? Tomorrow is my first prayer service here. How will I face all those people?"

"The bishop and my family are the only ones who know the whole story, but others may find out. Secrets rarely remain secret in a tight-knit Amish community. You must be prepared to face the talk, but I'll stand by you."

She gazed up at him. "I believe you will. *Danki.*"

"Of course. I'm your friend, remember? Let's go in."

The family, except for Moses, was gathered in the kitchen when Ash walked in with Mary. He noticed the card table was missing and realized the significance. His family accepted her as a member of the faithful. Gratitude overwhelmed him.

Ash squeezed her hand. Mary raised her chin. "Ash and I have agreed we are no longer courting."

He frowned. He wasn't expecting her to be so blunt.

"Oh, I'm sorry to hear that," his mother said. "I think the two of you are exactly right for each other."

Mary cast a startled glance his way. "I do care for Ash, but as a brother. He's been wonderfully supportive. Happily, we have put this courting nonsense behind us, and we're still friends. Right?" She punched his arm playfully.

"Right." He managed to keep his smile in place. Her feelings toward him were brotherly?

Chapter Six

Mary spent a restless night wondering how she could pretend she cared for Ash in a brotherly way. She was good at pretending, but not that good. It had been the only thing that had occurred to her when she heard his mother say they were right for each other.

She wasn't right for him. The bishop said they could continue the courtship, but she knew better. Now she understood why she had come to Maine in the first place.

She must have fostered a romantic relationship with Ash to flee the community that shunned her. Maybe she believed her shunning wouldn't become known in the far reaches of northern Maine. Ash deserved better than a woman with such a sly nature.

He might say it didn't matter, but it did. To her. What had she done? She needed to know.

From now on, she would treat Ash as a friend. Nothing more. For his sake and for her own. She knew how Ash thought. His overblown sense of guilt about the accident made him feel responsible for her. If he suspected her affections were deeper than friendship, that guilt might force him to press courtship again. It was up to her to convince him they should stay friends.

Denying her affection for him wouldn't work. They'd grown close in the days since her accident. Pretending otherwise would be impossible. Putting herself in a position where she could express some of her attachment to him was her best option.

It wasn't the perfect plan, but she couldn't give up her friendship with Ash. God had taken everything else from her. She needed Ash. To get through today and all the other days until her memory returned.

All she had to do was convince her heart to follow the plan.

The soft knock at her bedroom door told Mary she couldn't delay facing him any longer. "Come in."

Talitha opened the door. "We're almost ready to leave for church. Will you be joining us?"

Mary swallowed hard and nodded. She would be the oddity of the day. An object of speculation, covert glances, pity and outright curiosity. Ash had promised to stand beside her. She was counting on his strength to get through the ordeal.

Talitha came in and sat on the edge of the bed beside Mary. "You know you don't have to go."

"I'm physically able, and I have so much to be thankful for." She bit her lip and hoped Talitha would understand. "The real reason I'm going is selfish. I'm not sure that's the right frame of mind for worship."

Talitha smoothed a stray strand of hair from Mary's forehead and tucked it behind her ear. "You're going to have to explain."

"Every time I wake up, I have this feeling that what I'm searching for is right there. If I could just pull back the curtain and get a glimpse of my past, the rest would rush in to fill the void."

"I pray for that to happen."

"When I open my eyes, there's nothing. But maybe if I close my eyes while the congregation is praying and place my petition before *Gott* when we are gathered in His name, He will hear and answer my prayer. So I'm going because I want to be healed, and that is selfish. I should pray for His will to be done instead."

"I don't think you're selfish for wanting to be healed."

"You don't?"

"Nor do I believe *Gott* feels that way. We are all human. We pray for rain, for good crop prices, we pray our children will be healthy because we know *Gott* is a loving father who understands us and our frailties. Pray from your heart and know that He hears you. He will answer in His own time, not yours."

"I worry my faith isn't strong enough to endure the wait."

"I'm sure it is. What else is troubling you?"

"Everyone is going to stare." It seemed vain to say it out loud.

Talitha took Mary by the hand and helped her to her feet. "You won't be alone. Pamela, Esther and I will be beside you the whole time."

She couldn't stall any longer. "Then I reckon I'm ready."

Ash stood waiting for the women to come out by the family buggy. His brothers waited with him. He wasn't sure what to say to Mary after the events of yesterday. The one thing he was sure of was that he didn't see her as a sister. Her statement had shaken him.

Moses had been out doing chores when Ash and Mary made their announcement. "So the bishop gave you and Mary his blessing to continue your courtship. Her shunning in Ohio will be forgotten if she follows our Ordnung."

"That's right." Ash was happy for her. Whatever she had done would be forgotten, but he was still troubled. What had prompted such a serious step?

"But the courtship is off?" Moses looked puzzled.

Ash stared at his boots. "That's what she said."

"You sound disappointed. Are you?" Seth asked.

Was he? His feelings for Mary were still a jumble but being near her made him happy. "I'm not sure."

"What?" Gabe demanded. "Are you saying it could still happen?"

Ash shrugged. "You heard her. She thinks of me as a brother."

"Ouch." Moses shook his head. "That's a bad sign. A girl is over you for sure when she says one of two things. 'We can still be friends,' or 'I like you like a brother.' That's death to a romance."

"You aren't helping," Seth said between gritted teeth.

Moses aimed an annoyed glare his way. "I'm just being honest."

"He's right," Ash said. "I'm not the fellow who makes her heart race. I'm the guy who hid the truth and made a mess of things. She isn't what I expected, but I've come to like her. A lot. And not as a sister."

"Listen," Gabe said, casting a quick glance at the front door. "You went about this courtship the wrong way, but there is still time to fix it."

Seth nodded. "If you don't want to end the relationship, you need to start at the beginning. Catch her interest."

Ash shook his head. "We already know each other. It's not like seeing a girl at a picnic for the first time and wondering if there could be something between you."

"It's exactly like that." Gabe grinned. "Forget everything you thought you knew about Mary and start courting her."

"What are you two talking about? How can I undo what's happened?"

Gabe and Seth put their hands on Ash's shoulders. "You can't undo it but think of it this way. Now you know she is a fine eligible woman according to our bishop. You're going to say something sweet to her. Do something nice for her. Then you gauge how she reacts just as you would with any woman."

Ash gave a grunt of disgust. "If I was any good at that kind of thing, I wouldn't have started a long-distance relationship by mail." What his brothers were suggesting would never work.

"I'll help," Moses said with a sly grin. "I can tell when a woman is interested. I'll let you know if you're on the right track."

Ash rolled his eyes at Moses. "You always think the girl is interested in you. Remember when Waneta visited? You thought you had a romance going with Esther and Pamela's youngest sister, but once Nancy returned to Ohio, she got over you right quick."

"Moses has a point," Gabe said.

"I do?" Their little brother puffed up and grinned.

"It pains me to say it, but you do." Gabe turned to Ash. "We might be better at judging Mary's attitude toward you than you are. We can tell you what's working and what's not. Plus, Seth and I have wives who would be delighted with a bit of matchmaking. They can get the information you're after from the horse's mouth, so to speak."

Lifting his hat, Ash then raked his fingers through his hair and jammed his hat back on. "This is ridiculous. I don't want my family spying on Mary for me. I blew my chance with her. I have to accept that unless she tells me otherwise."

"Here they come. Say something nice to her," Moses muttered.

"You're being ridiculous," Ash said under his breath. He turned to smile at his father and the women coming down the porch steps.

"What have you got to lose?" Moses walked to the horses hitched in front of the family's largest buggy. It had three rows of seats and a storage box behind. Because it was a fine morning, they had rolled the door flaps up. They could be let down quickly if rain threatened. Moses wouldn't be riding with them. He was taking his courting buggy in case he had the chance to escort one of the single women home after the service.

Zeke helped his wife stow her baskets of food for the meal after the service. Esther and Pamela scrambled up into the center row of seats. Mary hesitated at the high step. Ash felt an elbow in his side.

He looked at Gabe, who nodded toward Mary. Maybe his brothers knew what they were talking about. He should at least explore the possibility.

Ash stepped forward. "Let me help."

She kept her gaze averted. "I'm not as agile as I used to be. At least I think I was nimbler."

He took her elbow to steady her as she stepped up. "Are your ribs paining you?"

"Only if I bend or stretch too far."

"Are you sure that you want to go to church?" He felt the nudge of another elbow and scowled at Seth behind him. Seth drew a grin on his face and smiled big.

"I'm glad you're coming," Ash said quickly. "I just hope it isn't too much for you."

He looked at Seth. His brother gave him two thumbs-up.

Mary took a seat beside Esther and looked down at Ash. She wore a guarded expression, but then she relaxed. "You're sweet to be concerned. I'll be fine."

He felt another elbow. He was going to have a dozen bruises if his brothers kept this up. Seth wagged his eyebrows toward the front of the buggy where Moses mimicked driving.

Ash smiled at Mary. "I can bring you home if you get tired. Moses will let us borrow his rig. That way the others don't have to leave early."

He almost laughed at his little brother's pained expression.

Gabe, Seth and Ash took their places in the rear seat. Their father spoke to the team to get them moving. The bimonthly prayer service was being held at the home of Jesse and Gemma Crump on the other side of New Covenant. The ride would take forty minutes.

"Say something to her," Seth whispered in Ash's ear.

"Like what?" he whispered back.

"Something funny or fun."

Ash drew a blank. He shook his head. Seth gave an exasperated huff.

Ash racked his mind for something to say that

wouldn't sound foolish. Why did he feel awkward with Mary now? He hadn't before. This was important to him. He didn't want to mess it up. A flash of red caught his eye between the trees. He quickly tapped Mary's shoulder. "Look, your fox is watching us."

"Where?" She sat up eagerly.

"To the left by that gray boulder. See her?"

"Oh, I do. And there is her kit, too." She watched until they were past, then she turned in her seat to smile at Ash. "You were right. She didn't go far."

"She must have a den nearby."

"Do you think we could search for it? Not today, but maybe tomorrow?"

He thought of all he had to do. "I really should catch up on my work."

"Of course." She turned back around.

He got another elbow from Seth. Glaring at his brother, he cleared his throat. "If you give me a hand with the inventory in the morning, Mary, we could scout around in the afternoon."

She turned to him quickly and winced. "I have to remember I can't do that yet."

She didn't want to work with him. Doing inventory wasn't anyone's idea of fun. "Never mind. I can manage by myself."

"*Nee*, I'd love to help if I'll be of any use with one hand."

She liked to tease. He'd give it a try. "Do you remember how to count past ten?"

"Ash! That was mean." Pamela glared at him over the seat back, but Mary wore a huge grin.

Laying a finger against her cheek, she looked thoughtful. "I reckon I can get to twenty by taking off my shoes." She couldn't hold back a giggle.

The sparkle in her eyes made his heart light. "That'll work."

His feeling of awkwardness evaporated. Teasing a woman wasn't something he normally did, but with Mary it seemed natural.

The women faced forward again. Ash elbowed Seth in the ribs this time and shared a grin with his brothers. Gabe gave him two thumbs-up.

That hadn't been so bad. Mary congratulated herself for maintaining the right tone with Ash on the ride to the Crump farm. Lighthearted and cheerful. He had responded in kind. He'd even made a joke. She smiled again at the memory.

Pamela leaned toward her. "I'm glad to see you and Ash are getting along."

She signed her comment for Esther.

"He's a fine man. You could do worse," Esther added.

Mary's smile froze on her face. "We're friends."

"Of course." Pamela and Esther shared a speaking look, signed something to each other, grinned, but didn't explain.

Mary looked out the door. Friends teased each other, right? It didn't mean there was an attraction between them. She certainly didn't want Ash's family to think there was. It might be best to ignore him for the rest of the day. Then Pamela and Esther would see she wasn't enamored with him.

When they finally arrived at the home of Jesse and

Gemma Crump, Zeke stopped the buggy in front of the house. Ash hopped out and offered his hand to Mary.

She held on to the carriage doorframe instead. "I can manage." Her tone was more abrupt than she had intended.

Nodding, he stepped aside, but she caught his puzzled expression. Had she hurt his feelings? This plan was turning out to be more difficult than she had imagined. She followed Pamela and Esther into the house.

The kitchen was a hub of activity as women set out food from various boxes and hampers while chatting and laughing. Mary stood back as Talitha bustled in with her baskets. She paused in the middle of the room. "May I have everyone's attention? Let me introduce Mary Brenneman from Ohio."

The room grew quiet as all eyes turned to her. Talitha put her basket down. "As I'm sure some of you have heard, she was in a terrible accident when a pickup truck struck her."

Murmurs of sympathy fluttered around the kitchen. Heat rose to Mary's cheeks.

"She has no memory of her life before waking up in the hospital. Not even her own name." Talitha paused.

The group remained quiet as they waited for her to continue. She took a step farther into the room. "The doctor called it traumatic amnesia. He believes her memory will return with time. She had been corresponding with my son Asher. We know she was coming to visit our community with the idea of moving here. We must pray for her recovery and do what we can to help her bear this burden as her new neighbors and friends."

A small red-haired woman with a sympathetic smile

stepped forward. "*Wilkumm*, Mary. I'm Gemma Crump. This is my daughter Hope." She placed her hand on the head of the toddler at her side. "We're glad you could join us."

"*Danki.*" Mary returned the woman's smile.

"Let me introduce you to everyone else." Gemma led Mary around the room. She met the bishop's wife and a dozen other women, including Gemma's mother. Esther and Pamela stayed by her side the whole time. It was overwhelming, but not as uncomfortable as she had feared. Talitha's announcement had set the right tone and delivered all the pertinent information so Mary didn't have to retell the story.

A short time later, Mary followed the Fisher women as they moved down to a large open basement for the service.

The men had lined backless wooden benches up either side of the center aisle down the middle of the room. Men and boys would sit on one side while women and girls sat facing them on the other side. The bishop and ministers would take turns preaching in the middle between them. Married women sat in the front rows while the unmarried women and girls sat behind them. One elderly woman sat beside the benches in a wing-backed chair. It surprised Mary there weren't more elders. Maybe it was because New Covenant was a new congregation settled by younger families.

Bishop Schultz and two other men entered the room. Mary assumed they were the ministers. Behind them came the men. They removed their hats and hung them from rows of pegs on the back wall in a quiet and orderly fashion. Married men sat in front. The youngest boys took up the last row nearest the door to make a quick escape when the service ended. Ash and Moses sat behind their father and married brothers almost directly across from her. She refused to look at Ash, keeping her gaze lowered.

The Volsinger, the song leader, announced the first hymn. A wave of rustling ran through the room as people opened their copies of the *Ausbund*. Mary picked up the thick black songbook beside her. It contained the words of all the hymns the Amish used in their services. Composed by early martyrs of the faith during their persecution and imprisonment, the songs told of sorrow, despair, hope and God's promise of salvation. The melodies, passed down through generations, were learned by heart in childhood. Singing was done slowly and in unison without musical instruments. Mary joined in the beautiful chant-like opening hymn, delighted to find she remembered it.

How was it possible she could recall words to a song, but not who she was or where she came from?

During the hymn, Bishop Schultz and his two ministers went out to counsel in a separate room in the house where they would discuss the preaching for the day. None had prepared notes. Amish preachers spoke as God moved them. They stayed out for an hour while the rest of the church sang hymns. Despite her best intentions, Mary found her gaze wandering to where Ash sat. Several times she caught him looking at her. She immediately looked away.

When the bishop and preachers returned, the sermons started. The men spoke Deitsh or Pennsylvania Dutch, but the Bible readings were in High German. After the readings, the men translated them into Deitsh so the young children could understand. Amish children didn't learn English and German until they started school. Deitsh was the language spoken at home.

The sincerity of the sermons moved Mary. She prayed earnestly with the congregation. She asked the Lord to heal her and show her His will. The hymns and prayers shared with the entire community filled Mary with a deep sense of peace, but her memory didn't return as she had hoped.

The service lasted for three and a half hours. During it she saw some of the youngest children sit with one parent for a while and then get up to sit with the other one. All the children were well-behaved. Gemma had set up a small table where the *kinder* took turns going to fill a baggy with animal crackers if they became restless.

When the service concluded, she went outside with Esther and Pamela while the men converted the benches into tables for the meal. The men would eat first and the women later. Esther and Pamela stopped to talk to several of their friends. Mary crossed to a small bench beneath an apple tree and sat down. Her ribs and arm ached after sitting up for so long. Her head started pounding, too.

Two young girls who looked about eight or nine approached and stopped in front of her. "Do you really have ambezzia?" one asked.

"Amnesia," Mary said. "And *ja*, I do. Who are you?"

"I'm Maddie Gingrich. This is my friend Annabeth Beachy. My very best friend used to be Bubble, but she moved to Texas because she was imaginary. If you forget your homework, the teacher can't be mad at you because it isn't your fault. Is that true?"

"I guess it would be, but I don't go to school."

A speculative glint appeared in Maddie's eyes. "How can someone catch ambezzia?"

A slender woman with honey-brown hair and eyes as green as grass walked up to the pair and planted her hands on her hips. "It isn't catching, and you will not forget your homework again."

Maddie looked disappointed, but she nodded. "Okay."

"Told you it wouldn't work," Annabeth said. "Come on, let's go play."

The two girls ran off.

Mary chuckled, her headache momentarily forgotten. "That one is a handful, isn't she?"

"You have no idea. I'm Eva Gingrich. I'm married to Maddie's brother Willis. We are raising her and two of his younger brothers."

"From your tone I thought perhaps you were her teacher."

"I used to be, but my brother Danny has that unenviable task now. Sadly, Maddie has him wrapped around her little finger. I hope she didn't upset you with her questions."

"Not at all."

"It must be terribly distressing for you. I can't imagine."

Mary adjusted the sling that pulled at her shoulder and made it ache. "The doctor advised me against trying to force my memory to return, but that's impossible. The longer it goes on the more I lose hope."

"Perhaps you need something to take your mind off it. We're having a work frolic at the school this coming Thursday. Spring cleaning in the schoolhouse and the teacher's home next door. Why don't you come and help? I'm sure the children will entertain you."

It felt good to be included in a normal activity. Mary cocked her head to the side and gave a nod. "I believe I will. *Danki.*"

"Don't thank me yet. You haven't met my brother Danny. He's one hard taskmaster."

"I'm not worried after you told me Maddie has him wrapped around her finger."

Eva laughed. "I look forward to seeing you then."

As Eva walked away, Mary slumped and rubbed her forehead. Why did she tire so easily? Why did her headaches keep coming back?

"You look about done in," Ash said, stepping around the side of the tree.

Her heart gave a happy skip at the sound of his voice. She should send him away, but she couldn't do it. "I love how you shower me with compliments."

He sat beside her. "You deserve every one. Are you ready to leave?"

"I want to stay. People are being kind. It hasn't been as hard as I imagined."

"Then stay."

"The truth is, I'm tired."

"And you have a headache."

"How did you know?"

He touched her forehead with his finger. "You're wearing your headache frown."

"I'm seldom without it, I'm afraid."

His dark brown eyes filled with concern. "Are they getting worse?"

"*Nee.* Mainly they come on when I'm tired."

"You need to rest more. I'll go get the buggy."

"I hate to take the buggy away from Moses. He

might want to take a girl home after the singing tonight."

Ash got to his feet. "Moses will survive. I'm taking my girl home first."

She saw Pamela approaching. "I'm not your girl, Ash," she said, loud enough for Pamela to hear.

"Right." Ash looked away, but not before she caught a flash of pain in his eyes. He walked off with his shoulders bent and his head down.

"What's wrong?" Pamela asked when she reached Mary's side.

"I have a headache. Ash is going to drive me home. Please tell everyone how much I enjoyed meeting them."

"I will. Is everything okay between you and Ash?"

"Sometimes he acts like we're still courting. I had to remind him we aren't. Tell Moses I'm sorry for taking his buggy."

"Don't worry about it. Give Ash some time to get over the relationship he thought he had with you. You don't remember any of it, but Ash had months to grow fond of the woman he was writing to and planning a future with."

"I'm sorry I wasn't honest with him then, but he needs to realize we're just friends now."

Pamela laid her hand on Mary's shoulder. "I understand."

Pamela walked away. Mary hoped she'd gotten her point across. She looked over to see Ash hitching Frisky to Moses's buggy.

"I can't be your girl, Ash. Not even if I want to be," she whispered.

Chapter Seven

Mary wasn't his girl. She had practically shouted it at him. Ash sat with his shoulders hunched against the sting as he drove toward home. He tried to ignore the pain, but he couldn't when she was sitting beside him. Why had he said that?

Because he wanted it to be true?

That was ridiculous. Completely ridiculous.

Mary remained withdrawn and silent as they headed home. She sat as far away from him on the buggy seat as she could get, looking lonely and dejected. The same way he felt. Was she still in pain?

"Are you okay?" he asked when they had been on the road for an uncomfortable two miles.

"I'm fine." Her curt reply wasn't encouraging.

"Is your headache worse?"

"*Nee*, it's fine." She stared off into the distance.

Ash pressed his lips together. He didn't need his brothers to tell him Mary wasn't interested in conversing with him. He glanced at her sad face. A new thought hit him. He was feeling sorry for himself, but

Mary was the important one. He needed to make this right between them.

"Are you still upset with me?" he asked.

That made her look at him. "Of course not."

He tipped his head in disagreement. "I think you are."

"What have I done that makes you say that?"

"It's not what you've done, it's just… Oh, never mind. I shouldn't have said anything."

She twisted in the seat to face him. "Tell me what you are about to say right this minute."

"Okay. This morning we were laughing together. I thought we were having a nice time. Then you almost took my head off for no reason. Now you can barely look at me."

She sighed and looked down. "I'm sorry, Ash. I didn't mean to hurt your feelings."

"Well, you did. I made a mistake when I said I'm going to take my girl home. I only meant I was going to take you home first."

"I understand that. Maybe I overreacted. It's difficult for me to know how to behave now. I enjoy your company, but I don't want people to assume we're courting when we aren't."

He was responsible for some of that. "By *people*, do you mean my family? Because nobody else knows that we were except the bishop."

"Your mother, Pamela and Esther have all hinted that we make a *goot* couple. It puts me in an awkward position."

Another glance at her forlorn face made his heart tighten. He couldn't bear to be the cause of her unhappiness. He wanted to see her smile at him the way she used to. They shared something special. He wasn't willing to lose that.

"I'm sorry if my family made you uncomfortable, Mary."

"It isn't your fault. You're just being nice, the way you always are, but they see something else."

"Do you want me to stop being nice?"

She arched one eyebrow in disbelief. "Is that possible?"

He wanted to hear her laugh. "I could try. You look haggard today, Mary. More than usual. Have you forgotten anything new lately? Do you recall what color the sky is? Shall I give you a hint?"

She choked on a giggle, then sat up straight. "I might forget I'm not mad at you."

There was the smile he was after. "If I'm rude and you're angry, that should get the point across."

"I'm not sure you'll be convincing." She gave a deep sigh. "Maybe I should ask the bishop to take me in."

Ash's heart dropped. He didn't want her to move out of his home. "Don't do that. I'll talk to my family. I'll make it clear that you and I are just friends. How does that sound?"

"Really?"

"Of course. I'll set them straight. No more talk about leaving, okay?"

"I appreciate that. You *are* still my friend, Ash. You know that, don't you?"

"Sure." He wanted to be more than her friend, but that was a lost cause.

"Danki."

"For what?" He glanced at her, and his heart turned over at the sight of her sweet smile.

"For understanding. You are a remarkable fellow."

It was a bittersweet compliment. Why couldn't she see him as a potential mate rather than a friend? He stared straight ahead not wanting his feelings to show on his face. "The most exciting man you know, right?"

"Not anymore."

"What?" He looked at her in surprise. Did she like someone else? Who did she know?

"I think Moses is more exciting."

She was joking, wasn't she? "Moses? Exciting? I wouldn't say that."

"He owns this fine high-stepping mare and plush courting buggy. I wouldn't be surprised to learn that he's got a stereo in here." She opened the glove box. "Aha. Just as I thought."

She pulled out a portable radio with two large speakers. "I'm sorry, Ash. Your little brother is *much* more exciting than you are."

Ash swallowed what was left of his pride. "I'll let him know you think so."

"Please don't do that." She put the radio back. "I don't need anyone asking to walk out with me, especially your baby brother."

He gave her a puzzled look. "You don't?"

"Absolutely not."

"But you are free to see any of the single fellows in the community."

She grew somber. "I won't go out with anyone."

"I don't understand. Why not?"

"Because I'm incomplete." She looked away. "I can't be a part of someone's life until I have recovered my own."

What if that never happened? Would she live alone

for the rest of her days? He grew sad at the thought. She had so much to offer. Surely that wasn't God's plan for her.

Ash wanted to reassure her, hold her close and tell her everything would be fine, but would it? He didn't have the right to do and say those things.

"Ash, stop!" Mary turned around in her seat.

"What? Why?" Ash drew back on the driving lines. Frisky came to a sliding standstill.

"I saw the little fox. It's hurt." She got down from the buggy.

"Mary, come back. An injured animal can be dangerous." She didn't heed him. He had no choice but to get out and follow her.

She stopped a dozen paces off the roadway and crouched down to peer under a fallen tree. "Oh, it has a broken leg. We have to help it."

The little red kit was huddled beneath the trunk, crying pitifully. Ash looked around. There was no sign of the mother or the other kit.

"We can't leave him here to suffer, Ash."

She was right. He knew what had to be done, although he hated the idea. "It will be kindest to put the poor thing out of its misery. I'll go home and get a gun."

She surged to her feet. "Asher Ethan Fisher, I will not allow such a thing!"

He'd never seen her so angry. "Mary, be reasonable. It's a wild animal."

"There must be something we can do. I know how much it is hurting, but bones will mend." Her voice broke.

"You can't take it home," he said as gently as he could. Surely she knew that.

Her chin quivered, but anger sparked in her eyes. "You just watch me, Asher Ethan Fisher. I am going to save this animal."

"Mary, please."

She ignored him, knelt beside the log speaking softly to the young fox. "It's okay. I'm going to take care of you."

She inched closer. The fox growled and snapped at her. She jerked back.

Why couldn't she be reasonable? Ash took off his jacket. "Get back before it bites you. I know Moses keeps a horse blanket in the boot. Get it for me."

"What are you going to do?"

"I'm probably going to get bitten. Do as I say. We need something to wrap him in."

Mary rushed to the back of the buggy and opened the boot. She found the horse blanket along with a tightly woven rattan box with a top. Inside was an assortment of tools. She dumped the contents and was able to drag it one-handed to where Ash lay sprawled on the ground with his head under the log. She heard a lot of snarling from the animal before Ash emerged with the young fox bundled in his jacket.

She opened the lid for him. "I found this in the boot, too. Careful. We don't want to hurt him."

"Too bad he doesn't feel the same about me." He laid the struggling bundle in the hamper and slammed the lid shut. "Now that you have your fox in a box, what would you like to do?"

She chuckled. "Nice rhyme."

"Mary?" She heard the annoyance in his tone.

"We need to take him to a veterinarian."

"That would be Doc Pike in Fort Craig, but it's Sunday. His office won't be open."

"Can we call his home from the phone shack?"

"We can. You must be prepared. He might say no to treating a wild fox."

"I understand. I won't let the poor little thing suffer longer than necessary."

"Okay. Get in."

After scrambling up into the buggy, she took the box when Ash handed it to her. *"Danki."*

"Don't thank me yet."

She looked down at him and smiled. "You were very brave."

He shook his head. *"Foolish* is the word I would use. I think you're rubbing off on me."

"We can't be practical all the time."

"I used to be. You're a bad influence." It didn't sound like he meant it, so she smiled. He walked around the back of the buggy and got in.

When they reached the phone shack near the Fisher farm, Ash got out to place the call while Mary held the hamper and talked softly to the little fox inside. "We're going to get you fixed up. It's going to be okay." She prayed she was telling the truth.

Ash came back after a few minutes. "Will he see us?" she asked.

"He's out on a call, but his wife told me where we can get help."

"Another vet?"

He shook his head. "There's a woman not far from here by the name of Walker. She takes in injured animals, nurses them and releases them back into the wild. I've never met her. She's something of a recluse."

"If she'll help, we have to ask."

"I agree."

Twenty minutes later, they turned off the highway where a crooked mailbox sat beside a large wooden crate with the word Donations crudely painted on it in white letters. They drove down a narrow, overgrown lane that stretched back into the forest. A small cottage came into view after a quarter of a mile.

The place had a neglected air about it. There were pickets missing in the fence that surrounded a tiny yard. The weathered siding needed painting, and the grass was overgrown. Across from the house were several large pens made of tightly woven wire. Some were covered with the same. Each held a large doghouse. A small deer lay curled up in one pen. Another held a bobcat watching the proceedings from the branches of a dead tree that had been placed inside the kennel. If the others had occupants, Mary couldn't see them.

A large mastiff lay in front of the cottage door. He gave a deep woof and sat up. The cottage door opened. A petite elderly woman stepped out. She wore blue jeans and a red flannel shirt. Her gray hair was pulled back in a long braid. She stood with her hands on her hips. "How can I help you?"

She didn't exactly sound welcoming.

"Are you Mrs. Walker?" he asked.

"I am."

"Mrs. Pike sent us. She thought you might be able to help." Ash stepped down from the buggy. He took the hamper from Mary, put it on the ground and then helped her out of the buggy.

"We found a little fox injured by the side of the road." Mary cautiously lifted the lid to peek inside.

Mrs. Walker came down the steps and crouched beside Mary. "How badly is it hurt?"

"It has a broken front leg. Can you help it?" Mary looked at the older woman's face. Up close, she could see Mrs. Walker had the most amazing deep violet eyes.

Suddenly Mary had a fleeting glimpse of a man with eyes the same shape and color in his tan face. Lines of worry creased his brow.

The vision vanished. Mary shot to her feet as pain stabbed her temples. A roar grew in her ears. Mrs. Walker stared up at her with a quizzical expression. "Have we met before?"

Mary stumbled back a step and turned toward Ash. She reached for him as everything went dark.

Ash caught Mary as she crumpled. He swept her up in his arms. Her face was deathly pale. Panic hit him so hard he could barely breathe. "Mary? Can you hear me?"

Mrs. Walker stood and frowned at them. "I don't normally treat people but bring her inside." She hurried ahead to the door and pushed the big dog off to the side.

Ash followed her into a dim room with a faded blue sofa beneath a single window. She picked up a yellow tabby cat off the couch and deposited the animal in an armchair. Ash laid Mary gently on the cushions. He knelt beside her and held her hand. His heart hammered wildly with fear. She had to be okay.

"What's wrong with her?" Mrs. Walker asked.

"I don't know." Her face was so pale. "Should we call an ambulance? Do you have a phone?"

"I don't. Young man, look at me."

He tore his gaze away from Mary's still countenance and focused on the older woman.

She eyed him intently. "She has a cast on her arm and old bruises on her face. What happened to her?"

He sank back and rested on his heels. "She was hit by a pickup truck about a week and a half ago. She has a cracked rib, and she gets bad headaches. She has only been out of the hospital for a few days, but she wanted to attend church services today. I could tell she was in pain after the preaching. She agreed to go home early."

Mrs. Walker went to the sink in the tiny kitchen and wet a dish towel. "Okay. It sounds as if she is trying to do too much too quickly. Is she your wife?" She brought the damp cloth over and laid it on Mary's forehead, then grasped her wrist.

"*Nee*, but she is staying with my family. She also has amnesia."

"Her pulse is fine." She lifted each of Mary's eyelids. "Her pupils are equal. That's a good sign. She doesn't remember the accident. That's not uncommon."

"Mary doesn't remember anything from before the accident. She didn't even know her own name."

Mrs. Walker frowned. "That is concerning."

"You wondered if you had met her before. She's from Bounty, Ohio. Have you been there?"

She picked up a black bag from beside the sofa and pulled out a stethoscope. "I have not. Why don't you step out so I may examine her? You can put the young fox in one of the cages in the barn for me."

"All right." He got up reluctantly. He didn't want to leave Mary.

"She'll be fine. I'll call you if she needs anything."

He took one step away and hesitated. Mrs. Walker

made shooing motions with her hand. "The sooner you go, the sooner you can come back. She'll be fine. I was a human nurse for many years until I discovered animals make better patients."

He nodded and walked out of the house. Standing on the porch, his feeling for Mary came into sharp focus. She was dear to him. Losing her would be unbearable.

The mastiff padded to his side and nuzzled his hand. He stroked the big dog's head. "You aren't much of a guard dog, are you?"

The dog sat beside Ash, wagging his tail.

Ash drew a shaky breath. How was he going to guard his heart now that Mary had found a way in?

She thought of him as a friend, someone as close as a brother. He couldn't even be sure she was a suitable woman. Where did that leave him?

Nowhere.

He walked over, picked up the wicker box and carried it to a small barn. Inside, he found one large room with a dozen small cages lined up against the walls. Some of them had openings through the wall where the occupants could go outside. One cage held a sleeping opossum with a bandage around its side. Inside another cage was an owl. He couldn't see what was wrong with it. In various cubbies between the cages there were bottles, rolls of bandages, assorted instruments and towels.

After unlatching one of the vacant pens, he laid several towels on the floor of it, then positioned his box so the young fox only had one place to go. It took several minutes for the animal to decide to leave the safety of the hamper. When he finally did, Ash quickly latched the cage shut. The fox limped around the enclosure several times before settling in a corner on the towels.

"You're a lot of trouble. If it wasn't for you, Mary would be safe at home, and I wouldn't know how much she means to me. I'd still be content being her friend instead of being sick with worry for her and wondering what I'm going to do. Bringing you here might be the biggest mistake I've ever made."

He checked on Frisky and then went up to the house. He had to step over the dog to get in the door. He breathed a sigh of relief when he saw Mary sitting up on the sofa. Some color had returned to her cheeks, but she still looked wan.

She smiled when she saw him. "I can't believe I fainted. I'm sorry I frightened you."

He moved the cat to the floor and sat down on the chair opposite her. "How are you feeling?"

"Foolish."

"I'll have tea ready in a few minutes," Mrs. Walker said from the kitchen.

"That isn't necessary," Mary said. "We should be leaving."

Ash wasn't taking Mary anywhere until she was fully recovered. At the moment, she looked like she would topple over in a strong breeze. "Tea sounds wonderful, Mrs. Walker, *danki*."

"Please call me Naomi. Your friend is obstinate, Mr. Fisher."

"I don't like to be fussed over," Mary said.

Ash nodded. "*Ja*, Mary has a stubborn streak all right."

Mary lifted her chin. "I do not."

She was looking better by the minute. He relaxed and

leaned back in his chair. "Who was it that insisted on crawling under a fallen tree to rescue a little fox when she was told she shouldn't?"

"I was merely concerned with the animal's welfare. And you were the one who crawled under the tree."

"Both you and that fox are *druvvel*."

Naomi laughed as she carried in two cups on a tray. "That will be a good name for him. Trouble."

Mary smiled at her. "You speak Deitsh?"

Naomi's grin faded. "I learned it as a child." Setting the cups down, she looked at Ash. "Make sure she drinks it all. I'm going to see if Trouble needs a cast. Sometimes in a young animal a leg break will heal without one if they can be kept quiet for a few weeks."

"We won't leave until she has finished her tea and is feeling up to the ride home."

"Good man." Naomi patted his shoulder and left the house.

Mary took a sip of her tea. Ash picked up his cup. "What happened, Mary?"

A faint frown creased her brow. "I'm not really sure. It was the strangest thing. Did you notice what bright violet eyes Naomi has?"

He shook his head. "I was too worried about you. You gave me quite a fright."

She blushed. "I am sorry. I didn't mean to."

"I know that. What about Naomi's eyes?"

"When I looked at her, I had a vision of a man with the same eyes."

"You saw a man with violet eyes?"

"It was more than the color. Their eyes were exactly the same. I don't know how to say it except if you look at Gabe's eyes they are exactly like Seth's."

"Identical."

She nodded. "I only saw it for a second before it faded. I tried to hold on to it, but then I had a sharp pain in my head. The next thing I knew, I was here on this couch. I think it was someone I know well."

He set his cup aside. "Then that is a good thing. Your memories are coming back."

Looking down, she shook her head. "I'd like to believe that, but the glimpses I've had are so few and vague that I have to wonder if I'm just imagining they are memories because I want them to be."

He slapped both hands on the tops of his thighs. "I say they are and that's that."

Rolling her eyes, she tipped her head toward him. "Not a rational conclusion, Ash. I disagree."

He liked the sparkle in her eyes when she teased him. "Finish your tea. If you're feeling well enough to argue, I think I can safely take you home."

"I'd like to visit Trouble first."

"Sure." He carried their cups into the kitchen and left them in the sink. When he came back, she was already on her feet. He eyed her closely. "Dizzy?"

"Not in the least."

"You will tell me if you start feeling poorly, *ja*?"

She stuck out her tongue. "You will stop coddling me, *ja*?"

He folded his arms over his chest. "Fine. Next time I'll let you hit the ground."

"*Nee*, you won't. You're too nice." She walked ahead of him out the door, patted the dog and then hurried toward the barn.

He stood on the porch and looked down at the dog.

"*Druvvel*. That's the word for her. She's trouble for my peace of mind and maybe for my heart."

The mastiff wagged his tail and gave a short woof as if in agreement.

Mary entered the quiet barn and immediately saw Naomi standing by the small fox. The animal was stretched out on the table. She was listening to it with her stethoscope. When she took the instrument out of her ears, Mary took a step closer. "How is he?"

"Stable for now. I had to tranquilize him. He's going to need a cast. I don't think the bone is broken, but it may be cracked. I suspect he was hit by a car."

Mary gave her a wry smile. "That makes two of us."

"Your friend told me."

"Did he also tell you that I have amnesia?"

"He mentioned it."

"Before I fainted, I think you asked me if we had met before?"

Naomi began soaking a roll of plaster in a basin of water. "I thought you looked familiar, but your friend said you are from Ohio. I've never been there. I'm sorry."

"Don't be. This is the burden *Gott* has asked me to bear."

"I'm sure it's a trial for you, but it would be a blessing for some of us."

Mary frowned. "I don't understand."

Naomi began wrapping the bandage around the young fox's leg. "Some of us have a past we would like to forget, but the Lord decrees we must endure the memories of our mistakes."

"I'm sorry."

Naomi looked up from her task. "Don't be. We all receive gifts and challenges from our Father. It is how we use them and how we face them that matters."

Mary walked around looking into the cages. "You use your gift to ease the suffering of wild animals. I'm sure that must please Him. They are His creatures, after all."

She stopped in front of the owl. "What's wrong with this bird?"

"Someone found her with an arrow through her wing. It's illegal to hunt raptors but some people are cruel, and others are simply ignorant of the suffering they cause. She hasn't been eating. I'm worried about her. She doesn't seem to have the will to get better."

"Maybe she just needs more space. She can't see the sky in here. Do you have somewhere for her outside?" Mary looked at Naomi.

The woman was watching Mary with an odd expression on her face. "I've been meaning to build a small aviary, but I haven't finished it."

Mary smiled. "I know several young men that I can coerce into lending you a hand."

"I can manage. But thank you." Naomi turned her attention back to the fox. "I'm sure your friend is waiting for you."

Mary heard the dismissal in Naomi's voice. She had worn out her welcome. "Thank you for helping Trouble and all the other animals. May I come back and see him sometime?"

"Suit yourself." Naomi picked up the kit and returned him to his cage. "There you go. Sleep well, little one and never fear—"

"Only pleasant dreams are allowed in here," Mary finished.

Naomi turned to stare at her. "That's right. How did you know that?"

"I don't know. I must've heard it somewhere. Goodbye and thank you."

"Mary. Please do come again. You're welcome anytime."

Surprised at the warmth and sincerity of the sudden invitation, Mary nodded. "*Danki*. I'll do that."

Mary walked out to see Ash waiting in the buggy. She stepped up and sat beside him.

He turned Frisky toward the lane. Mary looked back and saw Naomi come out of the barn to watch them drive away. "There's something familiar about that woman."

"In what way?" he asked.

"This is the first time we've met, but it feels as if I've known her before. I wish I knew why."

Chapter Eight

Ash sent Mary up to rest as soon as they reached home. For once she didn't protest, and he was grateful. He put a pot of coffee on to perk and sat at the table waiting for his family to get home.

When they filed in the door, he had worked out what he wanted to say. "I need to speak to all of you. I made coffee." He signed as he spoke for Esther's benefit.

"What's going on?" his father asked.

"I need to clarify some things about Mary and me."

His family took their places around the table and waited for him to speak. No one bothered to get coffee. Ash cleared his throat. "Mary and I had a long talk on the way home. Gabe, Seth and Moses, earlier today you suggested I try courting Mary. That's not going to happen." They were hard words to speak, but they needed to be said.

His mother leaned forward in her chair. "Ash, the two of you seem so right for each other."

"Let him finish, Mamm," Pamela said, keeping her eyes lowered. She had to suspect what he was about to say.

Ash needed everyone to understand. "We know Mary has had a difficult time. I don't want to make things harder for her. The point is, she's not comfortable walking out with me. She doesn't feel that way about me. She likes me as a friend. There's never going to be more between us. She's made that clear."

He would do his best to keep his newfound feelings hidden. From his family and from Mary most of all.

"She may feel that way now, but things can change," Gabe said.

Ash gave his brother a sad smile. "I don't think that's going to happen. What I need from all of you is to accept that Mary's feelings for me are not romantic. Don't hint that we belong together or try getting her to change her mind."

He looked directly at his mother. "Or scheme to put us together. I know you have the best intentions. I love you for it, but please don't. It makes her uncomfortable."

"What about your feelings?" his mother asked.

"Mary's happiness is important to me. I want her to feel welcome in our home for as long as she wishes to stay. She likes all of us and doesn't want to hurt anyone's feelings."

"We like her," Esther said.

"But we don't want to see you miserable," Seth said.

"You deserve happiness, too," Gabe insisted.

Ash loved his brothers more than ever at that moment. "Am I disappointed that Mary isn't attracted to me? I am. What man wouldn't be. I had an idea of how I expected my life to go. I wanted the same kind of relationship I see Gabe and Seth have with Esther and Pamela. I thought I was ready to start my own family.

I didn't want to feel left out. Someday those things will happen for me if *Gott* wills it. Just not with Mary. For now, I'm going to concentrate on helping her recover. I appreciate you hearing me out."

"You can't turn off your affections at will," Ash's mother said. "Trying to do so can lead to bitterness."

He shrugged. "I'm not denying how I feel about Mary. I like her tremendously. She's funny and unexpected. She's a sweet person and I treasure her friendship."

His mother's eyes narrowed. "It isn't that simple."

Ash's father rose to his feet. "Talitha, the boy has had his say. Leave him be. We will respect your feelings and those of Mary."

"Thanks, Daed."

His father nodded. "Come on, boys. The evening chores won't do themselves." He went to change out of his Sunday clothes. Everyone else did the same except for Ash's mother who stayed at the table.

Ash walked over and put his arm around her shoulders. "I'm okay. Don't worry about me."

"To worry is to doubt *Gott's* goodness and mercy. To fret a little for her children is a mother's duty."

"Well, please don't fret over me, then."

She reached up and cupped his cheek. "You might as well ask me not to breathe. I like Mary. She's teaching you to enjoy yourself. I've seen the two of you smiling and laughing with each other."

"That's what friends do."

"I reckon you must find your own way. Perhaps I'll write to Cousin Waneta and see if she has any advice."

Ash had to smile. "Save your matchmaking for Moses. Did you know he has a radio in his buggy?"

"Of course. I knew you boys had one in the barn during your *rumspringa*. Your father had one in his buggy when we were courting. We even danced a few times to the music when we were alone."

"Mother! I'm shocked."

She nudged him with her shoulder. "I wasn't born old, you know."

Ash laughed and hugged her again. "You aren't old. You are ageless."

"I enjoy a little flattery, but now it's time for you to get out of my kitchen. I must start on supper. Be assured that we will all help you take care of Mary."

"I know that." He started to leave the room then stopped on the threshold. "What do you know about Naomi Walker?"

"The woman who takes in animals?"

"That's the one."

"Not much. She came from Maryland about a year ago. I heard her husband walked out on her, but I don't know that for sure. I visited her once, but she isn't fond of company. She prefers her animals. Why do you ask?"

"Mary and I found an injured fox on the way home. We took it to her. Did she used to be Amish?"

"I've not heard that. I know she worked as a nurse and a missionary in Africa. If she was Amish once, she is *Englisch* now."

"Mary feels that she may have met Naomi before, but Naomi claims she didn't recognize her."

"Is that so strange? We all meet people who look familiar but aren't."

"Maybe you're right. It upset Mary."

"I pray her memory comes back soon. It's so hard on the child."

"I'd better get changed and help with the chores. Was Moses upset that we borrowed his girl-magnet?"

"His fancy horse and buggy? *Nee.* He spent the rest of the afternoon basking in the praise of several young women who mentioned how generous and unselfish he was."

Ash laughed. "Of course he turned it to his advantage. I pity the woman who falls for him."

His mother grinned. "She'll have her work cut out for her, for sure."

Mary joined the family for supper after a refreshing nap. Amish meals were for eating, not talking so it was a quiet affair. After supper, the family gathered in the large living room, as was their custom in the evenings. The French doors were opened. The breeze carried in the scent of roses and the sound of chirping birds gathering around the feeders throughout the garden. The evening light slowly faded. Ash went around lighting the lamps before he sat down with a book.

Zeke and Talitha were in their wing-backed chairs with the lamp table between them. Zeke read aloud from the Bible while Talitha relaxed with her knitting. Gabe challenged Seth to a game of checkers. Esther and Pamela got out a board game and invited Mary and Moses to join them. It was a game Mary knew. She was soon winning over protests from Moses.

When she looked up, she found Ash watching her. She wasn't sure if the soft light in his eyes was due to the lantern glow or some deep emotion. He smiled and her heart soared, only to plummet a second later. She wasn't his girl and never could be. No matter how much she wanted a life like this with him.

Talitha laid her knitting in her lap. "Ash told us you had an adventure after you left church, Mary."

She put away her sad thoughts and smiled. "We did, but Ash should tell it."

"Mary wanted to bring home a baby fox with a broken leg," he said.

"Where is it?" Pamela asked.

"We took it to Mrs. Walker," Mary said. "After Ash bravely crawled under a fallen tree to rescue it."

"This is a story we need to hear." Gabe turned in his chair to face Ash.

Mary and Ash recounted their experience with the injured fox. Gabe and Moses immediately started teasing Ash about being a fox terrier digging after his furry prize. Ash tolerated it with good humor. Mary had to add what she thought of his bravery. She didn't mention her fainting spell. Neither did he. She was thankful for that.

The many glances she intercepted between the family members led her to suspect Ash had already spoken to them about her concerns. Later, she took on Seth in a game of checkers and won. His defeated moan had everyone laughing. She glanced at Ash. He grinned and nodded encouragingly. She relaxed. It felt wonderful to be included in their warm family group. It was the best night she'd had since leaving the hospital. If only it could go on forever.

Early the next morning, she went out to the workshop to see if she could earn her keep by helping with his inventory.

Zeke and Seth were putting a red-hot metal rim on a wooden wheel outside the barn. Steam hissed and sputtered as they cooled it in a water trough. Moses was tacking black vinyl upholstery to a new buggy seat.

Ash was in the small office area with a large ledger open on the counter and a pencil tucked behind his ear. She knocked on the doorjamb. "Am I interrupting you?"

"Not at all. Have a seat." He indicated a high stool beside him. After pulling the pencil from behind his ear, he jotted several numbers on a scrap of paper. "Something isn't right."

"What's the problem?"

"The parts count is off. We should have five more wheel hubs. I'll need to order more if we don't, but they're expensive. I can't account for them."

"Have you asked the others?"

"I was getting ready to do that." He laid the pencil down. "What's up with you? How are you feeling today? You look less haggard. Have you forgotten anything new?"

"You are not being nice."

"I thought that's what we agreed on? Me not being nice. You being angry with me."

"That was plan A. Plan B was for you to talk to your family. I take it you did."

He nodded. "Everyone accepts that we'll remain friends. No one will suggest otherwise."

"Goot." She blew out a breath. There wouldn't be external pressure on her now, but she still had to deal with her own longings. He was such a wonderful man. Any woman would be blessed to have Ash walk out with her. Except the one who had schemed to gain his affection.

She smiled brightly to hide her somber thoughts. "How can I help today?"

"Find five wheel hubs."

"Okay? Where are your parts kept?"

"I'll show you. We have a separate storeroom at the back." He led the way past the glowing forge to another room filled from floor to ceiling with shelves and bins overflowing with bits and pieces of metal, wood and numerous bolts of fabric.

She could see organization wasn't a high priority for the Fisher men. "How can you find anything?"

"I have suggested we use a better system. I even labeled the drawers alphabetically, but it didn't help. This is just what everyone is used to. They claim they can't find anything when I put stuff away."

"Okay, am I searching for metal or wooden hubs?"

"Short metal. You look for them and I'll start counting the bolts and nuts. That takes the most time."

After searching through a dozen boxes, Mary located the missing hubs in an unmarked bin behind the door. "Found them!"

"How many?" He opened his ledger to the correct page.

"Four."

"Are you sure?"

"I didn't even need to take my shoes off to count that high."

He chuckled. "Fine. We're still missing one."

"One what?" Zeke asked from the doorway.

"One short metal wheel hub."

"Oh. I sold one to Willis Gingrich last week."

Ash pressed his lips into a tight line. "It's not written down."

"I was getting around to it." Zeke grinned at Mary. "Has he put you to work, too?"

"Just until the inventory is complete."

"I don't mind you taking over that task. Ash, Seth needs a leaf spring and a helper spring."

"Okay, I'll get them." Ash handed Mary his ledger. "Finish counting the six-inch bolts. I'll be right back."

She took the book from him and held it against her chest. "I know I said I wanted to look for the vixen's den this afternoon, but could we go back to Naomi's place instead?"

"Are you concerned about Trouble?"

She was more interested in talking to Naomi, but Trouble provided her a good excuse to visit. "I'm sure he's fine, but I would like to check on him."

Ash nodded. "Okay. I'll drive you over after lunch."

"If we're done with this." She patted the ledger.

"Even if we don't get finished, I'll drive you. The parts will still be here tomorrow. Unless Daed sells some while I'm not looking."

She grinned. "Take those springs to Seth. I can count faster if you aren't here."

"It's better to be accurate than fast," he cautioned as he went out the door.

Mary glanced at the book she was holding against her chest. She would do the best job possible because it was important to him. She eyed the floor-to-ceiling stack of bins. "Six-inch bolts, where are you?"

They finished the inventory by one o'clock. After a late lunch of cold cuts and lemonade, Mary eagerly climbed into the buggy next to Ash. "I'm sorry you have to drive me, but I don't think I can handle the lines with one hand."

"I'm eager to see how Trouble is faring, too. Are you sure you aren't too tired?"

"Not a bit. How am I going to pay for Trouble's care? I don't have any money."

"According to your letters, you do. You have a substantial amount in the bank from the sale of your husband's business."

Her mouth dropped open. "I have money?"

"That's what you wrote."

"What a relief. I don't know why I assumed I was poor. What type of business did my husband have?"

"I don't know. You never said."

"How can I get some of my money? Don't I need a checkbook or something?"

"The next time we go into Presque Isle, I will take you to our bank. Maybe they can arrange for a transfer of funds. It might be difficult without your ID and Social Security card. I reckon the police would have told us if they had recovered you purse."

She cocked her head slightly. "I wonder why I sold the business. Why didn't I continue to run it? Or hire someone to run it. Managing a business would be easier than being a farmhand for my father-in-law, don't you think?"

"That would depend on the business."

"You're right. This is so exciting. I have money! Are you sure I have a lot of money?" She saw he was trying not to laugh at her.

"Substantial was the word you used."

She tried not to get her hopes up. "That could be twenty dollars."

"I'm pretty sure 'substantial' is more than twenty

dollars, but I wouldn't start spending it until you know for sure you can get it."

"Of course not. I was thinking I could pay something on my medical bills." She turned in the seat to stare at him as a troubling thought occurred to her. "My old church won't take up a collection for me, will they?"

He shook his head. "I made other arrangements."

A sick feeling settled in her stomach. "You are paying my bills. Oh, Ash, I can't let you do that. It must be thousands of dollars."

"The hospital will work with you. Bishop Schultz can make a general appeal for assistance since he isn't supporting your shunning."

She sat back and rubbed her shoulder. "I'll repay you when I can. Which may not be soon. Well, it was fun having a 'substantial' amount of money for a bit. I think I'm used to being low on funds, anyway."

Sadness lowered her spirits as she wondered about the husband she couldn't remember. He must have been the love of her life. She glanced at Ash. When her memory came back, would she see him in a different light? Would her attraction to him pale against the love she'd had for Edmond Brenneman?

"Somehow it doesn't seem right to use the money when I don't remember the man who earned it. It was his business, his hard work."

Ash gave her a funny look. "You were his wife. I'm sure you helped."

"I hope so. I'd rather leave his funds alone for now and find a job. Start supporting myself instead of living off the charity of your family. I wonder what I can do?"

"Mary, I'm sure you can do whatever you put your mind to."

She smiled her thanks for his confidence. "Maybe someone local needs an experienced farmhand who can handle a team of four draft horses."

"It might be practical to wait until you get your cast off before you apply for that type of job."

Flexing her fingers, she gritted her teeth at the discomfort. They were still stiff. Her forearm ached when she moved them. "There you go being practical again, but in this case, I reckon you're right."

Dejected by the thought of waiting weeks yet before she could seek work, Mary fell silent.

It wasn't long before Ash turned off the highway at Mrs. Walker's lane. When they came out of the trees, Mary saw Naomi nailing a roll of chicken wire to a tall post.

She saw them and walked toward the buggy with her hammer in hand. "I wasn't expecting to see you so soon. Have you brought me another patient?"

Mary gazed at her face for some spark of recognition. Naomi's welcoming expression turned puzzled. "What is it?"

Mary sighed in disappointment. "Yesterday I thought I recognized you, or rather someone who looks like you. I was hoping that seeing you again would bring back that memory."

"I see by your face that it hasn't."

"*Nee.* That's always the way. I have flashes that I think are memories, but they never expand into something that I can be sure is real."

"You poor child. How terribly difficult that must

be for you. But you have come to see Trouble, too, I'm sure."

Mary smiled. "I have. How is he?"

"Hopping about a little. He's not happy with the cone I had to put around his neck to keep him from chewing his cast but otherwise he's doing well. I saw his mother hanging out beside the barn last night. She must've followed you here. I plan to move him to an outside pen so they can be near each other. I hope she doesn't abandon him. He'll need her when he's well and can be released. He's too young to manage alone."

Ash came to stand beside Mary. "Are you building him a bigger pen?"

Naomi looked over her shoulder. "That will be an aviary. I picked up enough wire to finish it yesterday."

"Is it for the little owl?" Mary asked.

"I got to thinking about what you said, and you might be right. She needs more space to stretch out her wings. Would you like some tea?"

"I don't want to take you away from your work," Mary said.

Ash held out his hand. "I can finish nailing up the wire if the two of you would like to visit for a while."

Naomi handed over the hammer. "I knew I liked you."

She tipped her head toward the barn. "Come see your Trouble first."

Mary and Ash followed her into the barn where the young fox was sitting up in his kennel looking a bit ridiculous with the white plastic cone around his neck and a cast on one leg.

Mary walked up to the cage, delighted to see the baby looking so bright-eyed. "Hello, beautiful *bobbli*.

I know it's awkward and uncomfortable, but in a few days, it will start feeling better. Then it will start to itch. I hope Naomi has something to help with that."

"He's growing fast so I'll have to change the cast in a week. I'll make sure to give him a good scratch while it's off."

The kit limped forward to sniff and then lick Mary's fingers. She looked at Ash. "Aren't you glad you rescued him now instead of the alternative?"

"You don't know how glad I am that I didn't have to choose the alternative." His relief was written on his face.

"Come up to the house when you're finished with the aviary, Ash," Naomi said. "I made fresh blueberry scones this morning. I love them but I don't need to eat them all by myself."

"Sounds *goot*."

Mary watched as he went out the door. The room seemed emptier without him.

"You have yourself a nice young man," Naomi said.

Mary turned to correct Naomi's assumption. "It's not like that. He is not my young man. He's a friend. That's all."

Naomi arched one eyebrow. "Funny, that's not the impression I get from the two of you."

"You're seeing something that isn't there." Mary couldn't look at Naomi. Was her attraction to Ash so strong that even a stranger could see it?

"Now you aren't being truthful."

Mary sighed deeply. "There can't be anything between us no matter how I feel about him."

"Is he married? Are you?"

"Neither one of us is."

"Then what's the problem?"

Mary stared into Naomi's sympathetic and somehow familiar eyes. A feeling that she could trust this woman filled her. She desperately needed someone to confide in. "It's so complicated."

"Aha. Then this conversation definitely calls for tea." Naomi marched out of the barn. Mary followed her up to the house.

Naomi pointed to the table. "Have a seat."

"Is there something I can do to help?"

"There's butter for the scones in the fridge. You can set that out. Some cups and plates, too."

When the table was set, Naomi brought a white china teapot decorated with pink roses there, filled the cups and sat down. She folded her hands. "Now, what seems to be the trouble between you and Ash?"

"Everything."

Naomi broke off a piece of scone. "This may call for two cups of tea. Try to be more specific."

Where did she start? Mary bowed her head. "I recently learned that Ash and I have corresponded for months before I came here. The relationship became romantic in nature. He proposed marriage."

"Before you met each other?"

"Apparently, I was coming to New Covenant to give him my answer. Why would I come all this way to tell him no?"

"Good point. You don't remember any of this?"

"Nothing."

"That must be disconcerting, but I'm still confused. You've met now. I can tell you like him a lot. Where's the problem?"

"I also learned I am shunned by my church in Ohio."

"Oh dear. I know what that means for an Amish person. I'm sorry."

"The thing is, I didn't tell Ash about my shunning in any of my letters. I was coming here under false pretenses. Maybe my letters were just a trick so I could start over in a new place."

"Seems a bit drastic. You don't strike me as the conniving sort."

"How can you say that? You barely know me."

"In my experience, which is vast compared to yours, child, conniving women rarely go out of their way to rescue an injured baby fox."

"But what if I'm not a good person? Don't you see? I can't allow myself to fall for Ash until I'm sure. Until my memory returns and I know what my feelings for him were, and why I tried to hide my shunning."

"*Were* is the key word in your argument. Aren't your current emotions more important than what you thought months ago?"

"I need to know, Naomi. I can't build a life with anyone until I know who I am."

"And if your memory doesn't return?"

"Then I'll have to go back to Ohio and learn what I can from the people who knew me."

"The people who shunned you. What if they won't speak to you? You know that's possible."

"I'll have to face that if it comes." Mary took a sip of her tea. It was lukewarm.

Naomi took a sip and put her cup down. "This is just my opinion, but I believe it is more important to be the best person that you can be now rather than worry about the past. I've made some heartbreaking choices in my life. I hurt the people I loved most. I lost the respect of my only son. We never spoke again and now he's gone so we never will."

Naomi reached across the table and laid her hand over Mary's. "But nothing in the past can be changed. When you accept that with your whole heart then you can begin to live as you should."

Was Naomi right? Could she let go of a past she couldn't remember? Or would it come roaring back and destroy her future?

Chapter Nine

Mary drew a shaky breath. She couldn't follow Naomi's advice. Knowing something from her past could hurt Ash made it impossible to reveal her feelings for him. Wouldn't it be less painful for him to lose a friend than the woman who cared so much for him?

"*Danki*, Naomi. I appreciate your concern."

"*Du bischt wilkumm.*"

"Your Deitsh is pretty *goot*."

Naomi looked toward the door. "Ash is taking a long time to finish that pen."

Movement caught Mary's eye. She turned to see a half-grown yellow tabby with white socks come staggering into the kitchen. The kitten came up to her, sniffed her ankle, then started purring and rubbing against her leg while struggling to stay upright.

"You poor little thing, what's wrong with you?" Mary picked her up.

"That's Weeble. Someone dropped her in my donation box. It was fortunate that I heard her cries when I went to collect the mail. She has CH. Cerebellar hypoplasia. More commonly called wobbly kitten syndrome."

"Will she get better?" Mary rubbed the kitten under the chin. A white bib that came up to her cheeks looked as if someone had glued cotton balls beside her nose. Weeble sat up and tried to bat the ribbons of Mary's *kapp*.

"She was born like this," Naomi said. "She may gain a little more muscle control, but she'll never get better. She's usually very shy and wary of strangers. I'm surprised she came out to meet you."

"I'm certainly glad you did, Wobbly Weeble. You're adorable."

Naomi looked at Mary intently. "Don't you feel sorry for her?"

The kitten had snagged Mary's ribbon and was trying to pull it to her mouth, but her head bobbed too much to bite it. Mary laughed. "Why should I? She doesn't know there's anything wrong with her. She just wants to play."

"Not everyone feels that way. I'm glad you do. Let's find out what's keeping Ash."

Mary put the kitten down and followed Naomi outside. The aviary was finished, but she didn't see Ash. The sound of hammering started behind the barn. The two women walked in that direction.

When they rounded the back corner of the building, Mary saw Ash fitting a top to a wooden box and nailing it in place. He looked up and smiled at her. "Did I miss the scones?"

"We saved you some. What are you doing?" Mary studied his project.

Naomi's face brightened with delight. "He's made an owl box."

He held it up. The rectangular box had a perch and a hole in the front. "I thought your feathered guest might like some privacy. My brother Gabe is an avid birdwatcher. We've got a few of these around the farm among other birdhouses."

"It's wonderful. Thank you, Ash. If you'll put it up, I'll get Bundi."

He chuckled. "You named your owl Bundi?"

She grinned. "It's a Swahili word. It means owl. So original. Mary, would you like to move Bundi to her new home?"

"Of course I would." She grinned at Ash. His smile widened, and Mary's heart beat faster. She was falling hard for Asher Ethan Fisher. That wasn't what she wanted.

But maybe Naomi was right, and it didn't matter what Mary had thought of him in the past or how she had acted. Could she accept that and live in the here and now? Could they be more than friends?

"What?" he asked, and she realized she had been staring at him.

What if they grew close and then something from the past hurt him or changed his feelings for her? She couldn't bear that. "Nothing."

"The owl?" Naomi prompted from the barn's doorway.

"Coming." Mary hurried to the door.

Inside, Naomi handed Mary a large pair of gloves. "Put on these gauntlets. They'll protect you from her talons."

Mary slipped her arm out of her sling. The large leather glove fit over her cast. She pulled on the other one. "I'm ready."

"Move slowly. Allow her to step onto your hand—don't grab her."

Mary did as Naomi told her and soon had a grip on the owl's feet. Holding her gently, she lifted her out of the cage and carried her outside to the new enclosure, speaking softly to ease the bird's anxiety. Bundi stayed calm. Ash had secured the box to the trunk of a dead tree inside the pen. Mary settled the owl on a branch next to the perch and stepped away.

Bundi looked all around, stretched out her wings and then scurried up the branch to the box. She checked it over carefully and then climbed inside. A second later she poked her head out the hole as if to say she approved.

"She looks happy." Mary prayed the little owl would feel at home under the starry sky tonight and grow confident again.

"You did well," Ash said.

Naomi nodded. "She has a gift. Animals seem to trust her."

Mary giggled. "A gift for handling owls. I wonder how I can translate that into a paying job?"

Naomi tipped her head. "Are you looking for work?"

"I haven't started, but I should. I've been living on charity for too long."

Naomi looked Mary up and down. "I know a crabby recluse who needs a part-time helper at her animal sanctuary. The pay isn't much, but you can set your own hours."

"You'd hire me?"

"On a two-week trial basis."

Mary couldn't believe her good fortune. "I accept."

"The animals will need to be fed and watered. Some

need medication, and that isn't always easy. You'll have to clean the cages and take care of new arrivals."

"I can do it. I may not be fast because of my arm, but I'll do a good job for you."

"Well, I'm willing to try it if you are."

Mary's excitement ebbed away. "I don't have transportation to get here and back."

"I can bring you in the mornings if Mrs. Walker can see that you get home," Ash said.

"My pickup is temperamental, but I'm sure it can make a short trip. When can you start?"

Mary looked at Ash. "The school frolic is Thursday. Why don't I come Friday and Saturday?"

"That's fine with me," he said.

Naomi nodded and smiled. "That works for me. Ash, I promised you tea and scones. Come on inside."

"You can meet Naomi's kitten. Her name is Weeble, and she is adorable. I might have to sneak her home with us."

Ash's eyes widened. "You're allergic to cats, Mary."

"I am?" That was a surprise.

"You wrote that your mother-in-law brought a cat into the house. You broke out in hives, yet she refused to get rid of the animal."

Naomi's eyes darkened with concern. "She was holding the kitten a few minutes ago. If it was a severe allergy, she would've had a reaction by now."

"I feel fine." Mary checked her hand and arm. "No itching, no red bumps."

Naomi put her fingers on Mary's wrist. "Any tightness in your throat or chest?"

"Nee." She took a deep breath to prove it.

Naomi released her hand. "Your pulse is fine."

Ash didn't look convinced. "You were a nurse. Can someone get over an allergy?"

"It occasionally happens. Some children outgrow their sensitivity."

Mary chuckled and nudged Ash. "Maybe my mother-in-law gave me hives, and I just thought it was her cat."

Both Naomi and Ash scowled at her levity.

"Monitor her for the next hour or so to see if she develops symptoms. Best not to expose her to the kitten again until we're sure she doesn't have a delayed reaction. I will see you on Friday, Mary. Be ready to work."

Mary impulsively hugged the woman. "I can't thank you enough."

"Just do your job. That will be thanks enough." She turned and walked into the house.

Mary grinned at Ash. "She tries to be gruff, but she isn't. Not really."

"Are you sure you feel okay? Can I get you some water?"

"Ash, you're doing that thing I don't like."

"Showing concern?" he snapped.

"Fussing. Will you stop!"

His frown deepened. "*Nee*, because you need someone to look after you."

She glanced at the house and then tried to sound calm. "I don't want Naomi to see us quarreling. Let's just go home."

He kept quiet until they were back on the highway. "Did you sense you know Naomi from somewhere today?"

At least he wasn't asking her how she felt again. That seemed to be the main theme of their relationship.

"I may have imagined that. I didn't have any kind of reaction when I saw her this time."

"The two of you seem to get along well."

"I know. I am glad she offered me a job. I'm employed. Isn't that great?"

"I'm not sure I've ever seen someone so happy to be cleaning out animal pens."

She wrinkled her nose at him. "You would point out the downside."

"I'm just being practical. I've got some rubber boots and gloves you can borrow."

"You can't burst my bubble. I'm going to love working with the animals and with Naomi. So there." She stuck her tongue out at him like he was a childhood friend.

That wasn't how she saw him, but she couldn't let him learn her true feelings.

Ash had never been so tempted to kiss a woman. Mary was impertinent and impractical. She annoyed him, and she was utterly adorable.

And that was not how he should be thinking about a sister or a friend. He concentrated on driving.

"I definitely want to repaint her donation box. I think she needs a sign by the highway telling people about her sanctuary. I'm sure not everyone knows where they can take an injured wild animal or injured bird."

"The vet sends people like us to her."

"True, but folks might be more inclined to help a wild animal if they know they won't have to pay a veterinarian to see it."

"You should discuss your plans with Naomi first.

She might not want more creatures. It costs money to take care of them."

"That's a good point. Perhaps we can have a fundraiser for her. I'm sure your mother will have a few ideas. I can't wait to discuss it with her."

That evening Ash sat in the corner with his book in his lap and watched Mary with his family. She and his mother had their heads together for a while discussing money-raising projects for the sanctuary. After that, Esther began teaching her the sign alphabet from a picture book. Mary had no trouble laughing at herself when she made a mistake.

Not serious, not practical, just charming. How could he have been so wrong about her? He wished he'd kept her letters. Now that he knew her, he wanted to re-read them and see if he'd come to the wrong conclusion, because that's what he thought he wanted in a relationship.

Gabe came over to sit on the arm of Esther's chair. *You should ask her to spell our announcement*, he signed.

Esther grinned and looked at Mary. "What does this spell?" Her fingers moved rapidly.

"Wait. Slow down."

Esther and Gabe grinned at each other. "Say the letters out loud," Gabe suggested. "It will help you visualize the word."

Esther signed the first letter.

"*B*. Is that right?" Mary looked to Esther for confirmation.

Esther nodded and signed the second letter.

"*A*. So *BA*."

Esther signed again. Mary grinned. "Another *B*? *BAB*?"

By now, everyone in the family was watching the exchange. Esther signed the next letter.

"I'm not sure about that one. Let me look it up." Mary thumbed through the book Esther had given her to study.

"*Y*," she announced. "*B.A.B.Y.* Your announcement is—baby?"

Esther nodded and blushed a pretty shade of pink.

"You're having a baby? That's *wunderbar*! I'm so happy for you." Mary jumped out of her chair to hug the mother-to-be.

Talitha put her knitting aside with a beaming smile. "Is this true? When? A grandbaby! My prayers have been answered."

Gabe slipped his arm around Esther's shoulders. "Early November we think."

Pamela rushed to her sister, and the two women embraced. Mary stepped back. Seth came over to pump Gabe's hand. "Congratulations. This is wonderful news, but you stole my thunder."

Gabe looked puzzled. Then he grinned. "You, too?"

Pamela slid her arm around Seth's waist. "October with our Lord's blessing. Esther and I agreed that she and Gabe should announce it first because he is the eldest."

"We'll need to start building you your own homes now," Zeke said with a wide grin. "I'm going to a *grossdaadi*. Daadi. I like the sound of that."

"I'm going to be an *onkel*." Moses grinned from ear to ear. "Women love men who like babies. I'll babysit whenever you need me."

"Great," Gabe said. "Mamm can teach you how to change dirty diapers. There'll be a lot of them with two infants in the house."

Moses's grin faded. "I might watch them when they're older."

Seth and Gabe burst out laughing. Ash smiled, but he couldn't help a twinge of envy. His brothers were moving into new territory. He would be excluded more than ever. They would be fathers. They would have their own homes.

The idea that having a wife might somehow keep him close to his brothers seemed ridiculous now. It couldn't be one for all and all for one with the three of them anymore. They were meant to grow apart. It was only natural that they lead different lives. Even if Mary agreed to marry him, it wouldn't change that.

He watched her smiling and congratulating his family. He didn't want what his brothers had now. He wanted Mary to be part of his life because he was falling in love with her. Not with some vague, inaccurate idea of her, but with the flesh-and-blood woman he saw before him. He wanted to walk his own path, the one the Lord had chosen for him, with her at his side.

Gabe walked over and stood in front of Ash. "Did we leave you speechless?"

"You did." Ash smiled, got to his feet, drew his brother into a bear hug and pounded his back. Seth came over. Ash wrapped one arm around him. "You two as fathers. It boggles the mind. Your poor *kinder*. Thank the Lord you both have responsible, bright wives to correct all the mistakes you'll make."

"So true," Pamela said, signing for Esther who laughed.

After congratulations went all around, Ash noticed Mary slip out into the garden. He followed her. She crossed to the rose arbor and took a seat on the bench. She seemed lost in thought. He walked over. "May I join you?"

She looked up with a soft smile. "Please do."

He sat and clasped his hands tightly together because he wanted to put his arm around her. "Happy news."

"Your *mamm* looked overjoyed. Your *daed* looked a bit stunned."

"I'm not sure he's ready to be a *grossdaadi*."

"How are you feeling?"

He looked down and chuckled. "I believe that's usually a question I ask you."

"Turnabout is fair play."

"I'm happy for them and grateful to *Gott* for this gift to our family. And you? You were looking pretty serious when I came out here."

"I was battling envy. It seems my husband and I weren't blessed with children. It must have pained us both. I would have loved to be a mother."

"It's not out of the question. You're young."

She cocked her head to the side. "How old did you say I am? Isn't it sad that I need to ask you instead of just knowing? When is my birthday? Did I have one and missed it?"

"You're twenty-nine. I have no idea when your birthday is."

"So I could be thirty even if I told you the truth."

"Of course you told me the truth."

"Not all of it. Maybe I fudged my age to sound more eligible."

"You don't look thirty. Except when you're looking haggard and worn. Then you look thirty-five, six, seven."

She fell against him laughing. "Ash, you are the best friend I've ever had. I'm sure of that even if I can't recall any other. You're the only person who can make me laugh by being rude."

A blush rose to her cheeks. She moved away and looked down.

"You should try insulting me in return. It's kind of fun," he suggested, hoping she would smile again. He loved her smile and her lilting laugh.

Keeping her eyes lowered, she shook her head. "I could never insult you. You've done too much for me. I'm so very grateful."

He didn't want her gratitude. He wanted her to like him for himself. "Forget about anything you think I've done."

Her gaze flew to his. "I pray to *Gott* I never forget a single thing about you."

Ash raised his face to the heavens. "That was a poor choice of words on my part." He glanced at her. "I'm sorry."

A smile crept across her lips. "Haggard and worn? I don't think saying *forget* is the poor choice you have to apologize for."

"Okay, I'm sorry for saying you look thirty-seven."

"Have you always been impossible?"

He got to his feet and held out his hand. "You'll have to ask my mother. Come back in. I think I saw Esther sign that she and Pamela made cake."

Mary grasped his hand and stood. "Cake sounds lovely."

Warmth spread from his hand holding hers until it filled his heart. He gazed in amazement at how beautiful she looked in the evening light. Her pupils darkened as her eyes widened. What was she thinking? Did she feel it too, this current that swirled, surrounded them like electricity?

What would she say if he asked to kiss her? Would she shyly agree or be horrified?

She lowered her eyes, breaking the connection between them. In that moment, he knew. He wanted her in his arms. Longed to kiss her sweet lips, to tell her she was beautiful in every way and that he thanked God for bringing them together.

She slowly slipped her fingers from his and the moment passed. She stepped away and went into the house. Missing her touch with a physical ache, he lingered for a moment to gather his composure. He never imagined it would be this difficult to remain her friend.

He fixed a smile on his face and went to join the celebration with his family.

Mary accepted a plate of cake from Talitha and moved to sit in the chair at the desk in the corner. Ash took his plate and stood across the room. Mary glanced his way once and then concentrated on her food. Something had passed between them in the garden. It changed her, made her deeply aware of him in a way she didn't know was possible.

She looked up and found him watching her. It wasn't friendship she read in his dark eyes. A deeper emotion pulled her toward him. It was frightening and exciting at the same time.

She looked away. Nothing could come of it. She couldn't allow it.

The front door opened, and Bishop Schultz came in. He greeted everyone, but his face was grim.

"Welcome, Bishop," Zeke said. "Come in and have some cake."

"I can't stay, *danki*. I've had word from Mary's bishop. I thought she would want to know. May I speak to her?"

Mary stood up. "Of course."

The bishop glanced around the room. "Should we talk in private?"

She couldn't look at Ash. "The Fisher family deserves to know what you have learned."

"As you wish." He pulled a letter from his pocket. "You were placed under the Bann for lack of humility, dishonesty in a financial matter, for defying your bishop and your failure to repent these sins."

"I don't see how that's possible," Talitha said. "Mary isn't like that. What are the details of her supposed dishonesty? He must have written more than that?"

The bishop waved the paper in his hand. "I'm afraid this is all he said. Mary, do you repent these sins?"

Even now, she had no real idea what she had done or why. Bowing her head, she nodded. "I do."

"Then my judgement has not changed. You are welcome here."

"I appreciate you coming by Bishop Schultz." She held her head up as she walked out of the living room.

Ash followed and caught her by the arm. "Mary, wait."

She couldn't bear to look into his eyes and see his disappointment. She fled up the stairs. Leaning against the door of her bedroom, she let her tears run down her face. Now Ash and everyone knew what kind of person she was.

The following day, overcast gray skies gave way to heavy rain. Mary stared out her bedroom window at the puddles growing in the gravel yard between the house and barn. The horses in the corral stood with their heads down and their tails toward the north wind, but they didn't seem to mind it enough to go into their dry stalls.

The entire family had gone to share their good news with close friends. Would they be sharing her story, too? No, she didn't believe that. They were too kind for that sort of gossip.

She should go stand in the rain. It couldn't be more miserable than doing nothing but thinking and wondering. Dishonesty, lack of humility, defying the bishop. As hard as she tried to remember the things she had done, all she accomplished was making her headache worse.

She had wanted to avoid the sorrow-filled faces of the Fisher family. Having endured enough of that at breakfast, she had pleaded a headache afterward and returned to her room, so she didn't have to go with them. They'd been trying their best to make her feel welcome and forgiven, but she just felt more like a fraud. She was a dishonest, prideful woman who had schemed to marry Ash.

Dearest Ash. Maybe it hadn't been a complete lie. Perhaps she had developed feelings for him from the letters he wrote. She could imagine them. He would've written about the farm, the family business and his brothers. It was possible she liked what she read and thought they would make a good match. It was less painful to believe that than thinking she had deliberately deceived him. Had she turned to him because she had no one else?

Ever since she woke up in the hospital, she had sensed something special between them. Something more than friendship. Ash had been there when she needed comfort the most. It was possible she had read more into his friendliness because she wanted to.

Those feelings had to stay buried. She wasn't right for him. He deserved so much better.

The patter of the raindrops on the window drew her attention again. What she needed was a walk in the rain. It always helped.

Mary inhaled sharply. *The rain. She used to walk in the rain.*

Racing downstairs, she flew out the door into the farmyard. Cold rain soaked her head and dress in a matter of moments as she turned in a circle, then strolled toward the barn. The smell of the rain and wet earth brought unexpected comfort in spite of the cold. She lifted her face to the sky and let the water cascade over her face.

"I hate getting wet, Daed. Please hurry."

"Nonsense." His laughter boomed as he held his arms wide. "We can't get any wetter than we already are. Lift your face to Gott's *blessing and let it renew your soul the way it renews the earth."*

"Mary, what are you doing?" Ash was covering her with a blanket that smelled like a horse.

She grinned. "I'm listening to my *daed.* I hear his voice."

Ash bundled her toward the barn. "You're freezing. Let's get you out of the rain. You shouldn't get that cast wet."

She looked at her arm. "I forgot about my cast. I like walking in the rain. He liked being in the rain."

"I don't." He pulled her into the workshop and led her to the glowing forge. He pumped the bellows, and the coals grew bright red. He pulled a bench over. "Sit here. This will get you warmed up."

Now that she was out of the rain she started to shiver. "I heard my father's voice, Ash. I remember a day with him." She could barely get the words out between her chattering teeth.

"We were riding home on the wagon. We got caught in a shower. I was miserable and told him to hurry. He laughed. Sa-said we couldn't get any wetter than we already were. He had a wonderful booming bi-big laugh, but I can't see his face."

She looked at Ash. "I want to see him again, but you said he died. I want to remember more things about him, but I can't. There's nothing else." She dropped to her knees and began sobbing. "I hate this. I hate it."

"It'll be okay. Hush now." Ash's gentle words pierced her sorrow. He wrapped the blanket firmly around her, lifted her from the floor and cradled her beside the warm forge.

Resting against his shoulder was wonderfully comforting. Her sobs died away into occasional hiccups. He didn't say anything more. He just held her. She never wanted to move.

Sandwiched between his warmth and the heat of the fire, her shivers lessened until they stopped altogether.

There was only the sound of the rain on the roof, the smell of smoke and the strength of his arms around her.

"How come you aren't with your family?"

"I didn't want you to be here alone."

She loved his compassion. "Why is this happening to me, Ash?"

"I don't know. It must be part of a greater plan because *Gott* allows it." There was so much sympathy in his soft words. It brought more tears to her eyes.

"He shouldn't," she mumbled.

"His reasons are beyond our understanding."

She sniffled. "I'm angry with Him for doing this to me."

Ash stroked her hair. "So am I, darling."

That drove a spike into her heart. "How can you call me that after what you know about me?"

"Oh, Mary, I can't change how I feel."

"You should. It's the only reasonable thing to do."

"That's not going to happen. I like you very much."

"No, you don't. You feel sorry for me." She scrambled away and ran to the house. In the safety of her room, she sat down on the bed and stared at the floor. Despite everything he knew, Ash still liked her. He had called her darling. Because he felt sorry for her or because he meant it?

She pulled the curtain aside and looked out her window. He was standing in the rain staring up at her.

What if he really meant it?

Chapter Ten

Mary remained in her room for the rest of the day with her hair down so it would dry. Brushing it soothed her. She wasn't hiding, but she wasn't ready to face Ash, either. Pamela brought a tray of food at suppertime. After that, no one pressed her to come out.

That night she dreamed she was again standing in the rain, only the water was rising quickly around her. The rain came in torrents. She had nowhere to go. She saw Ash trying to wade toward her. The current kept pushing him away. Crying out she reached for him, but the water closed over him, and he vanished. She woke sobbing and shivering. Huddled beneath the quilt, Mary knew it hadn't simply been a dream. Some part of it was true.

Early the next morning, there was a knock on her door. Talitha looked in. "Today is the school frolic, Mary. They're expecting your help." She shut the door without waiting for Mary's reply.

Was she ready to face the family and community? Mary pulled the quilt over her head. Silly question. Ash was the one she was afraid to confront. What if he'd realized he'd made a mistake yesterday?

What if he *meant* his words? What if he did care for her?

Knowing she wouldn't learn the truth in her room, she threw back the covers, dressed, pinned her *kapp* on straight and went down to face him. The men, except for Zeke, were already gone. It was a welcome reprieve.

An hour later, Zeke Fisher turned the family's buggy into the schoolyard and stopped the team beside the hitching rail out front. A half-dozen others were already lined up there. Ash and his brothers had arrived earlier and were beside a small barn unloading lumber from their wagon. It would be used to build additional playground equipment and benches for the ball diamond.

Mary watched them for a few minutes. It amazed her how handsome Ash looked in the early morning light. Dressed as the other men were in dark pants with suspenders, blue long-sleeved shirts and straw hats, there was nothing to make him stand out, and yet he did. She could pick him out of a hundred men or more.

He caught sight of her and smiled. She waved and felt the heat rush to her cheeks. Then she chided herself for acting like a smitten schoolgirl and quickly looked away, only to catch Pamela and Esther watching her with knowing smiles. Had Ash told them about his feelings for her? The sisters quickly sobered and continued unpacking the buggy.

Mary turned her attention to the school. The white one-story building with a steep roof had large windows across both sides of the building and a bell tower at the front. It sat back a dozen yards from the road. The playground consisted of a large patch of close-cut grass, A-frame swing set with four swings, a teeter-totter and a softball field with a chain-link backstop. Four young boys were throwing a ball around the bases.

Zeke went to confer with Bishop Schultz on what needed to be done. Talitha handed her basket to a young man who bore a striking resemblance to Eva Gingrich. "Welcome. We're glad you could make it. The women are gathered inside."

He helped Talitha and then Mary down. "I'm Danny Coblentz, the teacher. You must be Mary. I hope you're enjoying your stay with the Fishers. New Covenant has a lot to offer Amish folks interested in moving here."

"It certainly is beautiful." The school grounds backed up to the dense woods. A light breeze brought a piney scent that was mixed with another fragrance she couldn't identify. "What is that smell?"

He frowned for a second and then laughed. "Potato blossoms. The whole valley is covered with them this time of year. It's the main crop in our county."

One of the boys on the field yelled his name. Danny excused himself and jogged away to see what his student wanted.

Talitha leaned close to Mary. "He's a single fellow. He earns a nice living from the school board. The position comes with that sweet little house." She nodded to the home next door.

Mary rolled her eyes. "Am I going to be introduced to every unattached fellow in the community today?"

Talitha looked horrified. "Of course not. Several of them have jobs elsewhere and can't be here today. Danny is a good catch though. My cousin Waneta had high hopes for him and her daughter Julia, but sadly they fell out. Oh, there's Dinah. I must speak to her."

"Talitha?"

She looked back. "Yes?"

"Did Ash say anything about me yesterday?"

"He said you got caught out in the rain. Was there something else?"

"*Nee*, never mind."

"All right. I'll be in soon." She went to join her friend.

Mary picked up the last basket and carried it into the building. The school itself was a single room with wide, scuffed plank floors. Dust motes drifted in the beams of sunlight shining through the south-facing windows. At the front of the room was a raised platform with the teacher's desk. A dusty blackboard covered the wall behind it. Off to the side was a large bookcase completely crammed full of books. The student desks had been pushed against the walls. They would be taken outside to be cleaned while the ceiling, floor and walls were scrubbed.

The women of the community were gathered at the front. Eva Gingrich seemed to be in charge, dividing up the tasks and handing out supplies.

Mary walked up to the group. "What would you like me to do?"

Eva smiled at her. "I'm glad you could make it. Why don't you help Dinah and Gemma get the food ready and put out when it's time to eat? We have tables set up on the north side of the building. We'll clean the school this morning and then work in the house this afternoon. Please don't feel you have to stay and help the entire day. The house is open. Gemma is there making coffee. You might see if she needs help right now."

On her way out, Mary almost ran into a man carrying in a large box. She held the door open for him. He was tall and thin with a narrow face, close-set dark eyes and a hawk nose. He stopped to scowl at her. "You're new here."

She smiled. "I am. I'm visiting the Fisher family."

His expression brightened. "You're the one with amnesia. I was sorry to hear about your accident. The *Englisch* drive much too fast and have little regard for our people and especially our horses and buggies. Are you thinking of staying in New Covenant?"

"I'm afraid it's too soon for me to say that with any certainty."

He grinned and leaned toward her. "I'm Jedidiah Zook, by the way. Look forward to seeing you again. I plan to stop in and visit the Fishers real soon."

"I'm sure they are always happy to welcome a friend of the family." She slipped out the door and headed to the adjacent house.

Gemma was waiting for her on the porch. "I see you met Jedidiah. Did he say he'd drop by the Fishers' for a visit?"

Mary cocked her head. "As a matter of fact he did."

"You have sparked his interest."

Mary frowned over her shoulder. "Is he one of the fellows Talitha has lined up?"

Gemma contemplated the idea. "He might be. His brother-and sister-in-law in Pennsylvania recently died in a buggy accident and their two daughters have come to live with him. I pity them."

Intrigued, Mary eyed Gemma. "Why is that?"

"Oh, there's nothing wrong with the man. He's a successful farmer, but he doesn't have much personality. If you're looking for a no-nonsense, boring fellow with a big farm, he's your man."

"A big farm?" Mary giggled. "Then he definitely goes to the top. Oh, I shouldn't say that even in jest." Ash was the only man she wanted on Talitha's list.

Gemma took Mary's arm. "I can't see you settling for boring. The coffee is almost done. Would you mind taking some around to the men putting in the new playground equipment?"

Mary knew that was where Ash was working. She couldn't think of a reason to refuse. The truth was, she was eager to see him. She needed to know if his feelings had changed.

With a carafe of hot coffee in hand, she found a card table set up beside the barn. Someone had laid out foam cups, plastic spoons, sugar and a small pitcher of cream. Gemma followed her with a platter of baked goods. The men came up one at a time to get their coffee and rolls. Ash was among the last to make his way over.

She handed him a cup and his fingers closed around hers sending her pulse racing. This rush of emotion was not her imagination. They stared at each other until Gabe cleared his throat behind Ash.

Giving herself a quick mental shake, Mary stepped to the side. "Coffee, Gabe?"

"Danki." He took a cup and walked away after nudging Ash with his elbow.

Ash ignored his brother and stood sipping his drink by the table. She struggled to find something to say.

Finally, she looked at the wooden climbing area they were building. "How is it going?"

"You should know I don't feel sorry for anyone. I only hope things can progress from here. What about you?"

His eyes were filled with a soft expression that warmed her to her toes. Smiling, she looked down. "I think that could happen."

"Seriously? I'm mighty glad to hear you say that."

Gemma giggled and held out her platter. "Would you like a sticky bun, or is Mary the only sweet you're after?"

Ash blushed a deep red. "Thanks for the coffee." He hurried back to where his brothers were working.

Gemma gathered up the empty cups. "The two of you weren't talking about building the playground equipment."

Mary tried to bluff. "Of course we were."

"Nope. That man was looking at you the way Jesse still looks at me, and you were looking back."

Mary sighed. "I was, wasn't I?"

She had fought it long enough. She was falling in love with Asher Ethan Fisher. Admitting it to herself was freeing.

The rest of the day she enjoyed visiting with the women, helping keep track of the small children and watching Ash.

Bishop Schultz put him in charge of painting the small barn and corral fences. His crew of helpers were five boys ranging in age from six to ten. Ash patiently showed the youngers what needed to be done, helping the smallest one to hold his brush correctly and even lifting one child so he could paint the underside of the eves. Despite the amount of paint that landed on his clothes, he continually encouraged and praised the boy's work.

When the picnic-style lunch was served, he brought his plate over to where Mary sat in the shade with two infants. One on her lap and one on the quilt. He sank onto the ground next to her. "Who do you have there?"

"Charity and Jacob Weaver."

"Ah, the lumberjack's twins."

"Maisie asked me to watch them while she gets some food. Aren't they adorable? I love their red hair."

"Have you eaten?"

"I'll get something in a bit. I'm rather occupied at the moment." Jacob was up on his knees, crawling toward the edge of the quilt. Mary was trying to wrest a bug out of Charity's hand before she got it into her mouth.

Ash rescued Jacob and deposited him in the center of the quilt. The baby immediately headed in the other direction. Ash snatched him up again and settled the child on his lap. Unwilling to sit still, Jacob tried to climb up Ash's chest using his suspender. "Where is Moses when you need a babysitter?"

He looked completely at ease with a baby in his arms. "You must like children." Mary tossed the liberated bug away. "I saw you overseeing the paint crew."

"I do like kids. I look forward to being an *onkel*."

"And a father?"

He smiled at her. "Someday if all goes well."

Mary decided she and Ash were like two children sharing a special secret at breakfast the next morning. Every time she looked at him, he was smiling at her.

She grinned at him, too, but quickly lowered her eyes hoping no one else noticed. It was a forlorn hope. Esther and Pamela exchanged little comments in sign and giggled.

Gabe winked at her. "Beautiful morning, isn't it, Ash?"

"*Ja*, beautiful." His comment was followed by the rumble of thunder. Seth choked on a sip of coffee. Gabe pounded his back.

Ash scowled at his brothers. "What? We could use more rain."

"We will take what *Gott* sends," Zeke declared. "We've plenty of work to keep us busy inside the shop. We should get started. *Goot* meal, Mudder." He rose to his feet. Seth and Gabe did as well. Moses stuffed one more biscuit in his mouth and went out with them.

Ash rose. "I'll be in the shop when you're ready to go to Naomi's. I'll hitch up the buggy first thing."

They would be alone together on the ride to the sanctuary. Mary clenched her fingers together to still her jitters. "I'll be out when our morning chores are done."

After he left, Mary began humming as she helped gather up the dishes. She stopped when she discovered Talitha gazing at her with a self-satisfied smile. "What?"

Talitha raised both hands in the air. "I'm not saying anything. Except, sometimes I'm right even when other people refuse to see that."

Mary didn't reply. She hurried through her share of the housework and then gathered a few supplies to take along to Naomi's house.

When she stepped out the door, she saw Ash was

already waiting by the buggy. "I thought you were working in the shop?"

"Daed said I wasn't much use this morning. There was too much joking going on." He looked over his shoulder. Mary noticed all three of his brothers gathered in the doorway waving to them.

"Shall we go?" She hurried into the buggy. Her face had to be beet red.

Once they were out on the highway, she relaxed. The clip-clop of the horse's feet on the roadway and the jingle of the harness filled the quiet morning as they drove along. The storm clouds moved off. The sun came out making the raindrops on everything sparkle.

Ash cleared his throat. "I think we should talk about this."

"This what?" She waited to exhale.

He glanced at her. "Us."

She let out the breath she'd been holding. Why was she so nervous? "You mean our friendship?"

"Mary, I think we both know this has moved past friendship."

"What if it has? Nothing has changed except I know more about why I was shunned." Was she foolish to believe he could overlook that?

"I know those things trouble you. But none of that matters to me."

What wonderful words. Her heart filled with joy. She had to trust that God brought Ash into her life for a reason if she was going to take a chance on happiness. "I reckon if you can forgive my poor behavior, maybe I can look to the future instead of trying to see into the past."

He reached over and grasped her hand. "Does this mean you'll walk out with me?"

She nodded. "I believe it does."

His bright smile warmed her heart. "You won't be sorry, Mary."

Sitting up straighter, she looked ahead. "I have one condition."

He pulled his hand away. "Okay."

"You'll have to stop being rude to me."

"What do you mean? Oh, so I can't say you look haggard and worn-out anymore?" He jiggled the driving lines to speed up the horse.

"That's right."

He chuckled. "I can't tell folks your age might be thirty-eight or thirty-nine?"

Outraged, she stared at him with her mouth open. "Absolutely not."

"And no jokes about forgetting the color of the sky or how to count to ten?"

"Are you done?" She tried to sound miffed but couldn't.

"Sure. I won't use any of those innocent comments that you consider rude."

She turned her face away. "I believe I just forgot I was going to walk out with you."

He nudged her with his shoulder. "*Nee*, you didn't."

Casting him a sidelong glance, she knew she hadn't fooled him. "What makes you so sure?"

"Because of the way your eyes sparkle when you look at me."

She grew serious. "I pray my past never hurts you, Ash."

He covered her hand with his own and gave a gentle squeeze. "It won't."

"Then there is one more thing you need to know right now."

"It won't make a difference in how I feel." His earnest expression warmed her heart.

"I'm glad, but you just missed the turn to Naomi's place."

Chuckling, he slowed Dottie and brought her around. "I was wrong. Now I feel foolish."

Remarkable happiness churned in Mary. How was it possible to feel so blessed only two days after her darkest hour?

Ash had no intention of dropping Mary off at Naomi's and returning home. He hadn't needed to confide in his brothers. Apparently, his feelings were plainly written on his face. At their urging and with his father's consent, he had the rest of the day off to woo Mary. He wasn't going to waste it.

Naomi was in her front yard with her dog and eight ducks. Mary got out of the buggy and turned to him. "I wish you didn't have to leave."

"I don't. I am at Naomi's disposal for the day."

Naomi was trying to encourage her ducks into a pen. The ducks had other ideas. "That's a welcome surprise. I could use a hand right now."

It took the three of them twenty minutes and numerous attempts, several foiled by the dog's unwelcome assistance, to finally secure all eight ducks in their enclosure. Ash bent over with his hands braced on his knees and tried to catch his breath.

Naomi was panting as hard as the dog. "Mama Fox

got one of them last night. After this, I just might leave the gate open tonight."

"You don't mean that." Mary crouched beside the wire fence and let one duck nibble at her fingers through the wire.

"Let's just say I'm tempted."

Mary looked up at her. "Does that mean Trouble's mother is still coming around?"

"I can't be sure it was her last night, but I think so. I wish I knew where her den is. I would like to release Trouble near there when he's well enough."

"Mary and I can do some scouting later. We've seen her twice near our farm. I have a general idea."

Planting her hands on her hips, Naomi leaned back and stretched. "I'm too old for this."

Laughing, Mary stood up. "That's why you hired me."

"And why I'm here for free," Ash said.

Naomi arched one eyebrow. "I don't think you're here just to help an old lady, Ash, but I'll take what I can get."

Ash figured he was blushing, but he didn't care if Naomi knew how much he liked Mary. He wanted everyone to know. "Where should I start?"

She held up her arms and turned around. "Take your pick. The fence needs fixing and painting. A hinge came loose on the barn door. The weeds are getting taller than the dog. Have at it."

"And me?" Mary asked.

"Clean the cages in the barn. Don't let any of the animals out while you're doing it. I'm not going to run after another creature this morning." She headed into the house.

Ash folded his arms over his chest. "Are you sure you want to work for her?"

"Absolutely. I even brought rubber gloves and over-shoes."

"Then the sooner we get started the sooner we'll be done, and we can go looking for Trouble's home. I wonder if Naomi has any paint for her picket fence?"

Mary had some trouble managing the cage cleaning with only one good arm. Twice she had to get Ash to help her. He willingly dropped whatever he was doing and came to her aid.

She had been afraid that agreeing to date would impact their friendship, but she didn't see any trace of that. They were even better friends now that she didn't have to hide how she felt.

Naomi fixed them a lunch of wild rice with fresh mushrooms, a green salad from her garden and mixed-berry tarts for dessert. Then she brought out three paintbrushes, two oversized shirts to cover their clothes and a can of paint. Mary had to wonder if she had ever enjoyed an afternoon so much.

When the fence was done and left to dry, Ash took a walk around Naomi's duck pen and went a little way into the woods.

"I've found her trail," he said when he came back. "Are you too tired for a hike, Mary?"

Too exhausted to take a walk alone in the woods with Ash? She shook her head. "I'm not the least bit tired."

Naomi chuckled. "If you aren't back in an hour, I'll send a search party."

"We'll be back," Ash assured her without taking his eyes off Mary.

"Do look for the vixen's den while you're out there."
She gave him a hard stare.

Ash stood up straight. "Yes, ma'am. We'll be back in
an hour with a location where we can release Trouble."

He walked away from the sharp eyes of Naomi with
Mary at his side.

It was cool in the woods. The ground was damp
after the recent rains and held the footprints of numerous forest creatures. Backtracking the fox wasn't
difficult. Occasional white duck feathers proved they
were going in the right direction. The trees opened out
into a small clearing with a pond in the center. Just at
the edge of the forest stood a jumble of granite boulders. A few more duck feathers in front of a group of
low shrubs told him the den had to be behind them.

"Let's wait and see if anyone is about," he whispered.

Mary looked around with wide eyes. "What a perfect place for a home. The reflection of the trees and
sky in the pond is like a mirror. I can't imagine anything prettier."

Ash turned her face toward him with a finger under
her chin. "I don't have to imagine. I'm looking at something much prettier."

Her eyes darkened. "I think you should kiss me
now."

"My thoughts exactly." He leaned forward and covered her lips with his own. He meant it to be a brief,
chaste kiss, but the moment he tasted the sweetness of
her, that plan went out of his head.

Chapter Eleven

Mary knew his kiss would be wonderful. The touch of his warm mouth against hers sent her mind reeling. The sounds of the woods faded away. There was nothing but the need to be in his arms. His firm lips pressed against hers, tenderly at first, but growing more insistent as his arms encircled her to pull her close. She cupped his face with her hand and ran her fingers up into his hair, adoring the silky softness of it. His hat fell off and landed in the grass. She didn't care. She just wanted to hold him, be held by him and float together on the wonderous sensation of joy.

When he pulled away, she came drifting back to earth.

He tucked her head under his chin. His breathing was as unsteady as hers. "I think we should head back."

"Why?" She didn't want the moment to end. Had she ever felt this way before?

"Our hour will be up soon. I firmly believe Naomi will send out a search party."

A soft sigh escaped her tingling lips. "You're right. I

don't think she makes idle threats. I'm sorry we didn't see the foxes."

"I have a feeling they saw us first. It's hard to sneak up on a fox. They have big ears."

"And sharp eyes."

"And excellent noses. They will know we've been here if they didn't see us. Are you ready to go back?"

"Nee."

He cocked his head to the side with a smug grin on his face. "Did you forget the way?"

She jerked away from him. "You promised you wouldn't be rude to me anymore."

"Did I promise that?"

"You did." Frowning, she took a step away.

He caught her hand and pulled her back into his embrace. "Then I'm sorry. My mind is a muddle when I'm near you. Do you forgive me?"

How could she not? "I guess. On one condition."

"Another condition?"

She felt the rumble of his laugh deep in his chest. A sly grin curved her lips. "You'll like this one."

"Okay, what is it?"

"One more kiss."

"Don't the *Englisch* call that blackmail? But you're right. I do like your condition." He leaned toward her. Closing her eyes she raised her face. He planted a kiss on her forehead.

She pursed her lips in a pout. "That was not what I had in mind."

"But it's all you get." He took her hand. "Come on. Naomi is waiting for us."

With her hand in his, Mary walked along the trail, cocooned in contentment, surrounded by the earthy fragrance of the mossy woods she loved. She gazed up at the man beside her and wondered where this relationship was heading. How could she let it go further without repairing the damage she had done to her family and community back home?

He squeezed her hand. "What has you so deep in thought, Mary?"

"The past."

"I expected that."

"My shunning will always be a blight on my reputation, even if I'm accepted into the New Covenant church. We both know it won't remain a secret, and it shouldn't."

"What can you do?"

"I'm going to write to my in-laws. Tell them I'm sorry, that I repent and ask forgiveness. I'll ask to speak with them on the phone and hope they agree. Maybe hearing their voices will trigger some kind of recognition."

Ash squeezed her hand. "I think that's a fine idea. You can dictate it to me. I'll write it for you if that's acceptable."

She smiled at him. "*Danki*, that would be a great help. I might be able to scratch a note with my left hand, but I doubt anyone could read it."

It felt good to have a plan and to share it with Ash.

When they came out of the woods, they saw Naomi was indeed waiting on them. Seated in a rocker on her porch, she gave the impression of a ruffled mother hen. "About time. I have Search and Rescue on speed dial, you know."

"We're back safe and sound," Ash said. "We followed the trail of your visitor last night to a pond about a mile into the woods."

"I know the place. Be here tomorrow at noon, Mary." She rose from her chair to go in the house but stopped in the doorway and looked back. "You both did a fine job today. I appreciate it. Thanks." She went inside. The dog followed her.

Ash raised both his eyebrows. "A compliment from Naomi Walker. Those don't get handed out every day."

"You're too hard on her, Ash. She's a sweet lady. I wish I knew why she seems familiar."

"No more visions or flashes of memories?"

"None."

He folded his arms across his chest and stared at his feet. "I thought maybe when we kissed that you might remember kissing your husband."

She laid her hand on his arm. "*Nee*, I only thought how wonderful it was to kiss you."

Looking relieved, he grinned. "Then maybe we should try it again."

"First you'll take me home and help me write my letter. Ash, I need to reconcile with my church, my husband's family, my friends. You understand, don't you?"

"I'm not making any demands on you. Where we go from here is completely dependent on what you're comfortable with."

"You're a marvelous friend."

"Could you put *boy* in front of that?"

"You're a marvelous boyfriend."

He grinned. "I try. Let's go home and write your letter."

Mary pushed aside the sudden fear that gripped her.

It was the right thing to do. She couldn't move forward until she had repaired what she could of her past, so why was she afraid?

Ash helped Mary craft a brief but sincere apology to her in-laws, asking them to set a time when they could speak on the phone. After putting the letter in the mailbox, she turned to him with a broad smile. "I feel like I'm finally taking control of my life. Now we just wait."

"I admire your determination to reconcile with them." Ash didn't care if they accepted Mary's peace offering or not. But it was important to her. He was prepared to wait until she was ready to take the next step in their relationship, but the memory of the kiss they shared kept him awake at night.

What didn't make him happy was to see Jedidiah Zook show up on Sunday for a visit. He claimed he was taking his two nieces around to meet the other families in the district, but Ash saw Jed had his eyes on Mary.

The nieces were ten and eleven, somber, subdued children who seemed lost. Perhaps that was to be expected after losing both parents. Mary spent much of Jedidiah's visit talking to them and getting them to open up. Ash was amazed at her compassion and persistence. It was her story about the fox that caught their interest.

"She keeps a fox in her barn?" Lydia was the older of the two.

"It's the truth. A baby fox with an injured leg. His name is Trouble."

The younger girl, Polly, smiled sadly. "That was our *daed's* nickname for me."

Mary laid a hand on the child's head. "Then you must

come and meet Trouble. You are twins. He had red hair and so do you."

Polly turned to Jedidiah. "May we go see the fox, Onkel Jed?"

"If Mary has time one of these days. I'm sure we'd all enjoy spending more time with her."

Mary's smile slipped a little. "I'll have to check with Naomi."

When the visit was finally over, Ash accompanied Jed out to his buggy. The girls were saying goodbye to his family. He drew himself up to his full height, a good four inches taller than Jed. "I think you should know Mary is walking out with me."

Jed frowned. "I see. She seems like a nice woman. It's just that my nieces are going to need a mother. I don't know anything about raising girls. I can't teach them the things they need to know. If it doesn't work between the two of you, will you let me know?"

Ash learned he could experience jealousy and compassion in the same moment. He managed a smile. "Don't hold your breath, Jed. It'll work out for us. I'm sure of it."

Mary rode beside Ash on the seat of the family's wagon the next afternoon. He had several rolls of chicken wire, garden fencing and eight posts to build additional pens beside the barn so that some of the animals could enjoy the fresh air and sunshine.

When they reached the turnoff to Naomi's lane, Mary tapped his arm. "Stop a minute, please."

He did. She got down to examine the donation box. "We definitely need a larger sign here."

"I think I can find some scrap boards that will work.

In fact, I think I saw several behind Naomi's barn if she'll let us use them. A bigger sign might bring more animals as well as more donations. We should make sure she wants that."

"You're right." Mary tried to climb back up, but found she needed both arms.

"Step back," Ash said and jumped down when she was out of the way. "Come here." He motioned her closer.

Stepping behind her, he grasped her waist and lifted her up to the wagon seat. She gritted her teeth at the pain in her rib but kept a smile on her face. Her heart took a minute to settle down. He was so strong and gentle. She struggled to cover the effect he had on her. "I will be glad to get this cast off."

"How much longer?" He came around the wagon and got in on his side.

"The doctor said x-ray in four more weeks. Then I will know if it's healing right."

He drove up to the house and stopped the wagon beside the barn. It took him only a few minutes to unload, then he went to explore some of Naomi's scattered outbuildings.

Naomi opened the barn door. "I thought I heard someone out here. What's all this?"

"Ash is going to build some new pens for you. We thought you could use a bigger sign at the donation box, too, but wanted to check with you first."

"If he wants to do that, I guess that's okay."

"What name do you want on the sign?" Mary asked.

Naomi shrugged. "You think of something. Come with me."

Mary followed Naomi inside the barn. The little fox was pacing in a smaller cage.

"Why is he back in here?" Mary asked.

"I'm going to remove his cast and replace it with a splint. He'll have to be tranquilized. I don't want him struggling."

"Can I help?"

"You can. I'm not going to put him under deeply, but I will need you to watch and make sure he's still breathing or that he isn't waking up."

Naomi administered the drug with a small dart gun and waited until the kit leaned against the side of the crate and then slumped to the floor. The outside door opened. Ash came in.

"What are we doing?"

"Removing his cast," Mary told him.

"Ash, bring him over here," Naomi said. She stood beside a white folding table. Mary helped Ash slide the baby out of the kennel without hurting his leg and brought him to Naomi's workstation.

She handed her stethoscope to Mary. "Listen and tap out what you're hearing with your finger. That way I can see what his heart rate is. Ash, bring that little cutting wheel over here. Now hold his leg out straight for me."

Ash did as he was instructed while Mary tapped out to the baby's heart rate. It remained steady and strong until Naomi finished her work. She picked up her tools. "Go ahead and put him back, Ash. I need someone to sit with him until he comes around."

"I'll do it." Mary stroked the kit's thick, soft pelt.

"I'll stay with you," Ash said.

Mary smiled at him. "Don't you have a pen to build?"

"I'll get to it." He pulled up a folding chair that Naomi had leaning against the wall and brought over a three-legged stool for himself.

They sat beside each other in the quiet barn without speaking. The smell of animals, hay and old barn wood scented the air. Dust moats danced in the light shafts that came in through the gaps in the siding and the small windows. It was wonderfully peaceful and cozy. Mary was sorry when the little fox began to stir and sat up.

She stretched. "Did you find some wood for a sign?"

"Wood and blue paint, if that works."

"Sounds perfect. Let's go."

She felt like skipping as they walked along the lane. It was a carefree kind of day. She realized she hadn't struggled to recall a memory even once. She was coming to grips with the fact that her memory might not return ever. She glanced at Ash. She was making new memories just as he said she would.

They sketched out the sign in the dirt, deciding the lettering in size. They settled on Walker Animal Sanctuary. Ash nailed up the board while Mary painted the donation box. Ash painted the sign.

Mary walked over to him and studied his face. "You have a bit of paint here. Let me get it." She wiped his cheek with the corner of her apron. "Oops, I didn't get it all." She gave another wipe while trying mightily to keep the smile off her face.

"Let me see your other side." She put her finger under his chin and turned his face. "You have got some there, too." She gave a couple wipes to his cheek. "That's got it. Are we done?" She was already striding up the lane. When she reached the house, she doubled over with laughter.

Naomi opened the door. "What are you cackling about?"

"I found a new friend for Weeble."

Ash came walking up. Naomi clapped her hand over her mouth to hold back her laughter.

Ash looked at them both. "What's so funny?"

Mary couldn't keep her trick a secret any longer. "You have whiskers like a kitten only they're blue."

Ash rubbed at his face, but the thin smears of paint were already dry. Naomi went in the house and returned with a hand mirror. Ash looked at himself and then at Mary. "How did I ever get the impression that you have a serious nature? What hint in your letters did I miss?"

She raised her hands in an innocent shrug. "I don't know. Maybe I'm good at pretending."

Mary was outside with Esther watching her bring a bouquet of roses to life on her sketch pad when she heard a vehicle stop at the end of the lane. She tapped Esther's shoulder to get her attention.

When Esther looked over, Mary said, "I think I hear the mail truck. I'm going to see if there is a letter for me."

"It has only been a week."

"But it's possible I could get a reply this soon. I'm going to check."

Mary hurried out the gate and ran down to the highway. The white mail truck was pulling away. She opened the mailbox. It was stuffed full.

After pulling out the bundle, she sorted through it

as she walked back. Nothing for her, but there was a letter for Ash. The return address was Bird-in-Hand but no name. She carried the mail up to the house, trying not to be disappointed. Maybe tomorrow she would have an answer.

Ash was at the kitchen table with his mother and Gabe when Mary came in. He looked up and smiled, making her heart turn over with happiness. They had spent every evening together this past week, sitting in the garden, playing games with his brothers after supper, taking walks in the woods. She liked it best when they went up to the field of flowers and watched the sun go down. It was impossible to describe how happy she was. She might not remember her past, but a future with Ash was a wonderful possibility. Once she made amends.

"Anything?" he asked.

"Not for me." She didn't have to hide her disappointment. He understood all too well how important it was to her. "You have a letter from Bird-in-Hand. The rest are bills, magazines, the *Budget* and some junk mail."

He took the letter from Mary. "Bird-in-Hand? Who do we know there, Mamm?"

"Let me think. Your cousin Jeffery lives there."

"We aren't particularly close. Wonder why he would write to me?" Ash tore open the letter, unfolded it and began to read. His eyes widened. The color left his face. Something was wrong.

"Is it from Jeffery? Is it bad news?" Talitha asked with concern.

He blinked several times as he stared at Mary. "It's not from Jeffery." He held out the page to his mother. "It's from Mary Kate Brenneman."

Mary's heart pounded in her chest as he stared at her. This couldn't be right. It was a mistake. "I didn't write it."

"How is this possible?" Talitha took the page from him.

The blank expression in his eyes terrified Mary. "She apologizes for the delay in coming to stay with us, but she'll be here the day after tomorrow." He shook his head. "How did I not know?"

"Who would play a cruel joke like this?" Gabe snatched up the letter.

Mary couldn't breathe. "It must be a prank."

Ash never took his eyes off her. "It's no joke. That's Mary Kate's handwriting."

"What does this mean?" Her voice was a bare whimper. She stepped back until she came up against the wall. The room started to spin.

Ash propped his elbows on the table and rested his head on his hands. When he looked at her, his eyes were full of sorrow. "It means there has been a terrible mistake. You're not Mary Kate Brenneman."

She stretched one hand toward him. A muffled roar filled her ears. "If I'm not Mary, who am I? Ash, who am I?"

The spinning room tilted and went black.

Chapter Twelve

When Mary opened her eyes, she was in her room on the bed. The arrival of the horrible letter and the aftermath came rushing into her mind. Bile burned the back of her throat as her stomach lurched. Why couldn't it be a bad dream? Everything she thought she knew about herself was untrue.

Talitha sat beside her and placed a cool cloth on her forehead. "You fainted. How are you feeling?"

Like she was leaning over the rim of the huge, gaping dark hole, flailing her arms to keep from plunging into the darkness forever.

"I'm fine." It was a lie, but it didn't matter. Why worry Talitha?

"Mamm, I'd like to speak to Mary alone," Ash said from the doorway.

She turned her face toward the wall. "I'm not Mary. I'm nobody."

Talitha squeezed her shoulder. "You are someone. You're a child of *Gott*. You are special to Him. And to us. Do not forget that."

"Why? I've forgotten everything else."

"Mary, please speak to me," Ash pleaded.

She rolled away from the comfort Talitha offered, and the heartache Ash brought with him. "Don't call me that. Call me Jane Doe or Mary Nobody if you must call me something. I want to be alone, now."

"Very well." Talitha sighed heavily and got up from the bed. She and Ash left the room.

When Mary heard the door close, she wanted to cry, but tears didn't come. Knowing she wasn't the woman Ash had planned to marry devastated her. If there was one saving grace to the situation, it was that she had never told him she loved him. Telling him now would only hurt him. That secret would be hers alone until her dying day.

What did she do now? She didn't belong with the Fishers, kind as they were. She didn't belong to Ash.

Why had *Gott* allowed her to love him? His kiss had been so tender it made her heart ache to remember it.

She loved him. That wouldn't change because she wasn't his Mary Kate Brenneman.

A sense of calm settled over her. She sat up and wiped her face. If she loved him, she had to help him through this difficult time. She saw the pain on his face when he read the letter. He was suffering as she was. Now it was her turn to be strong. For him.

Ash paced across the kitchen and back. His brothers and his father sat quietly at the table watching him. He stopped when he heard someone coming down the stairs. His mother walked into the room. Her expression was grim.

He folded his arms tightly across his chest. "How is she?"

"Understandably upset. How could we have made such a mistake?"

He spread his hands. "How was I to know? I assumed she was Mary Kate because I was expecting Mary Kate. She had my letter in her hand."

"Perhaps she is a friend of Mary Kate's?" his mother suggested.

He pressed his palms to his temples. "I should've guessed. There were so many things about her that didn't make sense. She's not practical and serious."

She was funny, sensitive and utterly adorable. He was head over heels in love with her. And he might be engaged to the real Mary Kate Brenneman.

"What are you going to do?" Gabe asked.

"I have no idea. I'm in love with her, that much I do know. I think she loves me, too. My plan was to ask her to marry me as soon as her situation in Ohio was resolved. Only she doesn't have a situation in Ohio. There's nothing to hold her back now."

"She may already be married," Seth said.

Ash dropped onto the nearest chair with a weight like an anvil on his heart. He struggled to breathe. "You're right. Why didn't I think of that?"

She wasn't Mary Kate Brenneman from Ohio who had come to Maine to marry him. She had a family and a home somewhere. Perhaps even a husband and children. Were they searching for her, wondering why she hadn't returned or written, eaten up with worry as he would be?

He looked at the ceiling. "I should go up and try to talk to her again."

"Not yet," his mother said. "Give her a little more

time to take this in. The real Mary Kate will be here tomorrow. She may have answers to all of this."

Ash bowed his head. Her letter said she had the answer to his question. His stomach roiled at the thought. Nothing good ever came of impulsive actions.

Seth got to his feet. "We promised Jesse Crump his wheel today. We should go finish it. Come on, Ash. You can't do anything here. Mamm will let us know when Mary is ready to face you. I reckon we can still call her Mary, can't we?"

"You can," she said from the doorway. "There is more than one Mary in the world. If it would make you more comfortable, call me Mary. Ash, may I speak to you alone?"

Her face was pale, but her voice was steady. He got up. "Of course. Let's go into the garden."

She flinched but nodded and smiled. It didn't reach her eyes. There was no sparkle in them when she looked at him now. Ash followed her from the room feeling the gaze of his entire family on him.

In the garden she took a seat on the bench. He stood beside her with his arms folded. "I'm sorry about this, Mary."

"It's not your fault, Ash."

"I'm the one who told you and everybody else who I thought you were."

"Because that is what you believed. Enough wallowing in pity. This has happened and we must face it. I'm not Mary Kate Brenneman. She is on her way here expecting to meet the man she has grown fond of. Now I can start a search for my true identity. Perhaps the police can aid me. People must be searching for me. I hope someone is. This is a blessing. I wasn't shunned in Ohio but who knows, maybe I've been shunned somewhere else."

"How can you joke about this?" He sat down beside her and took her hand. "You know how I feel."

She pulled her hand away and placed her fingers on his lips. "Don't say anything. Knowing you has been wonderful. I will never forget you. Well, maybe I shouldn't promise that."

"Mary, please. I adore your quirky sense of humor but not now."

"I'm sorry. You will have a place in my heart forever, Ash. You'll get over this. In time what we had together will just be a beautiful dream."

"What do you mean?"

"I can't stay here, Ash."

"Of course you can. You're part of this family." His voice broke the way his heart was breaking.

She cupped his cheek. "I wish I could be, but I can't."

He pressed his hand over hers to hold on to her a little longer. "You're leaving? Where will you go?" He wanted her near, but he wanted her safe and happy even more. Why was God doing this to them?

"Naomi will take me in. With her help I can start searching for the place I belong."

"You belong with us." Tears welled up in his eyes. "With me," he wanted to shout but that wasn't possible unless Mary Kate was coming to refuse him. He prayed that would happen even as he accepted it was unlikely.

He had asked her to marry him, and he knew the honorable thing to do. If she accepted, he would be true to her no matter the cost to his heart. And the price would be high.

Mary's lip quivered. "Please, let me go. I have to find answers."

He sniffed and wiped his cheeks. "I want you to find them, but I don't want to lose my best friend."

"You won't," she said softly. "This isn't about you and me anymore. You have been part of Mary Kate's life much longer than you have known me. You had a connection that reached across a thousand miles before we even met. Don't discard what the two of you had because you and I were forced together by circumstances. Promise me you will give her a chance."

"I promise." He could feel his hope and happiness draining away. If he lost Mary, he would be an empty shell.

He gripped her hand between his. "Stay until Mary Kate gets here. She might have all the answers you need. You had her letter. She must have given it to you. Stay until then."

She might not want to marry me.

He didn't say the words aloud. He couldn't bear to give Mary false hope. If all he was given was one more day with her, he would cherish it.

Mary pulled her fingers away from Ash's hand. Lingering would only make her departure that much harder, but he was right. The real Mary Kate could have the answers she needed.

"I'll stay until she arrives. We should go in now. I want to tell the others what I've decided."

Sighing, he got to his feet and held out his hand for her. She didn't take it. If he touched her again, she would break down. This was worse than waking up in the hospital and finding everything was missing. Her old life was still a blank. The problem was she had started a new one with new friends and a new family. A new love. Now she was losing it all.

Inside, the family was waiting in the living room. They could've been gathered for a funeral by the looks on their faces.

"What will you do now, Mary?" Esther asked.

"Ash and I have talked it over. The best course seems to be waiting to find out what the real Mary Kate knows about me."

"You're the real Mary," Moses said. "She's the other one."

"After I speak to her, I'll be moving in with Naomi Walker. I know she'll have me."

"You should stay with us," Zeke said. Talitha patted his arm and nodded.

"There is an extra bed in your room," Pamela said.

Mary shared a sad smile with the family. "I don't think we'd be comfortable even if it turns out that I'm her sister or her best friend." She looked at Ash. "At least not for a while."

Moses walked across the room and enveloped her in an unexpected hug. "I'm gonna miss you."

She hugged him back. "I'll miss you, too."

"Mary isn't leaving yet," Ash declared loudly. Her heart broke into a hundred pieces at the pain in his eyes. If only she could fly into his arms and tell him everything was going to be okay.

But it wasn't.

"That's right." Talitha surged to her feet. "This will all work out as our Lord intends. We must be open to His will in all things and have faith in His mercy."

The Lord was challenging her mightily. Mary prayed she could survive the trial.

She didn't sleep at all that night. It was a little after four in the morning when she gave up trying and went down to the kitchen.

Her heart leaped when she saw Ash sitting at the table, but then it plummeted. His smile turned sad, and he looked away. "You can't sleep either."

She got a glass of water and sat at the table across from him. "The waiting is always the hardest part."

"I wish things were different."

"Don't say it, Ash. It's difficult enough. Let's just get through the day. What time will the bus arrive?"

"It should stop outside New Covenant about eight o'clock. It's raining outside. Would you like to take a walk? I know you enjoy walks in the rain. You love trees and squirrels. I've seldom seen you being sensible. See, I know a lot of things about you. I just don't know why we can't be together."

"We will know the answer in *Gott's* own time, Ash. Don't torment yourself."

"That's about as easy as not trying to make yourself remember. Did that work out for you?"

She had to change the subject. "Since I'm up I may as well start breakfast for everyone and give your mother a break."

"Sure. I'll go start with the chores. Bessie will be surprised to be milked this early, but I'm sure she'll cooperate. I'll get the eggs too, so you don't have to go out in the rain." He got up, put on his hat, slipped into a raincoat and went out the door.

Mary laid her head on her arms. "Why, *Gott*? This is so unfair."

No answer came to her. She rose and went to start on breakfast. Ash soon brought the eggs and milk in and left again. She was setting the table when the rest of the family came in. Esther and Pamela walked to her and put their arms around her. They didn't say anything, they simply held her, and she loved them for it.

Talitha went to the sink to look out the window. "Has Ash left yet?"

Mary wiped her eyes. "Not yet."

"Are you sure you want to go with him to meet the bus?"

She nodded. "The real Mary Kate may know who I am. I need to see her."

"The other Mary," Moses said.

Talitha lowered the window curtain. "It has stopped raining. Ash is hitching the buggy now."

"*Danki*. You have all been so kind to me. I'm sorry I'm not who you hoped I was."

"We pray you find all your answers today," Zeke said.

"So do I." Mary walked outside and saw Ash backing Dottie up to the buggy. He caught sight of her and stopped what he was doing. They stared at each other without speaking.

She looked down and waited. He finished hitching the mare and led her over. "I don't know what to say except that I'm sorry."

She was able to look at him then. "You have nothing to be sorry for, Ash. You have treated me with kindness and respect. I will treasure our friendship forever."

"You're more than my friend."

"I might be your married friend. Because I can't remember my vows doesn't mean I can brush them aside."

"I understand."

She didn't think she had any more tears left, but they welled up in her eyes. "You have to give Mary Kate a chance. She's come all this way. You were expecting a woman who seemed to be your perfect match. Maybe she still is."

Suddenly Mary didn't want to see their meeting. She couldn't bear knowing he belonged to another. "I've changed my mind. I'm not coming with you. The two of you need to meet without an onlooker. I'll speak to her when you bring her home."

"Are you sure?"

"I am. Don't keep her waiting." She spun away and ran around the side of the house to the garden at the back.

Ash reached the bus stop when it was still empty. He remembered the day he should have been at this place when Mary arrived. If only he had been.

The bus pulled in a few minutes later. A single Amish woman in a dark blue dress got off the bus. She was tall and sturdy looking with dark hair. She wore glasses and held a pair of suitcases. She spied him and immediately walked toward him. "Good day. Are you Asher Fisher?"

He nodded. "Are you Mary Kate Brenneman?"

"Indeed I am Mary Kate. I'm so pleased to meet you at last, Asher. You are exactly as I had pictured you from your lovely letters. I hope Mari explained everything, and you can forgive me for my delay. It was such an amazing blessing that she was on her way to Fort Craig, too. The Lord certainly put her in the right place at the right time for me."

"Mari? Her name is Mari?" He knew that much about her. She was going to be so happy.

Mary Kate scowled at him. "She called herself Mari Kemp. She did meet you and give you my message, didn't she?"

"I'm afraid things didn't go as planned. I'll tell you on the way to my home."

He explained what had happened as he drove toward the farm. Mary Kate was understandably upset by the events.

"And she has no memory of meeting me?"

"She remembers almost nothing before waking up in the hospital. The police found one of my letters in her hand at the accident. I was expecting you. I gave them your name. We all thought she was you."

"How horrible for the poor woman."

After that Ash couldn't think of a single thing to say to her. All he wanted was to see his Mary. His Mari.

"When I met my dear cousin so unexpectedly, I couldn't simply leave," Mary Kate said, her words running into each other in a rush. "We hadn't seen each other for eleven years and we were once so close. When Mari offered to explain the situation to you, I thought a few days delay coming here wouldn't make a difference. I knew you would understand. I didn't mean to linger so long with my cousin, but our visit was something I badly needed. The truth is, I was having second thoughts about coming here."

"You were?" His hopes rose. Maybe she had come to refuse him.

"In spite of my cousin's objections I realized this was the right thing to do." She turned in the seat to stare at him. "You haven't asked me what my answer is."

He knew what she was talking about. "I haven't forgotten about it."

"I certainly haven't, either. I've been giving it a great deal of thought and my answer is yes. Asher Fisher, I will marry you."

His heart dropped to his boots as his final hope died a painful death. "Don't you want some time to think it over? Don't you feel we should get to know each other better?"

"I feel I know you very well. We've been writing to each other for months. We have the same likes and dislikes. We're both practical people. I don't see any reason why this won't be a happy union."

Except that he was in love with another woman. "Do you know if Mari is married or engaged?"

"I have no idea. It didn't come up in our conversation. She did say she was coming here to find her grandmother, but she didn't mention a husband. Her poor family must be frantic after all this time."

"We contacted your family thinking they needed to know about your accident."

She made a sour face. "Oh dear. I'm sure you were shocked by what they said about me."

"I was."

"I can explain everything. It's not how they would've made it sound."

"I'm listening."

"Our bishop is my mother-in-law's brother. My in-laws and the bishop invested money in my husband's company when he was getting started. It became a wonderful success for a time. He paid them back every cent. Then the business started losing money. After he died, they claimed they each owned one third of the business and wanted to buy my third for a pittance. I refused and tried to run it myself but eventually I chose a more practical solution. I sold the entire company to one of my husband's *Englisch* friends."

Ash wasn't sure what to say. Silence seemed the best choice.

She drew a deep breath. "My in-laws were furious. They convinced people I had cheated them. I didn't, but none of the people in the community approved of my selling the company to an outsider instead of Ed's family. I regret that our family quarrel went so far. There were other problems, too, which I will tell you about later. Anyway, the Bann will be lifted if I admit I was wrong and share what I received for the business. I don't believe I was wrong, so I chose to leave." She clutched the strap of her purse tightly. "I have more to tell you, but perhaps it should wait."

They had arrived at the house. Ash stopped the buggy. Jedidiah Zook was standing by the front porch with Moses. One more problem to face.

"Asher, Moses says my wheel isn't done. You promised it would be ready today."

"We'll get it finished and deliver it to you. I'm sorry for the delay. I had to meet the bus. We have a visitor." Ash wasn't about to explain why he had another Mary Kate Brenneman staying with him.

Jedidiah tipped his hat and smiled. An unusual sight. Mary Kate smiled and nodded to him. She glanced around the property. "What a pleasant home you have,

Asher, although you might want to think about cutting back some of the forest. Those trees rather overwhelm the place."

"I've told Zeke Fisher that a dozen times," Jedidiah said.

Ash bristled. "I like the trees. I like all the trees just as they are."

Her eyes widened at his tone. "I'm sure the woods have many practical uses."

"The squirrels live there. They like their homes. I said I'd bring your wheel by later, Jed." Ash glared at him, got out of the buggy and helped Mary Kate down. Jedidiah strolled away, got in his buggy and drove off.

Ash reined in his temper. He never got this upset. "Mary, I mean Mari, is anxious to meet you. You are the one person who knows her. Please treat her gently. She has had a difficult time."

"Of course. Where can I find her?"

His mother came out of the house. Ash made the introductions. "Our Mary's name is Mari Kemp. Where is she?"

"She's in the garden. Ash, why don't you show Mrs. Brenneman the way."

Mary heard the door to the house open. She looked over and saw an Amish woman come into the garden. Tall and muscular, she moved with confidence as she approached. She sat on the bench. "Mari, you poor thing. Asher told me what happened."

Mary blinked hard. "What did you call me?"

"Mari. Your name is Mari Kemp."

She sucked in a breath. "I'm Mari Kemp, not Mary Kate. No wonder my name sounded only half right."

"All this time people thought you were me?"

Excitement poured through Mari's veins as pieces of her life popped into her head. "We were on the same bus. I remember. You were coming here, but you met someone while we were waiting to change buses."

"My cousin Sarah. I hadn't seen her in years."

"I said I would let Ash know why you weren't at the bus stop to meet him."

"You were searching for your grandmother near Fort Craig. Did you find her?"

Mari jumped to her feet. "Naomi Helmuth. I think I've met her, but her name is Walker now. Tell me where I'm from."

"Arthur, Illinois, I believe."

Mari paced back and forth. "I'm Mari Kemp. I'm twenty-three years old not twenty-nine. I'm from Arthur. There's nothing but cornfields for miles around our home."

A new memory struck her. She sat down, overcome with sadness. "My *daed* died three months ago. He drowned trying to rescue another man during a flash flood. Oh, Papa!" She doubled over in pain. It was the one memory she didn't want back.

Mary Kate laid a hand on Mari's arm. "I'm sorry to hear that."

Drawing a shaky breath, Mari sat up. "It was a shock when I found letters he'd written to his mother. They had all been returned unopened. I was alone in the world. I have no other family. I needed to find her. That's why I came."

She threw her arm around Mary Kate and hugged her. "I remember. Thank you so much."

When Mari opened her eyes, she saw Ash watching them from the doorway. Her heart sank. She wasn't married, but she remembered now why Mary Kate had come to Maine. The reason she needed to marry Ash.

He was too far away to overhear them. Mari sat back and braced herself to learn Mary Kate's decision. "Since you're here, I assume your reason for coming hasn't changed."

"It hasn't. I see no other choice. I spoke to the only friend I still have back home. She said my son Matthew cries for me all the time. We need to be together. I'll do anything to make that happen. I have accepted Asher's proposal of marriage."

"Do you care for Ash at all, or is he a means to an end?"

A soft smile transformed Mary Kate's face. "Asher's letters drew me out of a dark place. He wrote about his home and the wonderful people of this community, about his dreams and what he wanted his future to look like. His sensitive, caring letters made me believe that I could start over here."

"Have you told Ash about your son?"

She looked down. "Not yet. When we first started writing, I couldn't bring myself to share how I failed Matthew after my husband died. What mother wants to admit she couldn't take care of her own child? I was ashamed of myself. The troubles with my in-laws made it worse. I didn't want to burden him with the sordid details."

"He would have understood," Mari said.

"I know, but when I read Asher's letters, I could forget my own problems. After the bishop said I had to marry to get Matthew back, I was afraid Asher would stop writing if he knew the whole truth about what a mess I had made of my life. Then he proposed marriage in his last letter, and I saw a way out. I thought if I told him everything in person, I could make him understand. I'll tell him everything today. I pray he can forgive my omission and help me get my son back."

Mari faced the hardest choice of her life. If she told Mary Kate that she was in love with Ash she would ruin two lives by keeping a mother from her son. If she remained silent and left, Ash would gain a wife and a son the way he would have if her accident hadn't happened. If she'd simply given him the message and then gone on to look for Naomi.

He'd be a good father to a sad little boy.

"Ash loves children. He's a wonderful man, my best friend. We became very close. You must tell him the whole truth. It won't be easy for him to hear. He'll need time to adjust. Can you give him that time?"

Mary Kate gripped Mari's hand. "Of course I will. I'm so sorry this happened."

Mari gazed at Ash's troubled face where he stood by the house. "*Gott* allowed it. We trust it is part of His plan."

She walked toward Ash to say goodbye to her heart.

Chapter Thirteen

Mari Kemp. How long would it take him to get used to her name? How much time did he have? Was she about to vanish from his life? As she walked toward him, he knew she had the answers she had sought for so long.

When she stopped in front of him, the sadness in her eyes matched what was in his heart. "You remember."

"I do. Everything."

The lump lodged in his throat made him swallow hard. "And?"

"I'll be leaving today."

How could those simple words hurt so much? He closed his eyes and tipped his head back as the pain engulfed him. This wasn't happening.

"I'm sorry, Ash. My home is in Arthur, Illinois. I came here searching for my grandmother, Naomi Helmuth. I'm sure she's Naomi Walker. That's the reason she seemed familiar. My father looked so much like her. Their eyes are exactly the same. They were estranged before I was born. That's why she didn't recognize me. I'm told I take after my mother, and they never met. I plan to spend a few days getting better acquainted with her."

He knew the answer, but he had to ask. "Was there any chance for us?"

She looked down. "*Nee.* Mary Kate has some things she'd like to tell you."

He clenched his fingers into fists. "What's his name? The reason we couldn't be together?"

Mari laid her palm against his cheek. He'd never forget the feel of her small soft hands on his skin.

"It doesn't matter, Ash."

"I want to know."

She glanced over her shoulder at Mary Kate and then looked into his eyes. "Matthew."

So she had a husband, or she was promised as he was. Ash struggled to speak. "He's blessed. I hope he knows that."

A sad smile pulled at the corner of her mouth. "Dear Ash, I'm going to miss you so much. I can never repay what you and your family have done for me. I'll keep you and Mary Kate in my prayers every night of my life. Goodbye, Asher Ethan Fisher."

Tears filled his eyes and ran down his face. "Goodbye, Mari Kemp."

He couldn't bear it any longer. He turned and went into the house so he didn't have to watch her walk away from him.

Talitha, Esther and Pamela came out. Talitha wrapped her arms around Mari. "Our hearts are broken."

"Time will mend them." Mari didn't believe it. Her heart would never be whole, but she wanted to give these wonderful women some comfort.

"What can we do?" Pamela asked.

"Be kind to Mary Kate. She needs your help and support. Take care of Ash. I know he's hurting."

"You are, too," Talitha said.

"But I have my life back. All of it. From the window I broke at school during recess in the first grade, to sneaking out to see a movie during my *rumspringa*, to my father's tragic death. I'm going to see Naomi now. I'm sure she is my grandmother. I'll let you know where to send my things. Thank you for everything. I shouldn't say this, but I'll never forget you."

No one chuckled as she had hoped. Turning away, Mari hurried to the garden gate and let herself out. Running through the woods was awkward with her cast. She tried to outdistance her heartache but couldn't leave it behind. At the highway she slowed to a walk. She had done the right thing for everyone. That was what she needed to remember, not the look of pain on Ash's face.

It took her half an hour to reach Naomi's lane. She paused at the freshly painted sign for Walker Animal Sanctuary. She and Ash had painted it together. There would be reminders of their time together everywhere. As much as she wanted to stay in New Covenant, she realized it wouldn't be possible. To stay would mean seeing Ash and Mary Kate together.

She would go home and take up her life. Maybe she could get her old job back in the fabric shop where she had worked before her father's death. She wouldn't be alone anymore. She had a grandmother, even if she did live in Maine.

She didn't see Naomi in the yard or the pens. She walked up to the front door and knocked.

The door opened and Naomi stood there with flour on her shirt and arms. "Mary Kate, I wasn't expecting you today."

"My real name is Mari Kemp. I think you are my *grossmammi*."

Naomi grew deathly pale and pressed a hand to her chest. "You're mistaken."

Disappointment snatched Mari's breath away. She couldn't be wrong.

"You should leave now." Naomi tried to shut the door.

Why was Naomi, her friend, shutting her out?

Realization dawned. Because it was true. Mari stood her ground. "You knew who I was, didn't you?"

"I have no idea what you're talking about." She pushed on the door, but Mari pushed back.

"My father was Gerald Kemp. He was estranged from his mother. I thought she was dead, but when my father passed away, I found a bundle of letters tied up with a blue ribbon. They were all addressed to Naomi Helmuth. Twenty-three letters. Postmarked on my birthday every year and every one of them was returned unopened. Letters addressed to Africa, the Dominican Republic, other far-away places."

"Please stop." Naomi retreated into her kitchen.

Mari followed her. "I read them. They all started with the same sentence. 'My dearest mother, I forgive you.'"

Naomi braced her hands on the counter and bowed her head. "I don't know how he could."

"Did you know about me? Did you know you abandoned a son and a grandchild?"

Naomi shook her head. "I knew he married. I didn't

know about you until I read his obituary. I still take the Amish newspaper."

"Why did you return all his letters? That was so cruel."

"I wanted him to forget about me. I was never coming back. He had to accept that."

Mari gaped at her in disbelief. "He didn't forget you, but he never said a word about you. Why did you leave?"

"It's a long story. I can't bear to tell it."

"I'm not leaving until I understand."

"Oh, very well." Naomi turned around. "I was widowed when your father was five. I raised him alone until I met a wonderful man and fell deeply in love. We married when your father was fifteen. It wasn't what I had hoped for."

"In what way?"

"He and Isaac didn't get along. They quarreled often. Isaac felt strongly that God was calling him to the ministry. The Amish don't believe in such callings. Our bishop said Isaac was prideful for claiming God wanted him to become a preacher. After three horrible years of disagreements, Isaac was shunned because he wouldn't deny his belief."

Mari sat down at the table. "What happened?"

Naomi remained at the counter. "Isaac chose to join another faith, enter their ministry and become a missionary. I had a choice. Remain Amish or be shunned with my husband. I chose to go with Isaac. That meant turning my back on my friends, my vows to the church and it meant leaving your father. He was only eighteen. It was the hardest choice I ever had to make."

"Did you regret it?"

"That's a foolish question."

"I'm sorry." What choice could Naomi have made without regrets? What choice could Mari have made without regrets? "You must have loved your husband very much."

"Oh, I did. He was an amazing human being.

"Your father was forbidden to have any contact with me. If I had answered his letters, I would have risked him being shunned, too. I knew what the Amish faith meant to my son. I'm ashamed to learn my silence harmed him just as much."

"He forgave you."

"Hearing those words from you eases the ache that has never left my soul."

"How is it that your name is Walker now?"

"After we left Illinois, I went to school and became a nurse. Isaac and I worked together in Africa and at other missions for fifteen wonderful years. He died in Haiti. I was lost without him and lonely. I married again a few years later, but it didn't work out. He left me. I withdrew from the world after that. I was tired of being hurt. That's when I started taking care of injured animals. I found comfort in helping wild creatures and eventually I found healing. And then a little fox brought my granddaughter into my life in a most unexpected fashion."

Mari smiled. "*Gott* moves in mysterious ways."

"That He does. I'm thankful your memory has returned. How did that happen?"

"The real Mary Kate walked into the garden this morning and called me Mari. It was like a dam burst. Memories came flooding back so quickly it was hard to take them in. Then I remembered why I was coming to Fort Craig. To find you and get answers."

"I didn't know who you were when we first met. I only knew that you reminded me of my son. You have his smile and his ears."

"He had your eyes. The first time I looked at you, I had a vision of him. That's what made me faint. I think the pain I experienced was grief."

"You must miss him."

"I treasure every memory I have of him."

"I imagine Ash is thrilled for you."

Mari looked away. "He proposed to Mary Kate in one of his letters. She has accepted him. Things will go back to the way they should be if I'm not here."

"I'm so sorry. You love him, don't you?"

Mari's throat tightened. "I do. Ever since the day I opened my eyes in the hospital, and he became my whole world."

"What are you going to do now?"

"I'll go back to Arthur."

Naomi slipped her arm around Mari's shoulders. "I have room for one more in my collection of injured souls."

Mari sniffled. "Are you offering me a place to stay?"

"I understand if you would rather not. You know, because I left the Amish, and all."

Mari grasped Naomi's hand and squeezed. "My father forgave you. I would not be his daughter if I did any less. I'd love to stay with you for a few days."

"Even if I've been shunned? I belonged to your church district."

"We will work around it. We can't eat at the same table."

"I'll eat at the counter," Naomi said quickly.

Mari grinned. "Or I can. I can't do business with you so you can't pay me to work here. I can't ride in your truck, so you'll have to find someone else to take me to the bus station."

"Not too soon, I pray."

"This is the hard one. I can't accept anything from your hand. Not a fork, not animal feed, not a glass of water."

"I know. I must leave things so that you can pick them up yourself. There are no rules that say I can't hug you." She enfolded Mari and pulled her close.

This was what Mari had dreamed of finding. A loving grandmother. After a minute, she drew back. "You can always join a more progressive Amish church like the one here. That way your shunning in Arthur won't matter anymore."

"I'll think about it. I do miss worshiping with others. Bless you, child. Your kindness means the world to me. You can call me grandma if you want."

"I'd like that."

Naomi cleared her throat. "Since you're here, the animals in the barn need feeding and those miserable geese are out again."

"It will help to stay busy until I can get a bus ticket back to Arthur, but I can't stay long."

"I understand and I'm sorry. Trouble is doing well enough to be released in a few days. I hope you'll stay until then."

"I can do that." As long as she didn't have to see Ash.

Ash was stunned by what Mary Kate revealed to him in the garden that evening. She had a child she had failed to mention. Tearfully, she recounted the circumstances that led to her coming to Maine. He didn't know any Amish family as unkind to one another as hers had been. It wasn't the way a child should be raised.

"I'm deeply sorry for my deception. I grew to care for you when we wrote to each other. Please believe that part was true."

It was a lot to take in, but he heard the sincerity in her voice. "I do believe you, and I forgive you. A mother should have her child with her."

She smiled with relief. "Mari said you were a good man, that you would understand." Her smile faded. "If you don't wish to marry me, I will accept that."

Mari thought he was a good man. He wasn't. He was a hurt, angry, sad man. She had walked away from him because somewhere in her life was a man named Matthew. If he couldn't marry the woman he loved, then maybe he should help this woman who loved her son. "I haven't changed my mind."

"Are you sure? Mari said you would need time to think things over. She knew this would be difficult for you. I'm glad the two of you became friends. She's a very sensible woman."

"Actually, she isn't."

Ash left Mary Kate and spent the rest of the evening counting and recounting the bolts, springs, door handles and washers in the shop. He wasn't surprised when Gabe and Seth came in. They went to the bins and each opened a drawer.

"Ten left rear turn signals." Gabe closed his bin.

"Eight headlamps." Seth looked at Ash. "Did you get that?"

"You don't need to try to cheer me up. I'm doing okay."

His brothers looked at each other and chuckled. "Doing inventory cheers him up," Gabe said with a grin.

Seth pulled open another drawer. "This one is empty. We're missing one sweet, funny, impractical girl with her arm in a cast. What shall we do?"

Ash put his ledger down. "She's irreplaceable but unavailable."

"We're sorry, Ash," Gabe said. "What are you going to do?"

"Make the best of it. I'll gain a son and a wife."

Seth frowned. "You can't be serious."

Ash just wanted to be alone. "Go back in the house."

Gabe nodded toward the door. "Jedidiah Zook is here for a visit again. His girls were disappointed to miss Mary."

"Mari," Ash said through tight lips.

Gabe nodded. "They seem to like the other Mary Kate well enough. She's teaching them to play Settlers of Catan with Moses and Jed. You didn't mention she had a son before this, Ash. Apparently, it's his favorite game. She teared up when she said it. What's going on?"

Ash drew a deep breath. "I reckon she misses her boy."

"Jed was winning. We're not going back inside," Seth stated firmly.

Ash almost smiled. "Thanks for the warning."

Gabe opened the next bin. "Eight right rear turn signals."

"I think I'll go in and join the game." Ash handed

his ledger to Seth. Mari was out of reach. Accepting that was hard. He should at least get to know the real Mary Kate before they chose a wedding date.

Mari snuggled Weeble against her face and listened to the kitten's loud purring. She was always a happy little thing. Mari wished she could follow Weeble's lead. Waiting on Naomi to return with her clothing and things had Mari on edge. Would Naomi see Ash? Would he ask about her? Was Mary Kate settling in?

The battered brown pickup came rumbling down the drive. Placing Weeble gently on the floor, Mari then dashed out the door. When she reached the truck, she pulled open Naomi's door. "Did you see him? How is he?"

"I saw him all right. He's busy creating a storm in that family. Everyone is in an uproar."

"What do you mean?"

"He and the new Mary Kate are going to see the bishop tomorrow about setting a date for their wedding. Why is he jumping into a huge mistake so fast? I thought the man had more sense."

"He's actually going to marry her?" Deep in her heart, Mari had secretly cherished the hope that it wouldn't happen.

She had encouraged the relationship, but now she wished she had kept silent. When he married, he would truly be lost to her forever. "They've known each other a long time."

"That may be, but the boy is in love with you! He's not being fair to that woman."

"She needs a husband."

"What she deserves is a man who loves her beyond

all reason. A marriage based on anything less will struggle to survive."

"The Amish do not allow divorce."

"I'm not talking about splitting up. I'm talking about sharing hopes, dreams and sorrows with someone who understands and respects you. When that dies, a couple can stay together but the true marriage is dead. Then two people spend their lives in misery."

"That's not going to happen to Ash. He'll fall in love with Mary Kate again. He did once before."

"I pray you are right. His mother and brothers sure don't think so."

"Talitha can be wrong."

"We all can. I'm taking Trouble's splint off today. If he gets around fine without it, we can release him back into the wild tomorrow."

"That will be wonderful. Then can you arrange for someone to take me to the bus station?"

"No."

Mari frowned. "Why not?"

"Because you'd be jumping into a mistake, too. Why did Ash stop seeing you?"

"Because of Matthew."

"Who is Matthew?"

"He's the reason Ash and I can't be together."

"Are you promised to him?"

"*Nee.* I'll find someone who can take me to the bus, or I can walk."

"I read my son's obituary. It listed his daughter by her maiden name. No mention of a husband. Whoever Matthew is, he doesn't have a claim on you. Stubborn runs in your family, child. I should know. Don't let it ruin your life."

Tears gathered in Mari's eyes. "It's too late." She turned and ran into the house.

Naomi planted her hands on her hips. "Not while your grandmother is still breathing."

Ash went to hitch up the buggy after breakfast the next day and found a note on the seat with his name on it. Was it from Mari? He tore it open. The fine penmanship canceled that hope.

Ash, she isn't married. She isn't engaged. She loves you.

Would you want Mari married to someone who doesn't love her?

Do the right thing. Tell Mary Kate you're in love with Mari. Let her make the choice.

It wasn't signed, but he suspected Naomi was the author.

Would you want Mari married to someone who doesn't love her?

Never. Mari deserved so much better.

"I'm ready to go, Ash," Mary Kate said behind him.

He turned around and looked at the woman waiting for him. And so did she.

"Mary Kate, I have something important I need to say to you."

"If you're upset that Jedidiah Zook asked me to walk out with him, he didn't know about our engagement. I refused him, of course without giving a reason. I thought he should learn about it the same time as the rest of the community when our bans are announced in church."

"It's not that."

"Okay." She waited with a curious expression in her eyes.

"First you should know that I intend to marry you and reunite you with your son."

"That's reassuring."

"But you need to know that I'm in love with someone else."

Her eyes widened. "What did you just say?"

"I'm in love with Mari."

Mary Kate rocked back. "Well finally. I didn't think you were ever going to admit it."

"You mean you knew?"

"I strongly suspected. I watched the two of you together, trying desperately not to fall into each other's arms the first day I arrived. I felt sorry for the two of you, but I thought if it was true love, you wouldn't go ahead with our engagement. Now that I know the truth, I won't marry you. I hope you have told the poor girl how you feel."

"Actually, I haven't. I am engaged to you. Is our engagement off?"

"I suppose it is." Her eyes grew serious. "Do you truly love her, Ash?"

"More than my own life."

She blinked back tears. "Then I'm doing the right thing."

"Would you have married me suspecting that I love her?"

She tipped her head as she regarded him. "Love is a strange gift the Lord has given us. It expands as we use it. We love our parents when we are young. I love my son more than I can say. If we are blessed, we love our spouses.

"I loved my husband deeply. I never expected to feel that way about any man again. I thought I would be content with someone I liked and respected, who liked and respected me in turn. I would've tried to be a good wife to you, Ash. I suspect you would have tried to be a good husband to me. Thankfully, now neither of us has to try. It seems love is expanding again. I suggest you go find Mari and tell her how much she means to you. That kind of love should be cherished."

"But what about you and your son?"

"I will find a way to reunite with Matthew. I won't ever give up."

"Your son's name is Matthew?" he asked in surprise.

"It is. Didn't I mention that?"

"*Nee*, but Mari did." The name of the reason they couldn't be together. "You should walk out with Jedidiah if he asks you again."

She laughed. "I don't think that will take much encouragement on my part. I do kind of fancy him. He has the most amazing brown eyes and he's trying hard to be father to those adorable girls. I like him."

"He also has the largest farm out of all the Amish in the district."

"I suspected he had more good qualities. He needs some adjustments, but he may do."

"I wish you the very best, Mary Kate. If not for you I would have never met Mari." He bent and kissed her cheek.

"Finding a deep and abiding love is a great treasure, Ash. Never squander it, never hoard it. Give it freely and it will come back to you tenfold. I had it once. I would never take it away from someone else. I'm glad you said something before it was too late. Now go. I'm sure Mari is quite miserable believing that she is losing you forever."

He didn't need further urging. He hurried to the corral and harnessed Frisky to the buggy and drove out of the yard. He kept her to her fastest pace until he pulled up in front of Naomi Walker's front porch.

He jumped out and ran up the steps. Naomi was coming out the door just as he reached it. "I see you got my note."

"I have to see Mari. Where is she?"

"She's taking the little fox out to be released."

"Where?"

"Near where you found the den."

"Great. I know right where that is. *Danki*, for all you've done for her."

"She has done much more for me. I'm almost sorry to lose her to you."

He smiled. "You aren't losing her. I'll make sure of that." He jogged away from the house along the path that led to the pond where he had first kissed his Mary Kate. His Mari.

When he reached the clearing, he stopped. She was on her knees in the grass beside a pink dog crate. He could see that she was crying.

"I'm going to miss you, Trouble. But this is where you belong. You must promise to stay off the highway. Are you ready? I should be happy for you, my friend, but I'm not." She opened the cage door. The kit ran out and headed for the den. At the shrubbery, he stopped, looked back and made a series of clucking sounds before disappearing inside.

Ash walked up beside her. "That's the sound a fox makes greeting a friend. I'm glad I got to see that."

She wiped her eyes with the back of her hand and stood up. "I know what it is. What are you doing here? I thought you and Mary Kate had an appointment to see the bishop about the wedding date."

"We did, but the wedding is off so there's no point in going to see him. Are you ready to go back?"

Her eyes grew wide. "What did you just say?"

"Are you ready to go back?"

"You are a maddening man. Before that."

"You mean the part about the wedding being off?"

"Why? Mary Kate is perfect for you. She's practical and realistic and she doesn't rescue injured wild animals."

"Exactly." He stepped closer, wanting to pull her into his arms and hold her for a lifetime.

She took a step back. "I don't understand."

"It's simple, really. I'm not in love with Mary Kate. I'm head over heels in love with an impractical, funny, charming, adorable woman who likes to rescue injured animals and a stuffy fellow who didn't know he needed rescuing until she came into his life. Mary Kate has wisely chosen not to marry a man who is in love with someone else."

Her face lit up with the most amazing smile he had ever seen. "She has? You are?"

"I absolutely am in love with you. The only question I have is do you love me just a little?"

"No."

He drew back. "What?"

She threw her arms around his neck. "I don't love you just a little—I love you more than I can ever say.

But perhaps I can show you." She rose on tiptoe and pressed her lips to his.

Ash's heart soared with joy as he gathered her close. He hadn't known it was possible to be so happy.

Mari drew back and gazed at the man she loved, unable to grasp how her despair had turned into exhilaration in a matter of minutes. "I can't believe it. I thought I'd lost you forever."

He pulled her close and tucked her head under his chin. "I almost allowed that to happen."

"Is Mary Kate heartbroken?" Mari hated that her joy came at the price of someone else's pain.

"She isn't. She suspected that I was in love with you, and yet she was going to marry me."

"She was doing it for her son. A mother's love knows no bounds. Now what will she do?"

"Jedidiah Zook asked her to walk out with him yesterday. She told him no because we were engaged but now we're not. She likes the guy and his nieces."

Mari was skeptical. "She likes Jedidiah Zook?"

"Apparently, he has the most amazing brown eyes, and an exceptionally large farm. If it is meant to be, it will work out. Look at us. *Gott* in His wisdom brought us together."

"I understand the attraction of brown eyes with thick dark lashes. I also love brown hair that curls over my fingers when I slip my hands through it like this." She proceeded to toss his hat aside and run her fingers through his hair.

He gave a low growl and pulled her close. She winced.

He was instantly contrite. "Oh, Mari, I'm sorry. Did I hurt you?"

"My rib is still tender. But my face doesn't hurt."

He latched his hands behind her back but left a little distance between them. "It doesn't hurt here anymore?" He kissed her forehead.

"Not a bit."

"What about here?" He brushed his lips across her temple. A shiver ran down her spine.

"Didn't feel a thing." Did she sound breathless? Her heart was galloping.

"This spot still has a fading bruise." He kissed her cheekbone. "Is it sore?"

"A little, but my lips aren't." She licked them and pressed them together.

"I wouldn't want to neglect your lips if they don't ache."

"Please don't neglect them, Ash."

He chuckled. "I love you."

"I'm sorry I didn't quite hear that."

"*Ja*, you did."

"How do you know?" she snapped back.

"By the sparkle in your eyes when you look at me."

"Oh, that gave me away, did it? My lips are still waiting, darling."

"I haven't forgotten." He settled his mouth over hers tenderly. The warmth of his touch flooded her heart with delight.

He lifted his head to gaze at her. "I can't believe I almost let you walk out of my life."

"It was more my fault than yours."

"That's true. You have to make it up to me."

"I can do that." She grabbed a handful of his hair

and pulled his head down so she could kiss him. And keep on kissing him. Because nothing mattered but proving she loved him with all her might.

The uncertain path God had set before her brought her to the place where her heart belonged. She would never forget to give thanks for His amazing blessing.

Epilogue

Ash clenched and opened his icy fingers as his three brothers inspected him from all angles, smoothed his vest across his chest and brushed imaginary lint from the shoulders of his black *mutza* suit. He wasn't exactly sure how he'd gotten himself into this situation.

That wasn't true. God's plan, roundabout as it may have seemed, had brought him to this point.

Gabe took a step back. "You'll do."

Moses lifted Ash's black hat from the pegs by the door. "You're not nervous, are you?"

"Of course he is," Seth declared. "He's about to get married. He's bound to be nervous."

Ash snatched his hat from his little brother's hands. "I'm not nervous. I'm on my way to wed the most amazing woman who for some reason believes she is in love with me."

He jammed his hat on his head. What if Mari had changed her mind? What if he wasn't a good enough husband for her?

Those around him smothered their chuckles. He

glanced up at his brim and turned his hat the right way around.

"He's lying," Seth said.

Gabe nodded. "He's scared to death."

"Being the most sensible brother should entitle me to a little more respect," Ash said. His brothers laughed.

"You mean most stodgy." Gabe straightened Ash's bow tie, the one an Amish fellow only wore on his wedding day.

"He's the dull one, all right. She could do better." Seth shook his head sadly.

"Dull as ditchwater," Moses added with a chuckle. "But she couldn't do better. I hope Mari knows how fortunate she is."

Ash glanced at his brothers' faces. "She could do better, but no man could love her more. I will do everything in my power to make her happy."

He gazed out the front door standing open to a beautiful fall morning and took a deep breath allowing his heart to expand with pent-up joy. His bride was waiting for him at her grandmother's house.

Outside, Jedidiah Zook stood at the door of the buggy Ash's brothers had washed and shined until it gleamed. A young boy in a dark suit and hat stood at his side. Ash stopped beside the child. "Thanks for helping Jedidiah drive today, Matthew. Do you think the two of you can find Naomi Walker's house?"

"I'll make sure he doesn't get lost." The boy's solemn tone showed he was taking his responsibility seriously, but he grinned at his stepfather. Jedidiah snatched up the boy's hat and ruffled his hair affectionately.

Two months ago, Ash had stood beside Jedediah as

he wed Mary Kate. Today, Jedidiah would return the favor by being one of Ash's groomsmen along with his brothers.

A week after their wedding, Mary Kate and Jedidiah had arrived back in New Covenant with her quiet son. The community rallied to make the somber child feel welcome by holding a picnic at the school to introduce him to the other children. In the few short weeks that he had been with his mother and his new family, Matthew was coming out of his shell. Jedediah opened the buggy door, and the boy scrambled onto the front seat.

"Ready for this?" Jedidiah asked Ash.

Ash grinned and clapped his neighbor on the shoulder. "I've never been more ready for anything in my life. Drive fast."

"Are you sure I look okay?" Mari cast imploring glances at her *newehockers*—her side-sitters, the three women who would be her attendants during the ceremony and afterward at the wedding feast. Pamela, Esther and Mary Kate were all dressed as Mari was in identical pale blue dresses with white capes and aprons. As the bride, only Mari wore a black *kapp*. She would trade it for a white one later in the day.

"You look lovely," Mary Kate said. "Like a woman who is madly in love."

Mari closed her eyes. "I don't know how it is possible to love someone so much. *Gott* has blessed me beyond all measure."

"He has blessed both of us," Mary Kate said. "I came to Maine desperate to marry and get my son back. Instead of the loveless union I expected with Asher, I found Jedidiah, a kind and generous man who takes my breath away and two lovely little girls who asked me yesterday if they could call me Mother. I have my son and a new family I adore. I never imagined my life could be so wonderful."

Mari clasped Mary Kate's hands between her own. "I don't think I could have been truly happy knowing I took Ash away from you, but now I don't have to worry. I'll never forget the sacrifice you were willing to make for our love."

"I couldn't keep the two of you apart after I learned how Ash felt about you. Jedidiah was my reward for making the right decision. At least that's what he likes to tell me," she said with a chuckle as a blush stained her cheeks.

Naomi opened the door to her bedroom where the women were waiting. "Mari, your friends from Arthur have arrived."

"Wunderbar. Have them come in." She had written to the women she'd worked with in the fabric shop back home detailing her adventures and included an invitation to the wedding. Her three friends came in grinning from ear to ear.

"Mari, we're so happy for you." They each hugged her in turn. One handed her a package. "This came in the mail before we left."

"For me?" Mari looked at the return address. It had been mailed from the bus depot in Caribou, Maine. "I wonder what it could be."

She tore open the brown paper wrapping. Inside a cardboard box was a black bag. "My purse!"

She held it up. Until this moment she hadn't recalled anything leading up to her accident. "I remember now. I forgot my purse on the bus. I ran after the bus to try and stop it. That's why I dashed into the road. The man who hit me wasn't at fault. I was."

Inside was a note saying the purse had been turned into lost and found, and was being mailed to the owner's address found on her checkbook. Mari looked up at Naomi. "We must let the State Police know."

"We will. After the wedding. Ash is here."

Mari's heart gave a happy leap. "It's really happening, isn't it? I'm getting married."

Naomi grinned. She wore a dark green Amish dress and a white *kapp*. "Yes, and I am so grateful to be a part of your special day."

After weeks of soul-searching, Naomi chose to return to the Amish faith and was accepted into the New Covenant congregation. Her shunning was now a thing of the past and would never be mentioned again.

Mari stepped into her grandmother's embrace. "I can't believe how blessed I am to have found you."

"I love you. All I want is for you to be happy," Naomi whispered. "Ash does make you happy, doesn't he?"

"He does." Mari couldn't stop smiling. Ash was everything she could ever want. Just the thought of being his wife sent shivers of excitement down her spine.

"It's time to go," Pamela said.

Mari stepped back and clasped her hands together. "I guess I'm ready."

The others filed out of the room. Mari took a deep breath and followed.

Ash was standing by the front door. His eyes lit up at the sight of her. The attendants paired up and walked into the living room.

A grin curved Ash's lips. "You haven't forgotten that we are getting married today, have you?"

Her last bit of nervousness fled at the love shining in his eyes. "I knew there was something I was supposed to be doing this morning."

He held out his hand. She took it, and he squeezed her fingers. "This *is* the day *which* the Lord hath made."

"We will rejoice and be glad in it," she finished the verse, knowing it was impossible to be any happier.

Hand in hand they walked in to join the bishop where they declared their love in front of God and the whole church, to begin their new life together just as God had planned.

* * * * *

THEIR PRETEND COURTSHIP

Carrie Lighte

For every reader who has encouraged me
with generous, uplifting feedback—thank you!

Forbearing one another, and forgiving one another, if any man have a quarrel against any: even as Christ forgave you, so also do ye.
—*Colossians* 3:13

Chapter One

❧

"Sit down, Eliza. Your *mamm* and I have something important we want to discuss with you," Uri Gehman announced.

Eliza Keim could guess what her stepfather was going to say. Every summer since Eliza turned eighteen, he'd given her a different version of the same lecture. "It's time for you to get married and start a *familye* of your own in a *haus* of your own," he'd say. "I should be planting extra celery in my garden by now."

It was the beginning of July, more than two weeks past the time of year when young courting Amish couples in New Hope, Maine, informed their parents of their intentions to get married during the autumn wedding season. In turn, the couples' families planted extra celery because the vegetable was an essential ingredient in traditional Amish wedding meals. But for the fifth year in a row, Eliza hadn't approached her parents about increasing the size of their garden. Uri was aware that she'd been seeing her latest suitor, Petrus Kramer, since last July, so he undoubtedly wanted an update on the status of their relationship.

No one else I know is expected to discuss their court-ships with their eldre, Eliza silently brooded.

In fact, most couples she knew went to great lengths to keep their romantic relationships a secret from their peers, as well as from their family members. There were exceptions, of course; some young people were pleased to make it known they were courting. But Eliza was not one of them and she resented having to discuss the subject with her stepfather. However, even though she was twenty-three years old and even though Uri wasn't technically her father, Eliza respected the Biblical commandment that children honor their parents. She slid into a chair at the kitchen table.

"Aren't you going to sit with us, too, Lior?" Uri asked Eliza's mother, who was presterilizing jars in preparation for putting up strawberry preserves.

Can't he see she's busy? Eliza marveled to herself. Clearly, the timing of this discussion wasn't her mother's idea; she probably hadn't wanted to discuss the subject at all. But Lior hesitantly wiped her hands on her apron and took a seat beside her husband. Uri didn't waste any time getting to the point.

"We've been expecting you and Petrus to speak to us about your intention to marry," he said, the gruff tone in his voice matching the expression on his face. "We understand that he's up north in Fort Fairfield for the summer. Is that why you haven't spoken to us yet?"

"Neh." Eliza glanced down at her hands, folded atop the table, so she wouldn't have to look Uri in the eye. "Petrus and I aren't getting married. Our courtship ended before he left."

Petrus had been deeply disappointed when she'd told him she didn't want him as her suitor any longer.

Like Eliza's stepfather, he'd assumed that after almost a year of courting, they were on their way to marriage. *But she'd been very clear from the beginning that accepting him as a suitor didn't mean she was seeking to get married. She distinctly told him she'd like to get to know him better as a friend before they could even consider a romantic relationship.*

During the entire time they'd courted, Eliza had only walked out with Petrus on three or four occasions per month at most. And when they had socialized together, she'd always made a point of suggesting they participate in group outings, such as hiking or bowling with their peers. The only time they'd ever been alone was during their travel time in his buggy.

And although Eliza was a warmhearted person by nature, she'd been careful to never voice any special sentiments toward Petrus. And she'd certainly never allowed him to hold her hand, much less kiss her. In essence, she'd treated him as if he was a brother. A favorite brother, perhaps, but nothing more. So he'd had no reason to believe marriage was on the horizon for the two of them.

Still, when he'd brought up the topic a few weeks ago, Eliza was pained to discover how optimistic he'd been about sharing a future with her. That was why she'd broken up with him; she didn't want to give him false hope that if they continued courting long enough, she'd develop romantic feelings for him and eventually agree to become his wife.

Uri was drumming his fingers against the table, signaling he was impatiently awaiting an explanation, so she elaborated, "I didn't believe we were a *gut* match."

"In what way?" her stepfather asked, causing Eliza

to draw back her head in surprise. Even for him, the question was intrusive.

"Uri, if she says they weren't a *gut* match, we should trust her judgment. Eliza's almost twenty-four. She doesn't have to ex—" Lior began to defend her daughter's privacy, but her husband cut her off.

"That's right. She's almost twenty-four. She should be married by now. She should be raising her own family in her own home. And if she doesn't intend to get married, she ought to find a full-time job and contribute to our *familye's* expenses."

"But she already contributes to our expenses and I need her help here," Lior objected.

"Three of the *buwe* will be in *schul* all day once it begins in September," Uri pointed out to his wife. "So you'll only have two at home with you."

Eliza's five half brothers were three, four, six, eight and nine. While it was true that it might be a little easier for her mother to manage because six-year-old Samuel would start attending school in the fall, Uri clearly had no appreciation for all the effort it took to keep their household running smoothly. Especially since the youngest boys were also the most active of the bunch. And Lior struggled with low energy, which her doctor attributed to having a baby when she was forty-two and then another at forty-three, in addition to the three sons she was already raising.

"I could increase the number of rugs I make. Or increase their size so I could charge more for them," Eliza suggested. She consigned handmade rag rugs at the local Amish hardware store and then gave seventy-five percent of what she earned to her family's needs, ten percent to the needs of the church and the other fifteen percent she kept for herself. Her stepfather had never complained about this financial arrangement before now.

He ignored her offer and continued to harp on the topic of her courtships. "Every time you break up with a suitor, you give the same reason—you don't believe you're a *gut* match. It seems like it's a matter of *hochmut* for you to reject one suitor after the next."

Hochmut meant pride, and to be fair, Eliza could understand why Uri thought she was acting as if she was somehow superior to her suitors. But she honestly hadn't been rejecting any of *them*; she'd been rejecting their hopes of marrying her.

Why would I want to get married? she asked herself. *So I can be as overworked and underloved as my mamm is?* No, she'd much rather stay single. Besides, her mother needed help raising the five boys. If Eliza hadn't been trying to appease her stepfather, she never would have accepted an offer of courtship in the first place.

"I understand it might seem as if I think more highly of myself than of my suitors, but I truly believe Petrus would be better off with someone else. I couldn't agree to marry him simply because he wanted me to or because I'm almost twenty-four and it's expected of me." Eliza wanted to add, *Or because you want another* mann *in the* familye *to help you in the workshop.*

Uri made crates and pallets for local farmers to use for storing and transporting potatoes and other produce. Over the last few years, his business had become so successful that he'd had a difficult time keeping up with the demand. Eliza's mother had suggested he hire a couple of teenage boys to help him on the weekends, but Uri insisted that a family business should stay strictly within the family. The more orders he received, the more Uri pressured Eliza to get married.

"You still haven't said precisely *why* Petrus isn't a *gut* match for you."

Eliza stalled, trying to think of a convincing reason why she wouldn't want to marry Petrus, other than she had no interest in getting married at all. She didn't want to belittle Petrus, since she genuinely liked him as a friend. So she appealed to her stepfather's interests instead, and said, "It's not just that Petrus wouldn't be a *gut* match for me. He wouldn't be a *gut* match for our *familye*. You've indicated how much you'd like to have a son-in-law who could help you with the business, but Petrus's *daed* expects him to continue working on the dairy *bauerei* after he gets married."

"What about his older *bruder*?"

"He's moving to Minnesota, so he can help his wife's *daed* on the *bauerei* there."

Uri pulled on his long, white beard as he mulled over this information. Eliza's stepfather was sixteen years older than her mother, who was forty-six. She, too, was graying, which her daughter attributed to stress, rather than to genetics. Her mother's ashen appearance served as a visual reminder of how much Lior needed Eliza's help at home.

"If you didn't believe you were a *gut* match for Petrus, maybe it's best that you ended your courtship with him after all," Uri finally conceded and Eliza breathed a sigh of relief. Until he added, "Especially since I've recently been approached by someone else who is interested in courting you."

"*You've* been approached?" Eliza repeated, unable

to keep the scorn from her voice. Any man who would ask her stepfather's permission to court her, instead of asking her directly, was no man she'd ever accept as a suitor.

"*Jah.* Initially, I told him *neh* because I thought you and Petrus were still courting. But since you've ended your relationship with him, you should consider accepting Willis Mullet as a suitor."

Willis Mullet? He's closer to Mamm's *age than to mine!* The tall, overweight man had been a widow for eight years. He'd lived with his mother, who'd helped him raise his three sons, now eleven, ten and nine, until she died last winter. While Eliza could appreciate why he urgently wanted to remarry, she was alarmed to discover he was interested in courting *her.* Panicking, Eliza blurted out, "Willis is way too old for me."

"He might provide the maturity you need from a suitor. Besides, he's only thirty-six. That's thirteen years' difference between your ages. There's sixteen years separating your *mamm* and me."

That was exactly Eliza's point; she didn't want to follow in her mother's footsteps and marry an older man. She didn't want to marry *any* man. Or *court* any man. Especially not one who seemed as dull and needy as Willis Mullet. But since her stepfather wouldn't be satisfied unless she was walking out with someone, she figured the least she should be allowed to do was choose a suitor for herself. "I—I know, but... But lately another *mann* has been paying special attention to me and I—I think he's on the brink of asking to be my suitor."

Uri raised an eyebrow. "*What* young *mann*?"

Lior again tried to intercede. "Maybe she'd rather not say, Uri."

But he persisted. "Is it the Yoder *bu*?" he asked and Eliza shook her head. "One of the Kanagy *breider*?"

Eliza nodded. Two Sundays ago after church, Freeman Kanagy had offered to give her a ride home. And in New Hope, when a man invited a woman to ride in his buggy, it was almost always either because he was courting her or he *wanted* to court her. Thankfully, Eliza had had the perfect excuse to turn him down; two of her brothers had gotten sick to their stomachs during lunch, so she'd had to dash home to help her mother get them bathed and into bed. However, Eliza was relatively certain that with a little playful banter, she could encourage Freeman to offer her a ride again this Sunday.

Her stepfather looked skeptical. "Don't the Kanagy *breider* own a *blohbier bauerei*?"

Eliza realized Uri was worried that if she eventually married Freeman, he wouldn't want to abandon the blueberry farm that he and his brother Jonas owned and come work with Uri. Of course, she had no intention of ever marrying Freeman, but since she couldn't tell her stepfather that, she addressed his concern, as she reminded him, "*Jah*, but that's not their main vocation—it's only a seasonal occupation. They both work as independent carpenters."

Her stepfather slowly nodded. Eliza could almost hear him thinking that a carpenter would be the perfect match for *him* as a business owner. Granted, Willis Mullet was employed by an *Englisch* construction company and he undoubtedly would welcome the opportunity to earn a living by working within the Amish community instead. But Freeman was much younger than Willis, so Uri probably assumed that meant he'd be more compliant with Uri's way of doing things.

"Okay. If the Kanagy *bu* asks to walk out with you before Willis does, I'll respect your decision. Otherwise, I expect *you* to honor *my* request and accept Willis as your suitor...at least for a few months."

Eliza stole a glance at her mother for support. But Lior was nervously eyeing the pot of water boiling atop the gas stove. They both knew they had to get back to work in order to finish everything there was to do before taking a day of rest on the Sabbath tomorrow.

Walking out with Freeman is better than walking out with Willis, she mused, rationalizing. *And it's definitely better than working away from home full-time, which would mean leaving* Mamm *alone during the day.* Her other consolation was that blueberry season was only a week or two away, so hopefully Freeman would be too tired to take her out very often. Or at least, not until later in the summer, and maybe by then, Willis Mullet would be interested in someone else.

"*Jah*, okay," she agreed.

But even before Uri had pushed back his chair and stood, Eliza was silently praying something she never thought she'd pray. *Please, Lord, please, please, please let Freeman ask to be my suitor.*

Jonas Kanagy couldn't sleep. Right before he'd gone to his room, his brother Freeman had informed him that he was taking his own buggy to church the next morning instead of accompanying Jonas in his. *That confirms it*, he thought, brooding. *Freeman intends to give Eliza Keim a ride home. He wants privacy so he can ask to be her suitor.*

When the district members had met together for worship services two weeks ago, Freeman had announced he'd wanted to travel alone to church then, too. Jonas hadn't needed to ask him why: it was implicitly understood that when a young man or woman didn't ride with their family to or from church and didn't offer an explanation, it was because they intended to ride with one of their peers, usually of the opposite gender.

Not that Jonas would have questioned his brother, anyway—Freeman was twenty-three and he was free to go where he pleased. Besides, Jonas considered courting to be a private matter. But that didn't mean he wasn't deeply troubled by the likelihood that his younger brother was about to make a huge mistake.

He kicked off his sheet and flopped over in bed, thinking about the conversation he'd heard between Freeman and Eliza two weeks ago. Jonas hadn't meant to eavesdrop; he just happened to come around the corner of the church building at the same time Freeman offered Eliza a ride home.

"Maybe we can stop by Little Loon Lake on the way," his brother had suggested.

"*Denki* for asking, but I need to help my *mamm* with my *breider*. Peter and Samuel got sick after lunch and Mark looks a little green, too," Eliza had replied. Then she'd darted across the lawn and blithely called over her shoulder, "I hope you enjoy this beautiful weather!"

Jonas had managed to shrink back from view, so his brother hadn't known he'd overheard their brief conversation. Freeman had returned home a few minutes after Jonas and he'd been unusually quiet for the rest of the afternoon. But by Monday morning, he'd gotten his spring back in his step, and ever since then, he'd been whistling almost nonstop. Jonas suspected the cheerful tunes were a reflection of how hopeful Freeman felt about offering Eliza a ride home again this Sunday.

It wasn't surprising that he'd want to walk out with her. On the surface, Eliza was outgoing, gracious and quick to help whomever needed it. The way she interacted with her little brothers showed she possessed a lot of patience, as well as a good sense of humor. She was also unusually pretty, with chestnut-colored hair and amber-colored eyes, a heart-shaped face and very fair, flawless skin. So Freeman wasn't the only young man in New Hope who'd hoped to become her suitor.

Jonas knew this for a fact, because his closest friend, Petrus Kramer, had recently confided he'd courted Eliza for almost a year. According to him, the pair had never had a single argument during their courtship and Eliza had always seemed pleased to be walking out with him. So Petrus had felt blindsided when he'd brought up the topic of marriage and she'd responded by calling off their courtship altogether.

"I wasn't trying to pressure her—I told her I'd wait as long as it took until she was ready, but there was no convincing her," Petrus had said, bewildered. "I don't understand why just *talking* about marriage made her decide to break up with me."

Jonas didn't understand it himself. But he had an inkling of what was going on because he'd heard a rumor about something similar happening to another young man who'd once been Eliza's suitor. "It seems as if she's playing a game of some sort," he'd suggested.

"A game? What's her objective?"

"Who knows? But take it from me, it's better to find out sooner rather than later that she apparently didn't have any intention of marrying you."

Jonas knew that from personal experience. When he was twenty, he'd courted a woman from his home district in Kansas for eight months before learning she'd only entered into the relationship to make her previous suitor envious. Although she'd apologized profusely for her behavior and Jonas had forgiven her—he'd even attended her wedding—the experience had left him with a deep sense of distrust.

Four years later, he'd finally gathered the courage to ask to court another woman from his home district. He'd been her suitor for almost a year before she confessed she didn't care for Jonas the way he cared for her. She said she'd come to realize she'd primarily been walking out with him because her younger sisters were already married and she'd been worried she'd be a spinster forever. Although she hadn't deliberately meant to deceive Jonas, he'd felt tricked all the same. As well as hurt, angry and foolish. He decided the only way to guarantee that he wouldn't be used by a woman a third time was not to enter into a courtship again, period.

As it was, bachelorhood suited him just fine. It had been just two years since he and his brother had moved to Maine from Kansas. But he already liked it so much, and at twenty-seven he could imagine himself living alone here on the blueberry farm until he was old and gray, the way his uncle had done before him.

But Freeman has always wanted to get married and have six or eight kinner, Jonas thought. His brother had intended to get married when he was twenty, but the woman he loved had died unexpectedly from a congenital heart condition. Freeman had been absolutely despondent for a full year afterward. Then he and Jonas moved to Maine, and slowly the change of location and focus helped his brother recover emotionally from his loss. As far as Jonas knew, this was the first time Freeman was considering courting again.

After everything he's been through, I can't allow Eliza to break his heart the way she broke Petrus's, Jonas thought. But how could he stop her from doing that? He didn't want to tell his brother he'd overheard his conversation with Eliza two weeks ago. Nor could Jonas betray Petrus's trust by sharing what his friend had told him. Besides, even if he did, Freeman was very headstrong and he might not heed his warning.

If only someone else would become her suitor before my bruder *gets a chance to ask her to court her,* Jonas thought wistfully. *If I had any interest in a romantic relationship, I'd do it myself.*

All of a sudden, he sat up in bed. Actually, that wasn't a bad idea! The fact that Jonas had no desire to get married actually made him the perfect suitor for Eliza, because she couldn't possibly hurt his feelings by breaking up with him, no matter how long they courted.

Freeman would be disappointed, of course, but not nearly as crushed as he'd be if he walked out with her and then she broke up with him a year from now. Petrus was in Fort Fairfield for the summer, tending to his injured brother-in-law's farm. So Jonas figured his friend wouldn't find out about the courtship and feel as if Jonas had been disloyal to him.

Hopefully, before the summer ended, Freeman would set his sights on another young woman and forget all about Eliza. *Then I can call off our courtship without so much as a backward glance, just like she did with Petrus. Maybe a dose of her own medicine is the cure she needs to stop toying with* menner's *feelings...*

Of course, there was no telling if Eliza would accept Jonas as her suitor. Since he'd moved to Maine, he'd been on several outings with his single peers, including her. While she'd never exactly flirted with him, she'd always given him a winsome smile whenever they'd chatted. And she'd seemed genuinely interested in knowing how he was adjusting to Maine and what it was like to live in Kansas. *She may have just been acting hospitable and trying to make me feel* wilkom, he realized. *But since this the only plan I've got, it's worth a try.*

So the next morning, Jonas rose earlier than usual in order to take extra time making sure he smelled fresh, scrubbing his fingernails clean and shaving his face closely. When he was done, he lingered in front of the mirror, squinting his gray-green eyes as he examined both sides of his broad cheeks and jaw. He wiped a dab of shaving cream from one of the dark brown curls sticking out near his ear. Then he adjusted his suspenders evenly on his sturdy shoulders. There. That would have to do. Jonas donned his Sunday hat, said goodbye to his brother and went out the door.

In New Hope, as in the other Amish communities in Maine, every other week the district members met in an actual church building, instead of in each other's homes the way the Amish did in most states. The building had large windows, but there was no breeze circulating through the room. The weather was so warm that Jonas was perspiring by the end of the first hymn.

By the time the three-hour service was over, his hair was limp against his forehead and his back felt slippery with sweat.

If Eliza sees the damp marks on my shirt, she's going to think I'm nervous about offering her a ride, Jonas thought. Which he was, in a way, but that was mostly because his brother's happiness was at stake.

After he'd eaten the community lunch, Jonas wandered outside with the other men. But instead of heading toward the hitching rail, he dawdled near the staircase so he could intercept Eliza as soon as she came out of the building. Jonas noticed that Freeman was across the yard, loitering beneath a maple tree. No doubt, he was trying to appear as if he was enjoying a moment in the shade, but his brother knew he was waiting for Eliza to come out of the church, too. Since he didn't want Freeman to see him, Jonas ducked around the corner of the building.

To his surprise, he discovered Eliza dallying there, almost as if she was waiting for someone. Or hiding.

She started, seemingly as surprised to see him as he was to see her. "Hello, Jonas. How are you?"

"Hello, Eliza. I'm *gut,* but hot." He nervously tugged at his shirt collar, regretting that he hadn't planned exactly what he was going to say to her. "How are you?"

"I'm *gut*, too. But you're right, it's awfully steamy out today. I'm not looking forward to having my five *breider* climb all over me like little puppies in the back of our buggy."

Jonas broke into a smile; this might be easier than he'd expected. "Would you like a ride home in mine instead?"

"*Your* buggy?" she repeated, as if the idea was unthinkable.

Jonas wished he could take it back but he swallowed and uttered, *"Jah."*

Before Eliza could say anything else, Willis Mullet popped around the corner. He greeted the pair of them and then said, "Your *daed* has been looking everywhere for you, Eliza. He said your *mamm* needed to get your *breider* home for their naps, but they couldn't find you. I told him to go ahead and leave—I'd be *hallich* to give you a ride home. My *seh* are going to the Stutzman *familye's haus* for the afternoon."

Jonas caught his breath. *Is Willis interested in courting Eliza? That could work out even better for me, as well as for Freeman*, he thought. But Willis was much older than Eliza, so maybe he was only offering her a ride as a friendly favor to her father?

"Denki, Willis," she said sweetly, and Jonas's heart sank. Then she added, "But Jonas already offered me a ride, so I'm going with him."

Jonas's relief was short-lived because at that very second, his brother came jogging around the corner. He stopped short and his jaw dropped; there was no question he'd overheard what Eliza had said.

Freeman looked so crestfallen that Jonas was tempted to tell her he'd changed his mind and that she should ride with Willis instead. But that would have been rude. Besides, if it turned out that Willis wasn't interested in becoming her suitor—or if he was, but she said no—then there'd be nothing stopping Freeman from asking Eliza to walk out the next time he saw her.

No. Like it or not—and he didn't—Jonas was going to have to carry through with his plan.

Chapter Two

Eliza's heart was drumming in her ears like hoofbeats, so she was grateful that Jonas didn't say anything as the horse pulled his buggy down the church lane and onto the main road. She needed a moment to make sense of what had just transpired.

Less than ten minutes ago, she'd been helping the other women wash and put away the lunch dishes in the church's basement kitchen when Honor Bawell, one of the older singles in the district, had sidled up to her. "A certain *mann* is looking for you in the gathering room, Eliza," she'd whispered gleefully. Honor relished being involved in matchmaking. "I told him if I found you, I'd send you upstairs to see him."

Assuming Honor was referring to Freeman, Eliza was relieved; if he was bold enough to make it known he was looking for her, then that meant he wanted to speak to her about something important. Namely, courting. But since Eliza hadn't wanted Honor to know she'd been expecting Freeman to seek her out, she'd played dumb, and nonchalantly asked, "A certain man? Who is it, my step-*daed*?"

"*Neh*, but he's almost old enough to be." Honor had tittered. "It's Willis Mullet."

Eliza had lost her grip on the platter she'd been rinsing and it fell into the soapy water, splashing suds on both of them. "*Denki* for letting me know," she'd said, but she hadn't budged from in front of the sink.

"I'll finish washing the rest of these so you can go talk to him," Honor had insisted, nudging Eliza out of the way with her hip. "He said he'll be waiting near your *familye's* buggy, because he doesn't want to miss seeing you before you leave."

So instead of going up the main staircase to the gathering room, Eliza had escaped through the back basement exit. She'd crept around to the side of the building, with the intention of staying out of sight until she spotted Freeman Kanagy.

Before she'd left for church that morning, she'd spent fifteen minutes in front of the mirror practicing fluttering her lashes and twisting her prayer *kapp* ribbons around her finger, the way she'd seen some of her peers do when they were speaking with a man. That kind of flirting didn't come naturally to her, but she was so desperate to encourage Freeman to offer her a ride home that she was willing to use any trick she could.

However, when Honor had mentioned Willis was looking for her, Eliza's desperation intensified into full-blown panic. She would have preferred accepting a ride home on a motorcycle with an *Englischer* rather than going with him. So when Jonas discovered her lurking near the side of the building and offered her a ride home, she'd gladly accepted.

But now, seated beside him, she wondered how she could have misinterpreted Freeman's offer from two weeks ago. She supposed he could have asked to bring her home because he'd wanted to assess her interest in his brother, instead of in him. *I've heard that some* menner *are so shy, they ask a friend or* bruder *to speak to a* weibsmensch *on their behalf before they have enough courage to propose courtship directly to her*, she thought.

Jonas had never struck her as being bashful at all; in fact, they'd spoken several times, and if anything, he'd come across as more indifferent than shy. Not that he was arrogant, exactly, but that he'd never seemed to hang on her every word, the way some of her previous suitors had done prior to asking to court her. *Maybe the reason he wanted Freeman to get a sense of my interest has nothing to do with his being shy or saving face. Maybe that's just the custom in his home district in Kansas.*

Not that it mattered one way or another to Eliza whether she was courting Freeman or Jonas or any other bachelor in the district. All that mattered to her was that she didn't have to accept Willis as her suitor, as she'd promised Uri she would. *But if I don't think of a way to break the ice with Jonas, we'll be home before he gets the chance to ask me to walk out with him*, she realized.

Since he had to concentrate on guiding the horse along the road, it didn't make sense for Eliza to tip her head and bat her lashes the way she'd intended to do with Freeman. Instead, she tried to make her voice sound as coquettish as possible when she said, "It's so nice to have a chance to chat with you alone, Jonas. *Denki* for giving me a ride."

"You're *wilkom*."

His reply was so terse that Eliza wondered if she'd been reading too much in to his offer to bring her home, just as she'd misinterpreted his brother's overture. Or was Jonas simply nervous?

After a few more minutes of silence, she tried to draw him into conversation again, using one of the lines she'd rehearsed to say to Freeman. "I've actually been thinking about you a lot lately." Then she giggled, hoping to make it seem as if she'd unintentionally misspoken. "I mean, I've been thinking about your *blohbier bauerei.* It must almost be time for picking to begin?"

"*Jah.* We expect to open to the public a week from tomorrow."

"I'll be the first in line. All of my little *breider* love *blohbiere.* They love *blohbier* jam, *blohbier* pie, *blohbier* cobbler. They love *blohbiere* on ice cream and on cereal. I think they'd eat *blohbiere* on top of *blohbiere* if we'd let them."

Eliza laughed nervously. She realized she was rambling, but they were nearing the lane she lived on and she was becoming more and more fearful that Jonas wasn't going to ask to be her suitor after all. The thought briefly ran through her mind that if he didn't, maybe she could tell Uri that Jonas had given her a ride home and her stepfather would automatically assume that meant they were courting now. Then he'd back off about her considering Willis Mullet as a suitor.

Neh, Uri would never make an assumption like that—he's going to question me directly and I can't lie about it, she silently conceded.

As Jonas drew the horse to a stop at the end of her lane, she said, "So, anyway, you'll be seeing a lot of me on the *bauerei* this summer…" She let her sentence hang in the air. She'd done her best to set the tone for talking about courtship, but now it was up to him. As she waited for a response, Eliza actually did twirl her prayer *kapp* ribbon around her finger, but it was anxiety, not coyness, that made her fiddle with it.

Jonas shifted in his seat to face her. Sweat was dribbling down both sides of his face, but his mouth must have been dry because he licked his lips. In all of the times she'd spoken to him, Eliza had never really noticed how full his mouth was. Or that his upper lip formed such a perfect bow—it looked as if it had been stitched that way. It was a strange thing for her to notice now, but perhaps that was because she was so apprehensive about what he'd say next that she couldn't stop staring at his mouth.

"I think you'll find the *biere* are unusually sweet this season. They might not be quite as plump as last year's, but Freeman and I think the flavor is going to be more concentrated. Not quite as sweet as wild *blohbiere*, but still, very *gut*."

This wasn't the kind of sweet talk Eliza had hoped she'd hear from Jonas and she was losing heart. But she replied, "We can pick lowbush *biere* up the hill, right behind our barn. Oddly, my *breider* prefer the cultivated kind."

She told him the story about how the previous year, her mother had served the last of the berries to four of her brothers over ice cream as a special afternoon treat. The youngest boy, Mark, found out about it when he woke up from his nap, so naturally he wanted the dessert, too. Since they were all out of the cultivated berries, Eliza had sneaked up the hill to pick some of the smaller wild berries as a substitution. But when Mark saw them, he'd pushed away the bowl and said he didn't want baby berries, he'd wanted the grown-up kind.

Once again, Eliza recognized she was blathering, but she couldn't seem to make herself get out of the buggy without a courtship proposal. Thankfully, her anecdote seemed to put Jonas at ease. He chuckled and said, "I'd never even seen wild *blohbiere* until I moved to Maine, so I can understand your *bruder's* disappointment in being served the littler *biere*."

"Really? There aren't any wild *blohbiere* in Kansas?"

"*Neh*. It can even be difficult to grow the cultivated kind there, especially in the western part of the state. But we do grow lots of sunflowers. Fields and fields of them, taller than you and nearly as bright as, well, as the sun." Jonas rubbed his chin, a faraway look in his eyes. "I guess that's why Kansas is nicknamed the sunflower state."

"I didn't realize that. I've never been out of the pine tree state, so I always enjoy hearing you talk about Kansas." Eliza was being so sincere that she momentarily forgot about her mission to get Jonas to ask her to walk out with him. So she was surprised by the way he responded.

"I—I always enjoyed talking to you, too, Eliza. And actually, I'd like—I'd like to get to know you better," he said. She studied his expression, still unsure if he meant what she hoped he meant. Beads of sweat trickled down both sides of his face and he wicked them away with his palms before sweeping off his hat. His hair was plastered to his head and it seemed as if the poor man was melting before her eyes. But the gesture was so polite it made Eliza feel guilty that he was clearly trying to make a good impression on her. "I—I mean, I'd like to court you."

"That's *wunderbaar*!" she exclaimed. In her exuberance, she grasped his forearm. She released it just as quickly and drew back, trying to compose herself. No matter how relieved she was that he wanted to be her suitor, she couldn't allow Jonas to believe a courtship meant they were on a path to marriage. "I'd really like to get to know you better, too, Jonas. Although, I have to be very candid about something..."

As he cocked his head to the side and narrowed his eyes, a few droplets of sweat spattered from his hair onto his shoulder. "What's that?"

"I—I'd like our courtship to progress slowly. I want us to become better friends first. Without any expectation or pressure that..." She didn't even want to use the word *marriage*, so she said, "That we'll develop a closer relationship in the future."

She could barely meet his eyes. After flirting so blatantly with him, Eliza couldn't help but wonder if he felt as if she'd pulled a bait and switch. Was he going to rescind his offer of courtship now that she'd told him she essentially wanted to keep their relationship platonic?

Jonas had to bite his tongue so he wouldn't chuckle out loud. Partly, his urge to laugh was because he was relieved that Eliza had agreed to walk out with him. And partly it was because he was amused that she wanted their courtship to progress slowly. Jonas couldn't have hoped for a better response if he'd scripted it himself.

"I completely understand. We can develop our relationship as slowly as you'd like—you can set the pace," he told her. "In fact, with everything there is to do on the *blohbier bauerei*, I probably won't be able to walk out with you during the next few weeks. I'll be working until dusk every weekday evening and all day on *Samschdaag*, too."

"That's *wunderbaar*," Eliza exclaimed for the second time, before quickly explaining herself. "I mean, it's *wunderbaar* that you don't mind taking time to develop our friendship. And I have no expectation for us to walk out in the evenings, especially during *blohbier* season. I'll see you in *kurrich* and on the *bauerei*, which will be nice. But I know that being out in the sun all day can sap a person of his energy, so I understand if you're just too worn out to socialize afterward."

"*Gut*, it's agreed, then." Jonas realized he sounded as if he'd just confirmed a contract for a carpentry project for one of his *Englisch* customers. "I—I mean, I'm *hallich* we both understand one another's preferences and I look forward to courting you."

That sounded just as stiff, but Eliza didn't seem to mind; she was absolutely beaming. Jonas had to give her credit; the other two women he'd courted weren't nearly as easygoing about his schedule. They'd expected him to take them out every Saturday evening and for a buggy ride or picnic after church on Sunday, too.

"I'll hop out here," she said, indicating she didn't want him to pull all the way up the lane to her house. "Otherwise, my *breider* will see us and ask me a hundred questions about why I got a ride home from you instead of joining them in my *familye's* buggy. I'd like to keep our—our courtship as private as we can."

Jonas couldn't help but notice the word *courtship* seemed to stick in her throat. But maybe he was just imagining that because the word felt so strange to his own ears. Twenty-four hours ago, if someone had told him he'd be courting Eliza Keim—or anyone else—he would have checked the sky for flying pigs.

Yet now, as he rode home, he happily mused, *That was easier than I ever dreamed it would be. The way Eliza was flirting with me, it almost seemed as if she was as eager for me to become her suitor as I was to get her to walk out with me.* Then again, maybe Eliza would have been equally flirtatious with *any*one who'd offered her a ride home. Maybe that was part of whatever game she'd played with her previous suitors?

For someone who'd nearly bounced out of her seat when he asked to court her, she made a big point of emphasizing she wanted their courtship to progress slowly. Come to think of it, maybe she'd been *too* agreeable when he'd claimed he wouldn't be able to take her out very often this summer.

Suddenly, it occurred to Jonas that maybe she was toying with him, playing a game of cat and mouse. Perhaps that was what happened with Petrus and her other suitors, too… Perhaps she'd drawn closer and then distanced herself from them throughout their courtships, right up until the point when they'd wanted to discuss marrying her. But why would she do that? It seemed rather cruel.

I really shouldn't speculate, Jonas reminded himself. *Even if she behaves the same way toward me as her other suitors, I won't be affected by it, because I'm not going to get emotionally involved with her.*

As far as he was concerned, the more distance Eliza

wanted to put between them and the slower she wanted their relationship to develop, the better. In fact, he wouldn't mind if they didn't spend any time alone together until *blohbier* season was over at the end of August. And by then, it might not be necessary to take her out, because Freeman might ask someone else to court him.

Jonas pulled up the long, gravelly road leading to the house and farm. His happiness about how well things had turned out with Eliza was bittersweet, since he knew that the worst part of his whole scheme—facing his brother—was yet to come.

After unhitching the buggy and cooling down his horse, he meandered across the driveway. *Pretty soon, we'll have people coming and going in and out of here all day.* This would be his and Freeman's third summer running the "U-pick" blueberry farm they'd inherited from their uncle, and Jonas felt as excited about opening day now as he'd felt about it the first year they'd been here.

While he enjoyed the work he did as an independent carpenter—building decks, installing cabinets and laying floors—there was something about being outdoors all day tending to God's creation that Jonas liked just as much. Not that the work was that laborious. Although the men had to take care of pruning, irrigation, and disease and insect control, their uncle had done all the hardest work of planting and cultivating. By the time the Kanagy brothers inherited the land, the shrubs were fully productive.

The only improvement they'd made to the farm was to turn it into a U-pick operation. This not only saved them the time and effort of harvesting the fruit themselves, and the expense of hiring someone else to do it, but it also meant they didn't have to pay to have the fruit transported to nearby markets, since their horses could only travel so far in a day.

Their farm was very family-friendly, and *Englisch-ers* and Amish customers alike frequently brought their children with them to pick. The *Englisch* families especially enjoyed that Jonas or Freeman gave them rides in the horse-drawn flatbed "buggy wagon" to the barrens farthest from the parking area. The brothers employed a young Amish woman, Emily Heiser, to weigh the fruit, run the cash register and assist the customers as needed, but they didn't have any other employees. All in all, the Kanagy brothers' farm was a simple but satisfying business, and Jonas was grateful his uncle had bequeathed it to them, even though they missed their family and friends back in Kansas.

I should encourage Freeman to leave the bauerei *early on* Friedaag *and* Samschdaag *evenings so he can socialize with his peers*, Jonas thought. *It will give him the chance to become better acquainted with the young* weibsleit *in our district, now that he's ready to court again.*

As he neared the house, he spotted his brother relaxing in a glider on the porch. Freeman had changed out of his church clothes and was sipping homemade root beer that they'd bought in a big jug from Millers' Restaurant, which was owned by a local Amish family. "You're back sooner than I expected," he said when Jonas climbed the steps and sat down. "I thought you would have stopped off at Little Loon Lake on your way home."

"Why would I have done that?" Jonas asked, feigning ignorance. He needed to make absolutely sure Freeman was aware that he and Eliza were courting.

"Because I overheard you offering Eliza a ride in your buggy. She enjoys canoeing on the lake, so I figured you might have taken her there."

Little Loon Lake was accessible from a public parking lot at the town beach, but the Amish people in New Hope could also access it through the Hilty family's backyard. The district members had chipped in to purchase two canoes and a rowboat for the community's use. They stored the canoes, which could be used on a first-come, first-serve basis, in the Hiltys' shed near the water. Jonas had gone fishing on the lake several times and he'd enjoyed it, but he hadn't known Eliza liked canoeing, too. It made him feel a little guilty to realize his brother must have thoughtfully planned to take her there when he'd offered her a ride two Sundays ago.

"*Neh.* I just took her straight to her *haus.*"

"Then you didn't ask to court her?"

Jonas didn't have to pretend to be chagrined. Even though he expected Freeman's question, he was genuinely embarrassed to be talking with his brother about courting. Or maybe it was the shame of knowing he was being deceptive that caused Jonas's cheeks to burn. "That's—that's kind of a personal question."

"I promise I won't tell anyone at all. I just really need to know."

"*You* need to know? Why?" Jonas asked, although he could guess Freeman's answer.

"Because if you aren't courting her, I'm going to ask her to walk out with me. It's been over three years since…" Freeman's voice faltered, and as he took another sip of root beer, Jonas looked out over the lawn so he wouldn't have to see the flicker of emotion darken his brother's expression. But he recovered quickly and started over. "It's been three years since Sarah passed away and I feel ready to court again. I've spoken to Eliza several times and I think highly of her."

Freeman's lingering sadness over Sarah's death confirmed for Jonas that he was doing the right thing by preventing his brother from getting hurt again. But he still felt terrible admitting what he'd done. "I—I actually *did* ask Eliza to court me."

"Did she say *jah*?"

He nodded, still unable to meet his brother's eyes.

To his surprise, Freeman chortled. "You look so miserable, I was sure she'd turned you down."

Surprised, Jonas glanced at him. "You're not disappointed that I asked her to walk out with me?"

"Actually, I'm glad you beat me to it. If she said *jah* to you, obviously you're the one she's interested in. So you spared me the humility of being rejected face-to-face." Freeman's mouth curved into a self-conscious smile. "I actually kind of wondered if there was someone else she wanted to court or if she was already courting. I offered her a ride home two weeks ago and she turned me down. She said she had to help take care of her sick *breider*. I couldn't quite tell if she was being genuine or if she was just making an excuse to spare my feelings. It's been so long since I've courted that I feel like I don't trust my intuition about *weibsmensch*."

Freeman's good-natured concession made Jonas feel even worse about the situation. "I'm *hallich* you feel ready to start courting again. Some *weibsmensch* is going to be very blessed to have you as her suitor. In fact, I was just thinking that if you want to spend more time socializing, you don't need to stick around the *bauerei* until closing time on the weekends. I can manage on my own."

"What about Eliza? She's going to expect you to take her out."

"*Neh*, she won't. I already explained to her that I'll have a lot to do on the *bauerei* and I probably won't get to see her too often until *blohbier* season is over."

Freeman's eyes widened. "You told her that? What did she say?"

"She completely understood."

His brother lifted his hat and rubbed his forehead as if he had a headache. "Wow, and I thought *I* was out of practice as a suitor... Listen, Jonas, you can't ask to court a *weibsmensch* and then tell her you don't have time to see her for a couple of months. She might have indicated she was fine with that arrangement, but trust me, she isn't. Or even if she is right now, it won't last very long. The entire point of a courtship is getting to know each other, and you can't do that if you don't spend time together."

But she said she wanted to take our courtship slowly, Jonas thought. Aloud, he argued, "I've known several long-distance courtships that have resulted in marriages. And those couples spent very little time with each other because they lived so far apart."

"They may have lived far apart, but you can believe they were writing letters almost every day. Or spending lots of time at the phone shanty calling each other." Freeman swallowed the last of his root beer. "Trust me, if you don't take Eliza out at least once a week, your courtship will be over before it begins... And if that happens, don't blame me if I make a second attempt to court her myself!"

Even though he was sure—or almost sure—that his brother was joking about becoming Eliza's suitor if she broke up with him, Jonas didn't find Freeman's remark to be one bit funny.

I'm actually going to have to treat this arrangement more like it's a real courtship after all.

The realization was so nerve-racking that if Jonas hadn't already been perspiring for hours, he would have broken out in a cold sweat.

Chapter Three

"Your *mamm* and I noticed you stayed in your room last evening," Uri said to Eliza a week after Jonas asked to court her. Since it was an off-Sunday, they'd just finished holding their home worship service. The boys had been dismissed to play outside and Eliza was edging out of the living room toward the kitchen so she could help her mother prepare a light lunch.

"*Jah*, that's right, I did." She explained that she'd been working on knotting an oversize rag rug that she'd hoped to take to Harnish Hardware Store on Monday morning for consignment. However, she'd gotten too tired and hadn't been able to finish it before going to bed. Since today was the Sabbath and the rugs were a source of income, she couldn't work on it this afternoon, either.

Uri thrummed his fingers against his knee, the telltale sign he was impatient or displeased, but Eliza couldn't figure out why. She thought he'd be happy she was trying to earn more money to contribute to their household expenses. "Are you going out this afternoon?" he asked her.

"I don't know." Her friend Mary Nussbaum sometimes stopped by on Sunday afternoons. On occasion, if her two youngest brothers were napping, Eliza would accompany Mary to Little Loon Lake, where the two women would go canoeing. But if all of the boys were awake, Eliza preferred to stick close to home, so she could help her mother keep an eye on them. "Why do you ask? Do you and *Mamm* need me to watch the *buwe* at home so you can go pay someone a visit by yourselves?"

"*Neh.* I wanted to know if the Kanagy *bu* was coming to take you out since you said he asked to be your suitor," Uri replied, referring to Jonas as "the Kanagy boy" because he couldn't remember either of the brothers' names, she was sure.

"Jonas *did* ask to be my suitor." Eliza struggled to keep any hint of defensiveness out of her voice. Firstly, because Uri had almost made it sound as if she'd been making up the fact that she and Jonas were courting. And, secondly, because it wasn't any of his business how many times a week they went out. But since she knew that wouldn't stop her stepfather from questioning her further, Eliza provided the explanation he was seeking. "He's been busy preparing to get the *blohbier bauerei* ready. Opening day is tomorrow."

Uri made a disgruntled sound. "He can't work on a farm after dark, nor can he work on it on the *Sabbaat.*"

Aware he was implying that Jonas should have been available to take her out in the evenings or on the weekend, Eliza said, "I don't mind. I appreciate that he's such a hard worker."

"A young *mann* should show more interest in the *weibsmensch* he's courting," Uri grumbled, almost as if *he* was the one who felt slighted by Jonas's inattentiveness. "He might not be a *gut* match for you, either. I believe you would have been better off with Willis Mullet."

Please, Gott, *help me not to respond in anger,* Eliza silently prayed before she spoke. "Jonas has only been my suitor for a week. It will take time for *me* to discover whether he's a *gut* match or not." Emphasizing the word *me* was as close as she dared come to telling Uri he didn't have any say in the matter. Eliza excused herself and went into the kitchen to help her mother make peanut-butter-and-strawberry-jam sandwiches for the boys, and ham-and-cheese sandwiches for the adults.

"Did I hear you say tomorrow is opening day for the *blohbier bauerei*?" Lior asked her. "I don't know where my mind is—I'd completely forgotten."

"*Jah.* I plan to go picking at around nine or ten o'clock. I can take the three older *buwe* with me, so they can help me pick."

"Wouldn't you rather go by yourself so you can talk to Jonas without your *bruder* interrupting?"

"*Mamm*, you sound just like Uri, trying to rush my courtship," Eliza complained. "I wish neither of you knew Jonas asked to be my suitor."

An injured look crossed Lior's face. "My intention wasn't to interfere in your courtship, Eliza. I only want you to feel free to socialize without always having to take care of your *breider*."

Eliza regretted hurting her mother's feelings. She wished she hadn't reacted so strongly, especially since it was really Uri's meddlesomeness she found so exasperating, not her mother's. "*Denki*, I appreciate that you were trying to be helpful, *Mamm*. But I honestly didn't intend to go to the *bauerei* to socialize with Jonas. I want to pick *blohbiere* so we can get started making jam, as well as all the other treats the *buwe* like so much. Besides, Jonas is going to be too busy to stand around chatting with me."

"Oh, he might be busy, but any suitor worth consideration will go out of his way to spend time with the *weibsmensch* he's courting, even if it means working twice as hard when she's not around."

Lior's comment was almost exactly the same as what Uri had said, but this time Eliza didn't take offense because she noticed the dreamy expression on her mother's face. She assumed Lior was thinking about being young and courting Eliza's father. Henry Keim had died when Eliza was six. Since she hardly had any memories of him, she loved hearing her mother reminisce about what he was like or tell her stories about things he'd done.

"When you and *Daed* were courting, did he always take time to chat with you, even if he was busy?" she asked.

"*Jah.* And so did Uri. I remember when he spent an entire afternoon taking me on errands because our *gaul* had thrown a shoe and the farrier was in Canada visiting relatives. It was your twelfth birthday and the weather was bitterly cold. I decided to walk into town because I needed to pick up the winter boots I'd ordered for your present, as well as purchase cocoa so I could make your favorite chocolate-buttercream frosting for the birthday cake. I'd just recovered from the flu and Uri didn't think I should be walking so far in that kind of weather. He insisted it wasn't a problem for him to

take me into town. I didn't find out until much later
that he'd had a big order to fill for a customer by the
next morning, so he'd worked until midnight to make
up for the lost time."

"I didn't know he did that," Eliza said. Although the
anecdote was admittedly sweet, she was disappointed
that her mother had told a story about Uri instead of
her father.

"*Jah*, he did a lot of thoughtful things like that when
we were courting."

It's too bad he doesn't still *do thoughtful things like
that for you*, Eliza thought. *But once you married him,
he probably figured he didn't have to try so hard to
win your affection anymore.* That was another reason
she had no intention of getting married—she doubted
most men could sustain the romantic, thoughtful gestures they practiced when they were courting.

"Lior!" Uri called from the other room. "I'm *hungerich.* Is lunch almost ready?"

"*Jah*, it's all set." Lior turned to her daughter. "Could
you please go round up the *buwe*?"

Eliza hurried outside and circled the house, where
she spotted the boys at the bottom of the small hill
in the backyard. "Mark, Eli, Samuel, Isaiah, Peter!
Time for lunch!" she called. All of them except Samuel charged past her to go inside. The six-year-old had
just rolled down the hill and he must have still been
dizzy because he only took a few cautious, crooked
steps like a newborn foal before falling onto his bottom. Eliza had to stifle a giggle as she went over to
help him up again. As they walked, she held his sweaty
palm to keep him steady.

"*Denki*, 'Liza. The ground is tipping," he said.

"The ground isn't tipping—*you* are. It's called being dizzy," she explained. "I'm surprised you don't have a *bauchweh*, too."

"*Neh,* my *bauch* is empty, so it doesn't hurt. What did you and *Mamm* make for lunch?"

"*Aebier*-jam-and-peanut-butter sandwiches. I know those aren't your favorite, but guess what?"

"What?"

"Tomorrow I'm going *blohbier* picking, so pretty soon we'll have *blohbier* jam and peanut butter sandwiches, instead of *aebier.* You can *kumme* with us and help me pick this year. I think you're tall enough now."

"I can? Wait until I tell the other *buwe.*" Samuel dropped Eliza's hand and started to run. He staggered for a few steps and she thought he would take another tumble, but he quickly straightened out and made it to the porch without falling.

Watching him, she couldn't help but smile. Although her little brothers were a handful, they were also a delight. *They're one of the few reasons I'm glad* Mamm *married Uri,* she thought.

After Eliza's father, Henry, had died in a tree-falling accident, Eliza and Lior had moved back in with Lior's parents. Lior's father had passed away two years after that, and her mother perished within months of him. So Eliza and Lior had lived by themselves from the time Eliza was nine until she was thirteen. The two were very close, and in some ways, they felt more like sisters than mother and daughter. As far as Eliza was concerned, they could have happily lived alone like that forever.

Lior's parents had left her a small house and their modest savings. Times were tight, but it wasn't as if

Eliza's mother urgently needed to get married for financial reasons. But Eliza supposed she must have been desperate for adult company—that seemed the only logical reason she would have ever courted someone like Uri. And he'd clearly fooled her into thinking that he'd be as kind and considerate a husband as he'd supposedly been as a suitor.

Not that he was ever really *mean*… But in Eliza's eyes, he was never really pleasant, either. Although she felt guilty for thinking it, sometimes it seemed to Eliza that her stepfather had always resented how close she and her mother were. *That's probably one more reason he's so eager to marry me off and get me out of the* haus. *He'd rather have* Mamm *all to himself, even if it means she'll have no one here to help her with the* buwe.

Well, he could pressure Eliza until the cows came home, but there was no way she was ever going to get married. And *pretending* to court was as close as she was ever going to come to actually courting.

But considering how closely Uri is monitoring this courtship, I'm afraid I'm going to have to do a better job of pretending. And I can't do that unless Jonas starts showing more interest in me.

It was only ten o'clock on Monday morning and the parking area near the barn was already almost filled with *Englisch* vehicles. Jonas realized he was going to have to set out orange cones and rope off a section of the yard to indicate additional spaces the customers could use. While he was thrilled that the business was off to such a great start, he felt a little overwhelmed.

Despite their best preparations, Jonas and Freeman

had suffered an unexpected setback yesterday. After they'd worshipped together and eaten lunch, Jonas had announced he was going to the phone shanty to call his family in Kansas at two o'clock, the way he usually did on off-Sundays.

"When you're done talking to *Mamm*, are you going to pick up Eliza and take her canoeing or on a picnic?" Freeman had asked.

"Whether I am or not, it's none of your concern," Jonas had replied. Even though he'd had no intention of going anywhere with Eliza, he didn't want Freeman to know that. "I hope you're not going to be checking up on me throughout my courtship, because I won't appreciate it."

"Okay, okay, I'll back off. I just want to make sure Eliza doesn't feel ignored, that's all."

Jonas would much rather have gone hiking in the gorge with Freeman and other singles from their district, but if he had done that, his brother definitely would have known that Jonas hadn't gone out with Eliza. Of course, there'd been the possibility that *she* might have shown up for the hike by herself, but there was nothing Jonas could have done about that.

When he'd arrived at the phone shanty, he'd discovered a message on the voice-mail system from Emily, the young woman Jonas and Freeman had hired to work the cash register on the farm. She'd said she was visiting relatives in Serenity Ridge and her return trip to New Hope was going to be delayed because her mother had the flu and was too sick to travel. Emily had said she wouldn't be able to come to work until Tuesday or Wednesday morning.

So, because they were short-staffed, opening day

at the farm was a little more hectic than usual. Freeman had to stay at the cash register booth so he could weigh the fruit and collect money from the customers. Jonas, meanwhile, had been trying to manage the daily chores and upkeep of the barrens in between giving customers rides to and from the parking lot in the buggy wagon. He'd quickly realized that transporting *Englischers* such a short distance wasn't a good use of his time, and decided they'd just have to walk, the way the Amish people did.

However, half a dozen customers complained that their children had been waiting all year to ride in the buggy wagon because it was such a novelty to them. Some *Englischers* even hinted that the horse-drawn ride was the reason they patronized the Kanagy brothers' farm, instead of the U-pick farms closer to where they lived. So Jonas resumed shuttling them back and forth, and he even took an extra lap around the perimeter of the farm just for fun as a way of retaining customer satisfaction.

But now, he was ready to switch responsibilities with Freeman for an hour. As he neared the cash-register booth, Jonas noticed his brother was talking to an Amish woman who had several small children with her. He was approaching them from behind, so at first he couldn't tell who it was, but when he got a little closer he recognized Eliza and her little brothers.

"Do you *menner* want your own baskets, or are you going to put the *blohbiere* you pick in your *schweschder's* basket?" Freeman asked the boys.

"Our own," the two tallest ones replied in unison, so Freeman handed them each a wooden basket that had a length of rope looped through the handle for tying the container around their waists.

"How about you?" Jonas's brother crouched down to speak to the smallest boy. "Do you want your own basket to put your *blohbiere* in, too?"

"Neh," he said seriously, shaking his head. "I'm not going to put mine in a bucket. I'm going to put them in my *moul*."

Freeman and Eliza cracked up together. Then Freeman teased, "In that case, you'd better hop up on this scale so I can weigh you. Then, when you're done picking, I'll weigh you again."

"Why?"

"So I know how much to charge you for all the *blohbiere* you ate."

Once again, Eliza laughed. Actually, she cracked up harder than Jonas would have expected her to. It wasn't *that* funny, at least not to Jonas, who had heard his brother make a variation of that same joke several times before now. He cleared his throat and stepped forward, interrupting their chatter. "Hello, Eliza."

She glanced up from helping one of the boys tie the basket around his waist. "Oh, hello, Jonas. It looks as if you're having a very successful opening day so far."

"Jah. There are a lot more customers than we expected."

"They probably want to get a head start on perfecting their recipes for the *blohbier* festival."

The *Englischers* in New Hope hosted a blueberry festival the second weekend in August. Held on the town's fairgrounds, the festival was an opportunity for farmers, bakers and vendors to sell blueberries by the pint, as well as blueberry jams and desserts. Nonedible items for sale included blueberry-scented candles, hand towels embroidered with blueberries, photographs of local blueberry barrens and other decorative household knickknacks. The festival also offered various activities and events, live music performances, a road race and, of course, a blueberry-pie-making contest—which was followed by a blueberry-pie-*eating* contest.

It would have been considered *hochmut* for Amish women to enter the baking competition, but several of them chipped in to share a rented space at the festival so they could market their blueberry confections and other handiwork.

"Are you participating in the festival, Eliza?" Freeman asked.

"*Neh.* My *bruder* love *blohbiere* so much that we have to use every *bier* we pick for jams or treats for our *familye.* There's never anything left over for us to sell."

"What about the rugs you make—don't those have *blohbiere* on them?"

Jonas thought, *I wasn't aware she made rugs for sale—how is it Freeman knew that about her?* It concerned him that his brother was so familiar with Eliza's preferences and hobbies.

"*Neh.* They're rag rugs, not embroidered," she answered. "In order for me to be able to sell them at the festival, they're supposed to be related to *blohbier* season."

"Aren't any of them the color *bloh*?" Freeman joked.

Eliza smiled. "*Jah*, but I don't think that counts. You'd be surprised by how seriously the festival organizers are about these things. Last year they closed down the stall next to ours because the vendors were selling *aebier* jam, if you can believe it."

Freeman's eyes got big. "You're kidding, aren't you?"

When Eliza giggled, Jonas decided he'd better do something to interrupt their banter a second time, so he told his brother it was his turn to shuttle the customers between the parking lot and the barrens.

"Sure," Freeman said good-naturedly. "I'll wait to give Eliza and her *breider* a ride, too. They've walked all the way from her *haus* so they're probably hot and tired."

Jonas didn't want to appear rude by suggesting his brother should leave without her, but he really wanted to speak to Eliza by himself. Given the way Freeman was kidding around with her, Jonas was starting to feel nervous that she might decide she preferred his brother's company to Jonas's. *I've got to arrange to spend time with her alone very soon*, he thought. But how could he do that if Freeman whisked her away?

Thankfully, Eliza said, "That's okay, there's no need to wait, Freeman. The more worn out my *breider* are, the less likely they are to wander away and get lost in the *blohbier* bushes. Besides, I think I need a longer rope for my basket. This one doesn't go all the way around my waist."

"That's because that one is for a *kind's* basket. Just a second—I'll find you an adult-size piece," Jonas offered. But first, he turned to his brother and pointedly dismissed him. "See you later, Freeman."

After Freeman had left and Jonas retrieved a longer piece of rope for Eliza, he was still at a loss for how he was going to manage to set a date with her in front of her little brothers. He could tell they were antsy to start picking berries and he knew he had to think quickly, but his mind drew a blank.

"Oh, *neh*, I'm all thumbs," Eliza said, reaching around behind her back. "I tied my basket on too tight, but I think it's in a knot, so I can't loosen it. Could you please help me with it, Jonas?"

She's been tying an apron around her waist every day since she was a maedel—*certainly she should be able to work a knot out on her own by now,* he thought. But then it occurred to Jonas that she was *flirting* with him. Once again, she'd presented him with a better solution for his dilemma than he could have ever thought of on his own.

"Sure, I'll give it a try," he said. As he loosened the knot, he was close enough to lean forward and whisper in her ear. "I'm sorry I didn't get to see you yesterday, but may I take you for a ride next *Sunndaag* after *kurrich*?"

"I'd like that a lot," she whispered back, turning her head ever so slightly. Her face was so close to his that if they'd actually been courting and no one else had been around them, he might have been tempted to kiss her cheek.

The unbidden thought was so disquieting to him that Jonas stepped back and said to her brothers, "If your teeth are *bloh* when you *kumme* back, I'll know what you've been eating!"

When Eliza laughed just as hard at his joke as she'd laughed at Freeman's, Jonas breathed a sigh of relief. He didn't have anything to worry about…at least, not until next Sunday, when he had to take Eliza out for the first real date of their fake courtship.

Chapter Four

"Stay on the grass, *buwe*, or else you'll have to *kumme* back here to hold my hand and walk with me!" Eliza called for a second time to three of her brothers, Peter, Isaiah and Samuel. It was Thursday morning and the boys were gallivanting up ahead of her and Mary on their way to the Kanagy brothers' blueberry farm. Even though the quiet country road had a wide, gravelly shoulder, Eliza felt they couldn't be cautious enough around *Englisch* traffic. The boys obeyed and moved farther to the left, onto the grassy field. To Mary, she said, "Sometimes I feel like I'm herding goats."

Mary chuckled. "Don't you mean sheep?"

"*Neh.* It would be much easier to herd sheep."

"I wish I had little *breider* to herd." Mary was the youngest of seven daughters, all of whom lived out of state. So she didn't even get to see her little nieces and nephews very often. "Better yet, I wish I had *kinner* of my own." Unlike Eliza, she'd occasionally indicated that she was eager to get married and start a family, but she'd never had a suitor.

"One day soon, you will. But this morning, I'm *hal-*

lich you're here to give me a hand with my *breider*. When we went picking on *Muundaag,* Peter got stung by a bee and Isaiah accidentally spilled all of the *bloh-biere* out of his basket when he bent over to pick up a snake."

Mary stopped short in her tracks as if she'd just seen a reptile herself. "You saw a snake in the *blohbier* barrens?"

"I didn't—Isaiah did. It was only a green snake. They hardly ever bite."

"Even so, their slithering bothers me." Mary shuddered and then resumed her pace beside Eliza. "Do you suppose you can *kumme* canoeing with me and a few others from *kurrich* this *Sunndaag*? Honor is getting a group together. I think Keith, Glenda and Ervin intend to go."

"I, um, I wish I could, but I can't." This Sunday after church, Eliza's mother, brothers and Uri were going kite flying with a few other couples who had young children. So it would have been an ideal time for Eliza to accompany her friend—if only she hadn't already committed to going for a buggy ride with Jonas.

"Oh, that's too bad. Do you have to watch your *breider* again?"

"*Neh.* I…" Eliza hesitated. Mary was her closest confidante besides her mother, so she'd told her about each of the suitors she'd had in the past. Although she hadn't confided the *reason* she'd agreed to be courted by them, she'd let Mary know when she was courting and when her courtships had ended. But after having five suitors in as many years, she felt a little self-conscious admitting to Mary that she was courting a sixth, when her friend hadn't ever courted anyone at all.

However, Mary guessed the reason for Eliza's pause. "Don't tell me—you have another suitor, don't you? And you've already made plans with him for *Sunndaag*."

Eliza nodded and replied in a low tone so her brothers wouldn't hear. "*Jah*. He asked to be my suitor about two weeks ago, but we haven't gone out anywhere together yet. So he's taking me for a buggy ride after *kurrich*."

"I see." Mary pressed her lips together, and for a while, the only sound between the two young women was the crunching of the gravel beneath their sandals as they strode toward the farm. Eliza glanced at her friend's profile and recognized the disappointed expression on her face.

"Please don't be upset." Eliza assumed Mary felt let down that she couldn't go canoeing with her. "I know I've only been able to go to the lake with you once this summer, but unfortunately, I have to honor the first commitment I made."

"*Unfortunately?*" Mary repeated incredulously. "If you feel it's unfortunate that you're going to spend time with your suitor, why did you agree to walk out with him in the first place?"

Eliza quickly backtracked, and stammered, "I—I didn't mean it's *unfortunate* I'm spending time with him. I meant it's unfortunate that I already made a commitment to him because I'd prefer to go canoeing with you and everyone else on *Sunndaag*." Her explanation did little to appease Mary, who seemed uncharacteristically expressive this morning.

"I don't understand you, Eliza. You're my closest friend and I'm *hallich* that you appreciate the *schpass* we have together… But if the shoe were on the other foot, I'd rather go out with my new suitor than spend *Sunndaag* canoeing with you and the other singles," she admitted.

"Thanks a lot," Eliza said drolly.

"All I mean is that it's perfectly natural for a *weibsmensch* to be excited about going out alone with her new suitor. But you seem to act as if it's a dreaded chore," Mary said. "Maybe that's because when a person has had as many suitors as you've had, courting loses its shine."

"You're making me sound like an *Englischer* who dates someone different every couple of months," Eliza protested. "I haven't had *that* many suitors."

"You've had a lot more suitors than I've ever had—although I guess that wouldn't be difficult to do." Mary whisked her fingers over her cheek and Eliza couldn't tell if she was brushing away a tear or shooing a fly. "I hoped to be married and have a *kind* by now. I never thought I'd get to be this age without ever even having a suitor. It makes me wonder if *Gott's* will is for me to be single the rest of my life."

"Don't be *lappich*. You're only twenty-two."

"My *schweschdere* were married by the time they were twenty-one and they'd all had their first *bobbel* within a year."

"It isn't a race," Eliza reminded her, even though she understood why Mary might feel as if it was. "You shouldn't feel pressured to get married just because other *weibsleit* our age are married."

"I don't feel pressured. I feel *envious*," Mary confessed. "I know I should be content with my life, whether I'm single or married. But I truly hope it's

Gott's will for me to fall in love, get married and become a wife and a mother—and the sooner, the better."

Even though Mary had sometimes mentioned that she wished she'd had a suitor and she'd occasionally commented that she couldn't wait to become a mother, she'd never spoken about it as openly and with such longing as she did today. Although Eliza didn't want to get married herself, she wanted her friend to have the deep desire of her heart. "If that's what you really want, then I'll pray the Lord will allow it to happen," she offered.

"Denki." Mary was quiet for a moment, then ask, "Now, are you going to tell me who your suitor is?"

Knowing she could trust her to not tell anyone else, Eliza said, "Jonas Kanagy."

"Really?"

"Why do you sound so surprised?"

"Well, it's just that…" Mary stopped to shake gravel from her sandal, then replied, "To be frank, Honor mentioned that Willis Mullet was looking for you after *kurrich* the other week. She had the notion he was going to ask you to walk out with him. But you know what she's like—anytime a *mann* and a *weibsmensch* so much as glance at each other, she assumes they're courting."

Eliza didn't bother to acknowledge that in this instance, Honor was more right than wrong about Willis's intentions. *"Neh*, it's Jonas who's courting me."

"Oh." Mary gave a funny little laugh. "I actually thought his *bruder*, Freeman, might be interested in you. At the risk of sounding like Honor, the few times when he has stopped to chat with us after *kurrich* lately, I've noticed how attentive he always is to everything you say."

Although Eliza had thought the same thing at one point, she now realized she'd made the wrong assumption, too. "He's just a *gut* listener."

"Mmm-hmm. If you say so," Mary teased.

"What does that mean?"

"It means I wish *menner* would fawn all over me the way they fawn all over you."

"Don't be *narrish*. *Menner* would fawn all over you if they had the chance to get to know you better. I've grown up with the *buwe* in our district, but you're a relative newcomer to Maine."

"A newcomer? I moved here six years ago! The *menner* in our peer group have had plenty of chances to get to know me better. If they really wanted to, they would have done it by now."

Eliza had to weigh her words carefully before she replied, since she didn't want to hurt her friend's feelings. Mary was a warm, thoughtful, lovely person, but when she was around men, she had a tendency to withdraw. During their outings with their male peers, she was so reserved that at times she almost seemed disinterested. Additionally, she was very pretty, with ash-blond hair and big blue eyes that appeared even larger when she wore her silver-framed glasses. Eliza suspected that the men their age felt somewhat intimidated about approaching her, so they mostly kept their distance.

"Maybe—maybe they just need a little encouragement," she tentatively suggested.

"You think I should *flirt* with them?" Mary said the word *flirt* as if the idea was completely appalling to her. Eliza wasn't sure that was because Mary came from a very conservative background or because she simply found flirting to be too disingenuous for her personality. It was probably a little of both.

"*Neh*, not necessarily. But sometimes *menner* don't know how to get a conversation started or they lack the confidence to speak with a *weibsmensch* one-on-one. If you initiated a conversation with one of them, it might put him at ease." Up ahead, Eliza's brothers were turning onto the dirt driveway, heading for the booth to collect baskets to put their berries in. She called out, reminding them to keep an eye out for *Englisch* vehicles. Then she asked Mary, "Is there any *mann* in particular you'd consider accepting as a suitor?"

"I—I guess so," she admitted, her cheeks going pink. Her voice dropped even lower as she said, "Lately I've noticed that Freeman has been attending more social events. There's something about him that seems kind of, well, different from most of the other *menner* our age. But like I said, he only seems to have eyes for you—at least, that's what I thought."

Eliza snapped her fingers. "I have an idea. I'll suggest to Jonas that we should go canoeing, too. You, Freeman, Jonas and I can all ride together to the lake on *Sunndaag* after *kurrich*." Not only would riding there together give Eliza the opportunity to facilitate a conversation between Freeman and Mary, but it would also prevent the conversation from becoming too personal between Eliza and Jonas. The longer she could keep their discussions on a superficial level, the better.

"But how are you going to get Freeman to agree to go, too?"

They were within a stone's throw from the booth where Emily Heiser was tying a blueberry bucket around

Samuel's waist. Eliza answered Mary in a whisper. "Just leave it to me. I'll think of something."

"Look who's here." Freeman elbowed his brother. It was almost lunchtime and they were returning from the northern-most section of barrens, where Jonas had been showing Freeman that the birds had been feasting on blueberries.

"*Jah,* I see her," Jonas replied noncommittally. He'd noticed when Eliza, her brothers and Mary Nussbaum had arrived earlier that morning, but he hadn't sought out Eliza to talk to her for several reasons. Firstly, he was too busy. Secondly, he didn't want to show her any special attention in front of Mary, since he didn't want Mary—or anyone else—to suspect that they were supposedly courting. Thirdly, and most importantly, Jonas was at a loss for trivial topics to discuss with Eliza; he actually hoped to "save" his small talk for when he took her for a buggy ride on Sunday.

However, there was no avoiding chatting with her now because she had spotted him and Freeman, and was lifting her hand in a wave. The littlest of the three boys, Samuel, also waved and smiled a blue-toothed smile. Jonas couldn't help but chuckle.

The Kanagy brothers headed toward the booth, where the group was clustered around the scale. Everyone exchanged greetings as Emily weighed their berries and carefully poured them into the buckets Emily and Mary had brought to transport the fruit home.

"Looks like you picked enough to make several pies," Freeman commented to Eliza. "If your *breider* here are tired of eating *blohbiere,* feel free to bring any leftover pie to Jonas and me. It's my favorite."

Eliza answered, "My *blohbiere* are for making jam, not pie. But Mary's baking pies and they're always *appenditlich*. It's a *gut* thing for the *Englisch* that she can't enter them in the contest at the *blohbier* festival, because she would win, hands down."

"*Neh*, there's nothing special about my pies," Mary said modestly, shaking her head as she looked down at her shoes.

"I'd be happy to be the judge of that," Freeman offered with a laugh. "And when I'm done eating, I can tie the empty pie tin to a post to frighten away the birds."

"Oh, *neh*. Have they been eating the *biere*?" Eliza asked.

"*Jah*. They've helped themselves to that entire area over there." Jonas waved his hand to indicate the northern section of the farm. Then he turned to Eliza's brothers and asked, "Can you guess what kind of bird has been eating the *blohbiere*?"

Isaiah shrugged and Peter shook his head, but little Samuel took a guess. "The *hungerich* kind?"

Jonas, Freeman, Eliza and even quiet Mary burst out laughing. "That's a better punchline than what I was going to say," Jonas admitted.

"What kind of birds were you going to tell us ate the *blohbiere*?" Eliza asked.

"Why, bluebirds, of course," Jonas replied with a friendly smirk and she chuckled at his joke. "Although I think the bluebirds had some help from their friends, the robins and starlings. The damage is pretty widespread."

"That's a shame." Once again, Eliza sounded very empathetic. "If it would be helpful, I could make a scarecrow for you?"

"*Denki*, but there's no need to go to that trouble," Jonas said, declining her offer, although he was grateful for it. "We'll pick up some scare tape at Harnish Hardware Store."

"What's scare tape?" Samuel asked, wide-eyed, as if he were imagining something very frightening.

"It's a kind of shiny ribbon that we can fasten to the *blohbier* bushes," Jonas explained. "Kind of like the tinsel that *Englischers* decorate the *Grischtdaag* tree with in the center of town. The ribbon reflects the sunlight, and when the wind blows, it dances around and makes a crinkling sound, which the birds don't like. So it keeps them away from our *blohbier* bushes."

As Jonas was talking, he noticed two *Englisch* women and about half a dozen children gathering around the buggy wagon near the other side of the parking lot, apparently waiting for a ride out to the barrens. So he suggested to Freeman, "Looks like you've got customers waiting for you. And I should get back to work, too."

Freeman started walking toward them, then called over his shoulder, "Don't forget—if you need anyone to eat leftover baked goods, I'm up for the job. It doesn't have to be pies, either. I also like *blohbier* muffins and *blohbier* crumble."

Jonas ruefully shook his head at his brother's blatant hinting, but Eliza just giggled. "We'll remember that, won't we, Mary?" she said.

Mary didn't seem as amused as Eliza was. Ignoring the question, she said, "It's almost lunchtime. We should be getting back or your *breider* will get so *hungerich* they'll eat half the *blohbiere* before we make it to your *haus*."

"Okay. But I was just going to ask Jonas if I could have a glass of water before we leave. The *buwe* guzzled down the entire jug we brought and I'm so thirsty." She looked directly into his eyes and Jonas could tell she wanted to discuss something in private with him. He dared to hope she was going to tell him she had to cancel her plans with him on Sunday after all.

"Sure. Do you need a drink, too, Mary?" he asked, but she said she'd brought her own thermal bottle of water, so she had plenty to drink. So Jonas led Eliza toward his house, careful to keep at least three feet of distance between them so no one—Amish or *Englisch*—would suspect they were a couple.

"I always thought the *buwe* walked quickly, but I can hardly keep up with you," Eliza said when they'd gotten halfway across the lawn, so he slowed his pace a little, but not so much that they could easily make small talk.

"I'll be right out," he told her when they reached the porch. He took the steps two at a time, then dashed into the house and back out a moment later with a tall glass of water, which he extended to her.

"Denki."

As Eliza tipped her head upward and slowly drained the glass, her reddish-brown hair glinted with sunlight. For a second, Jonas pictured her shiny locks loosened from the bun she wore at the nape of her neck and blowing in the breeze. Quickly looking away, he dismissed the image as something that had simply popped into his head because they'd just been discussing reflective scare tape.

After she handed the glass back to him, he set it on the bench where he and Freeman had left their root-beer glasses the previous evening. "I'd better get going," he remarked, hastily hopping down the stairs.

"Wait, just one second, please." Eliza hurried down the stairs, too. Shielding her eyes, she looked up at him. "I was wondering if you had a particular destination in mind for our buggy ride on *Sunndaag*?"

Jonas's thought about how pretty Eliza's hair was had left him feeling so unsettled that he'd completely forgotten she must have had an ulterior motive for asking for a drink of water. Without thinking, he answered bluntly, "*Neh*, not yet. But I will." Once the words were out of his mouth and Eliza discovered he hadn't put any consideration into planning a special outing for them, Jonas expected her to scowl or frown. Instead, she smiled.

"Actually, since you don't have specific plans yet, I was wondering if we could go canoeing at Little Loon Lake," she suggested. "Honor is getting a bunch of people together and I thought it would be *schpass* if we joined them."

Jonas couldn't believe it. For what must have been the third or fourth time, Eliza was providing him with an easy road out of his predicament. "Sure. If that's what you'd prefer to do instead of going for a ride, I'd enjoy it, too." *Socializing with a group of people will be a lot more* schpass *than spending the afternoon pretending to be romantically interested.*

"*Wunderbaar.*" She smiled and added, "I know Mary would like to go, too. If she rides with us, people won't suspect that you and I are courting."

Jonas just *knew* there had to be a catch. "I, um, well..." he stuttered. It wasn't that he minded giving Mary a ride, too, but showing up to a group event with two women just wasn't something a typical Amish man in this district did. At least, not unless one of the women was his sister. It seemed to him that Eliza should have known it wasn't a custom here, too. But since she apparently didn't see why he might think it was inappropriate, he said as tactfully as he could, "I'd feel kind of outnumbered by *weibsleit*."

"Oh, *jah*. You're right, I can see what you mean." She nodded in agreement and took a few steps, but then stopped and held a finger in the air. "I have an idea. If Freeman doesn't already have other plans, maybe he could *kumme* with us, too? No one would give it a second thought if the four of us traveled there together."

Even though she was acting as if the thought had just occurred to her, there was something about Eliza's solution that just seemed a little *too* convenient, as if she'd had it in mind all along. Was he imagining it, or was it possible that Eliza was becoming more interested in keeping Freeman's company than in keeping Jonas's? She certainly seemed to enjoy talking to Freeman and kidding around with him. But then again, Eliza was generally a very amiable person and she'd laughed at Jonas's corny jokes, too, so maybe he was misreading the situation.

Still, he was tempted to tell her that he'd changed his mind about going to the lake after all. But he'd already agreed to it and if he broke his word, he might lose her favor altogether. So he did the only thing he could. "Sure, I'll ask him if he wants to *kumme*."

"Great. I'll let Mary know I mentioned the outing at the lake to you and that you and your *bruder* are going and you agreed to give us a ride. We'll meet you at your buggy after *kurrich*."

That wasn't exactly how the conversation had gone, but Jonas said, "Sounds *gut*. See you then." As he strode off, he thought he heard Eliza say something else, but he didn't catch it because he was silently praying that Freeman had already made plans to do something else on Sunday afternoon.

Chapter Five

"**W**on't you please *kumme* fly kites with us, too?" Samuel pleaded to Eliza as they rode to church on Sunday morning.

She shifted her youngest brother, Mark, to her other knee. At three years old, he was still just small enough that he had a difficult time staying seated on either of the narrow benches facing each other in the back of the buggy, so it was safer for her to keep him firmly in her arms. Rather than tell Samuel she was going out with Jonas, Eliza replied, "If I *kumme*, there won't be enough kites for everyone."

"That's okay. I'll share mine with you. *Mamm* says *Gott* likes it when we share with a cheerful heart."

Eliza smiled at the dear little boy; she should have known not to give him such a feeble excuse. "*Denki.* That's very generous of you. Next time we have a breezy *Sunndaag,* maybe I'll be able to join you. But today I'm going canoeing with my friends."

"Your friends?" he asked. "Mary?"

"*Jah*, she'll be there," Eliza answered.

At the same time, Lior gently scolded him from the

front of the carriage. "Samuel, that's none of your business."

Generally speaking, it was considered impolite for Amish children to question adults about their plans. However, Eliza found her six-year-old brother's curiosity more understandable and less intrusive than her stepfather's, who asked, "What do you mean, Mary will be there? I thought you were going out—"

Eliza noticed her mother tap Uri's shoulder and raise her finger to her lips. So Uri was quiet a moment before he rephrased his question in a way the boys wouldn't understand. "I thought you were going out with your other...*friend*."

"*Jah.* I am. There is a group of us going," Eliza cryptically assured him even though she resented the infringement on her privacy. She'd told him earlier in the week that she and Jonas were spending Sunday afternoon together. That was already more information than Eliza felt she should have had to share. Couldn't he just leave it at that?

She silently asked the Lord to give her patience and to take away her resentful feelings, but she still felt annoyed all the way to church. Those feelings lingered throughout the worship service as well. She felt like canceling her plans with Jonas just to prove to Uri that he wasn't in control of her social life. But that was just it: Uri *was* in control of her social life, at least to the extent that he insisted Eliza should have a serious suitor.

Besides, she really was looking forward to canoeing, and she was committed to helping Mary get to know Freeman better. Her friend, however, had expressed second thoughts about going when Eliza told her about the arrangement she'd made with Jonas to invite his brother.

"Oh, *neh*!" she'd cried. "I didn't realize you were going to speak to Jonas about it directly. He probably thinks *I* put you up to matchmaking. If Freeman finds out, he'll think I'm being very forward. Now he's going to avoid talking to me altogether."

"Don't worry. I made it seem as if I was the one who wanted you to *kumme* along so no one would know Jonas and I are courting. He and Freeman won't suspect a thing. When it comes to courting and romance, *menner* can be completely oblivious about a *weibsmensch's* interests," Eliza had said. She should know; she'd been tricking her stepfather about *her* interest—that is, her lack of interest—in suitors for over five years.

Thinking about it now, as the minister read a passage from the third chapter of Colossians that included a verse about not lying to one another, Eliza felt a little twinge of shame. Not about matchmaking for Freeman and Mary, but about purposely misleading Uri. But she quickly dismissed her qualms, rationalizing that her stepfather was so controlling that he left her with no other choice. Besides, it wasn't as if she'd been outright lying to him—or to her mother—anyway.

Nor have I been lying to my suitors, she silently justified. *I've always been very straightforward about not necessarily wanting anything more than an opportunity to develop friendships with them.*

Indeed, judging from the few interactions she'd had with Jonas so far, she believed she genuinely would enjoy becoming friends with him. Eliza liked the way he engaged with her brothers, and she appreciated how agreeable he was about going to the lake on Sunday, instead of for a ride. Also, her connection to him was already allowing her to help Mary get better acquainted with Freeman. *For all I know,* Gott *has allowed Jonas to be my suitor just for that very purpose*, she told herself.

Yet if that was true, then why did she still feel so relieved when the minister's sermon about truthfulness was finally over?

"You want to sit in the front with Eliza?" Freeman asked out of the corner of his mouth as Eliza and Mary approached Jonas's buggy after church.

"Neh," Jonas whispered urgently. "Remember, you have to pretend you don't know anything about us courting. That's the entire reason Eliza wanted you and Mary to *kumme* with us—she doesn't want anyone to know I'm her suitor, including *you*."

"Hello!" Eliza called, and Mary echoed her greeting. They were each carrying an insulated half-gallon jug, which presumably contained water or lemonade for the group to share.

The brothers hardly had time to say hello back before Honor came dashing toward them from the opposite direction, a sizable cooler bag in hand. "Oh, *gut*—you haven't left yet," she said, panting. "I was going to ride with Glenda, Ervin and Keith, but Keith's *groossmammi* and *groossdaadi* arrived yesterday as a surprise for his *daed's* birthday. So he's staying home with them. I didn't want to ride alone with Glenda and Ervin because I'd feel like a third wheel, if you know what I mean." She gave an exaggerated wink, which was unnecessary because everyone knew exactly what she'd meant.

"You're *wilkom* to join us," Jonas said. Eager to get on the way before Honor could catch her second wind and continue gossiping, he said, "I can hold your bag while you get in."

"*Denki*, Jonas. You're such a gentleman." Honor's syrupy tone made Jonas regret offering.

"And I can take those for you." Freeman held out his hand to take the jugs from Eliza and Mary, then joked, "I'm just as much of a gentleman as my *bruder* is."

Eliza laughed and handed over the bottle before climbing into the back of the carriage, but Mary held on to hers and stated, "It's only a half gallon of water. I think I can manage, *denki*."

On the way there, Honor talked so much that no one else got a word in edgewise. Not that Jonas minded; it was actually kind of a relief to have her do all of the talking because he was preoccupied with other thoughts.

Eliza certainly seems to be amused by Freeman, he mused. *Or does it just seem that way because Mary is so reticent by comparison?* In either case, to be on the safe side, he decided when they reached the lake, he'd try to keep as much distance between Freeman and Eliza as possible. But how could he separate the two of them in a way that wouldn't result in him winding up alone with Eliza?

Thankfully, an opportunity presented itself almost as soon as they arrived at the lake and met up with Glenda and Ervin. "Glenda's wrist is still healing from when she fell and sprained it last week, so she shouldn't paddle. I can take her in the rowboat. That means there will be three of you in one canoe and two in the other, okay?" Ervin suggested, making it clear he preferred to be alone with Glenda in the rowboat, even though it had room for three people.

"Sounds *gut*," Jonas agreed. "You and I can share a canoe, Freeman. The *weibsleit* can go in the other one together."

Freeman looked incredulously at his brother and opened his mouth, undoubtedly to object, but Honor beat him to it. "It's so rare for even one of you Kanagy *buwe* to *kumme* on an outing with us. How will we get to know you better if you only keep company with each other?"

"*Jah.* She's right. I talk to you morning, noon and night. It's time for us to chat with someone else," Freeman said to Jonas, smirking. "I'll take two of the *weibsleit* in my canoe and you can take one in yours."

Jonas knew Freeman was setting it up so that it wouldn't seem suspicious for Jonas to go alone in the canoe with Eliza, and for once, he didn't mind his brother's interference in his supposed courtship. However, before he could answer, Honor again piped up. "I'll go with Jonas. Mary and Eliza, you can go with Freeman."

Jonas shot his brother a pleading look but Freeman gave him a shrug as if to say "Sorry, but what can I do?"

Eliza said the arrangement was fine with her and hurried to put on a life vest. She seemed more eager than disappointed to be relegated to Freeman's canoe with Mary. *Is that because she doesn't want Honor or the others to figure out we're courting, or is it because she prefers Freeman's company to mine?* Jonas wondered, irritated that such thoughts were plaguing him.

"Let's head toward Pine Island," Ervin suggested a few minutes later as the three vessels shoved off from shore.

Pine Island was how they referred to the little clump of land in the middle of the lake. Surrounded by jagged rocks and densely populated with pine trees, the rectangular-shaped island was probably only seventy feet long and thirty feet wide, but it was a popular picnicking spot because it afforded a cool, shaded resting or fishing area in the middle of the lake.

"Okay," Jonas agreed, then pointedly added, "After we take a break there, we can switch paddling partners."

"Are you tired of me already?" Honor asked, sounding dejected. "We haven't even gotten our paddles wet yet."

Realizing he'd insulted her with his suggestion, Jonas joked, "*Neh*, but my *bruder's* arms will probably be tired so he'll want someone else to paddle by then."

"*Voll schpass,*" Freeman remarked from his canoe, where he was sitting in the back. Mary was in the middle and Eliza was paddling in front. "If my arms are so weak, why are we ahead of you?"

"You won't be for long," Jonas quipped. "We'll race you to the island, won't we, Honor?"

"*Jah.* Let's go!"

Jonas put all of his strength into paddling, and Honor was a strong, confident paddler herself. The pair quickly overtook and then outpaced Eliza, Mary and Freeman's canoe. Ervin and Glenda apparently decided not to race at all because when Jonas glanced over his shoulder, he noticed they were lagging so far behind that it was clearly intentional.

"We won!" Honor exclaimed when she and Jonas reached the shallow, rocky area surrounding Pine Island several minutes before anyone else did.

"*Gut* paddling," Jonas acknowledged. He navigated them around the boulders jutting up above the water and situated their canoe parallel with the embankment. He told Honor she should get out first, but when she stood she said she felt "too tippy" and promptly sat back down. So Jonas got out and dragged the boat about fifteen yards through shin-deep water to where there was a flat, sandy area, so Honor could easily step onto it. Regardless, as she stood up, she extended her hand to him. Reluctantly taking hold of it, Jonas thought, *She didn't have any difficulty balancing when she was getting* into *the canoe.* As soon as her second foot hit dry land, he released her fingers.

It wasn't that he disliked Honor, but he did recognize that she'd earned the reputation she'd developed for being rather bold in her behavior toward the bachelors in the New Hope district. He supposed it was understandable; Honor was one of the older single women and she clearly wanted to get married soon. But the community was small so she probably didn't have a lot of options for suitors. However, Jonas didn't want to do anything to encourage her to think *he* might be one of those options. *I'm not even interested in being* Eliza's *suitor...and I'm actually courting her,* he thought wryly.

So when Honor suggested Jonas should sit with her on a large log in the shade, he declined, making a joke at Freeman's expense to soften his refusal. "*Denki*, but I'd better not. I've got to stand here and make sure my *bruder* doesn't capsize his canoe on a rock."

Honor giggled. "Do you really think he might tip it over?"

"*Neh*, probably not," Jonas admitted. "But better safe than sorry."

Shading his eyes as he peered out over the water, he watched Freeman and Eliza paddling toward the island, with Glenda and Ervin's rowboat still far in the distance behind them. As Freeman's canoe came closer, Jonas could see Eliza was scowling. *Maybe she doesn't enjoy being with my* bruder *so much after all.* And although he wouldn't have deliberately *wished* a bad time on her, Jonas couldn't help but feel a little bit relieved.

This is not *how I envisioned spending the afternoon,* Eliza thought as she silently brooded. She was hot, sweaty and annoyed that Jonas had suggested racing across the lake. *How is Mary supposed to chat with Freeman when he's so intent on getting to the island? Honor and Jonas already won the race and Glenda and Ervin aren't even trying, so what's the big rush?*

Not that Mary could easily chat with him, anyway, since she deliberately sat facing forward instead of facing Freeman, but she could at least say something over her shoulder. Instead, Eliza's friend had been virtually silent for the entire excursion toward Pine Island. *How does she expect Freeman to be interested in her when she's acting as if she wouldn't give him the time of day?* Eliza wondered.

But what really had gotten her goat was that Jonas seemed to be showing Honor an inordinate amount of attention. Granted, there was little he could have done when Honor declared she was going to paddle in the same canoe with him. And Eliza figured he was just being polite by holding Honor's bag for her when she got into the buggy—after all, Freeman had done the same for her. But Eliza had distinctly spotted Jonas taking Honor's hand and helping her out of the canoe when they'd reached the island just a moment ago.

I know I said I didn't want anyone to find out we're courting, but that doesn't mean I want him to show special attention to Honor, she thought. *If he's not careful, she'll think he's interested in her.* It wasn't completely far-fetched for Eliza to imagine that Honor might tell her mother about her misperception, and that Honor's mother would be so delighted that she'd share the news with someone who'd share it with *Eliza's* mother. Or worse, that Uri would somehow hear the rumor.

I can't allow that to happen, Eliza thought. So when they approached the embankment and were ready to disembark from the canoe, she sweetly asked Jonas, who was standing close to the water's edge, "Could you take my hand, please? I feel shaky, probably from all that exertion."

Eliza was almost certain she heard Mary snicker behind her—after all, they'd both hopped in and out of the canoe easily without assistance countless times before. But there was too much at stake for her to care if her friend thought she was acting sappy. Jonas took her fingers in his, and she was surprised by the softness of his touch. After holding his hand a moment longer than necessary, so Honor would see them, Eliza finally let go.

But Honor was bending over her own canoe, fishing her cooler bag out of it, and she apparently hadn't even noticed. Eliza realized she'd forgotten the jug of iced tea she'd made for everyone to share in the canoe. "Oops," she said. "I forgot—"

"It's okay. I'll carry it. I know how dizzy you are," Mary said drolly. Then she hopped out of the canoe, a jug in each hand, without so much as a wobble.

"Wow, Mary. You have the balance of a cat," Freeman remarked as he clumsily hefted himself onto dry land.

Not exactly the most romantic compliment, but it's a start, Eliza thought, pleased. It seemed Mary was pleased, too, because even though she didn't respond aloud, a blush rose on her cheeks and forehead.

Once Glenda and Ervin had come ashore, the group climbed farther up the embankment to sit on an old fallen tree and on the numerous rocks or stumps in the area. Mary and Eliza distributed paper cups of water or iced tea to everyone, while Honor passed around a tin of blueberry muffins that she'd made. Everyone except Freeman refused the offer, saying they were still full from eating lunch at church.

"More for me," Freeman said gratefully. "I'm starving and I love any dessert made from *blohbiere*."

How is it possible that Freeman has lived here for over two years and has attended dozens of kurrich *potlucks and yet he doesn't realize what a* baremlich *baker and cook Honor is*? Eliza wondered to herself. She wasn't being unkind: Honor's cooking was notorious in New Hope. In fact, it was even notorious in the surrounding communities of Serenity Ridge and Unity. To be sure, her lack of simple culinary skills was an anomaly among Amish women, much like it would have been for an Amish man to lack basic carpentry skills.

Yet even more unbelievable was the fact that she

seemed oblivious to how bad the food she prepared actually tasted. Despite several frank comments from her mother and others in the community, Honor's enthusiasm for cooking and sharing the desserts and dishes she'd made never waned. So Eliza watched intently as Freeman took his first bite of a muffin.

Honor was also watching intently. "How is it?" she asked.

"Mmf," he mumbled, still chewing. He swallowed and then downed a big gulp of iced tea. "I've never tasted *blohbier* muffins quite like these."

Eliza recognized he was being as diplomatic as he could while still being truthful, and she momentarily felt bad for Honor, who really did try very hard. However, Honor appeared clueless as to what he really meant, and commented, "I'm *hallich* you like them. You and Jonas should take the rest home with you. Since you're bachelors, it's probably rare for you to eat homemade treats."

"*Neh*, that's okay," Freeman replied, a little too quickly, waving his hands for emphasis. "One is enough for me."

Honor quizzically wrinkled her brow. "But you just said you loved *blohbier* desserts."

Freeman avoided answering by taking another swallow of iced tea, so his brother chimed in, "*Denki*, Honor. That's very considerate of you."

She beamed at him and then someone brought up the subject of the blueberry festival. As everyone else was talking, Eliza mulled over Jonas's response to Eliza. It was clear to her that he was covering for his brother's impoliteness and she was impressed by this small kindness. She tried to catch his eye so she could smile at him, but he was gazing out at the lake. As she studied his profile, she found herself thinking, *For someone with such a prominent, masculine-looking jawline and forehead, he sure does have soft, pretty eyelashes...*

The seven of them must have relaxed on the island for a good hour, joking, telling stories about what they'd been doing over the summer and even singing a few contemporary worship songs together. Eventually, they made their way back down to the water and waded around the rocks for a while before Glenda said she had promised to be home before suppertime, so she needed to leave.

"I'll take you back," Ervin quickly volunteered before anyone else could lay claim to the rowboat.

"I need to head home, too," Mary said, to Eliza's dismay. Although no one would have considered her friend to be gabby, she'd certainly been engaging in the conversation more than she usually did when men were included. Eliza could tell she was having a good time and Eliza was enjoying herself, too. She'd forgotten how carefree she felt when she didn't have to keep an eye out for her little brothers.

"Okay. But I know how much you like to paddle and you haven't gotten a chance yet," she replied to Mary. "My arms are tired, so I'll sit in the middle of the other canoe with Jonas and Honor, as long as they're willing to do all the work." This seating arrangement seemed like the best of both worlds. It would give Mary the opportunity to visit with Freeman, while preventing Eliza from being alone with Jonas.

"Sure, I'll paddle," Honor agreed. "Jonas seems to steer us exactly in the direction I want him to go, without my even telling him to head left or right. We make a really *gut* team, don't we, Jonas?"

He shrugged. "You are a strong paddler, but for my part, there's not much I have to do to guide the canoe. It's pretty much a straight line from the Hiltys' beach to the island."

For some reason, Eliza felt bothered by his response. *I'm a strong paddler, too,* she thought, even though she knew it was prideful, regretting that she'd pretended her arms were tired. Which was odd, because it wasn't as if she had anything to prove to Jonas. "I hope you don't plan to race again," she remarked, knowing that if they raced, Mary wouldn't be able to enjoy a leisurely discussion with Freeman.

"Why not? You'll be on the winning team this time," Honor teased.

"Suit yourself, but you'll be paddling into the wind." She climbed into the canoe and sat with her back toward Jonas. There was no sense facing him since they weren't going to converse, anyway. *I know I asked him not to let anyone know we're courting, but he has spent more time chatting with Honor than with me. What if he's as interested in her as she apparently is in him?* she thought, worrying.

As they set out for the opposite shore, it occurred to her that while Honor may have won the previous race to the island, Eliza couldn't allow her to win over Jonas's affections. It wasn't that she wanted him to develop any romantic feelings toward *her*—after all, that was what had happened with Petrus and it had ended in him being bitterly disappointed. But she couldn't risk Jonas dropping her to court Honor.

If that happens, I'll be stuck walking out with Willis.

So from now on, no more group outings—Jonas and I are going to go out alone, she resolutely decided.

Freeman and Mary easily won the race. Once both teams had crossed the lake and everyone had disembarked at the Hiltys' property, Glenda and Ervin had to leave right away. So the other three women put the paddles and life vests into the storage shed while Freeman and Jonas hoisted the canoes onto the storage rack.

As they were dragging the rowboat to drier ground, Freeman whispered, "On the way back, you can let me off at Abram's *haus*—I'll say I want to drop in and see if he's home. That way, you'll have some time alone with Eliza."

"*Neh*, I won't—she lives farther away from our *haus* than Honor does." Jonas intended to drop off the women according to the proximity of their houses from the lake. Which meant first he'd stop at Mary's house, then Eliza's and then Honor's.

"You still don't get it, do you?" Freeman muttered. "Anyone can tell by her expression that Eliza's annoyed at you. You've been paying more attention to Honor than to her this entire afternoon."

His comment really riled Jonas. Partly because he knew his brother was right. But mostly because Jonas felt like *Freeman* was paying even more attention to Eliza than Jonas had been paying to Honor. "What excuse will I give for dropping Honor off first and then circling all the way back to drop off Eliza? It will be obvious that I want to spend time alone with her, just like it's obvious that Ervin wants to be alone with Glenda. If you think Eliza seems upset with me now, how do you think she'll feel if Honor finds out I'm courting her?"

"*Jah*, I guess you're right." Freeman lifted his straw hat to wipe his brow. "But mark my words, Eliza is not *hallich* with you."

It's not my fault she wanted to go on a group outing, Jonas silently observed. Regardless, for his own sake, he couldn't allow their afternoon to end on a sour note. So when he stopped at the end of Eliza's lane, Jonas made a point to get out of the buggy and give her his hand to help her down, something he'd never ordinarily do if they were just friends. At least, not unless she cajoled him into it, the way Honor had done.

He was worried that Eliza would push away his arm or ignore him, but she slid her hand into his. Just as when he'd helped her out of canoe, he was aware of how slender and silky it felt. Instead of letting go when both of her feet touched the ground, he led her to the side of the buggy, out of Honor and Freeman's range of view, and then he released her fingers.

In a hushed tone, he said, "I had *schpass* at the lake today. But I think it would be nice if we went out alone next time, if you wouldn't mind?"

"*Neh*," she replied firmly and Jonas's stomach dropped. Was she really *that* annoyed at him? But in the next breath she clarified, "I wouldn't mind at all."

"*Wunderbaar*," he uttered in relief. "I'll pick you up next *Sunndaag* at two o'clock and I'll have something special planned."

In a saccharine voice that rivaled the tone Honor had used when he'd held her bag for her, Eliza cooed, "Anything we do together will be special, Jonas."

He should have felt reassured by her sentiment, but he didn't trust the abrupt shift in her demeanor. Also, she was speaking too loudly for someone who'd claimed she wanted to keep their courtship private. It seemed as if she wanted Freeman and Honor to hear her. Jonas could only think of one reason for that: she was trying to make his brother envious that they were walking out.

Neh, that's narrish, he told himself. She already had the opportunity to walk out with him—or at least, to accept a ride home from him—and she'd turned him down. Then again, maybe now that she'd spent more time with Freeman, had she changed her mind? Or was the volume of her voice simply a reflection of her enthusiasm about going out alone with him? It was irritating to Jonas that he felt he had to keep second-guessing her motives, yet something about her behavior just didn't add up. But he forced himself to respond. "*Gut*. I'll see you then."

Turning to saunter away, Eliza gave him an over-the-shoulder smile. "Hopefully we'll see each other on the *bauerei* this week, too."

"I'll keep an eye out for you," Jonas replied. As he returned her smile, he thought, *Two can play this game...* even though he couldn't be sure whether she was actually playing a game or not.

Chapter Six

"*Guder mariye,* Mary," Eliza and four of her little brothers sang out together as they saw her coming up the lane on Wednesday morning. It had been raining since Monday, so it was the first time this week they were able to go blueberry picking. After being cooped up in the house for what seemed like a long time, they were all glad to be outside again and were eager to start their trek to the farm.

"*Guder mariye.*" Mary bent down and patted Eli's head. The four-year-old was sitting in a red wagon, with an empty pail for transporting the berries home on his lap. "Are you coming to pick *blohbiere,* too?" she asked him.

"*Jah,*" he exclaimed.

Samuel elaborated, "He's not tall like me because he's only four and I'm six. So he can't reach the high *biere.* But I'm going to show him how to pick the low *biere.*"

"That's very helpful of you," Mary said. "Is Eli going to be kind in return and let you ride in the wagon with him?"

"*Neh.* I don't need a ride. I'm going to run with my

other *breider.*" Samuel promptly galloped off to catch up with his older brothers, who were already starting down the dirt lane.

"My *mamm* is feeling under the weather and Mark has a slight fever, too. I thought it would be a *gut* idea if I brought Eli with us so she and Mark could rest." Eliza pulled the wagon behind her as the women began walking. Speaking in *Englisch* so Eli couldn't understand, she said, "I've been curious to hear about how it went on *Sunndaag.* Did you enjoy being in the canoe alone with Freeman? Did the two of you get a chance to chat?"

"*Neh.* Not really. He was too focused on racing you, Honor and Jonas back to the other side of the lake."

"*Ach.* That's exactly what I thought may have happened, especially when I saw how fast you two were paddling."

"I don't think we were paddling any faster than Honor and Jonas were," Mary answered modestly, as usual. "I think we were quicker because we had one less person in our canoe."

"That's what Honor said, too. She seemed a little indignant that you and Freeman beat us." Eliza muttered beneath her breath, "I guess it was hard for her to accept that she and Jonas weren't as *gut* of a paddling team as she thought they were."

"Is that envy I hear in your voice, Eliza?" Mary asked, gently reproaching her.

"Why would I be envious?"

"Because Jonas seemed to be paying more attention to Honor than to you."

Uh-oh, did Mary notice that, too? "Well, it did bother me a little that Honor was being such a flirt, but I wouldn't say I was envious. I think Jonas was just being careful about how much he talked to me so no one would guess we're courting. Because when he let me off at my *haus*, he made a point of mentioning he wanted to go out alone with me next *Sunndaag.* So it's not as if I'm worried that he'd prefer to be Honor's suitor instead, or anything like that." Even as she was speaking, it occurred to Eliza that she was trying a little too hard to assure Mary that she wasn't concerned.

"That's *gut.*" Mary chuckled to herself. "Although I have to admit, I'd rather Honor pursue Jonas than Freeman. She's so determined that I'd never stand a chance if he became the object of her affection."

"Well, you *might* stand a chance if you opened up to Freeman a little," Eliza suggested, repeating her earlier advice. "Give him a little sign that you're interested."

"You mean I should act like Honor does around *menner*? No, *denki*," Mary said firmly.

"You don't have to be that bold. But maybe you could… I don't know. Bring him some *blohbier* pie? He said he loved it…and you know your pie is so much better than anything Honor could ever make."

"You're *baremlich*," Mary said, but she giggled.

"*Neh*, I'm just being honest. One taste of your pie and Freeman would literally be eating out of your hand." Eliza playfully cautioned, "Just please don't give Jonas any, or he'll fall for you, too. Then you'll have both Kanagy *breider* vying for your attention, and who would that leave me for a suitor?"

"Oh, I wouldn't worry about that if I were you," Mary said wistfully. "If Jonas ever ended your courtship, there'd be someone in line right behind him eager to become your suitor."

Jah, that's what I'm afraid of—and it would be Willis Mullet, Eliza thought. *And that's why I'm not going to let Jonas break up with me...even if it means acting bolder and more flirtatious than Honor acts.*

Jonas stepped out of the barn, smack into Honor's path. She was carrying a flowered plastic container similar to the one she'd given him on Sunday.

"There you are, Jonas. Emily told me she saw you go into the barn. I have something for you." She held out the container and Jonas hesitated to take it. Even if Honor was the best baker in all of the New Hope district, he would have been reluctant to accept whatever goodies she was offering because he didn't want to do anything to encourage her apparent interest in him. But neither did he want to be rude, so when she pushed the container into his hand, he accepted it. "It's *blohbier kaffi kuche.* I figured the muffins I made you on *Sunndaag* are long gone by now."

"*Jah,* you're right, they are." Jonas had fed them to the chickens, who'd gobbled them up in no time. "That was thoughtful of you. I'll, um, I'll just tuck them back into the barn so they aren't sitting out in the sun. I don't have time to run over to the *haus* to put them inside."

"That's a *gut* idea. Maybe we can enjoy one together later, when you're ready for a *kaffi* break. I'll be here on the *bauerei* picking *biere* for a while, so just give me a shout." Before Jonas could tell her he wasn't planning to take a coffee break, something caught Honor's attention. "Look, there's Eliza and Mary. I'm going to try to catch up with them so I have someone to chat with while I'm picking."

She flew across the dirt driveway calling their names,

and Jonas went back into the barn and set the container of blueberry coffee cake inside an empty wheelbarrow by the door. Then he hastily made his way to the western corner of the farm, carrying the jar of nails he'd forgotten the first time he'd gone into the barn to retrieve his hammer and some boards.

Earlier that morning, he'd discovered a portion of the fence around the perimeter of the property had been damaged in the previous night's thunderstorm. The wind had snapped a large, rotting branch off a maple tree and it had landed on the fence, breaking several boards. Jonas had spent the early morning hours cutting up and clearing away the fallen limb. Now it was necessary to repair the fence, which discouraged deer from visiting the blueberry farm.

It's too bad I can't build a fence to keep the birds away, too, he thought as he began replacing the splintered boards. While some people recommended netting, it was too expensive and time-consuming to install on a farm this size. He'd spoken to an *Englisch* farmer who'd told him that birds were able to tear or peck their way through it to get to the fruit, anyway. The reflective scare tape Jonas and Freeman had used apparently didn't work as well when the sun wasn't out, either—they'd found evidence the birds had been eating the berries during the rainy weather.

So Freeman had insisted on buying several rubber snakes, as well as a plastic red-tailed hawk, to use in addition to the scare tape. The problem with using fake predators was that they frequently needed to be moved so the birds wouldn't get used to them being in the same spot and figure out they weren't real.

It occurred to Jonas that he was a bit like a scarecrow himself, trying to keep Eliza from getting too close to Freeman or vice versa. *I've got to keep on my toes so they don't realize* I'm *a phony, too,* he thought. *And that includes coming up with a special date for this* Sunndaag.

He'd been brainstorming about it ever since he'd dropped off Eliza at her house, but so far, the only activity he knew she'd really like was canoeing on the lake. But that didn't seem very original, since they'd just been there with their peers. He supposed they could go for a hike at the gorge, although that wasn't exactly a unique outing, either. In fact, hiking there was such a popular Sabbath recreational activity that they were bound to meet their peers or other district members out on the trails. So Jonas mentally crossed that option off his list, too.

Why did I ever say I'd plan something special? he asked himself. *Now she's going to have high expectations, even if she did claim she'd consider anything we did together to be special.* But Jonas didn't know her well enough to come up with an activity or a destination that he was certain she'd really enjoy. It was getting to the point where he wondered if pretending to court her was worth the stress it was causing him. *Maybe I should just step aside and let my* breider *find out the hard way what Eliza is really like*, he mused.

But just last evening Freeman had mentioned Sarah, his fiancée who had died. It was during the thunderstorm and he'd remarked that she'd always relished it when storms rolled across the plains in Kansas. Freeman had commented that she'd said she'd liked it because the thunder and lightning were such remarkable displays of God's power and majesty. "I still think of her whenever it storms..." he'd admitted, his voice trailing off as he stared absently out the window.

Recalling how doleful he had sounded, Jonas knew he couldn't back out of his courtship with Eliza. Freeman was still too emotionally vulnerable. As his older brother, Jonas would always consider it his responsibility to try to protect him from getting hurt, no matter how old they were.

By the time he'd finished repairing the fence, Jonas still didn't have any clue where he'd take Eliza on Sunday. *Maybe I should go find her now and just ask her what she'd prefer to do*, he thought, since that seemed like the most practical solution. But then he'd run in to Honor, too, and she'd probably invite Mary, Eliza and her brothers to join them for coffee cake in the barn. Worse, she'd suggest that she and Jonas should go take a break alone and Eliza would hear. *I'm still trying to make up for canoeing alone with Honor on* Sunndaag. *I don't want to upset the apple cart again*, he lamented to himself.

So on his way back to the barn with the extra boards, he circumvented the section of the barrens where the customers were picking today. Instead, he cut through an area that was still off-limits and continued brooding. *How did I get myself into a position in which I'm avoiding not one but two* weibsleit *on my own* bauerei?

"You *buwe* have done a *gut* job. Those *biere* are nice and plump and I don't see any green ones," Eliza said as she surveyed the fruit the boys had picked. After helping Eli and Samuel untie their baskets, she told her four brothers, "I packed a snickerdoodle for each of you, so you can have a rest in the shade beneath those trees at the end of the row. Mary and I will be done in a few minutes and then we'll go home."

After the boys had trotted away to enjoy their snack, Honor said, "It's probably almost time for me to *absatz*, too. I brought Jonas some *blohbiere kaffi kuche*, and we're supposed to take a break together."

"You and Jonas?" Eliza echoed incredulously.

"*Jah.* Why is it so surprising he enjoys my company? Is it just because I'm a few years older than he is?"

Eliza glanced to her right at Mary, who discreetly rolled her eyes. Deep down, Eliza suspected that it was probably Honor, not Jonas, who had initiated getting together with him for a piece of coffee cake. But it still rankled Eliza and she knew she had to say something to put an end to Honor's pursuit of him. Exaggerating her pout, she said, "Your age has nothing to do with it. I'm surprised Jonas would agree to take a break alone with you because he's walking out with *me*."

"He *isn't*!" Honor exclaimed, clapping her hand over her mouth. Mary didn't even bother to pretend that this was the first she'd ever heard that Eliza and Jonas were courting.

"*Jah*, he is. He asked to be my suitor a couple of weeks ago."

"Oh, Eliza. I'm so sorry," Honor apologized. "I never would have asked him to take a *kaffi* break with me if I had known you two were courting. I feel *baremich*."

I knew *she was the one who initiated it*, Eliza thought. But Honor's apology sounded so heartfelt that she couldn't hold the trespass against her. "We were doing our best to keep it a secret, so you're not the one who should feel *baremlich*—Jonas should. I can't understand why he'd agree to spend time alone with you, knowing that it might give you the impression he's not already courting someone. Namely, *me*," she stressed.

She wasn't truly annoyed at him, nor was she even perplexed. Eliza had witnessed Honor's behavior around bachelors often enough to understand if Jonas had felt cornered. But she had to at least act put out, the way she might have felt if she'd authentically liked him as a suitor.

"Please don't be angry at Jonas on my account," Honor pleaded. "To be fair, I didn't really give him much of a choice in the matter." Her eyes began to well, so Eliza reached over and patted her shoulder.

"I believe you. I suppose I don't even need to mention it to him. It's a simple misunderstanding, that's all. It's nothing to get so upset about."

"That's not what I'm upset about. I'm upset because no matter how hard I try or how clever my schemes are or how often I create opportunities for the singles in our district to socialize, I still don't have a suitor. I feel like I'm never going to have one." Honor sniffled and blotted her eyes with the hem of her apron.

"I know how you feel, Honor," Mary admitted, leaning forward to see past Eliza. "It's difficult to want something so much and not know if you'll ever have it."

"*Jah*, I've been asking *Gott* to bless me with a suitor for years and years. It makes me question whether He wants me to get married and have *kinner*. I start to wonder if I should stop asking and accept that the answer is *neh*."

As Eliza listened to her friends share their disappointment, she was struck by the realization that they both dearly wanted a suitor and she dearly wished she *didn't* have one. It didn't seem fair. She was already doing everything she could to help Mary foster a connection with Freeman, but what could she do to help Honor? *Should I break up with Jonas so he can court her?* she wondered.

Yet Eliza couldn't bring herself to entertain that idea for very long. She hated to admit it, but her fear of winding up with Willis was too great. Besides, there was no guarantee that Jonas would want to court Honor if he wasn't courting Eliza.

"I don't think you should stop asking the Lord for what you want," she advised. "And I'll pray about it for you, too."

"Denki." Honor wiped her hands on her apron. "All right, I'm done picking for the day. Now that I know Jonas is courting you, I'm so embarrassed that I just want to leave the *bauerei* before he sees me again."

Her friends said goodbye to her, and a few minutes later Eliza announced it was quitting time. "These *blohbiere* are practically falling into my basket, so I wish I didn't have to leave. But I'd better bring the *buwe* home for lunch."

"I only need about a cup and a half more," Mary said, plucking handfuls of ripe fruit from the branches as she stepped farther down the aisle. "By the time you round up your *breider*, I'll be ready to go, too."

"Okay." Eliza exited the row of blueberry bushes and she was adding her basket to the other baskets in the wagon when Mary let out an ear-piercing shriek.

Jonas distinctly heard a woman scream and he charged in the direction of the noise. Halfway across the barrens, he discovered Eliza peering down a row, her hand covering her mouth. Three of Eliza's brothers were clustered behind her, the smallest one holding on to the skirt of her dress as he peeked down the row.

"What's the matter?" Jonas asked, looking over her shoulder to see what she was seeing. Peter, Eliza's oldest brother, was inching down the path between the blueberry bushes wielding a long stick.

"Mary saw a snake," Eliza answered softly without turning around. "She said it's right in front of her and she's too afraid to back away."

Indeed, some twenty feet beyond Peter, Mary was standing as still as a statue. She had one foot in front of the other; apparently she'd been in the middle of taking a stride when she'd become paralyzed by fear.

"Peter, don't go any farther," Jonas instructed the young boy. There weren't poisonous snakes in Maine, but he still didn't want the child to accidentally provoke the creature into biting him. "Just stay right there. I'm coming down the aisle behind you. Don't make any sudden movements."

Jonas crept toward Peter and took the stick from his hand. He figured he'd use it to push the snake out of Mary's path. The thick, coiled reptile was partially obscured by the long grass, but from what Jonas could tell, it had a dark zigzag pattern on its back. It actually looked a lot like a rattlesnake he'd seen once in Kansas, but Jonas knew that was impossible; there weren't any rattlesnakes in Maine. Even so, he proceeded cautiously, tiptoeing past Peter and down the aisle, holding the long stick out to one side. He was halfway to Mary when he heard his brother's voice from behind him, at the end of the row.

"I heard a scream. Is someone hurt?"

"Neh," Eliza replied. "There's a snake blocking Mary's way. She's too scared to move and the snake won't budge, either."

"It *can't* budge—it's not real!" Freeman hooted with laughter.

By this time, Jonas was within a few feet of the serpent and he could clearly see that it was one of the toy snakes his brother had mentioned he'd purchased at the discount store in town. But Mary was still frozen in the same position, so Jonas comforted her. "It's not real, Mary. It's rubber. See?"

When he tapped on the snake with the stick to demonstrate, the toy bounced a little, causing Mary to flinch. She was so pale that for a second Jonas thought she might faint. Instead, she burst into tears, twirled around and bolted down the aisle in the opposite direction so quickly that she jostled the basket still tied to her waist, scattering berries in her wake.

Jonas felt awful that his brother's careless placement of the snake had resulted in Mary being so frightened. And he felt even worse that Freeman had laughed about it. He turned around to address him, but Eliza beat him to it. Actually, she was addressing her little brothers, but her remark was clearly intended for Freeman.

"Kumme, buwe. It's not kind to laugh at another person when they're scared or upset, and I don't want you to ever do that. Do you understand me?" All the boys nodded except for the littlest one, Eli, who was reaching up to let Eliza put him in the wagon along with their baskets of berries. "Let's go make sure Mary's okay."

"I'm sorry, Eliza. I didn't mean—" Freeman began, but she cut him off.

"I'm not the one you should be apologizing to," she snapped as she started down the center aisle with him close on her heels. "But I doubt Mary wants to speak to you right now, so please stop following us."

"*Jah.* Okay. I'll speak to her later." Freeman took off his hat and wiped his brow as he watched Eliza and her brothers tramp toward the checkout booth. When he turned to face his brother, his cheeks were red and his eyes were clouded. "I wouldn't have placed this snake here if I knew anyone was going to be picking in this section today. I thought we agreed to direct customers to the eastern half of the barrens until tomorrow or the next day."

"I know you didn't do it on purpose." Jonas sighed. "But you really shouldn't have laughed at Mary when she was already upset."

"I wasn't laughing at Mary!" Freeman protested. "I was laughing at *you.* It was funny to see such a big strong man tiptoeing down the aisle and brandishing a stick to fend off a *toy* snake!"

"I wasn't *brandishing* the stick, I was just carrying it so I could direct the snake away from Mary. Besides, I didn't know it wasn't real at the time," Jonas reminded him, but he had to chuckle, too. "I suppose I can see why you thought I looked pretty funny, though."

"And I can see why the *weibsleit* thought I was laughing at Mary," Freeman acknowledged ruefully. "Do you think I should try to catch them before they leave so I can apologize?"

"*Neh.* Like Eliza said, Mary probably needs a little time to recover. She's likely embarrassed, and if you talk about it right now, she may feel even worse," Jonas suggested. His brother hung his head, looking so dejected that Jonas felt bad for him. But he felt even worse knowing that deep down, he was kind of relieved Freeman had fallen out of favor with Eliza.

Almost immediately, Jonas regretted having such thoughts about his brother, so he offered, "Listen, you can take these boards and nails back to the barn and I'll go smooth things over with the *weibsleit* for you."

"Are you okay, Mary?" Samuel asked, tugging her hand when the group caught up with her near the checkout booth.

"Jah." She glanced down and gave him a weak smile. "I feel a little *lappich*, though. Whoever heard of being afraid of a toy snake?"

"I thought it was real, too," Peter said, consoling her. "And I was a little bit scared also, because it didn't look like any snake I ever saw before."

Mary affectionately patted his shoulder. "You were very brave, Peter. *Denki* for being willing to protect me."

"You're *wilkom*," Peter said. "I can carry your basket of berries to the scale for you, too."

"I'll pull the wagon," Isaiah offered. So Eliza allowed the boys to hurry off in front of them toward the checkout booth.

"They're such sweet, thoughtful *buwe*," Mary remarked. "Unlike some *menner* who are three times their age."

"Jah, I was surprised by how Freeman acted, too," Eliza agreed. "It was immature, as well as rude."

"I thought he was different than that, but maybe it's better I found out what he's really like now, before I got my hopes up that he might make a *gut* suitor."

There was a hint of disappointment in Mary's voice that showed she'd *already* gotten her hopes up. So even though Eliza was offended by Freeman's behavior toward her friend, she suggested Mary not give up on him altogether.

"I know he shouldn't have laughed, but sometimes *menner* just have a different sense of humor than *weibsleit* do. I think he felt really bad that he hurt your feelings. He started to say he was sorry but I wouldn't let him finish."

"Nice of him to apologize to you, but you weren't the one who was utterly humiliated after being scared half to death," Mary pointed out.

"He wanted to apologize to you, but I told him you probably didn't want to talk to him right now. I figured you needed to gather your composure first." Eliza couldn't help but giggle as she added, "Meanwhile, it will do him *gut* to sweat it out a little, not knowing whether you'll accept his apology or not."

"Of *course*, I'll accept his apology, because the Bible tells us to forgive one another just as *Gott* in Christ has forgiven us," Mary asserted. "But that doesn't necessarily mean I'd want him for a suitor anymore."

"Don't make up your mind just yet," Eliza advised. "Because now that Honor knows Jonas and I are courting, she might turn her focus on Freeman and then you'll regret not giving him another chance."

"I doubt that Honor would ever like Freeman. He wasn't very polite to her about her *blohbier* muffins, either."

Eliza couldn't argue with that, so she continued walking in silence until they reached the long line at the checkout booth. By the time they'd paid for their fruit, little Eli was asleep in the back of the wagon. The other three *buwe* were energized from their snicker-doodles and they abandoned the responsibility of pulling him in favor of springing alongside the driveway like grasshoppers.

Just as they reached the end, Eliza heard Jonas's voice, as he called, "Eliza, Mary, wait!"

They stopped and turned to see him jogging in their direction. In one hand, he held a large plastic jug. In the other, he was carrying a flowered container that Eliza immediately recognized as belonging to Honor's mother. *That must be the* blohbier kaffi kuche *she made for him. I hope he's not going to be as rude as his* bruder *was and ask us to give the* kuche *back to her.*

"I wanted to be sure you're all right, Mary," he said, squinting against the sun at her. "You had a bad fright and I thought you might need something to eat or drink."

Mary smiled at him. "I'm fine, *denki.* And I appreciate the offer but I'm going to have lunch soon, anyway."

"Are you sure?" he said and when Mary nodded, Jonas asked, "What about you, Eliza? Or the *buwe*?"

"*Neh.* We'd better not. As Mary said, it's almost time for lunch and a treat would spoil their appetites."

"Oh, okay." Jonas seemed disappointed and Eliza didn't know if it was because they'd turned down his hospitality or because he'd hoped to get rid of the muffins. But she thought his gesture was kind, either way. "Well, I—I also wanted to say how sorry I am about what happened. We never would have put that deterrent where we knew someone was going to be picking. We didn't intend for anyone to harvest that section until tomorrow."

"There was a group of *Englisch* teenagers picking in the eastern area," Eliza explained. "They were pretty boisterous and I was concerned about the kind of language they were using. I didn't want the boys to hear it, so Emily said we could move to the other section. Not that it's her fault—I was the one who cajoled her into it."

"I'm *hallich* you moved—I wouldn't have wanted you or your *breider* to hear foul language," Jonas said, knitting his eyebrows in consternation. "If that happens again, please let me know. I'll remind the customers that this is a *familye bauerei*. I'm sorry you had to listen to that kind of talk, even for a moment. And I'm sorry about the rubber snake, too. My *bruder* also wants to apologize for his response, but I'll let him do that in person the next time you're here... You will be coming back, won't you?"

Moved by how concerned and apologetic Jonas was, Eliza answered, "*Jah*. Of course, we'll *kumme* back, won't we, Mary?"

"I suppose that depends on how many more pies I need to make," Mary answered noncommittally. Then she pointed to Peter, who was attempting to climb a tree at the end of the lane by standing on the fence railing. "Looks like the grasshoppers have decided they'd rather be squirrels instead."

"*Ach*. Would you mind keeping an eye on them, Mary? I need to rearrange these *biere* so they don't tip over if Eli shifts positions in his sleep." She gestured to the pails they'd brought to transport the berries home.

"Sure. 'Bye, Jonas."

"'Bye, Mary." He lifted the jug in a sort of wave,

and as Mary walked toward the boys, he asked Eliza, "You need a hand with those?"

"Please. I just need to make sure they're nice and snug."

Jonas set down the muffins and plastic jug. They both reached for one of the pails at the same time and his palm momentarily covered Eliza's. On Sunday, he'd taken her hand when she'd asked him to help her out of the canoe, and again when he'd assisted her out of the buggy. So why did his touch suddenly make her feel so tremulous? And why didn't the feeling pass even after he'd lifted his hand from atop hers and reached for a different container?

"There," he said, after expertly repositioning the pails. "They should be nice and secure now."

"Denki." Eliza looked into his eyes, which were more green than gray in this light. "And *denki* for coming to check on Mary. That was thoughtful of you."

"No need to thank me. I do hope the, ah, incident with the snake won't keep her from returning to the *bauerei.*"

"I think she just has to get over feeling *lappich* about being afraid of a fake snake."

"She has nothing to feel *lappich* about—I'm the one who was preparing to fend it off with a stick." Jonas chuckled at himself. "It looked like a rattlesnake I saw out on the prairie in Kansas once."

"Really?" Eliza gulped. "Did you fend that off with a stick, too?"

"Neh. I backed slowly but surely away. And as soon as I'd put enough distance between us, I hightailed it out of there like a black-tailed jackrabbit."

"Schmaert mann!" Eliza said with a chuckle. She

appreciated Jonas's candid admission of how fearful he'd been, and she wished she could ask him more about the wildlife in Kansas. But she could see that Mary was having a difficult time wrangling her brothers. Gesturing toward the group, she remarked that she probably should get going now.

"*Jah,* me, too." Jonas bent down and picked up the plastic jug and container of muffins. When he straightened up again, he said, "But I look forward to continuing our conversation the next time we see each other."

"You want to talk more about snakes?" Eliza teased. She couldn't help herself; she just felt very lighthearted all of a sudden. But she made Jonas blush.

"*Neh*, I meant—" he began.

"It's okay. I know what you meant—and I feel the same way. I'm really looking forward to talking more to you, too, Jonas." And for the first time since he'd asked to be her suitor, there was nothing phony or exaggerated about her sentiment.

Chapter Seven

"Mamm?" Eliza placed her hand on her mother's shoulder. Lior was snoring softly, her head tucked into her folded arms on the table. *"Mamm?"*

She roused and rubbed her eyes. "Did I fall asleep?"

"Jah. Why don't you go lie down while I get supper ready?" Eliza suggested. Over the week, her mother had become increasingly fatigued as the flu drained her energy. Now, on Saturday, she could barely keep her head up.

"I can't. I've got to finish reconciling these accounts."

Eliza doubted she had the presence of mind to calculate the charges for Uri's customers accurately. *How could he possibly expect* Mamm *to do the bookkeeping in her condition?* she wondered. *He should just wait until* Muundaag. *Better yet, he should do it himself.*

"I can take care of the books after the *buwe* go to bed," Eliza offered.

"Denki, but *neh.* You've got your hands full looking after your *breider."*

Peter, Isaiah and even little Samuel had spent the better part of the day helping Uri clean the workshop.

Eli was now sick with the flu, too, just like Mark. So all five of the boys would undoubtedly be exhausted and go to bed early, leaving Eliza plenty of time to work on the accounts. So she knew her mother was just making an excuse; the real issue was that Uri didn't want anyone except Lior to manage his books.

Eliza understood it was useless to try to persuade her to relinquish the responsibility. But with some persistent coaxing, she at least managed to convince her to lie down until supper was ready after all. "You'll be able to think more clearly once you've had a *gut* rest and a bowl of *hinkel supp.*"

The weather was so hot and humid that the mere mention of soup made Eliza wish she could go dip her feet in Little Loon Lake again. Thinking about the lake made her think about Jonas, which in turn made her curious about what he had planned for their "special" date.

After setting a glass of water on her mother's nightstand and checking on Eli and Mark, Eliza returned to the kitchen and began preparing soup for her mother and youngest brothers. She was also making meat loaf and mashed potatoes for Uri and the three older boys. She intended to make plenty so she could reheat the leftovers tomorrow, since cooking full meals was prohibited on the Sabbath.

As she peeled the potatoes, Eliza's thoughts strayed again to her date with Jonas the following day. Ordinarily, she might have used her mother's illness as a convenient excuse to stay home and avoid spending time alone with a suitor, especially so early in a courtship. But in this instance, even though she had a legitimate reason to cancel her date with Jonas, she decided not to.

Uri isn't working tomorrow, so he can take care of Mamm *and the* buwe. *Maybe if he has to manage the household on his own, he'll have a better sense of how challenging it can be,* she thought. *Then he won't insist I get married and move away or find a full-time job outside the* haus.

But Eliza knew that was the wrong attitude to have toward her stepfather. Furthermore, the real reason she didn't want to miss her date had very little to do with Uri—it was that she honestly *did* hope to get to know Jonas better. In her eager anticipation, she wondered whether she should take her own advice to Mary and make a *blohbier* dessert for them to enjoy during their outing. And since he was going to the trouble of planning a special activity for them, she resolved to make the dessert a special one, too.

Eliza was leafing through her recipe cards when the mudroom door opened and Uri stumbled into the kitchen, leaning on Peter and Isaiah's shoulders. His expression was grim and his breath labored. Eliza's stomach dropped and she was instantly wracked with guilt for all of the ungenerous thoughts she'd been entertaining about him.

"What is it? Are you injured?" she asked as she helped ease him into a kitchen chair.

"I think I have the flu," he answered grimly. "It just hit me like a ton of bricks."

"Oh, *neh*!" Eliza uttered, both in sympathy for Uri and in disappointment for herself. Now there was no way she could go out with Jonas tomorrow.

On Sunday afternoon, Jonas set the bag containing marshmallows, graham crackers and chocolate bars

beside him on the buggy seat. He'd already put his
tackle box and two fishing rods in the back of the carriage. After agonizing over what "special" activity he
and Eliza could enjoy together, he'd finally decided to
take her fishing in Crooked Creek. Afterward, they'd
roast marshmallows over a campfire.

Fishing isn't exactly a popular courting activity, he
conceded a few minutes later as he guided his horse
along the main thoroughfare. *Most people usually don't
roast marshmallows or have campfires until after dark,
and I intend to take Eliza back to her home long before then.* But unless another, better idea struck him
between now and the time he arrived at her house, he
had no choice but to carry out his plan and hope she'd
enjoy herself.

*Otherwise, she might not give me the chance to go
out with her again*, Jonas thought. But his desire to
show Eliza a pleasant afternoon wasn't simply because
he was worried she might break up with him. He also
wanted her to have a good time because *he* wanted
to have a nice afternoon *with* her. Just because their
courtship wasn't real didn't mean they couldn't have
schpass as friends. And it didn't mean he had to dread
spending time with her, either.

Jonas hadn't seen Eliza—or Mary, for that matter—
back on the farm since the incident with the rubber
snake. But since then, he'd reflected on the conversation they'd had that morning many times. He couldn't
put a finger on it, but something about Eliza seemed
different as they'd talked that day. She seemed more
natural somehow, as if she wasn't making such an effort or being flirtatious. And he didn't feel as if he had
to work so hard to come up with small talk, either.

It reminded him of the few times they'd socialized together shortly after he had arrived in New Hope, before he'd had any notion of pretending to court her. On those occasions, he'd share what he missed about Kansas and she'd tell him what she enjoyed most about living in Maine.

That's the kind of light, relaxed conversation I hope we have today, Jonas mused, turning down the side road leading to her house. As agreed, he waited at the end of the lane for her, a common practice for young Amish men and women who didn't want their families to know they were courting. With the exception of telling his brother he was Eliza's suitor, Jonas intended to do his best to protect their privacy. So he was caught off guard when Peter and Isaiah came loping down the lane at quarter past two, fifteen minutes later than Eliza had agreed to meet him. Samuel was trailing them in the distance.

"*Guder mariye*, Jonas," Peter and Isaiah greeted him.

"Hello, *buwe,*" he replied, wondering the best way to explain why he was idling in his buggy at the end of their lane. However, he quickly learned there was no need for an explanation.

"Eliza wanted me to give you this." Peter reached up and handed him an envelope. Puzzled, Jonas tore it open. The note inside read:

Jonas,
My mother, Uri, Eli and Mark are all ill with the flu, so I'm afraid I have to stay home and take care of them. I'm sorry. I know you had some-thing special planned and I was really looking forward to spending the afternoon together.

I hope to see you again soon.

Eliza

PS Don't worry, the boys are too young to suspect we're courting.

Jonas pushed back his hat to scratch his head. He couldn't help it—the first question that entered his mind was, *Is her* familye *really so sick that she has to stay home to care for them? Or did she have a change of heart about going out alone with me and her* fami- lye's *illness was just a convenient excuse?* He regret- ted not trusting Eliza enough to take her at her word, but he still had his doubts.

"Let's go back to the *haus*," Peter told Isaiah.

"But Eliza said we should wait to see if Jonas wants to give her a message, too."

"Bobbelmoul!" Peter elbowed Isaiah. "She said we weren't supposed to *ask* for a message—we were only supposed to wait to see if Jonas *offered* her one. Oth- erwise, it's rude, like asking for a piece of *kuche* when you go to someone's *haus*."

Jonas smiled to himself. He could tell from Eliza's words to her brothers that she was hoping for a re- sponse from him. And that meant she truly must have been disappointed she'd had to cancel their plans. "I actually would like you to give her a message, but I need a second to think what I want to tell her."

Isaiah raised his hat and slid a pencil from behind his ear. "Eliza said if you wanted to give her a mes- sage, you should write it instead of tell us because we might get distracted chasing a toad or a butterfly and we'd forget by the time we got back."

Now Jonas was really grinning. *Eliza is so hopeful*

I'll reply to her message that she even made sure her breider *took a pencil with them so I could write back to her.* He hopped out of the buggy and accepted the pencil from Isaiah. Jonas was about to start writing when he noticed Samuel shuffling toward them, his head hanging so low that his chin nearly touched his chest.

He called hello and when the little boy glanced up, Jonas could see that his eyes were watery and his eyelids were swollen. He couldn't tell if he was coming down with the flu, too, or if he'd been crying. "Are you okay? You look a little under the weather."

Samuel tipped back his head and squinted at the sky, obviously confused by the idiom. "What weather? It's sunny out."

Jonas suppressed a chuckle, but Peter and Isaiah laughed aloud…although not unkindly.

"Jonas doesn't mean the real weather," Isaiah explained knowingly. "It's just a saying. It means you look like you're about to cry."

Samuel's eyes flooded even as he protested, "I do *not*." He dropped his head again and kicked a pebble to the side of the driveway.

"He's upset because he didn't get to carry Eliza's note," Peter said quietly.

"Or the pencil," Isaiah added.

"I am *not*." Samuel lifted his head, his chin quivering. "I'm sad because *Daed* is sick and he can't take us to the lake and now I'll never get to go canoeing."

"Remember what Eliza told you?" Peter asked. "She said you can go when *Daed* gets better."

"What if he doesn't ever get better?" Samuel wailed.

Recognizing that the child was at least as upset about his father's illness as he was about his canceled canoeing excursion, Jonas was struck with an idea. *I could take the* buwe *fishing this afternoon. I'm sure it would be helpful to Eliza.* But first, he needed to get her approval. Jonas didn't want to present the idea only to have to disappoint Samuel again. "I think your *daed*—and your *mamm* and *breider*—will recover from the flu in a little while. And we should pray about that every day until they do," he suggested, touching Samuel's shoulder.

The child nodded. "That's what Eliza said, too. At breakfast we asked *Gott* to make them all better. And at lunch. But *Daed* is still sick and he can't get out of bed."

Noticing that Samuel was more worried about his father than he was about the other members of his family, Jonas assumed it must have been rare for Uri to be ill. He remembered how frightened he'd been the first time he'd ever seen his own *daed* laid up in bed; until then, Jonas had naively believed his tall, strapping father was impervious to almost any illness or injury. "It's *gut* that he's getting lots of rest because that's what will help him feel healthy and strong. But it might take a few days before he's one-hundred-percent better."

"Eliza said it might take this many." Sniffling, he held up six fingers. "That's how many years old I am, too."

"You're *six*?" Jonas pretended to be surprised. "I didn't know you were six. I thought you were only five. But if you're six, maybe you can help me with an important task."

That seemed to perk Samuel up. He wiped his cheek and asked, "What task?"

"I need to ask Eliza something. I was going to write

her a note, but I really need to talk to her in person. While I'm hitching my *gaul* could you run and ask her if she has a moment to *kumme* out to the porch so I can speak to her?"

Samuel nodded, but he looked crestfallen, as if he was disappointed because the task wasn't as important as he'd hoped it would be. So Jonas leaned down and whispered, "And here's the hard part—you have to be really careful not to let anyone else hear you, because we don't want to disturb their rest." It was true that he didn't want the child to wake anyone up, but Jonas also didn't want them to know about his request to talk to Eliza in private. If she agreed to allow him to take her brothers fishing, then he'd leave it up to her to explain why he'd dropped by the house in the first place. "Do you think you can do that?"

"*Jah.* I'll be as quiet as a mouse. Just like when we're in *kurrich* and I need to ask my *schweschder* a question," Samuel solemnly promised before he pivoted and shot up the driveway.

"Could you two show me where I can tie my *gaul*?" Jonas asked Peter and Isaiah, who readily led him to the hitching post. Then they accompanied him to the porch steps before meandering around to the backyard, leaving Jonas alone to nervously await Eliza's arrival.

Eliza hummed as she pushed the rocker back and forth, cradling her youngest brother. Three-year-old Mark was the last of her "patients" to finally fall asleep. But she was concerned that if she set him down, he'd wake up again and start crying, which just might make *her* start crying, too. She'd been up half the night caring for her family and she was exhausted.

Even in her feeble condition, her mother had tried to help Eliza comfort Eli and Mark when they'd woken up crying and feverish in the middle of the night. But Lior's legs were so weak that she'd barely made it halfway up the stairs before collapsing into a sitting position. She'd made such a racket that Eliza had feared she'd actually fallen *down* the staircase. Surprisingly, Uri had never even roused; he'd been so wiped out that he'd been sleeping ever since he'd returned from the workshop on Saturday afternoon.

Thankfully, Eliza had already had the flu earlier that summer and so had the other three boys. *I don't know what I would have done without them this morning,* she thought. Peter had helped her make breakfast, Isaiah had read to Eli and Samuel had kept Mark entertained with a hand puppet so he wouldn't fuss and wake up Lior and Uri. The three boys couldn't have been more helpful. Yet after their brief home-worship service, Eliza had snapped at Peter for dropping their copy of the hymnal, *The Ausbund,* as it had narrowly missed her bare foot. And then she'd scolded Samuel for whining because Uri couldn't take him to the lake.

Of all people, I should be more understanding about how disappointed he is, because I felt the same way when I realized I couldn't go out with Jonas, she silently chastised herself. She just hoped Jonas didn't feel equally let down, especially after making special plans for their date. Eliza glanced toward the window. *I suppose the* buwe *would have* kumme *inside by now to relay a message if Jonas had asked them to pass one along.*

Just after the thought ran through her mind, she heard the door open. A few seconds later, Samuel crept into the living room. "It's okay. You don't have to tip-toe, honey," she told him. "Mark is sound asleep now."

But Samuel approached the rocking chair, then whispered, "I promised to be very quiet so no one would hear when I told you something."

"You have a secret?"

"*Neh.* A message." Even though they were the only two people in the house who were awake, Samuel cupped his hands around Eliza's ear. "Jonas wants to know if you can talk to him on the porch."

Eliza turned to face her little brother, their noses just inches apart. "He's on the porch?"

"Not yet. He's hitching his *gaul.*"

Eliza had been hoping for a verbal message or a note from Jonas, but she couldn't imagine why he'd need to come talk to her on the porch, unless it was to express his annoyance that she'd canceled their plans. But he wouldn't do that, knowing her family was sick, would he? Either way, she had to find out and then send him home. What if Uri woke up and managed to drag him-self out of bed and saw or heard Jonas talking to her? He'd insist Eliza tell him what was going on.

So she whispered, "*Denki* for telling me Jonas's message, Samuel. That was a big responsibility. Could you help me with something else that's a very big re-sponsibility?"

"*Jah,*" the child agreed.

"While I go speak to Jonas, could you please stay here and listen in case *Mamm* or your *daed* or *breider* wake up? And if they do, can you *kumme* get me as quick as a bunny so I can bring them whatever they need?"

"*Jah.* I'll listen very carefully."

"*Denki*. I'll be right back."

Eliza gingerly rose, set Mark on the sofa and tucked a quilt around him. Then she hurried out to the porch, where Jonas was pacing. As soon as she'd shut the door behind her, she assured him she didn't have the flu, but suggested he might want to keep his distance as a precaution.

"It's okay. I already had that flu earlier this summer. It was awful. I hope your *familye* isn't suffering too much?"

He didn't seem annoyed that she'd canceled the date. He just looked concerned about her familye's well-being. "They're having a rough time of it, especially my *mamm*. But they'll be okay in a few days, *Gott* willing."

"I'll keep them in my prayers." Jonas shifted his stance and rubbed his jaw, which Eliza noticed was clean-shaven. Suddenly, she felt very frumpy by comparison. She'd been in such a rush to check on Eli and Mark this morning that she'd donned yesterday's apron instead of putting on a clean one. And she hadn't even looked in the mirror when she was pinning her prayer *kapp* to her hair, so for all she knew, it was crooked and she probably had blueberry jam on her face, too.

"*Denki*," she said. While she appreciated his concern and was glad he understood why she'd broken their date, Eliza didn't have a lot of time for chitchat. She said, "I really should go back inside to make sure my little *breider* are still asleep, so…"

"Right. I figured you might need some help or a little rest yourself. So I was wondering if I could take Samuel, Isaiah and Peter fishing at the creek for a couple of hours?"

Eliza was so taken aback she could hardly reply. She

never would have imagined a suitor proposing such a generous offer, especially after she'd just canceled a date with him. "I—I couldn't ask you to do that," she stammered.

"You didn't ask. I offered. I promise I'll keep a very close eye on the *buwe*. I won't let them fall in the water or *kumme* into contact with any rattlesnakes," he said, his lips twitching with an impish smile.

"In that case, *jah*. It would really be *wunderbaar*," she said. "I know they'll love it, especially Samuel. Uri was supposed to take him canoeing for the first time today and he was crushed he couldn't go."

"So I gathered," Jonas said. "I'll round up Peter and Isaiah from the backyard, if you send Samuel out."

Eliza practically skipped into the house. Samuel was also beside himself with happiness when she told him that Jonas wanted to take him and his brothers fishing in the creek. He bounded out of the house and down the porch steps so quickly that his hat flew off. When he turned back to get it, Eliza waved at him from the doorway.

"If *Daed* wakes up, tell him I didn't go canoeing without him," he called, holding up six fingers. "I'm waiting 'til he gets better in this many days."

Hopefully it won't take that long, Eliza thought. As she watched Jonas's buggy pull down the lane, she murmured a prayer for her family's health, as well as for the boys to have an enjoyable time. Then she went into the house and lied down on the other end of the sofa where Mark was sleeping.

Just before she dozed off, she thought about how grateful she was for Jonas's presence in her life. Because while she originally may not have wanted a suitor, today she was in dire need of a nap, and she never would have been able to take one if it hadn't been for him.

When Jonas brought the boys back to their house shortly before five o'clock, Eliza was sitting on the porch swing reading to Eli and Mark. "You didn't catch anything?" she asked her empty-handed brothers as she stood up.

"*Jah*. I caught a brook trout but it was too little so I couldn't keep it," Isaiah answered.

"I caught three but they were all too little, too," Peter said.

"I caught a frog with my hands. It was almost bigger than Peter and Isaiah's fishes," Samuel boasted. "But I put it back because the creek is its home and I wouldn't want someone to pick me up out of my home and put me down someplace else."

"I see. Well, if you've been handling frogs and fishes, you'd all better go wash your hands before supper. Please help Eli and Mark wash theirs, too," Eliza instructed the boys.

Jonas had noticed how frequently they'd quoted their older sister, and he could see clearly she was like a second mother to them. *She probably wants to have* kinner *of her own soon*, he thought as the boys obeyed her request and went indoors. *She'd make a* wunderbaar mamm.

"Jonas?" she asked, her voice interrupting his reverie.

"I'm sorry. What did you say?"

"I said it's obvious the *buwe* had a lot of *schpass*. I hope they behaved themselves."

"*Jah*. No problems at all," he replied.

"*Gut*. I can't thank you enough for taking them to the creek. It gave me the opportunity to take a nice long nap, which I desperately needed."

"You look a lot more rested," Jonas remarked, noting that her eyes were brighter now. In fact, they appeared to be sparkling.

"*Jah*, with my stained apron and uncombed hair, I must have looked like I was coming apart at the seams earlier," she admitted, self-consciously smoothing down the skirt of her dress.

"I didn't mean that. You could be wearing a gunnysack and you'd still look pretty." The unbidden thought seemed to leap from his mind to his tongue, and once spoken, it made both of them blush.

"*Denki,*" Eliza murmured.

Jonas quickly attempted to cover up his embarrassment as he confessed, "By the way, if the *buwe* don't have big appetites, I'm to blame. I gave them s'mores for a snack."

"Wow. No wonder they're so *hallich*. Fishing in the creek and roasting marshmallows is a *wunderbaar* way for young *buwe* to spend an afternoon," she declared. "But how did you happen to have the makings for s'mores in your buggy?"

Chagrined that she considered the activities he'd planned for their date to be more suitable for young boys to enjoy, he stuttered. "I—I…"

"Oh, I see!" She giggled. "You had the treats on hand because you were planning to go fishing and roast marshmallows with *me*."

"*Jah,*" he admitted. "I suppose that probably doesn't seem like a very special activity for adults, though."

"Are you kidding? S'mores are my favorite and going to the creek would have been so refreshing," she insisted. Peering into his eyes, she lowered her voice and added, "But being able to take a nap when I desperately needed one was more special than any other activity you could have planned, Jonas."

There was something about the sincerity of her tone and the way she was looking at him that made Jonas feel ten feet tall, and yet weak-kneed at the same time. His mouth was so dry he had to lick his lips before replying. "I'm *hallich* to hear that. But I hope I didn't put you in an awkward position with your *mamm* and Uri. I mean, because if the *buwe* mention our outing, your *eldre* will probably figure out we're courting."

"I don't mind if they know," she said with a shrug. "As long as it doesn't bother you."

"*Neh.* Not at all. I'm proud to be your suitor." Once again, the words flew from Jonas's lips, but this time he didn't feel embarrassed after he said them. He felt happy—although more than a little bit vulnerable—because they were more true than not.

Chapter Eight

On Monday, Eliza ended up doing the bookkeeping for Uri, anyway. She also used his cell phone—which the *Ordnung* permitted for business purposes, provided it was used more than five hundred feet away from their house—to call customers and inform them their orders might be delayed until Uri recovered.

Thankfully, his bout of the flu passed a lot quicker than Lior's. On Tuesday morning, he startled Eliza by walking into the kitchen from the mudroom. "I didn't realize you were outside. I thought you were still sleeping," she said.

"*Neh.* I felt well enough to milk the *kuh*. Peter and Isaiah have been taking care of the livestock for the past few days, so I thought I'd let them sleep in."

"I'm *hallich* you're doing better, but I didn't expect you to recover so quickly." Eliza hesitated before telling him that she'd called a couple of his customers to explain their orders might be delayed. She had tried to speak to her parents about it first, but they were both either sleeping or too groggy throughout the day to hold a conversation. Uri was so territorial about his business that she expected him to be angry she'd made the decision to contact his customers on her own, but instead, he thanked her.

"I appreciate that you took the initiative to do that. Even though I feel okay now, I might run out of steam by lunchtime, so the orders might wind up being delayed, anyway." He averted his eyes and contemplatively stroked his beard. Eliza had rarely seen him appear self-conscious, and she thought it was because he was embarrassed that he was going to be late fulfilling orders. But then he said softly, "I—I might need your help with the bookkeeping, too. Your *mamm's* mind is too foggy to do it right now, but you've always been *gut* with numbers."

Surprised to receive both an expression of gratitude *and* a compliment from her stepfather in one morning, Eliza beamed. "I already took care of the books, too."

"You did? But I didn't give you per—" Uri began, his tone gruff. But he stopped in midsentence and simply mumbled, *"Denki."* Then he poured himself a large cup of coffee and said he would drink it on the porch until breakfast was ready.

Within minutes, everyone except Lior was seated at the table. Uri said grace, thanking the Lord for their food. When he'd finished praying, just as everyone else was lifting their heads, Samuel chimed in, "And *denki* for making *Daed* all better. Please help *Mamm* feel all better, too."

Once again, Eliza expected a stern reaction from Uri, since it was considered inappropriate for an Amish child to interject a remark into an adult's conversation, and especially into a conversation with the Lord. But something about Samuel's prayer must have touched

Uri, because he reached over and tousled his hair. Then he served himself three heaping spoonfuls of breakfast casserole, a sure sign he was on the mend.

The boys quietly devoured their meals and afterward Eliza excused them from the table to go brush their teeth. "Peter, you can help Mark with his toothbrush and Isaiah can help Eli, please. Afterward, you may quietly put together a puzzle or read in the living room so you don't disturb *Mamm*'s rest."

Only Samuel remained at the table, clearly dawdling on purpose so he could talk to his father. "Guess where we went on *Sunndaag, Daed*." The boy didn't wait for his father to reply as he told him, "Jonas took us fishing at Crooked Creek."

Uri raised an eyebrow at Eliza. "Jonas?" he repeated.

She nodded and Samuel innocently elaborated, "He's Eliza's friend from the *blohbier bauerei*. And he's our friend, too. We had s'mores, but only one each because he didn't want Eliza or *Mamm* to be upset that they made supper and then we didn't want to eat it. 'Cept he got to have two because he doesn't have a *mamm* or wife to make him supper or *appenditlich* treats. He only has a *bruder* and his *bruder* can't bake any desserts a person would ever eat. Not even if it was the only dessert on a dessert island."

When Samuel stopped talking to take a drink of milk, Uri caught Eliza's eye and then covered his mouth with his arm, coughing into the crook of his elbow. When she rose to bring him a glass of water, she realized he wasn't coughing—he was laughing. Eliza didn't know whether it was Samuel's mangling of the phrase *deserted island* or the fact that he had clearly quoted Jonas verbatim that tickled her father's funny bone, but suddenly she could hardly suppress her own laughter. She managed to dismiss Samuel from the table before dropping into her chair and cracking up into her hand so no one else would hear.

In all the time she'd known Uri, she'd rarely seen him laugh like that, and she'd certainly never laughed that long with him. Their shared amusement made her feel closer to him, and some of her previous resentment seemed to melt away. When their laughter subsided, he pushed back his chair and stood up. "That was thoughtful of your suitor to take the *buwe* to the creek. Maybe this time you've chosen someone who'd make a *gut* match for you after all."

Normally, Eliza would have bristled at Uri's comment because she would have considered it to be intrusive. But today she took it in stride, preferring to think of it as a compliment instead of as her stepfather's attempt to pressure her into getting married. "We'll see," she replied lightly.

After Uri left for the workshop and Eliza began doing the dishes, she found she couldn't stop thinking about Jonas's positive attributes. As Uri mentioned, he was very thoughtful. He was also funny, kind and hardworking, not to mention he had an affable, easygoing way with her brothers. She could almost picture him cradling a baby of his own in his strong, muscular arms someday...

"Are you okay?" Lior touched her shoulder, startling Eliza from her daydream.

"Oh, *guder mariye, Mamm.* I'm fine," she responded. Although she was glad to see her mother out of bed and dressed in her regular clothing, Lior still had dark circles beneath her eyes. "How are *you* feeling?"

"Better. I even have a bit of an appetite this morning."

"Then sit down and I'll fix you *oier* and *kaffi*. I need a second cup myself."

"*Gut.* You can fill me in on what's been going on around here. I feel as if I've been away on a long trip. It even seems as if the *buwe* have gotten taller in my absence."

Eliza chuckled. "Considering how many *blohbiere* they've been eating lately, they probably *have* grown."

She spent the next ten minutes telling her mother about Eli and Mark's recovery from the flu, how she'd taken over the bookkeeping and customer calls for Uri and what the other three boys had been doing the last few days, including their fishing trip to the creek with Jonas. Finally, she confided, "Now I understand better why it was so meaningful to you when Uri took you shopping so you could get the ingredients for my birthday *kuche*. That kind of thoughtfulness really endears a *mann* to you, doesn't it?"

"Mmm-hmm," Lior murmured, partially obscuring her smile behind the rim of her mug.

"What are you laughing at?" Eliza asked.

"I'm not laughing. I'm smiling because I've never heard you speak so fondly about one of your suitors."

Embarrassed, Eliza poured another splash of milk into her coffee and stirred it so she wouldn't have to meet her mother's eyes. "You've hardly ever heard me talk about my suitors at all."

"Exactly. You must really like Jonas."

"I like him for as much as I know him, *jah*. But I still don't know him all that well." She was trying to remind herself of that fact as much as she was her mother.

"I don't want to get carried away with my emotions just because he did one very thoughtful thing for me."

"I agree. It's *gut* to take time to get to know him better. Maybe by next *Muundaag*, I'll be feeling well enough that you can return to the *blohbier bauerei* and spend time with him again."

"Muundaag?" Eliza exclaimed. "That's almost a full week away!"

Lior burst out laughing. "I was only teasing so I could determine how eager you really are to see him."

Eliza could feel her cheeks and ears burning. She was going to insist that she'd only meant she hoped her mother would feel better long before Monday, but she couldn't deny she was also eager to see Jonas again, too. Especially since he'd left her house the other day without arranging to take her out after church this coming Sunday. It was possible he hadn't asked her out because he was going to be out of town or had other plans, but she suspected he'd simply been counting on seeing her again and asking her then. So she wanted to be sure they had another opportunity to chat before Sunday rolled around.

"You're right, *Mamm*," Eliza admitted. "I would like to see him again once you're well enough to manage the *buwe* on your own."

Lior leaned forward and took her daughter's hand. In a serious voice, she said, "I appreciate everything you do around here for me. For all of us. But there will *kumme* a day when we'll have to manage without you. It will be an adjustment, but we'll be fine. So when you're ready to get married and have a *familye*—"

"Who said anything about getting married?" Eliza protested, withdrawing her hand from her mother's.

"Just because my feelings for Jonas are different from my feelings for past suitors doesn't mean I hope to marry him."

"I understand that, Eliza," her mother stated firmly. "But what I need you to understand is that when you do fall in love and want to get married and start a *familye*, you have my blessing. I wouldn't ever want to stand in the way of your happiness and *Gott's* will for your life."

Eliza slowly nodded. "I understand, *Mamm*." Rising to her feet to scramble a couple of eggs for her mother, she added, "But right now I'm perfectly *hallich* with the way things are."

Yet for the first time, when Eliza thought about what it might be like to be married, she didn't imagine it making her *un*happy.

"Is that all you're going to eat?" Freeman asked his brother on Thursday after Jonas crumpled his napkin and dropped it onto his plate. They were eating leftover barbecued chicken they'd bought from Millers' Restaurant on Wednesday evening. "You're not sick, are you?"

"Neh." Jonas wasn't physically ill, anyway. But from his previous courting experience, he recognized that he was suffering from lovesickness. Ever since Sunday, he'd lost his appetite, he'd had trouble sleeping and he couldn't stop thinking about the woman he was courting.

How did this happen? he asked himself, just as he'd done when he'd gotten the flu earlier in the summer. He'd thought he'd taken the most important precaution—namely, remaining emotionally distant—so he wouldn't fall for Eliza. In fact, he'd thought he was *immune* to her charms. But here he was, feeling almost as if he was in physical pain because he hadn't seen her for four days.

Or maybe he was achy because he recognized that his feelings for Eliza were in conflict with his better judgment. Jonas knew that his past courting experience should have been enough to deter him from becoming vulnerable to a woman again. And *Eliza's* past courting experience definitely should have reinforced his reluctance. Yet it was as if he'd lost sight of the reason he'd asked to be her suitor in the first place—because she was a heartbreaker and he didn't want his brother to get hurt. And somehow, he'd pushed the fact that this was supposed to be a fake courtship to the back of his mind.

"*Gut.* That means all the more for me." Freeman helped himself to the last two pieces of chicken. "I haven't seen Eliza on the *bauerei* this week. Did you two have an argument on *Sunndaag* or something?"

Although on Sunday Jonas had mentioned he was going to Eliza's house, he hadn't shared any other details about his afternoon with his brother. Until now, Freeman hadn't asked him about it, either. So his sudden interest in Eliza put Jonas on edge. Was his brother *hoping* Jonas wasn't getting along with her? "*Neh.* Her *familye* has the flu, so she's had to stay home to care for them. I'm sure she'll be back once her *mamm* feels better." Then he pointed out, "Not that it would be any of your business if Eliza and I *did* have an argument."

"*Neh*, it wouldn't be," Freeman agreed amiably. He speared several green beans with his fork, chewed them and swallowed, then added, "I wasn't trying to be nosy. I only wanted to know because I haven't seen Mary around here since the day she got scared by the snake.

Since she's Eliza's friend, I was concerned that my behavior might have reflected poorly on you. That it might have caused a problem between you and Eliza."

Jonas relaxed his shoulders. "*Neh*. Things are going well between us. Very well."

"I'm *hallich* to hear that." Freeman didn't sound very happy, though; he sounded forlorn. Was that because he was holding out hope that things wouldn't work out for his brother and Eliza? Or was it simply because he wished he could be courting someone, too?

Jonas cleared his throat. "Did you, uh, did you meet anyone new at the singing last weekend?" On Sunday evening, Freeman had attended a big regional singing with young singles from the New Hope, Unity and Serenity Ridge districts. But until today, Jonas had deliberately avoided questioning him about it, since he hadn't wanted Freeman to turn the tables and start asking him about his date with Eliza.

"*Jah*. Lots of new people. It was three districts," Freeman answered.

"You know what I mean. Did you meet any *weibsleit* who captured your attention?"

"Look who's being nosy now!" Freeman replied, needling him. "*Neh*, I couldn't picture myself in a courtship with any of the *weibsleit* I met there."

Once again, Jonas experienced a pang of insecurity. Was Freeman uninterested in anyone else because he was still carrying a torch for Eliza? Or was it simply that he didn't seem to have anything in common with any of the young women he'd met?

As if he'd read Jonas's mind, Freeman elaborated, "I know Serenity Ridge and Unity are only a day trip from here, but I'd rather not have a long-distance courtship."

"Well, have you ever considered courting... Honor Bawell?" Jonas had just said the first single woman's name that popped into his mind, and Honor was an obvious choice since she was clearly interested in being courted.

"Honor? No way!" Freeman said, and guffawed. "I'd only want to court someone with the intention of eventually marrying her. And I could never marry Honor—I'd starve to death if she were my wife!"

Jonas had to chortle at that, then he suggested, "How about Mary Nussbaum? I don't know her very well, but since she's a friend of Eliza's, she must have some *wunderbaar* qualities."

"I have considered her, *jah*. But she barely spoke to me that day we went canoeing. And now, after what happened with the rubber snake, I doubt she'll even say hello to me again."

"Sometimes the most unlikely people make the best couples." *And I should know*, Jonas thought.

"Since when did you become New Hope's resident matchmaker?" Freeman quipped. "Just because you're smitten with Eliza doesn't mean I have to be in a courtship to be *hallich*, too."

"I never said I was smitten with Eliza!" Jonas objected.

"You didn't have to say it. It's written all over your face."

"Well, you've got barbecue sauce written all over yours," Jonas joked, getting up to take his plate to the sink. "I'm going to hit the hay."

"Already? The sun hasn't even set."

But after four nights of tossing and turning in bed, Jonas was beat. Even if he didn't wind up getting any more sleep tonight than he had gotten earlier in the week, he didn't care. All that mattered was that the next day brought the possibility he'd see Eliza on the blueberry farm. Because as soon as he saw her, he was going to ask her to go out with him after church on Sunday.

By Friday, Eliza was champing at the bit to get to the blueberry farm. She'd hoped to go on Wednesday, or Thursday at the latest. But she could see that her mother was still fatigued on Wednesday, and on Thursday, Almeda Stoll, the deacon's wife, stopped by with two meals for their family, since she'd heard Lior and the boys had been ill.

It would have been rude if Eliza hadn't offered her hospitality in return. So she'd poured sun tea and served Almeda, Lior and herself slices of the blueberry-cream-cheese cake she'd intended to bring to Jonas. Moments after Almeda left, Uri came into the house carrying two business ledgers. Apparently, Eliza and Lior had duplicated several entries and it had taken him an hour to reconcile their mistakes.

Uri had complained, "This is why only one person should work on the accounts."

It's also why you should only keep one business ledger, Eliza had thought. By that time, it was almost two thirty, which wouldn't have allowed her time to get to the farm, pick berries and return in time to have supper on the table by six o'clock.

On Friday morning, however, she was bound and determined to leave her house by eight, even if it meant taking all five of her brothers with her. Thankfully, it didn't come to that. Quite the opposite: Uri decided he needed Peter and Isaiah's help in the workshop. And Lior insisted the other three boys stay with her, despite Eliza's expressed concern for her mother's health. So a few minutes before eight o'clock, she started off for the farm on her own. She'd barely made it down the driveway when she spotted Mary heading toward her, swinging a big plastic bucket.

"What a *wunderbaar* surprise. It's such a treat to be able to spend time alone with you on a weekday!" Eliza exclaimed. "I was beginning to worry you'd never *kumme* picking *biere* with me again."

"To be honest, I wasn't sure I was going to return to the *bauerei*, either. But then I decided I was being prideful because I'd felt so *lappich* and that I really should give Freeman another chance." Mary giggled. "Plus, I need to make more jam to sell at the *blohbier* festival. How has the picking been this week?"

"I don't know. I haven't been back since we went last *Mittwoch*, either." Eliza explained that Uri had gotten ill, in addition to Eli, Mark and Lior. Then she told Mary about how Jonas had taken her brothers fishing at the creek on Sunday so Eliza could have a break. "Wasn't that considerate of him?"

"I suppose." Mary's response was barely audible.

"Jonas also made a campfire and they roasted marshmallows and had s'mores, since that's what he had planned for us to do on our date. The *buwe* are still talking about how much *schpass* they had."

"Apparently, they're not the only ones still talking about it."

Eliza had never heard Mary use sarcasm before and she felt stung by it. Her eyes brimming, she asked, "Why are you being like that, Mary? First you complained I acted as if it was a chore to have a suitor. And now that I'm excited about courting Jonas, you still seem critical. I thought you'd be *hallich* for me."

Turning to her, Mary immediately apologized. "*Jah*, you're right. There's no need for me to be so surly. I am *hallich* for you, Eliza. It's just that…well, it's difficult for me to hear about how *wunderbaar* Jonas is because I want a suitor to do those kinds of things for me, too." She flicked her prayer *kapp* string over her shoulder and acknowledged, "But that's a very self-centered way for me to behave. I'm sorry."

"*Ach*." Eliza groaned. "I'm the one who's being self-centered, as well as insensitive. I know how much you want a suitor and here I am, babbling on and on about Jonas. It's just that I've never felt this way about anyone I've courted before, and I feel like I can hardly contain myself. But from now on, I promise I'll try."

"*Neh*. You can't do that," Mary objected. "Otherwise if I get a suitor, I won't feel free to gush about him to you." She grinned.

"First of all, it's not *if* you get a suitor—it's *when*," Eliza emphatically corrected her. "And secondly, I'm not *gushing*."

Mary gave her a knowing look. "Okay, you might not be gushing about Jonas. But take my word for it, you're definitely *blushing*."

Eliza didn't have to take Mary's word for it; the closer they got to the Kanagy brothers' farm, the hotter her cheeks and forehead felt. And her stomach swirled with a kaleidoscope of butterflies. In all her years of courting, she'd never been so anxious to see her suitor.

As they turned up the driveway, Eliza remarked that the parking area seemed very crowded for so early in the morning. "There are probably so many *Englisch* customers here because they're preparing their baked goods for the *blohbier* festival the weekend after this one," she ventured.

"Probably. But it also might be because next week we're supposed to get a lot of rain."

"Really? I didn't know that." Eliza was disappointed. She'd already missed seeing Jonas every day this week, and now she wouldn't see him next week, either? It made her even more eager to chat with him today and find out if he wanted to make plans with her for Sunday.

When they reached the booth to retrieve the kind of baskets they could tie around their waists, Eliza and Mary discovered a handwritten sign posted over the scale. It said:

> The cashier will be unavailable to check out customers until 9:30. We apologize for the inconvenience. Please help yourselves to baskets.

There was also a map indicating which area of the farm was open for picking.

"Of all the days for Emily to be late, it's a shame it's today, when there are so many customers here," Mary commented as they tied their baskets around their waists.

"*Jah*, that's too bad," Eliza agreed absentmindedly as she looked around for Jonas, who was nowhere in sight.

"I'm sorry—we only take checks or cash," Jonas informed the *Englisch* customer who handed him a credit card.

There was a big sign posted over the crate of baskets that plainly stated this policy. If Emily had been distributing baskets, instead of home in bed with the flu, she would have reminded the customers of this fact, too. The Kanagy brothers had always tried to make sure people understood *before* they started picking berries that credit cards would not be accepted.

Although the *Ordnung* permitted certain businesses in town to use credit-card processors, Jonas and Freeman had decided long ago they weren't going to use one. They didn't want the hassle of installing an electrical line or getting an internet connection, which so many of the machines required in order to work. Most of the local customers were accustomed to bringing checks or cash to Amish businesses and very few took issue with their payment policy. However, the woman standing in front of him was the third customer who had complained about it this morning.

"But *I* never carry cash or checks," the woman retorted. "I don't think it's fair to impose *your* religious beliefs on me. It's not a very good business practice, either."

Jonas could feel his eye twitch and he sensed a headache wasn't far away. Rather than tell the customer he wasn't trying to impose his beliefs on her, he offered, "If you'd like, I can put aside your fruit for you until you're able to return with cash or a check?"

"I don't have spare time in my schedule to be running back and forth like that!" she objected, even though she clearly had spare time in her schedule to argue with Jonas.

The woman standing beside her seemed embarrassed. "I've got plenty of cash with me, Beth. Why don't I pay for yours and you can pay me back later?"

"I'm tempted to just put this basket down and walk away in protest of the payment policy. But after all the work I put into picking these berries, I won't give him the satisfaction," she said to her friend as if Jonas couldn't hear her.

Please, Gott, *give me patience and an attitude that reflects Your mercy*, he silently prayed as he turned to set the second customer's berries on the scale.

Freeman had sometimes suggested they were over-paying Emily, who often sat idly in between check-ing customers in or out. He'd thought that they should give her additional responsibilities on the farm to keep her busy, such as picking berries to sell to people who wanted to buy them by the pint instead of picking their own. "We could put a bell on the booth for custom-ers to ring when they're ready to pay for their fruit. That would alert Emily to return to her station," he'd suggested.

But Jonas had always insisted that customers would be frustrated if they had to wait for Emily to return from a distant part of the farm. Furthermore, he wanted her to remain at the booth to be a welcoming presence, to answer customers' questions and to direct them to the picking area or inform them they could get a ride in the buggy wagon. Now that Jonas had manned the booth and dealt with several unreasonable *Englischers* in Emily's absence, he had an even greater apprecia-tion for the service she provided, both to the customers and to Jonas and Freeman. *Maybe if Freeman spends a few hours doing her job, he'll have a better under-standing of how challenging it can be, too*, he thought.

But that would mean Jonas would have to switch responsibilities with him and transport customers across the farm in the buggy wagon. He was reluctant to leave the booth because he'd hoped to see Eliza the moment she arrived on the farm so he could ask her if she'd spend Sunday afternoon with him. Usually, she and her brothers didn't arrive until nine thirty or ten o'clock, but Jonas had been at the booth since nine twenty and he still hadn't seen her. Now it was almost noon and he was beginning to lose hope that she was coming to the farm at all today.

He continued weighing the fruit and collecting payments, but the line appeared to be growing longer instead of shorter. No doubt that was because most of the customers wanted to get out of the hot sun and go home to eat their lunches. While Jonas was waiting on a pleasant group of young adults wearing T-shirts from the local university, he noticed Freeman across the driveway, returning from a buggy run. He waved him to come over so they could switch places.

After the group of college students paid for their fruit and moved on, Jonas was astonished to recognize who was next in line. "Eliza and Mary, I didn't know you were here!" he exclaimed.

They both greeted him, and then Eliza explained, "We got here bright and early. We had to make up for lost time." Her skin was dewy and flushed and she had dirt smudged across her cheekbone, but she looked absolutely luminous and Jonas couldn't stop grinning. As he was weighing her fruit, she asked, "Is everything okay with Emily?"

"She has the flu."

"Ach. Poor *maedel*." Eliza clucked her tongue. "And

poor you, too—it seems like a busy day to be short-staffed."

"*Jah*, but I'd rather have too many customers than too few," Jonas replied in *Deitsch*.

As they were speaking, Freeman came up beside Jonas and greeted Mary and Eliza. Then, still speaking *Deitsch*, Jonas told him it was his turn to wait on the customers and he'd give them buggy rides.

"*Gut.* I'd prefer to sit in the shade for a while. But after you drop the customers off, take a look at the left-hand corner of the barren near the woods. I think something's been eating our *biere* again," he replied, also in *Deitsch*.

"Birds?" Jonas asked.

"*Neh*. Bears."

Mary's hand flew to her cheek. "Bears?"

"Don't worry, it's probably only *one* bear. And judging from how many *biere* he ate, he'd be way too full to take a chomp out of you." Freeman chuckled nervously. Jonas knew how troubled he'd been about upsetting Mary a while back and how eager he was to apologize to her, but once again, it almost seemed as if he was making light of her fear. She pinched her lips together in a tight seam. Jonas noticed Eliza's smile had faded, too.

Thinking quickly, he said, "Most of the customers are going home for lunch, so I think I have time for a quick bottle of root beer before we have a big enough group to take a buggy ride. Would you like a cool drink before you walk home, Eliza and Mary?"

"*Jah,* please," Eliza replied.

"*Neh, denki,*" Mary answered at the same time. She quickly added, "But you go ahead, Eliza. I'll wait over there in the shade beneath that maple." She gave Freeman and Jonas a curt goodbye and started across the lawn, barely allowing Eliza time to reply.

Jonas was concerned she would change her mind and leave with Mary, but she said, "Okay—I'll only be a minute. I can take the bottle with me."

As Jonas and Eliza were walking toward the house, they were stopped twice by customers asking when they could get a buggy ride out to the barrens. Jonas assured them the buggy wagon would leave within the next five minutes. Once they were out of earshot of the second person, Eliza said, "*Ach.* I'm keeping you from your work. I don't really need a drink. I should leave so you can go serve your customers."

"I will serve them—after I've served you a cold drink," he insisted.

They reached the porch and he hopped up the stairs, went inside and promptly came out with two opened bottles of root beer.

"*Denki.*" Eliza took a sip of the beverage he handed her.

Even though he had no reason to fear she'd say no, Jonas felt more nervous asking Eliza to go out with him now than he'd felt when he'd asked to court her the first time. His mouth was so dry he swallowed down half of his root beer. He wiped his lips with the back of his hand before speaking. "I—I was wondering if you have plans for *Sunndaag.*" Without waiting for her to answer, he eagerly added, "Because if you don't, I'd like to go canoeing with you after *kurrich.* My *bruder* ate the rest of the chocolate and marshmallows, but I could buy more and we could make a campfire on the island, since we didn't get to have one last *Sunndaag.*"

Eliza's smile told him everything he needed to know, even before she answered. "I'd really like that, too. But please don't get ingredients for s'mores—I'll bring a special dessert for us to share."

"Sounds *wunderbaar*," he replied. Although, if he still felt the way he was feeling now, Jonas knew he'd probably be too lovesick to eat anything on Sunday.

Chapter Nine

❦

"What's in there? Is it for lunch?" Samuel asked, pointing at the thermal bag Eliza was holding on her lap as the buggy carried their family to church on Sunday morning.

"*Neh*, it's dessert for a friend and me. We're going canoeing after *kurrich*," Eliza replied softly. She hoped Samuel wouldn't ask which friend was going canoeing with her, because she didn't want Uri to overhear and scold him for being nosy again. But the boy was more interested in her snack than in her social life.

"Is it *blohbier* muffins?" he asked.

"*Neh.*"

Isaiah took a turn guessing, too. "*Blohbier* crumble?"

"*Neh.*"

"Maybe it doesn't even have any *blohbiere* in it at all," Peter informed his younger brothers. "It might be chocolate *kuche*."

"But I didn't smell chocolate *kuche* baking last night after we went to bed. I smelled something with *blohbier* in it," Isaiah explained.

Eliza chuckled. "I can't sneak anything past your noses, can I?"

"*Neh.* My nose is awake even when my eyes are asleep," Eli said, wrinkling his nose and causing Eliza to chuckle.

Isaiah was right about what he'd smelled: Eliza had made lemon blueberry cake after the boys had gone to bed last evening. And since she couldn't justify unnecessary food preparations on the Sabbath, she'd also made hand-whipped cream to put on top of the cake, even though she would have preferred to make it fresh in the morning. Since this would have to do, she'd included the cream and cake in the thermal bag, along with two ice packs from their diesel-powered refrigerator and freezer. She hoped Jonas liked the dessert, because after the two of them had a slice, she intended for him to take the rest home.

"I'll tell you all a secret," she whispered. The boys leaned toward her so they could hear. "I made a separate *blohbier* dessert for you, too. Tonight after supper, you'll find out what kind it is."

The boys grinned appreciatively and then leaned back in their seats again. "I wish it was after supper already," Eli whispered.

"I wish I could go fishing again at the creek," Isaiah said in normal speaking volume.

"*Jah,* me, too," Peter echoed.

"I wish we could go kite flying with you, Eliza," Samuel added wistfully. "Remember you said you would take me on *Sunndaag*? Today is *Sunndaag*."

Uri must have heard him because he scolded Samuel from the front of the buggy. "You *buwe* need to stop pestering your *schweschder*."

They aren't pestering me, Eliza thought, but she knew it would have been rude to contradict her stepfather. So she quietly whispered to Samuel, "I will take you kite flying, but remember that I said it has to be a breezy *Sunndaag*? There isn't any breeze today at all."

In fact, the air was so still it felt stifling, and the sky was an unbroken field of white clouds. Eliza had been fretting ever since she woke that morning that it would rain and her canoeing trip with Jonas would be canceled. *Maybe if it rains he'll be willing to do something else instead*, she thought. *Even taking a buggy ride around town would be fine with me, as long as we get to spend the afternoon together.*

She was so eager to see him again that when she got to church and was seated alongside her family, she had to resist the urge to peek over her shoulder to see where he was sitting. *I'm worse than my* breider, *fidgeting like this*, she thought, as she tied a kerchief into bunny ears to keep Eli distracted during the long sermon.

After the worship service ended and Eliza was downstairs in the kitchen, helping the other women prepare lunch, Honor greeted her and Mary. "I'm rounding up people to go hiking at the gorge after lunch. So far, Glenda, Ervin, Freeman and Jacob all said *jah*. Do you two want to *kumme*?"

Secretly happy that the group was going to the gorge instead of the lake, Eliza blurted out, "It's nice of you to invite me, but I already made plans."

"Somehow, I knew you'd say that." Honor gave her a smug look. "How about you, Mary?"

"Well…*neh*. I don't think so. But *denki* for asking."

Honor's eyes went wide and she asked in a conspiratorial whisper, "Why not? Do you have *plans*, too?"

She emphasized the word in a way that made it clear she really wanted to know if Mary was going out with a suitor.

"*Neh.* It's just that it looks like it's going to rain. I don't want to make the trip out there only to have to turn around," Mary said.

Her answer seemed to satisfy Honor's curiosity. She lifted two pitchers of water from the counter to carry upstairs. "Okay, but if you change your mind, we're meeting at Freeman's buggy," she said before leaving the room.

Eliza suspected the real reason Mary didn't want to go hiking had less to do with the weather than it did with the fact that Freeman would be there. On the way home from the farm on Friday afternoon, Mary had commented that she'd decided she definitely wasn't interested in him as a suitor any longer.

"Is it because he didn't apologize to you for laughing about the snake?" Eliza hadn't even waited for her friend to answer before she'd said, "Because I'm sure he will—there were just too many customers around today for him to get the chance."

But Mary had dismissively waved her hand, saying there really wasn't any need for him to apologize and she wasn't holding anything against him. She'd said she just thought his sense of humor was too different from hers. Eliza had tried to persuade her to keep an open mind, but Mary had pointedly changed the subject.

At the risk of irritating her friend now, Eliza tried one more time to get her to reconsider. "I'm surprised you're not going to the gorge," she whispered. "I thought you love it there, even when the sun's not out."

Mary hesitated and Eliza could tell she was ambivalent. "I do, but…"

"You still feel uncomfortable around Freeman?" Eliza queried and Mary nodded. "He probably feels more uncomfortable around you than you feel around him. The sooner he gets a chance to apologize to you, the sooner you'll both be able to put the incident behind you."

"*Jah*, maybe." Mary gave Eliza a little nudge from the side. "But since when are you so interested in what happens between Freeman and me?"

"Since I started praying that the Lord would provide a suitor for you," Eliza answered. *And since I've found out how much* schpass *courting can be when your suitor is someone you actually like.*

As Jonas and Eliza started out for the lake in his buggy, he was at a complete loss for words. Which was silly, considering he'd been daydreaming throughout the three-hour worship service about all the things he wanted to ask and tell her. But after church and lunch were finished and she'd come walking across the lawn toward his buggy, the sight of her sparkling smile had him completely tongue-tied.

So sitting beside her now, all he could think to ask was "Do you think the weather is going to hold until we're done canoeing?"

"I don't know. But as long as there's no lightning, I don't mind if it rains a little bit while we're out on the lake. We won't melt, right?"

"Right, we won't melt." Jonas chuckled. "That's the same thing your *breider* said when I told them to be careful not to fall in the creek. They quote you a lot, you know. It's clear they take everything you say to heart."

Now it was Eliza's turn to chuckle. She said, "*Jah.* They took what *you* said to heart last *Sunndaag,* too." She proceeded to tell him that Samuel had repeated word-for-word Jonas's justification for eating two s'mores, while the boys were only allowed one apiece.

"*Ach.* My secret's out." He momentarily covered his face with one hand. "I suppose I should have set a better example for them and waited until I got home to have seconds."

"Don't be *lappich.* You're a *wunderbaar* role model and they're still talking about all the things you taught them about fishing." Her compliment made him sit up straighter. "Besides, you couldn't help it if you were *hungerich,* considering you don't have anyone to make *appenditlich* treats for you."

Jonas's mouth watered. He'd deliberately eaten a light breakfast and he'd hardly been able to finish a bologna sandwich during the church lunch because he was so nervous about his outing with Eliza. But as he began to feel a bit more relaxed, his appetite was kicking in again. "What did you make?" he asked.

"You get three guesses," she playfully replied. "And I'll even give you a hint. It contains a yellow fruit and a—"

"You made banana cream pie? That's my favorite dessert in the world!" he interrupted, turning to watch her reaction. "How did you know?"

"Oh, *neh*?" She looked crestfallen. "If banana cream pies is your favorite dessert, then you're going to be very disappointed in what I made. It's lemon *blohbier kuche.*"

"Aha! I knew I could get you to tell me what it is." Jonas slapped his knee in amusement.

"Hey, you tricked me." Eliza bumped her shoulder against his, affectionately chiding him. "Is banana cream pie really your favorite?"

"*Neh*. In fact, the only part of banana cream pie that I actually like is the whipped cream on top."

"In that case, you'll be happy to know that I brought lots of whipped cream for our *kuche*." Eliza abruptly clapped her palm against her forehead. "Uh-oh. I just realized I forgot to bring a spoon. Or any utensils at all."

She sounded so distraught that Jonas tried to comfort her. "We can eat the *kuche* with our hands." It wasn't uncommon for the Amish in their community to eat a slice of cake or pie with their hands, just as they'd eat a cookie, provided the cake or pie crusts were the type that held together well. The custom was just more practical than using plates and utensils, especially when they were eating outdoors or in big groups, because it saved them the effort of washing extra dishes, which they had to do by hand.

"*Jah*, that's fine, but we can't very well use our fingers to put a dollop of cream on top of the *kuche*," she lamented. "I'm sorry, Jonas. I wanted to make something you'd really like."

Touched, Jonas said, "I already *do* really like the dessert, simply because of how much care you put into making it. *Denki* for doing that for me, Eliza."

"You're *wilkom*," she replied. The note of relief in her voice almost instantly turned to dismay as a bright white flash lit the air around them. "That was lightning I just saw, wasn't it?"

Before Jonas could answer, thunder resonated overhead, followed by a barrage of raindrops against the roof of the buggy's carriage. There was no way they could go canoeing in this weather, but Jonas had another idea. "This looks like it's just a passing shower. I know a place where we can wait it out, if you're willing?"

When she readily agreed, Jonas took a short detour, directing the horse off the main street and onto a winding side road. After about a half mile, he turned into the lot of an abandoned fuel station, bringing the animal to a halt beneath the metal canopy where the out-of-service gas pumps stood. The crumbling asphalt was littered with empty beer cans, the windows of the station were boarded up and there was graffiti scribbled across the wall.

"It's certainly not as scenic as the lake, but at least my *gaul* will be sheltered from the storm," he said.

"*Jah.* But if any *Englischers* see us here, they're going to think we're *narrish*," Eliza remarked. At first Jonas didn't know what she meant, but she explained that it might look as if they'd pulled up to the pump to get gas for their buggy. Her humorous observation made him crack up.

"Laughing like that makes my *bauch* hurt," he said, holding his stomach. "Or maybe I'm just *hungerich* for dessert."

"I am, too. I deliberately didn't eat much at lunch," Eliza admitted as she unzipped the thermal bag. "I'm glad I sliced the *kuche* already, but I really do wish I had a spoon for the topping."

"Who needs a spoon? Why can't we just dip the cake into the whipped cream?"

Eliza looked dubious, but she agreed it was worth a

try. So after she'd given him a slice of cake, she opened the container of cream and extended it to him. Using his cake as a sort of scoop, Jonas pushed it through the cream, until the entire slice was slathered with it. "Are you sure you got enough?" she teased.

"I can *never* get enough whipped cream," he replied, grinning.

Then she dipped her cake into the container, too. They ate hungrily and messily, laughing about how difficult it was to take a bite of the treat without spilling the whipped cream on their clothes.

"It was definitely worth the effort, though," Jonas remarked, wiping his fingers on the napkin Eliza handed him after he finished eating his second piece. "That was *appenditlich*."

"I'm *hallich* you like it, because the rest is for you to take home."

"*Denki*. I might have to hide it before my *bruder* returns this afternoon."

"Oh, that's right. He went hiking at the gorge, didn't he?"

Even though Jonas was the one who'd mentioned Freeman, the fact that Eliza knew his whereabouts gave him pause. Narrowing his eyes, he said, "*Jah*. How did you know he was going hiking?"

"B-because Honor mentioned the outing. She asked me if I wanted to go, too." There was no mistaking that Eliza sounded uncomfortable answering his question, and her cheeks were turning pink, too.

"Do you wish you'd gone hiking with them after all?" Jonas queried.

Eliza drew back her chin in surprise. "*Neh*, of course not. Why? Is that what *you* would have preferred to do?"

He instantly felt foolish for doubting her and terrible for making her doubt *him*. Trying to lighten the moment and reassure her at the same time, he said, "*Neh*. There's nowhere I'd rather be than here with you at this abandoned fuel station, eating *kuche* and whipped cream with our hands."

"There's nowhere else I'd rather be, either," Eliza echoed with a smile. She'd just been making small talk when she'd mentioned hiking at the gorge, so she was surprised Jonas had seemed offended by her comment. *Was he uncertain about whether she was enjoying their time together just because the date wasn't going according to plan? Or was he unsure about whether she truly wanted to be alone with him, because when he first asked to court her, she'd made a point of saying she was only interested in developing a friendship first?*

While it was true that Eliza still wanted to get to know Jonas better, she no longer considered him just a friend; she definitely thought of him as a suitor. A *real* suitor. And if he should want to hold her hand or move closer to her on the seat, she wouldn't object. In fact, she *wanted* him to. But how could she let him know that without being too forward? She turned to face him fully and said, "I like being here in the rain—it feels so cozy." She'd stopped short of using the word *romantic*, but she hoped Jonas understood it was what she'd meant.

"*Jah*, it does," he agreed, his eyes settling on her mouth. For a second, Eliza wondered if he was thinking about kissing her, but to her embarrassment, he pointed to his own lips and said, "You have a little bit of cream on your face."

She wiped her fingers across her mouth, her face burning. "Did I get it?"

"*Neh*. Here—can I?" Jonas asked and she nodded. He lifted his hand and cupped her cheek in his fingers and palm, dabbing the skin near the corner of her lip with his thumb. His touch was so gentle it made Eliza shiver. He must have thought she was trying to wiggle away from him, because he dropped his hand. "Sorry."

"*Neh*. It's okay," she said quickly. It was better than okay—it was absolutely wonderful. "You have soft hands."

He turned up his palms and inspected them. "That's because for the past couple of months I've been working on the *bauerei* instead of doing carpentry. Usually I have a lot more calluses than this," he said. For a second Eliza was sure he'd missed her hint entirely, but then he reached over and interlaced his fingers with hers. "So I'm *hallich* we started courting in the summer or I'd feel too self-conscious holding your hand for the first time."

"I wouldn't have minded," Eliza said, feeling rather self-conscious herself. On occasion, her suitors may have taken her hand to keep her from slipping on the ice or for some practical reason like that, but she'd never allowed any of them to hold her hand the way Jonas was doing now. It made her feel so breathlessly giddy, she could hardly talk, and could barely concentrate on what he was saying. So for the next half hour, she answered questions when he asked her, but mostly Eliza let Jonas carry the conversation. He amused her with stories about his family and friends in Kansas.

Finally, he said, "It doesn't look like the rain is going to let up. I'm afraid I should probably get my *gaul* home and wipe him down. He had a case of rain scald from the humidity recently, so I have to be extra careful about his skin so he doesn't get it again."

"Oh, right. You wouldn't want that happening to the poor animal again," Eliza said, even though she was disappointed that their date was ending already. Jonas let go of her hand to release the buggy's parking brake and pick up the reins, but to her delight, once they'd pulled onto the main street, he took hold of her fingers again. "I didn't see Emily in *kurrich* today. She must be really sick," Eliza commented, since Amish people only missed church when it was absolutely unavoidable.

"*Jah.* Her *mamm* told me she'd probably stay home from work all week," Jonas replied with a sigh. "It's going to be awfully hectic without her. After *kurrich* I asked a couple of *meed* if they could fill in for her, but no one is available."

"*I* could fill in for her," Eliza volunteered without thinking twice about it.

"You?" Jonas's voice was incredulous.

Eliza pulled her hand away so she could turn sideways and look at him. "*Jah.* Why not me? I'm capable of weighing fruit and making change."

"I have no doubts about your abilities. It's just that I didn't realize you wanted a job," he explained. "I have to warn you, the position doesn't pay very much."

"I don't want a *job* and I don't want to get paid. I just want to help you on the *bauerei* for a few days."

"But I couldn't let you work without paying you. It wouldn't be right."

Eliza crossed her arms over her chest. "And I couldn't allow you to pay me. I have no interest in becoming your employee, Jonas. You and I are courting, and this is the kind of thing that people who—who care about each other do. I didn't pay you for babysitting my *breider* last *Sunndaag*."

"That's different. I did that to help your *familye*, not your business. And it was only for one afternoon."

"Okay, fine." Eliza shrugged, as if it didn't matter, but she actually felt a bit put out. "If you don't want my help—"

Jonas cut her off. "I *do* want your help. I would *love* your help. But are you sure your *mamm* is well enough to manage your *breider* on her own?"

Eliza honestly hadn't even considered that, but now that Jonas mentioned it, she stammered, "I—I think she should be okay."

"Well, when I swing by to pick you up, you can let me know one way or the other. How does seven thirty sound?"

"You don't need to pick me up. I walk to the *bauerei* all the time," she said.

"I know you do. But we're courting and that's the kind of thing people who care about each other do," Jonas countered, using Eliza's words against her.

He would have to get up awfully early to get all of his chores done on the bauerei before picking her up. It was another example of his willingness to go out of his way for her and she couldn't refuse. "Okay," she agreed. *"Denki."*

"You're *wilkom*." He gave her shoulder a little tap, and when she unfolded her arms and dropped them to her sides, he reached for one of her hands and held it firmly all the way back to her street.

"Since your *eldre* already know that we're courting,

I might as well bring you to your door so you won't get wet," he said as they turned in the driveway. "Unless you don't want your *breider* to find out, too?"

"As I've said, they're too young to suspect us of courting, so it's fine if they see you dropping me off." Eliza giggled. "But I can't promise they won't run out and ask why you didn't take them with you, too. They think they're friends with you now."

Jonas chuckled. "Who knows? Maybe one day we will take them with us."

"Maybe," Eliza said. Previously, she would have welcomed it if a suitor had invited her brothers to join them on an outing because the boys would have kept the conversation from getting too personal. But today she was in no hurry to relinquish her time alone with Jonas.

He directed his horse to the turn-around at the end of the driveway, which was as close to the front porch as he could get. Then he hopped out into the rain and took her hand as she climbed out, too. "*Denki* for spending the afternoon with me. It was *wunderbaar*," he said.

"I thought so, too." She gave his fingers a quick squeeze before reluctantly dropping his hand. "'Bye, Jonas. I'll see you tomorrow morning."

When she went inside the house, it was unusually quiet. *The* buwe *must be napping*, she thought as she tiptoed into the living room. Her mother looked up from the letter she was writing at the desk and greeted her. Uri was seated in an arm chair, reading *The Budget*. He said hello but didn't lower the newspaper.

"Are the *buwe* asleep?" she asked.

"Eli, Mark and Samuel are," Lior answered. "Peter and Isaiah went home with the Mullet *buwe* after *kur-*

rich. They were supposed to try out the Mullets' new trampoline, but I'm sure they had to change their plans once it started raining."

"Oh, I don't know about that. I think the rain might make jumping on the trampoline even more *schpass* for them," Eliza said with a laugh. She was relieved that Willis Mullet's sons hadn't come *here* instead of her brothers going to their house. Otherwise, she would have been expected to join Willis and her parents for tea and dessert when he arrived to pick up his sons. This way, Uri would be going to pick up Peter and Isaiah from the Mullets' house instead.

"You came home early," he remarked, peering over the top of his newspaper. "Didn't you have a *gut* time with the Kanagy *bu*?"

"Uri," Lior said, addressing her husband under her breath. "That's Eliza's private business."

Although Eliza appreciated her mother's support and agreed it was none of Uri's business why she'd returned home early this afternoon, this was one of the rare occasions when she didn't mind telling him about her date. "Actually, we had a *wunderbaar* time. Jonas's *gaul* has suffered from rain scald recently, so he had to cut our outing short so he could go home and care for his skin. But I didn't mind, because I plan to see Jonas tomorrow, too." Eliza was nearly gloating as she explained she'd agreed to help on the farm during Emily's absence.

But Uri burst her bubble when he asked frankly, "How much is he going to pay you?"

"He—he's not," she stuttered. "He wanted to, but I'm not doing it for the money. I'm doing it because… well, because he's my suitor and I want to help him."

"That's very kind of you, Eliza," Lior said, nodding at her daughter. "I'm sure Jonas appreciates it, and working together can be a *gut* way for a *mann* and *weibsmensch* to develop a stronger relationship."

"What about helping your *mamm*?" Uri asked. "She's been ill and she still needs a lot of rest."

I'm well aware of that, Eliza wanted to retort. *But if you're so concerned about* Mamm's *health, then why don't you handle your own bookkeeping so she doesn't have to stay up late in the evenings to work on it? Or why don't you take the* buwe *outside so they're not underfoot after supper, or put them to bed in the evening?*

Instead, she quietly said, "That's true. And Jonas already knows I might not be able to *kumme* if *Mamm* is still too weak. He's going to stop by in the morning, when we'll have a better idea of how much energy she has."

"She might have energy in the morning, but that doesn't mean she'll be able to manage on her own for the entire day," Uri said, which Eliza found maddening, considering he'd been pushing her to find a full-time job. Was he just objecting to Eliza being gone for eight or nine hours because she wasn't getting paid? Or was it that he was truly concerned about Lior because he'd been sick, too, so he finally had a better understanding of how fatigued his wife was?

Lior rarely raised her voice, but now she barked, "Stop talking about me as if I'm not here, you two. And stop acting as if I'm incapable of running this household and taking care of the *kinner* by myself." She set down her writing tablet and rose to her feet. "If I'm sick or too tired to manage, then I'll send one of the *buwe* to the workshop to get *you* to help me, Uri. But

Eliza is going to go assist her suitor on the *bauerei* this week and I don't want to hear another word about it."

As her mother went into the kitchen, the only word Eliza wanted to utter was *denki*. Instead, she turned and padded down the hall and up the stairs to her room, where she stretched out sideways on her bed for a nap. Pressing one hand to her cheek, she fell asleep to the pleasant sound of the rain against the roof and the memory of Jonas's touch against her skin.

Chapter Ten

Jonas got up so early to finish his chores that he actually had half an hour to spare before it was time to go pick up Eliza. He poured himself a second cup of coffee and took the remaining slice of lemon blueberry cake out onto the porch, where he sat down on a wooden glider.

Not two minutes later, Freeman came around the corner of the house. Before Jonas could say good morning, his brother pointed to the plate and asked, "What's that?"

Jonas slid the last bite of the cake into his mouth, chewed and swallowed it before answering. "Lemon blueberry *kuche*. Eliza made it."

"Is there any more?"

"*Neh*. Sorry." Jonas had eaten the rest the previous day, while Freeman was out socializing with his peers. "Didn't Honor send you home with any treats yesterday?"

"*Jah*. I was just feeding them to the *hinkel*."

Jonas chuckled. Patting his stomach, he said, "Eliza is a *wunderbaar* baker."

"*Gut*. Maybe if we drop a few hints, she'll bring extra desserts to work with her this week."

"*Jah*—for me." Jonas may not have been concerned any longer that Eliza was interested in his brother, but he did feel the need to remind Freeman of that fact. "*I'm* her suitor, not you. But there's no way we're going to suggest she should do some baking—she's already doing us a big favor by working on the *bauerei*."

His remark seemed to go right over his brother's head. "I didn't say we should *suggest* she bake something. I just said we should drop a few hints."

"*Neh*, we're not going to do that," Jonas emphatically repeated. "And you're not going to treat her like an employee or make any other demands of her, either."

"Am I allowed to talk to her at all?" Freeman retorted.

"Of course you are. But I want Eliza to know we appreciate her presence here. So be careful about what you say. You've already offended her friend—I don't want you to say something that might insult Eliza, too." Standing to leave, Jonas noticed Freeman's expression had clouded over, and he realized his brother probably still felt bad about upsetting Mary. "Sorry, Freeman. I shouldn't have rubbed that in."

"*Neh*, you're right—I do need to be more sensitive about what I say. I wish Mary would *kumme* back to the *bauerei* so I could let her know I wasn't mocking her or making light of her fears."

"Well, she said she was making jam to sell at the festival, so she's got to return soon for more *biere*," Jonas said encouragingly. "Maybe today's the day." He clapped his brother's shoulder before leaving to go hitch the horse and buggy.

As he headed toward Eliza's house, Jonas prayed that her mother would be well enough that Eliza could work on the farm. "I know it's selfish of me, Lord," he confessed aloud. "But we need her help and I really enjoy her company."

He arrived at the end of Eliza's lane to find her waiting for him there. She was holding a plastic jug in one hand and a thermal bag in the other—a promising sign. "*Guder mariye*, Eliza. What's that you're carrying?"

"Just my lunch. Why? Were you hoping it was more *kuche*?" Eliza had a twinkle in her eye as she tilted her cheek toward him. She was obviously teasing, but his reply was heartfelt.

"Well, I admit the *kuche* was *appenditlich*, but I'm even happier to know it's your lunch because that means you're able to spend the day on the *bauerei*."

"*Jah*, I am. My *mamm* feels much better this morning."

"That's great news." Jonas caught a whiff of lavender as she slid into the seat next to him. Giving her a sidelong glance, he realized it was probably her shampoo. Her hair was so shiny, she must have just washed it.

"What's wrong?" she asked and he realized she'd caught him eyeing her.

Abashed, he blurted out, "Nothing's wrong. I was just thinking about how pretty you look and how *hallich* I am to see you. I mean, not because you look pretty. I would be *hallich* to see you even if you looked *baremlich*. Not that I can imagine you ever looking *baremlich*…" The more Jonas said, the worse he sounded. *And I had the nerve to tell Freeman not to offend Eliza today*, he lamented. "I just mean I really appreciate your coming to the *bauerei* today."

Eliza giggled, sounding more amused than insulted. "It's my pleasure."

"I hope you still feel that way at the end of the day. I anticipate there will be a lot of customers trying to get their picking done in preparation for the festival. Most of them are very friendly and cooperative, but I have to warn you, there are always a few demanding ones in the group as well."

"That's okay. Interacting with them will give me practice in case I get a job working with *Englischers*."

Jonas was perplexed. Hadn't she told him just yesterday that she didn't want a job? It was a minor inconsistency, but it still gave him pause. If Eliza wasn't being honest with him about her employment interests, how could he trust that she was being honest about her interest in *him*?

Giving her the benefit of the doubt, he thought, *Maybe yesterday she was just insisting she didn't want a job because she didn't want to accept payment from me.* If that was the reason, then Jonas couldn't exactly hold the little white lie against her.

Either way, he had to be sure. "I thought you told me you weren't looking for a job," he challenged.

Why did I blurt that out? Eliza silently scolded herself. *I am such a* bobbelmoul. *How am I going to explain?* She couldn't very well tell Jonas about her stepfather's demand that she either find a job or get married, because Jonas might think she was hinting that their courtship should head in that direction. And while she was growing to like him more and more every minute she spent with him, Eliza certainly wasn't anywhere near considering marriage, and she doubted he was, either.

She decided to gloss over her slip of the tongue, and

said, "I'm not *looking* for a job. But you never know what the future might bring. It's *gut* to have experience dealing with different people and situations." Her explanation seemed to satisfy Jonas, who nodded, so she quickly changed the subject. "What will I be doing today besides waiting on customers?"

He described the various responsibilities of the position, then said, "You can always flag down me or Freeman if you need anything or if the customers get out of hand."

"Trust me, if I can manage my five little *breider*, I can manage this."

"I do trust you, but I'll still drop by to see if you have any questions or want to take a break or anything." Jonas added, "I usually have lunch around twelve thirty. I thought maybe you and I could both eat at the same time? Freeman can take your place waiting on the customers at the booth."

"Then who will give the *Englischers* rides in the buggy wagon?"

"No one. This morning I posted a sign saying that buggy rides won't be offered between noon and one o'clock, due to a staffing shortage."

Eliza couldn't help but smile. *He arranged all of this in advance just so we could eat together.* She was pleased he wanted to spend time with her in the middle of his working day as much as she wanted to spend time with him.

Once they reached the farm, Jonas stabled his horse, since Freeman's horse would be pulling the buggy wagon today. They'd barely made it to the booth when the first car pulled into the driveway and parked. Two young girls got out and skipped over to the booth, followed by a woman who was talking on a cell phone. Eliza had seen Emily at work often enough to know how to welcome the customers, provide them with baskets and answer their questions. Since the girls said they wanted to ride in the buggy wagon, she directed them to wait across the driveway for Freeman, who was nowhere in sight at the moment.

After the customers walked away, Jonas remarked, "Looks like you already have the hang of this. Can I bring you a cup of *kaffi* before I leave?"

Eliza couldn't recall Uri ever asking Lior if she needed anything to eat or drink, much less volunteering to bring it to her, so she was tickled by Jonas's offer. "*Denki*, but I try to limit my *kaffi* to just one cup a day…and I've already had two," she said with a giggle. "There is, however, something else I might need…"

"Anything at all. Just name it."

He leaned in expectantly, and as she watched his full, pink lips pronounce the words, Eliza thought, *A kiss. I'd like you to give me a kiss, please.* She had *never* entertained that thought about a suitor before now, and the longing was so staggering that she was sure Jonas could read it in her eyes. In fact, she *wanted* him to read it in her eyes. *Don't be* narrish. *He can't kiss you right here, in front of* Englischers *and in broad daylight*, she reminded herself.

Blinking, she cleared her throat and said, "The cashbox."

Jonas straightened up and smacked his forehead. "*Ach.* I usually bring that out and hide it on that little shelf behind the booth for Emily. But my body must have been awake before my mind was this morning, because I forgot all about it. I'll run up to the *haus* and get it."

Just as Jonas was turning to leave, Freeman came out of the house and moseyed down the porch stairs and across the lawn, holding up a brown metal box. "You missing something?" he called, and Jonas gave him the thumbs-up signal. When he was close enough that he didn't have to shout to be heard, Freeman greeted Eliza and handed her the cashbox. "It looks as if I've got customers waiting, so I'd better go. If you have any questions, just holler."

After Freeman left, Jonas said he had things to take care of on the farm, too. "Last chance to change your mind. Are you sure there's nothing else I can get you before I head out?"

Once again, Eliza was overwhelmed with the inappropriate temptation to hint that she'd like a kiss. *So this must be what romantic attraction feels like*, she marveled to herself. Aloud, she said, "*Denki*, but I have everything I need."

For now, anyway, she thought as she watched Jonas amble away. *But I still hope to receive a kiss from you. And I hope to receive it sooner rather than later...*

As much as Jonas already enjoyed working on the blueberry farm, he enjoyed it even more with Eliza working here, too. He kept finding excuses to walk by the booth, where he'd spy her counting out change for customers or helping the children tie their baskets around their waists. She always seemed to have a smile on her lips and a lilt in her voice. Jonas didn't want to disrupt her work, but he'd try to catch her eye in passing. If he did, he'd touch the brim of his hat, tipping it ever so slightly, and she'd give him a tiny nod. These brief exchanges made him feel as if they shared a secret, which put an extra spring in his step.

Jonas's only complaint was that time seemed to pass too slowly until their lunch break and too quickly during it. It felt as if they'd hardly sat down before Freeman was waving them back over to the booth because it was past one o'clock and customers were lining up at the buggy wagon. Eliza and Jonas had been so absorbed in their conversation that they'd neglected to eat, so they had to gobble down their sandwiches as they were walking across the lawn.

For the rest of the afternoon, the hours dragged by again until it was finally almost five o'clock. When Jonas approached the booth, he noticed Eliza happened to be weighing fruit for Almeda Stoll, the deacon's wife.

"*Guder nammigdaag*," he greeted the older woman.

"Why hello, Jonas," Almeda said as Eliza handed her a bill and several coins in change. "The *biere* are really bursting with flavor this year, aren't they?"

"*Jah*. The Lord has blessed us with abundant and *appenditlich* fruit."

"Have you heard about the tropical storm coming our way on *Samschdaag* evening?" Almeda inquired. "We're only going to get the remnants of it, but the heavy rain is supposed to stick around for four or five days afterward."

Jonas winced. "That's what I heard, too. All that rain at once isn't *gut* for the *biere*—they'll go bad. But hopefully, the upcoming festival will continue to bring a lot of customers here to harvest as many ripe *biere* as possible before the storm."

"*Gott* willing," Almeda said, nodding. She turned to Eliza. "If you're done here, I can give you a ride home since your *haus* is on my way."

Jonas's shoulders drooped. He'd been waiting for hours to be able to spend time alone with Eliza again. *Please say* neh, he silently pleaded with her.

"*Denki,*" she said. "But there are still customers out in the barrens, so I'll be here for a while. I don't want to keep you."

"I see." Almeda raised an eyebrow and Jonas got the sense she really *did* see what was going on, but she graciously bade them both goodbye before going on her way.

Freeman strode up to the booth from the opposite direction with a heaping basket of berries in hand. "There you are," Jonas commented. "Can you check out the last few customers when they *kumme* in from the barrens? I'm going to give Eliza a ride home."

"Now?" Eliza sounded surprised. "The *bauerei* doesn't close until five thirty." Technically, it closed at five, but there were always a few people who took their time coming in from the barrens, so it seemed as if she had fully expected to be on the farm until five thirty.

"*Jah*, but I know you need to get home to help your *mamm* make supper." He turned to his brother. "Freeman doesn't mind, do you, Freeman?"

"*Neh*, not at all. We really appreciate the work you've done for us, Eliza… Here are the *biere* I mentioned I'd pick." He thrust the basket of blueberries into her hands.

Jonas didn't know whether he was grateful for the gesture or resentful of it. On one hand, he *had* asked his brother to be especially polite to Eliza. On the other hand, Jonas wished that he would have thought of picking berries for Eliza, since that was the kind of thing a suitor should have done for the woman he was courting. Then again, throughout the day Jonas had asked Eliza if there was anything he could get for her. So why had she asked for Freeman's help, instead of Jonas's?

"*Wunderbaar.* See you tomorrow," she replied casually, and just as Jonas was pivoting to cross the driveway, he noticed that she winked at his brother. It was a brief wink, but it was undeniably a wink.

His legs felt like lead as he wordlessly trudged toward the barn with Eliza at his side. Jonas hated entertaining the kinds of suspicions that were running through his brain. *They're acting as if they have a secret. Is she going to end our courtship so Freeman can be her suitor?* Jonas couldn't ever imagine his brother betraying him like that, and he'd come to believe Eliza wasn't capable of doing such a thing, either. But he'd been blindsided before. Besides, how else could he account for what he'd just seen?

"Why are you walking so quickly, Jonas?" Eliza asked breathlessly as she tried to match his strides. "I'd like to talk to you about something before you take me home, but I can hardly keep up with you."

Jonas slowed down. He could sense what was coming and he figured he might as well hear it now rather than on the way to her house. If she broke up with him midway, it would be awkward taking her the rest of the way home. At least if she let him know now that their courtship was over, then Freeman could give her a ride. "What is it?"

"Well, it's about your *bruder.* I'm not sure if he wants me to tell you this, but he didn't specifically say I shouldn't, so…" she began and Jonas's heart suddenly seemed as heavy as an anvil inside his chest. How could this be happening to him a third time? "Freeman picked these *biere* for Mary because he feels like it's his fault she isn't returning to the *bauerei* and he knows she wants to make a lot of jam to sell at the festival. So I told him I'd give these to her. I know it's out of our way, but I wonder if we can swing by there either this evening or first thing tomorrow morning so I can drop them off at her *haus*?"

Jonas had to refrain from throwing his hat in the air and cheering. Eliza had no intention of breaking up with him! *Why did I ever worry she was interested in Freeman?* Jonas asked himself. He was flooded with shame because he'd doubted her integrity, as well as his brother's. Yet he was also deeply relieved that he hadn't made a fool of himself by expressing his doubts.

"Of course. No problem." And as soon as they were both seated in the buggy, he finally took Eliza's hand in his, just like he'd been yearning to do ever since he'd let go of it the previous day.

Eliza was so buoyant that if Jonas hadn't held her hand all the way home, she felt as if she might have floated away. Working at his farm was even more fun than she'd expected it to be, primarily because he kept dropping by to ask how she was doing, or to bring her a bottle of root beer, or to deliver the bowl of blueberries he'd picked and washed just for her to eat as a snack.

However, upon returning home, she was dismayed to see how frazzled her mother appeared. Eliza blamed herself. *If only we hadn't stopped at Mary's* haus *to drop off the* biere, *then I would have been home to help with part of the supper preparations.* She knew they could have waited until the following morning to deliver them; the fruit would have kept. But she'd selfishly wanted to prolong the time she spent holding hands with Jonas as they rode through New Hope.

So after supper, she insisted she'd take care of clearing the table and washing and drying the dishes by herself, since she hadn't been home to help prepare supper. Now, as she scraped buttery residue from the bottom of a frying pan, she thought, *If Uri was as helpful and attentive toward* Mamm *as Jonas is toward me, she wouldn't be so run-down.* Eliza couldn't picture her suitor ever becoming as demanding as Uri seemed to be now. *If anything, Jonas has become more attentive and considerate the longer I've known him.*

"Can I, Eliza?" Samuel's imploring voice brought her back to the moment. "Please?"

"Can you what?"

"Go to the *bauerei* with you tomorrow. I can help you pick lots of *biere*."

"I won't be picking *biere*, remember? I'll be waiting on customers."

"I can help you wait on customers then. I know lots of words in *Englisch*." The Amish children in New Hope didn't formally learn *Englisch* until they started school, but they picked up words and short sentences from overhearing their parents speaking with *Englischers*.

"Okay. How would you tell a customer their *biere* cost seven dollars and forty cents?" she asked her little brother.

"I don't know *money* words," he objected. "But I can say *Englisch* food words, like *milkshake* and *cheeseburger* and *French fries*."

Tousling the boy's hair, Eliza suppressed a smile, recalling how he had learned those particular words. His older brothers had gone to a drive-thru restaurant in the buggy with Willis and his sons a year ago. Peter and Isaiah had been talking about the experience ever since. "That's excellent pronunciation, Samuel. But the only food the customers can get on the *bauerei* is *blohbiere*."

"Oh. Well, I could… I could stand in the shrubs and scare the birds away for Jonas," he insisted, wheedling her.

"That's a job for a scarecrow on a pole, not for a *bu* like you," Eliza said. She was trying to be firm, yet she was torn because she recognized how proud he'd felt that he was finally old enough to accompany her to the blueberry farm. "*Buwe* like you need to run around in big fields. It's supposed to rain this weekend, but maybe the next *Sunndaag* we can go to Hatters Field and play kickball."

"And fly kites?"

"Absolutely," she confirmed. "We might even climb trees, too—if the kites get stuck in their branches. How does that sound?"

"*Gut.*" He was smiling again as his mother called him upstairs for bed.

However, Eliza belatedly realized that if she went kite-flying with Samuel on the Sunday after next, she wouldn't be able to go out with Jonas. The thought made her frown. But in the next moment, she recalled what Jonas had said about possibly taking the boys out with them. Her smile returned, and by the time she'd finished drying and putting away the dishes, she felt as if she might float away again.

Chapter Eleven

"Today will probably be really busy again," Jonas said as they neared the farm on Tuesday morning. "But in the future, you might want to bring your rugs with you."

"My rugs?"

"*Jah.* If there's a lull between customers, you might get bored just sitting there at the booth, so you could work on your rag rugs," he explained. "Or you could bring a book to read. Or whatever else you'd like to do."

Once again, Eliza was impressed by Jonas's thoughtfulness toward her. "*Denki*, but I've *kumme* to help. So if *you* have something else you'd like *me* to do during lulls between customers, just say the word."

"In that case…" He faced her, a sheepish, lopsided smile on his face. "I'd like you to take a break with me around ten o'clock this morning. I bought donuts on my way to your *haus.*"

There isn't a bakery on the way to my haus, Eliza thought. *He must have gotten up even earlier this morning and gone all the way into town just to have an excuse to take a* kaffi *break with me.* Usually when Eliza realized one of her suitors had schemed in order to spend more time with her, it had made her feel uncomfortable. Trapped, even. But when Jonas did it, it just made her feel special, and she wanted him to know how eager she was to spend time with him, too. "That was very thoughtful of you." Looking up at him from beneath her lashes, she coyly added, "I'll be counting the minutes."

However, the farm was so busy that Eliza lost all track of time. Both Amish and *Englisch* customers swarmed the barrens like bees on a hive. And everyone was abuzz with talk about the upcoming festival, as well as about the tropical storm that was working its way up the coast. Eliza was surrounded by so much commotion that she hadn't realized Jonas had sidled up to her, sometime after ten o'clock. Pivoting to set the fruit on the scale, she bumped into him, nearly upending the basket. He caught her arms on both sides to steady her, but his touch only made her feel more light-headed.

"I'm sorry," she whispered in *Deitsch*. "This line is growing by the minute. You'll have to take a break without me."

But Jonas insisted on staying to help until the crush of customers eased to a manageable number. Before leaving her on her own again, he joked, "We can eat our donuts at lunchtime…unless my *bruder* discovers them first."

As it turned out, there was another large influx of customers during the noon hour, with an equally large group checking out so they could go home and eat their own lunches. Meanwhile, Freeman's horse had become overheated and he needed to take the animal to the stable. So rather than sitting down to enjoy a leisurely meal and conversation, Jonas and Eliza worked side by side, which wasn't nearly as private, but was satisfying in its own way.

By five o'clock, there was still a handful of customers out in the barrens. While Eliza was waiting for Freeman and Jonas to circle around to the booth so Jonas could bring her home, an *Englisch* woman wearing high heels and a short skirt came tiptoeing across the dirt driveway.

"Oh, no," she whined when she reached the booth. "Are the berries sold out for the day?"

It took a moment for Eliza to understand what she meant. "I'm sorry, but we don't sell berries by the pint. This is a U-pick farm only."

"That's a shame," the woman replied. "There are half a dozen large businesses right down the road from here, including my employer's office. You could make a lot of money from people who enjoy fresh, locally grown produce but who don't have the time to pick it themselves. They'd appreciate being able to swing by the farm on their way home from work and grab a pint of berries."

That actually wasn't a bad idea, but Eliza knew Jonas and Freeman would have had to hire more staff members to harvest the berries, since they were too busy to do it themselves. Besides, Jonas had mentioned they didn't have the funds for additional employees. However, Eliza offered, "I could probably pick a pint or two and set them aside for you, if you'd like to return at this time tomorrow."

"Aren't you sweet!" the woman exclaimed, obviously delighted.

Eliza's motivation wasn't solely to please the customer; it was also to help Jonas and Freeman. Every pint of berries sold was one less pint that would go to waste if the weather turned bad. Eliza figured if she arrived just fifteen minutes earlier tomorrow or stayed just fifteen minutes later now, she could pick more than enough berries for the *Englisch* customer.

But when Jonas heard of her plan, he objected, saying *he* should be the one to pick the berries and that he'd do it after he'd dropped her off.

"How about if we both pick the *biere*, once Freeman gets here?" she suggested. "It'll take half as long if we're working together. And we've hardly had a chance to chat all day."

"That's true. But don't you have to hurry home to help your *mamm* with supper?" Jonas asked.

"*Neh.* As long as I do the cleanup, my *mamm* will be fine managing the preparation." At least, Eliza hoped her mother would be fine, because there was nowhere else she wanted to be right now than alone with her suitor. And as Mary had once told her, that was perfectly natural, wasn't it?

"I was *hallich* that Mary returned to the *bauerei* today," Freeman said to Jonas on Wednesday evening as they ate their supper. "I crossed paths with her out in the barrens. She seemed pleased about the *biere* Eliza gave her from me."

"*Jah*, Mary mentioned that when she ate lunch with Eliza and me, too."

"O-o-hh," Freeman uttered, nodding knowingly. "So that's why you were glum this afternoon—you didn't get to take your lunch break alone with your girlfriend."

That was *part* of Jonas's disappointment; the other reason he was down in the mouth was because one of Emily Heiser's sisters had stopped by to tell them that Emily would be coming back to work on Friday. Of course, he was pleased about Emily's recovery, but Jonas regretted that tomorrow would be his last day working with Eliza. While it was possible she might return to the farm to pick berries for her family, that wouldn't be the same.

"I wonder if Mary plans to *kumme* to the *bauerei* tomorrow, too," Jonas muttered, not realizing he'd spoken aloud until Freeman chuckled.

"How about this... If she does, I'll ask her to have lunch with *me*. That way, you and Eliza can take your break alone together."

Jonas raised an eyebrow. "Mary might think you're interested in her romantically, you know."

"That's a risk I'm willing to take if it'll wipe that frown off your face," Freeman quipped.

Jonas couldn't tell whether his brother was sincerely being altruistic or if he was trying to disguise the fact that he truly *was* interested in Mary. Either way, he appreciated the offer, which actually did put a smile on his lips. "*Denki*. I think I'll take you up on that," he said.

"No need for thanks. Just remember this the next time Eliza bakes a dessert for you," Freeman replied, grinning as he patted his stomach.

The following morning Eliza wasn't at the end of the lane when Jonas arrived. He was so eager to see her that he got out of his buggy and paced back and forth near the fence. Through a clearing in the trees, he caught a glimpse of her hanging laundry on the clothesline, her back turned toward him. *She must have gotten up very early to have already washed and wrung the clothes.*

After she'd pinned a final pair of trousers to the line, she darted back into the house. A moment later she emerged, carrying her lunch bag. "Guess what I made yesterday evening?" she asked once they were seated side by side. Without waiting for him to answer, she said, "*Blohbier* buckle. I brought some for us to have for dessert...and a square for Freeman, too."

"*Gut.* Now I have *two* reasons to look forward to lunch—seeing you and eating *blohbier* buckle." Jonas took her hand and wiggled so close to her that their knees were touching. "I'm going to miss taking my breaks with you once Emily returns."

"*I* won't miss taking breaks together," she retorted.

He turned sideways and noticed her mischievous smirk. "You won't?"

"*Neh,*" she said, nudging his knee with hers. "Because I intend to *kumme* back tomorrow."

Jonas grinned. "You're coming to the *bauerei* to pick *biere* for your *familye* tomorrow?"

"*Neh.* I'm coming to the *bauerei* to pick *biere* for *you.*" In a bubbly voice, Eliza told Jonas that she'd been thinking about the customer's suggestion that they sell berries by the pint. "It seems like a *gut* idea, since the *biere* will just go to waste if they ripen and then we get so much rain that they go bad on the bushes before anyone can pick them. We could post a big sign at the end of the driveway alerting *Englisch* passersby that we're temporarily selling picked fruit, too."

Jonas found her use of the word *we* endearing; it showed how invested she was in the farm, and how connected she felt with him. However, he couldn't allow Eliza to continue working on the farm for free. "I agree that it would be *baremlich* for the *biere* to go to waste, which is why Freeman and I were already planning to pick them whenever we have spare time. We're going to ask if one of the *weibsmensch* from *kurrich* would sell them at the festival on *Samschdaag*—"

"Ooh, *jah*!" Eliza interrupted him, snapping her fingers as if something just occurred to her. "We could sell them at both places—the festival *and* the *bauerei*! I'm sure Mary would let us sell them at her booth. We could take turns managing the sales. She could attend the festival in the morning and I could attend it in the afternoon. I'll ask Uri for some pallets to transport the fruit, but we'll need to buy some pint-sized cardboard produce baskets at the farmer's exchange today after work."

"Wait a second," Jonas objected. "I don't want you to have to go through all that trouble for me and Freeman. The *bauerei* is our responsibility, not yours." Out of the corner of his eye, he noticed Eliza's shoulders slump.

"Oh. Okay," she replied in a small, quavering voice. "I was only trying to be helpful. I didn't mean to step on your toes."

Jonas slowed the horse, bringing him to a stop on the shoulder of the road. Angling sideways so he could look straight into her big brown eyes, which were brimming with tears, he touched her shoulder. "You didn't step on my toes, Eliza, and you *have* been incredibly helpful. But to continue to accept your help without giving you anything in return makes me feel like I'm taking advantage of your generosity. I don't believe that's the way people should treat each other. And it's certainly not the way a *mann* should treat the *weib-smensch* he's courting."

"I understand," she said, sniffing. "And I respect that more than you know. I really do."

But she still looked dejected, so Jonas suggested, "Maybe if I were to do something for you so your efforts didn't seem so one-sided. Is there anything you'd like me to help you accomplish?"

"Well…" Eliza tipped her head to the side, her face brightening. "You could take my *breider* kite-flying with me the *Sunndaag* after this one?"

"Pshaw." Jonas waved his hand. "I'd do that, anyway. How about something like… Like for the rest of the season, you and your *breider* can pick—or eat— all the *blohbier* you want, no charge? And whenever I can, I'll help you."

She tittered. "Talk about taking advantage of someone. You have no idea how much those *buwe* can consume! Why don't we just agree that my *breider* and I can have one morning of free picking?"

Relieved to see a smile on her lips again, Jonas countered, "*Neh*. The rest of the season or nothing. That's my final offer. Take it or leave it."

"In that case, I'll take it," she agreed.

"*Gut.* But would it be okay if you didn't tell your *breider* about our arrangement until next week?"

"Are you afraid they'll eat too many of the *biere* before the festival?"

"*Neh.*" Jonas leaned toward her and openly admitted, "I just really enjoy being alone with you. And if they're around, I wouldn't be able to do this…" He lifted his hand from her shoulder to her face. Cupping her cheek in his palm, he gazed deep into her eyes. She seemed to understand the question he was asking because she nodded ever so slightly against his hand. Or was the motion he felt only his own fingers trembling?

He paused, unsure, until her eyelids fluttered closed. Then Jonas drew closer and pressed his lips to hers for a soft, lingering kiss, the first of many they'd share during the next three days.

"But today is *Samschdaag*," Uri objected after Eliza told him where she was going. He'd been heading into the house as she was going out of it, and they'd crossed paths on the porch steps. "I didn't realize you were going to spend the afternoon at the festival."

Eliza had to hold her tongue so she wouldn't sound as impatient as she felt. Jonas was undoubtedly already waiting at the end of the lane to bring her to the festival. "I thought I told you when Jonas picked up the pallets yesterday morning."

"You didn't say anything about *you* going to the festival," Uri insisted. "Only that Jonas needed to borrow the pallets for the day."

"I'm sorry. I thought I told you," she repeated. "But I don't see what difference it makes. *Mamm* doesn't mind me going." *And you'd better get used to my not being around if I end up getting married like you've always wanted me to.* And, for the first time, like *Eliza* was beginning to want to.

Uri gruffly replied, "I was planning to surprise your *mamm* by taking her out to supper. She's been running herself ragged and I thought it would be a nice change for her."

Eliza felt as if someone could have knocked her over

with a feather. *Uri wants to do something thoughtful—and even* romantic—*for* Mamm? "Don't worry. I'll be home by five thirty sharp, and you can leave then. Tell her not to make anything for the *buwe*. I'll take care of fixing their meal when I get home."

After Uri grunted his agreement and went into the house, Eliza flew down the driveway to the end of the lane, where Jonas was waiting for her. Earlier that morning, Freeman had delivered the fruit to Mary's booth at the festival while Jonas managed the farm. Jonas was using his lunch break to bring Eliza to the festival, and he'd also bring her—and the pallets—home at five o'clock. Thanks to Uri, they were already a few minutes behind schedule, yet almost as soon as they pulled onto the main road, Jonas turned off onto an unpaved path. Virtually never traveled, the tree-lined dirt road was only a quarter mile long and it didn't so much come to an end as it dwindled into a grassy field.

"Why are you turning here?" Eliza asked, even though she knew exactly why he was turning here. This was the same place they'd turned for the last three days, both on the way to the farm and on the trip back so they could snuggle and kiss without being seen by passersby. "We'll be late for the festival."

"Just a few kisses," Jonas pleaded, nuzzling her ear.

"That tickles," she complained, though jokingly, as she scrunched up her shoulder. *"Absatz."*

But she only half meant it. Although she'd never been kissed before Wednesday, now that she had, she couldn't seem to get enough of Jonas's lips on hers. She'd thought about his kisses long after she'd gotten home each evening and she'd anticipated them long before she saw him each morning. However, she also recognized that as much as she enjoyed it, there was a time and a place for kissing and it couldn't be the focus of their courtship. Rather, it *shouldn't* be. But Eliza liked this aspect of having a suitor so much that she gave in and allowed Jonas to brush his lips against hers.

"Really, Jonas," she scolded after he'd kissed her. "We need to get to the festival so Mary can go home and eat lunch. And we can't stop here on the way back, either. I promised Uri I'd return by five thirty, on the dot."

"All the more reason to give you another kiss now." Jonas proceeded to give her *three* more kisses before picking up the reins and guiding the horse back to the main road. Within fifteen minutes, they'd arrived at the fairgrounds where the festival was being held. Jonas dropped her off in the parking area, promising to return a few minutes before five o'clock so he'd have plenty of time to load the pallets into his buggy and still get her home by five thirty.

"There she is!" Mary exclaimed when Eliza arrived at her table. Half a dozen other women from their district were selling their blueberry confections, linens and crafts beneath the same tentlike canopy. "It's nearly one thirty. I thought something may have happened to you and Jonas on your way here."

Eliza could feel her cheeks going red. Even if it might have seemed logical for Jonas to give her a ride since it was his blueberries she was selling, she knew how quickly people jumped to conclusions in New Hope. In this instance, they would have been right if they assumed the pair was courting...or if Honor had already spread the rumor. But Eliza didn't appreciate her friend drawing attention to the fact she was late, probably because she already felt guilty that she and Jonas had stopped to steal a few kisses.

Before she could respond, Honor's mother, Lovina, nudged Almeda Stoll and gestured toward Eliza with her chin. "I think someone must have taken a detour," she teased. "Look how she's blushing."

Eliza wished she could have dived beneath the table. Instead, she pretended she hadn't heard and said to Mary, "You must have been very busy. It looks like most of your jam is gone already and there's not a single pie left." Over three quarters of the blueberries were gone, too.

"*Jah.* It should be slow for the rest of the day." After Mary showed Eliza which cashbox she was using for own sales and which she was using for Jonas's berries, she left. Eliza spent the afternoon chatting with the other women from her district in between sales. By four o'clock, everyone had completely sold out all of their baked goods and preserves, and they'd sold most of their embroidered products, too. One by one, their husbands or children arrived to pick them up, and although they offered Eliza a ride home, she declined, saying she had to wait for Jonas, since he was transporting the pallets back to her house.

"I could load them into the back of our buggy. We have plenty of room," Almeda's husband offered, to Eliza's dismay.

"*Neh*, Iddo. Then Jonas will have made the trip out here for nothing," Almeda interjected, winking at her. "Just be careful with those detours—they can be treacherous."

Understanding exactly what the deacon's wife

meant, Eliza felt the color rise to her cheeks. But she nodded at the older woman's gentle but wise admonishment. "We're not taking any detours—I'm going straight home."

"*Gut.* Better to avoid them altogether." She smiled. "We'll see you in *kurrich* tomorrow."

Once Iddo and Almeda walked away, Eliza began stacking the pallets so they'd be easier for Jonas to bring to the buggy.

"Eh-hem." A man cleared his throat behind her.

At first she thought it was Jonas, but when Eliza spun around, she found Willis Mullet standing on the other side of the folding table. "Oh…hello, Willis."

"I see I'm too late to buy one of Mary's pies. Or a jar of her jam."

"You're too late to buy anything at all." She extended her arms, indicating the empty tent.

"*Jah.* I guess I am. Well, do you need help carrying those pallets to your buggy?"

"*Denki*, but my suitor—I mean Jonas—will be here at any moment to pick them up." Eliza averted her eyes, pretending to be embarrassed that she'd disclosed her secret, but she hadn't actually made a slip of the tongue. She had intentionally revealed that Jonas was her suitor so Willis would know she still wasn't available for courting. He didn't seem surprised, however, nor did he appear ready to leave. So she hinted, "There might be a couple of *Englischers* who are still selling goodies near the entrance to the fairgrounds. Their pies won't be as *appenditlich* as Mary's, but they might hit the spot."

Willis shifted his weight from one foot to the other. "Actually, I—I'm not that interested in pie." He leaned closer and said in a low voice, "I stopped at your *haus* and Uri told me you'd be here. I wanted to ask you something."

It ruffled Eliza's feathers to hear that her stepfather had told Willis her whereabouts, but she kept the annoyance from her voice. "What is it?"

"I—I wondered if you…" He paused for what seemed like an insufferably long time. "If you know if Mary is courting anyone?"

Willis was interested in Mary? Eliza was so astounded she couldn't speak. She just stood there, squinting at him. Eliza knew from previous conversations that her friend had absolutely no romantic interest in Willis, but how could Eliza tell him that? At one time she'd resented him for asking Uri if she'd consider courting him instead of speaking directly to Eliza about it. But now she now realized it was because Willis was shy. Or maybe he lacked confidence, since he probably hadn't courted anyone for a long time. In any case, Eliza was overcome with compassion for the widower who'd already lost so much in his life.

"Willis," she said softly, looking into his eyes. "I can't speak for Mary, but isn't she kind of…immature for you?"

"You mean young, don't you?" Willis asked. When Eliza nodded, he heaved a sigh. "*Jah*, I suppose she is."

"Have you considered courting someone closer to your own age?"

"The problem is, the only unmarried *weibsmensch* closer to my age in New Hope is Honor Bawell. And it's obvious why I could never be her suitor."

Eliza took a step backward. *What a* baremlich *thing to say. Is it just because she can't cook?* "What exactly do you mean by that?" she snapped. He must have felt ashamed because he looked down at his round stomach. So Eliza repeated her question. "Why would you say such a thing?"

"B-because, you know. Honor's so…outgoing and—and popular," he stammered. "And since she's still not married, it's clear she's very particular. She must have turned down quite a few suitors over the years. Suitors who had a lot more to offer her than I do."

Once again, Eliza was dumbfounded that she'd completely misjudged him. "You have plenty to offer a *weibsmesnch*, Willis. But the only way you'll know if Honor would agree to walk out with you is to ask her."

"I could—I could never ask to be her suitor. It would be too humiliating if…" Willis shook his head, as if imagining Honor turning him down.

"How about if you write her a note? I'll deliver it to her for you," Eliza urged him, tearing a sheet of paper off the little pad she'd been using to keep track of sales. "You can fold it up and I promise not to peek or to say a word about it to anyone."

Willis appeared dubious, but he accepted the pen and piece of paper and leaned over the table. Eliza busied herself with restacking the pallets, so he wouldn't feel as if she was hovering. When she looked up a few moments later, he was still hunched with his pen above the paper, but apparently he hadn't written anything yet. Out of the corner of her eye, she could see Jonas heading toward them.

"You'd better hurry. Jonas is coming," she warned. He scrawled his message and hastily folded the note in fours and then in fours again. He hesitated to give it to her.

"I'm not so sure about this," he said.

"It's worth a try. And I happen to think Honor would really like to be courted by you," she reassured him.

"Not as much as I'd like to court her." He pressed the little square of paper into Eliza's hand as Jonas reached the canopied area. She slipped it into her canvas bag just in the nick of time.

Jonas had seen Eliza and Willis talking from a distance, and initially, he'd thought nothing of it. But as he drew nearer, it became clear from how close they were standing that they were engaged in a very personal conversation. He'd tried not to let it bother him, but when he'd gotten even closer, he thought he'd heard Eliza tell Willis it would be an honor to be courted by him. And he was almost certain that Willis had said how much he'd like that, too. Jonas's heart had quickened as he tried to convince himself that he couldn't have heard what he thought he'd heard. *I was too far away to catch every word they said*, he'd reasoned—right until this very moment, when he'd undeniably witnessed Eliza and Willis squeeze each other's hands.

Yet even though he'd seen this with his own two eyes, Jonas knew there had to be a logical explanation. He *wanted* there to be a logical explanation. *She just kissed me on the way to the fairgrounds this afternoon. I refuse to believe Eliza would do that and then suddenly decide she's interested in Willis instead.*

However, both Willis and Eliza appeared embarrassed when he greeted them, which did little to allay his concerns. "Do you—do you need help carrying these pallets to your buggy?" Willis stuttered.

"*Neh.* I'll manage," Jonas answered curtly, even

though it would take him two trips. He bent down and lifted a stack of the pallets. Without saying anything else, he turned and carried them to his buggy. He was so appalled by what had transpired between Eliza and Willis he could hardly see straight. He could hardly *think* straight. *How could I have been so* dumm? he lamented. *This whole time, I was worried about Freeman, when it appears it's actually Willis that Eliza was trying to make envious.*

But she wouldn't do that to Jonas, would she? He resolved not to let his imagination run away with him, just because one of his former girlfriends had used Jonas to make another man jealous.

By the time he returned to the canopied area a second time, Willis was gone and Eliza was snapping the legs of the folding table flat against its underside so she easily could carry it. He picked up the remaining stack of pallets, and she accompanied him to the buggy. "Guess what? All the *biere* sold out over two hours ago!" she exclaimed as she traipsed alongside him.

"That's *gut*," he said numbly, barely hearing her blithe chatter about how big the crowd was and about how he should consider selling berries there every year. He secured the pallets in the back of his buggy, and after he climbed into the seat beside her, she handed him a small, heavy cashbox.

"This one's yours. Mary and I figured it was easier to keep the purchases separate."

"Denki." Jonas took a deep breath and began, "I noticed you and Willis seemed to be deep in conversation when I arrived…" He figured he'd give her a chance

to explain before he commented that he'd also noticed she'd squeezed Willis's hand.

"*Jah*. He wanted to buy one of Mary's pies, but he arrived too late. They sold out even before the *biere* did. She's going to be so *hallich* that every single jar of her jam sold, too. She was worried that—"

Jonas didn't have the patience to listen to Eliza prattle on about Mary's pies or jam. He interrupted her in midsentence and bluntly asked, "What else were you and Willis discussing?"

Eliza drew back her chin in surprise. "Why are you so interested in my conversation with him?"

The very fact that she'd responded to his question with a question made Jonas even more suspicious. Yet he didn't want to come right out and accuse her of behaving flirtatiously toward Willis, so he said, "Because the two of you looked awfully…*cozy* talking together."

"Cozy?" She gave a little snortlike laugh that sparked Jonas's temper. Was this all just a joke to her? Jonas decided to cut to the chase.

"It's not funny, Eliza. You squeezed his hand. I saw you."

She made a loud, exasperated huffing sound, as if he was being ridiculous. "I did *not* squeeze his hand."

"So you're saying I was imagining it? You're honestly telling me that you two didn't deliberately touch each other's hands?"

The indignation completely melted from Eliza's expression. Apparently, she decided to take a different tack. In a patronizing voice, she said consolingly, "Our hands may have touched but not in the same way I hold hands with you, Jonas. There's no need to be envious." She reached over and squeezed his fingers but he yanked his hand away.

"I am *not* envious." Jonas's adamant tone of voice made his horse's ears twitch; he had yet to signal the animal to walk on. "You still haven't answered my question. If you have nothing to hide, you'd just tell me what you two were talking about."

She crossed her arms against her chest. "And if *you* trusted me, you wouldn't insist I tell you about a private conversation."

Jonas was so frustrated that he muttered, "I *did* trust you—which was my mistake. I should have known better than to get involved with someone who likes to string men along just for the sport of it."

"What are you talking about?" Eliza's eyes looked ready to overflow with tears, but Jonas wasn't going to allow himself to be deceived by her innocent, wounded appearance.

"Everyone in New Hope knows what kind of games you play with your suitors. You pretend to like them and just when they get serious about you, you break up with them to court someone else," Jonas retorted. "If you want to court Willis Mullet, go ahead and be my guest. I was only courting you so you wouldn't court my *bruder* and break his heart the way you did to Petrus."

Color rose in Eliza's cheeks, and her tearful expression was replaced by a steely glare. Her nostrils flaring, she snapped, "For your information, I am *not* interested in a courtship with Willis Mullet. And as of this minute, I am even *less* interested in a courtship with you, Jonas Kanagy. Or a friendship, for that matter."

"That makes two of us," he said, but she had already hopped out of the buggy and was storming across the parking lot.

Eliza saw red as she wove a path around the parked *Englisch* vehicles toward the road. She was furious at Jonas for so many reasons, she could hardly absorb them all. How dare he accuse her of stringing men along? Obviously, Petrus had told him about their courtship. Or at least, he'd told Jonas about his version of their courtship and breakup.

It's so unfair for Jonas to accuse me of breaking his friend's heart when I made it abundantly clear I only wanted a friendship with Petrus, she thought angrily. *If anyone has broken anyone's heart,* Jonas *has broken* mine. *What right does he have to act so distrustful of me?* He's *the one who was being deceptive. The one who was pretending to like me when his only intention in courting me was to protect his* bruder. *Which is absolutely* lecherich, *anyway.*

Eliza felt completely foolish that she'd gone to such lengths to help Jonas with his blueberry crop. And she felt absolutely disgusted that she'd allowed him to kiss her. *He has probably been laughing up his sleeve this whole time. Making a mockery of me because he thought* I *was using* him *when it was completely the other way around.*

How could she have been so gullible that she'd believed he was genuinely as considerate as he'd seemed? She should have known that kind of thoughtfulness had to be an act. *Jonas's behavior was even worse than Uri's.* But at least her stepfather was openly demanding and interfering, whereas Jonas had deliberately tried to trick Eliza into believing he was kind, appreciative and warmhearted. *I suppose I should consider it a* gut *thing that I found out his true colors sooner rather than later,* she told herself. Otherwise, she'd feel even more disappointed—and more infuriated—than she did now. As if that was even possible.

Trudging along the shoulder of the road, Eliza lugged the canvas bag with Mary's cashbox in it. It kept knocking against her leg, which made her feel even more miserable, and soon she was weeping. She tucked her chin to her chest so passersby wouldn't see that she was crying.

Hot, sticky and both emotionally and physically drained, Eliza arrived home more than an hour later to find Uri sitting in a glider on the porch. "You promised you'd be home at five thirty so I could go out with your mother," he reminded her. "It's almost six thirty now."

Eliza paused on the top step. Couldn't Uri see how upset she was? For all he knew, she'd been in a buggy accident. Couldn't her stepfather have at least inquired about her welfare before lecturing her about being late? Without looking at him or offering an explanation, she said, "I'm sorry. I'll fix the *buwe's* supper as soon as I wash my hands. You and *Mamm* can leave whenever you're ready."

"There's no point to it now—your *mamm* heated up stew for all of us."

Eliza took another step closer to the door, but Uri wasn't finished with his lecture. "You've been spending entirely too much time with your suitor lately and neglecting your responsibilities here. It's not acceptable."

Clenching her hands into fists at her sides, Eliza refrained from saying, *Nothing I ever do is acceptable to you. When I don't have a suitor, you lecture me about getting one. When I am courting, you complain I'm not home often enough. There's just no pleasing you.*

Instead, she said, "I promise it won't happen again." And as she yanked the door open, she added silently, *Because I'm not courting anyone for the rest of my life.*

Chapter Twelve

Eliza woke on Sunday morning, still dressed in the clothes she was wearing on Saturday evening when she'd dropped onto her bed, crying. She must have been more tired than she'd realized.

Closing her eyes again, she listened to the heavy rain hitting the roof, which reminded her of sitting in Jonas's buggy with him at the deserted gas station. She groaned and shifted into a sitting position, banishing the memory from her mind. There was no sense in starting today as miserably as she'd ended yesterday.

I've shed enough tears over Jonas, she told herself when she saw her puffy eyelids in the bathroom mirror. *I'm not going to waste another minute thinking about him.*

After washing her face, brushing her hair and changing into fresh clothing, she headed downstairs. As much as possible, Eliza and her mother didn't cook on the Sabbath, so breakfast on Sunday usually consisted of little more than toast and boiled eggs. In the kitchen, her mother was already laying the bread on a cookie sheet to slide into the oven, which was how the Amish toasted their bread.

"Guder mariye," Eliza cheerfully greeted her, hoping Lior wouldn't notice that her eyes were pink-rimmed. Before retreating to her room the evening before, Eliza had managed to compose herself long enough to apologize to her mother for ruining her plans with Uri. But she hadn't explained *why* she'd returned home later than she'd said she would, and she didn't want to elaborate on it now, either. "What can I do to help?" she asked.

"Could you please get another jar of jam from the basement? The *buwe* have nearly polished off this one already." Lior scraped a spoon against the bottom of the jar. "I hope you plan to go picking for us this week, now that the festival is over?"

"Neh." Eliza's answer sounded too brusque, even to her own ears, so she added, "It's supposed to rain."

"Jah, but only through *Mittwoch.* Then the skies should be clear for the rest of the week. I'm sure the *buwe* will be *hallich* to help you…if you don't mind taking them along, that is."

"Mmm," Eliza responded vaguely and scurried from the room. As she went downstairs to retrieve a fresh jar of jam, she recalled Jonas's offer for her and her brothers to pick as many blueberries as they wanted, without charge. It added insult to injury that she'd toiled for a full week for the benefit of his farm, yet he was getting out of holding up his end of the bargain.

I have half a mind to show up with the buwe *to pick* biere *from eight in the morning until five at night every sunny day from now until the season ends,* she thought. But what would be the point in that? All the free blueberries in the world wouldn't be enough to make up for how he'd treated her. How he'd *tricked* her. Besides, being around Jonas would only make her *think* about Jonas, and thinking about Jonas would only make her mad. Or sad. *And I've already cried enough over him*, she reminded herself again as she brought the jam back upstairs.

After the family had eaten breakfast and held their home-worship service, Eliza's brothers quietly drew pictures and played with their blocks while the adults read the Bible to themselves. Then Eliza and Lior made sandwiches for lunch. "Uri and I are taking the *buwe* to the Mullets' *haus* this afternoon. Lovina Bawell's *kin-skinner* are visiting so she's bringing them over, too."

"That's a lot of *kinner* in one *haus* on a rainy afternoon."

"*Jah*. But Willis has that large basement where they can play while the *eldre* are visiting upstairs," Lior replied. "You're *wilkom* to *kumme* with us, but I imagine you have plans?"

"Mmm." Once again, Eliza didn't directly answer her mother's question. She figured that even though Willis hoped to court Honor, there was no guarantee she'd say yes, and if Uri found out Eliza and Jonas had broken up, he might still try to push Eliza and Willis together.

However, Eliza was struck with an idea about how she might help hasten Willis and Honor's courtship along. So before her family set out for the Mullets' house, Eliza wrote a note to Honor indicating Willis had asked her to pass along the enclosed message. Then she put both pieces of paper in a sealed envelope and gave it to her mother to give to Lovina, so she in turn could pass it to Honor.

Please, Gott, *if it's Your will, let Honor give Wil-*

lis a chance, she prayed silently as she watched Uri's buggy pull through the deep puddles on the driveway before turning down the lane. Eliza's intention in making this request to the Lord wasn't primarily because she wanted to eliminate the possibility that her stepfather would cajole her into courting Willis. It was that she truly wanted her friend to have the desire of her heart. *I just hope her heart doesn't wind up broken, like mine did*, Eliza thought bitterly.

This was the first time in ages that she'd been alone in the house for an entire afternoon and she felt at a loss for how to occupy her time. If the weather had been better, she would have walked to Mary's house, but the rain was coming down in sheets. So Eliza decided to read a novel she'd checked out of the library so long ago she'd forgotten which character was which and she had to start reading it from the beginning again.

As hard as she tried to focus on the storyline, intrusive thoughts about Jonas kept interfering. *I can't believe he'd think I'd kiss him in one moment and then break up with him in the next just so I could court Willis*, she grumbled to herself. *He's as mistaken about* my *character as* I *was about his. He sure had me fooled about what a* wunderbaar mann *he was!*

Just as tears threatened to spill, Eliza heard footsteps on the porch. For a split second, she thought, *It's Jonas—he's* kumme *to apologize.* She rose and went to answer the door, pausing before she opened it to pull back her shoulders and hold her chin high. She didn't want him to get the impression she'd been wallowing in sorrow.

But instead of Jonas, she found Mary on the porch, which made her feel both disappointed and relieved at once. "Hi, Mary. Am I ever *hallich* to see you. *Kumme* in," she urged and her friend closed her umbrella and stepped indoors. "It's raining buckets out there—how did you ever manage to stay so dry walking all the way from your *haus*?"

"I didn't walk. I got a ride." Mary hesitated, glancing over Eliza's shoulder before she whispered, "Can I talk to you in private?"

"Don't worry, we're the only ones here. *Kumme* sit in the kitchen. I'll make tea."

"*Denki*, but I can't stay," Mary replied in a normal volume. She gave Eliza a shy smile, then blurted out, "Freeman is waiting for me at the end of your driveway. Yesterday morning when he dropped off the *biere* at the festival, he asked me to walk out with him!"

"He did? How *wunderbaar*!" Eliza exclaimed, genuinely happy for her friend. *I only hope Freeman treats you better than his* bruder *treated me.*

"That's why I may have seemed impatient when you showed up late to the festival yesterday—I was dying to tell you. But there were so many *weibsleit* from *kurrich* nearby that I ended up keeping it to myself, because I didn't want them to hear," Mary explained. "Freeman doesn't know I'm confiding in you about it, though. I made an excuse to stop here. I told him I needed to pick up my cashbox, which I actually do since I'd like to deposit my earnings in the bank tomorrow."

"*Schmaert* thinking. I'll go get it." Eliza dashed up to her room and returned a moment later with the box, which she extended to her friend.

As Mary accepted it, she said, "*Denki* for this. And

denki for praying that I'd meet a suitor. I'm really *hallich* you convinced me to give Freeman a second chance."

"You're *wilkom*." Eliza frowned, thinking about how she wished she'd never given Jonas a *first* chance.

Mary must have noticed her expression because she asked, "Is something wrong?"

"I just...never mind. I'll tell you about it later." She didn't want to delay her friend's outing with Freeman.

"But I feel guilty leaving you all alone, knowing something's troubling you."

"Well, you shouldn't. It's perfectly natural for you to be excited about spending time alone with your suitor," she insisted, quoting what Mary herself had previously said. "Go have *schpass*. I'll be fine."

But as soon as she'd closed the door, Eliza crumpled into a heap on the sofa and wept herself to sleep.

On Saturday during supper, Jonas poked his fork into a small square of ham, but instead of lifting it to his mouth, he mindlessly pushed it around in circles on his plate. Ever since he'd broken up with Eliza, he'd had a bitter taste in his mouth and a churning feeling in his stomach that had made it nearly impossible for him to eat.

Jonas had tried to tell himself that this physical response to their breakup wasn't because he was sad—it was because he was *angry*. He was angry at Eliza for denying that she was interested in Willis, even after he'd caught her cozying up to him and directly confronted her about it. But he was even angrier at himself for becoming romantically involved with her despite his better judgment.

As he'd done countless times during the last week,

he silently berated himself for losing sight of the very reason he'd started to court her in the first place—to keep her from playing games with his brother's heart. Instead, she had played games with *Jonas's* heart. And deep down, beneath all his anger, he had to admit how much it hurt to discover she'd just been toying with him. *It serves me right for being so* dumm. *I knew better than to allow myself to get close to another* weibsmensch. *Especially one like Eliza.*

"If you don't finish your supper, you won't get any dessert," Freeman joked, interrupting his thoughts. "And you'll definitely want dessert tonight—it's pie that Mary baked."

Jonas's brother had confided that he'd asked to be Mary's suitor the previous weekend, and she'd said yes. She'd come to pick blueberries on Thursday and Friday mornings, once the rain finally stopped, and the couple had eaten their lunches together on both days. Freeman had taken her out yesterday evening, too. He seemed happier than he'd been in years. In fact, he seemed every bit as happy as Jonas was *un*happy.

"No pie for me, *denki*. I'm not very *hungerich*," he said with a sigh.

Freeman narrowed his eyes, scrutinizing him. "Why are you so glum? Is it because Eliza wasn't able to *kumme* to the *bauerei* this week? You should have taken her out one evening after work. I know you've been concerned about your *gaul* getting rain scald again, but the weather was dry last night. And the night before."

Jonas avoided the topic of Eliza, and simply answered, "My *gaul's* skin is completely healed now."

"Then why have you been moping around ever since

the blueberry festival? Did you and Eliza have an argument?"

"That's none of your business," Jonas barked. Then he dropped his fork onto his plate and leaned back in his chair in resignation. "But since you're going to find out through the grapevine soon enough, anyway, I might as well tell you. We're not courting anymore. She's interested in someone else."

"Wow." Freeman set down his utensils, too. Shaking his head, he added, "I'm really sorry to hear that. I've been praying that your relationship would continue to grow deeper."

"You have?" Jonas was moved that his brother had such a magnanimous attitude toward him, considering Freeman was interested in becoming Eliza's suitor before Jonas began courting her.

"*Jah.* I know you've been…well, disappointed by relationships in the past, but you seemed really joyful while you were courting Eliza. And she's so different from the other *weibsleit* you've courted that I was hoping your relationship would last for the long haul." He chuckled ruefully. "And for the short term, I also thought it would be a lot of *schpass* if you and Eliza and Mary and I raced canoes at the lake together tomorrow afternoon."

Maybe you and Mary can go canoeing with Willis and Eliza instead, Jonas thought bitterly as he rose to bring his plate to the sink. "If you're going to the lake, I assume that means we'll be riding to *kurrich* in separate buggies?"

"*Jah.*" Freeman got up to remove a large glass container from the fridge. "You sure you don't want pie?"

Jonas shook his head. "I'm going to go take a shower,"

he said before lumbering down the hall. But instead of ducking into the bathroom, he continued to his room, where he dropped onto his bed with a moan. Knowing what he knew from his previous breakups, he anticipated that even catching a glimpse of Eliza in church tomorrow was going to be an awkward, uncomfortable experience. It would undoubtedly trigger all sorts of uncharitable thoughts and feelings that Jonas was aware were displeasing to the Lord. It was bad enough that he'd been wrestling with those emotions all week, but somehow it seemed even worse to be troubled by them during worship services.

Although he recognized he ought to ask the Lord for a more forgiving attitude, Jonas's anger was still smoldering deep within his heart. Quite frankly, he wasn't ready to even *want* to forgive Eliza yet. Besides, he was exhausted. So instead of praying, he rolled over, closed his eyes and went to sleep.

After she'd helped her mother get the boys into bed, Eliza sat down at the folding table in the living room, where she'd been braiding rugs every spare moment she had this week. *I'll be able to take these to Millers' Restaurant on* Muundaag *for consignment,* she thought as she surveyed her handiwork. *This has been a much better use of my time than working on Jonas's* bauerei *for free.*

As much as she'd been trying not to think about him, Jonas kept creeping into her mind. She shook her head, as if to clear her brain of him. "I think it's supposed to be breezy out tomorrow," she commented to her mother, who was sipping tea on the sofa beside Uri as he read *The Budget.* "I'd like to take the *buwe* kite flying at Hatters Field after we return from *kurrich*, as long as you don't mind if I use the buggy."

"*Neh.* That's fine. It would be a treat to *kumme* home and take a nap in peace, wouldn't it, Uri?" Lior nudged her husband.

He lowered his newspaper and peered at Eliza. "Don't you have plans to go out with the Kanagy *bu* tomorrow?"

Her stepfather's nosy question instantly riled Eliza. *He's not a* bu, *he's a* mann *and his name is Jonas. But, neh, I'm not going out with him ever again.* Instead of voicing her response aloud, she merely shook her head and began twisting a length of fabric for the new rug she was beginning.

"You haven't seen him for quite a while," Uri remarked. Eliza knew this statement was really meant to be a question; it was his way of asking *why* she hadn't seen Jonas lately. As usual, she didn't think the details of her social life were any of Uri's business, so Eliza just shrugged without looking up. But Uri didn't take her silence as a hint that she didn't want to discuss the matter with him. He persisted, and asked, "When do you think you'll go out with him again?"

Maybe it was because she was worn out from struggling to work through her anger and sadness all week, but Eliza could no longer seem to hold her tongue. "Never. I am *never* going out with Jonas Kanagy again," she declared, jumping to her feet. "I'm not going out with *any* suitor ever again. So if you want me to move out of the *haus,* I'll move out. But I'm not going to court someone and get married just so *you* can have a partner to help you run your workshop."

Eliza turned and fled to her room before either her

mother or stepfather could reply. She must have sobbed into her pillow for fifteen or twenty minutes before there was a knock on the door. Eliza invited her mother to enter, but she didn't sit up or turn around. She anticipated Lior crossing the room to sit beside her on the bed, but her mother kept her distance. She didn't speak, either, so Eliza began the conversation.

"I'm sorry if I sounded disrespectful, *Mamm*, but I can't tolerate the way Uri interferes in my private matters anymore. My courtships—or lack of courtships—are none of his business."

She heard a cough, and in the next instant Eliza realized she'd made a mistake; it wasn't her mother who was standing in the doorway, but Uri. "You're right. Your courtships *aren't* any of my business—that's a point your *mamm* has repeatedly tried to drill into my thick noggin. However, I've been a slow learner," Uri said. Eliza was so stunned to discover it was her stepfather, not her mother, in the doorway that she couldn't reply. But she was even more astounded when he actually apologized to her. "I'm sorry for prying."

Eliza rolled over and sat up, placing her feet on the floor. Too embarrassed to meet his eyes, she looked down at her knees and nodded, indicating she had accepted her stepfather's apology. But he wasn't done explaining.

"I realize I've pushed you into courtships. And you're right, it's been because I've wanted a *mann* in the *familye* who could run the business in the event that—that something happens to me." Uri pulled on his beard. "I'm not a spring *hinkel* anymore, you know."

Although Eliza realized he was trying to lighten the mood, her eyes teared up. *He's been worried about who*

would provide for our familye *if he became ill or died,*
she realized. *That's probably why he wanted me to get
a full-time job, too—so I could provide an income if*
Mamm *and the* buwe *needed one.*

Her stepfather continued, "However, your *mamm*
has been reminding me that I don't know what the future holds, but *Gott* does. And He will provide for our
familye, no matter what… That's why Lior and I decided last week that rather than increase the number
of my employees, I'm going to decrease the number of
orders I accept. At least until the *buwe* are older and
they can help in the workshop."

"That sounds like a *gut* plan," Eliza murmured.

"*Jah*—and I have your *mamm* to thank for coming
up with it." Uri paused, a contemplative look on his
face, and it occurred to Eliza how much he seemed to
respect Lior's quiet but persistent advice. "So that's
why I was asking when you were going to see Jonas
again—I need him to return the pallets he borrowed.
As long as they aren't stained from the *blohbiere*, I can
include them as part of an upcoming order."

"Oh, I see," Eliza quietly replied. "Do you suppose
you could ask him for them after *kurrich* tomorrow?
We're not exactly on speaking terms right now."

"I'm sorry to hear that," Uri replied, shaking his
head. "I really thought he was a *gut* match for you. I
had high hopes that this courtship might even result
in marriage."

Exasperated that her stepfather was already slipping into his old habits again, Eliza protested, "But
you just said—"

Uri cut her off. "I didn't want you to continue to
court him for *my* sake or for the sake of the business.

I hoped you'd continue to court him because you've never seemed so *hallich* about spending time with one of your suitors as you did with him."

That's because I never fell for one of my suitors before, Eliza thought. And she'd never fall for another one again, because she never wanted to *have* another suitor again. Nor would she need to, now that Uri had decided not to pressure her into a courtship. The thought should have made her feel comforted, but as she followed her stepfather back downstairs to have a piece of blueberry cheesecake, Eliza could barely hold back her tears.

After lunch—he'd barely eaten half a sandwich— Jonas was one of the first men to reach the hitching rail on Sunday. Seeing Eliza sitting two rows up from him had made him want to flee ever since he'd first arrived at church three and a half hours earlier. Especially since he'd noticed Willis Mullet and his sons were sharing the pew with her family.

Jonas had almost finished hitching his horse and buggy when he realized he'd forgotten his Bible inside, so he had to go back in to look for it. He'd gotten sidetracked by Iddo Stoll, who'd engaged him in a fifteen-minute conversation. By the time Jonas had retrieved his Bible, there were only a few buggies still hitched to the post...and to his dismay, Honor Bawell was waiting next to his.

"*Guder mariye,* Jonas," she said gaily. "Have you seen Eliza? I can't find her and I was sure she'd be with you."

"What makes you think that?" Jonas asked.

"Oopsie. I guess she didn't tell you I found out that you're courting." She giggled. "Don't worry, I haven't told anyone, even though I'll personally never understand why some people are so secretive about who they're courting."

Jonas didn't feel like telling Honor, of all people, that not only was he *not* courting Eliza, but they also weren't even on speaking terms any longer. "I think Eliza already left," he said flatly. "In any case, she's not with me."

"That's too bad." Honor winked at him as if she assumed he was going to meet up with Eliza later but was pretending he wasn't for the sake of privacy. "But if you happen to see her, could you please tell her I said *denki* for encouraging Willis to ask if he could be my suitor?"

Jonas inhaled sharply. "Willis is courting *you*?" he clarified, barely able to keep the incredulity out of his voice.

"Don't sound so surprised!" Honor stuck out her bottom lip.

Jonas rushed to apologize. "*Neh*, I didn't mean it like that. I just thought that Willis was…" He stopped short, unable to explain why he was so baffled. Thankfully, Honor jumped to her own conclusions about what he'd meant.

"I know. I thought the same thing—Willis is so shy." Honor beamed. "And he is, too. If Eliza hadn't suggested he write me a note, he probably never would have asked me to walk out with him. So be sure to tell her I said *denki*."

As Honor turned and practically skipped toward Willis's buggy, Jonas felt as if the earth was spinning. *Was* that *what Eliza had been speaking to Willis about at the festival?* he wondered. If it was, then Jonas could understand why she had refused to tell him the details of their conversation.

His mind reeling, he pulled himself into his buggy. But instead of picking up the reins, he covered his face with his arm, blocking out the bright sunlight. Yet he couldn't block out the realization that he had wrongly accused Eliza of being a game player.

His stomach felt like it was turning somersaults as he recalling how baffled—how *hurt*—she'd appeared when he'd said that everyone knew she strung men along for sport. Even if that had been Petrus's perception of his experience courting Eliza, it hadn't been Jonas's experience. He'd had no right to accuse her of such behavior. Even worse, he'd wrongly accused her of flirting with Willis. Of being romantically interested in him. *I essentially called her a liar*, he realized, mortified.

Jonas picked up the reins and signaled his horse to walk on. There was absolutely no reason he should expect Eliza to accept his apology. But that didn't mean he wasn't going to beg her forgiveness.

"Look at how high my kite is, Eliza!" Samuel exclaimed, releasing one hand from the spool to point to the sky.

"Hold on tight with both hands or you'll lose it," she warned.

"Okay. I will," the child promised as he slowly walked closer to where Peter and Isaiah were flying their own kites.

As it happened, both Eli and Mark had fallen asleep on the way home from church, so Eliza had only taken the three eldest boys to Hatters Field. They couldn't have been more delighted, and she tried to match their enthusiasm about the activity, but her mind drifted back to the pastor's sermon today. He'd read the third chapter of Colossians and Eliza was struck by the thirteenth verse, which urged believers to forbear and forgive one another, just as Christ had done for them.

I suppose I could forgive Jonas for thinking I was flirting with Willis, she reasoned. After all, it probably had looked like they'd been holding hands and Eliza was very secretive about their discussion. But she didn't know how she would ever forgive Jonas for using her. *I don't care if Petrus may have told him, it wasn't right for Jonas to kiss me if he didn't truly like me. It wasn't fair for him to let me think we had a romantic future together. I never misled any of my suitors like that. I didn't even hold their hands.*

Noticing her brother's string was going slack as the breeze let up, Eliza called to him, "Wind it tighter, Samuel!" But it was too late—the kite dropped to the ground in the distance. As he was running to retrieve it, Eliza noticed movement in the corner of her eye. "Uri? What are you doing here? Is *Mamm* okay?"

"*Jah.* She's still napping and so are Eli and Mark. I decided I wanted to fly kites with the *buwe.*"

"You walked all this way from the *haus*?"

"*Neh.* I…" He paused, adjusting his hat. "I got a ride from Jonas."

"Oh." Eliza figured Uri must have asked him to drop off the pallets he had borrowed. "I'm surprised he delivered the pallets on the *Sabbaat.*"

"He didn't. He came to our *haus* looking for you. He's waiting for you in the parking area over there." Uri pointed to a row of trees at the edge of the field.

"At the risk of interfering in your personal business, I agreed to give you the message that he'd like to speak with you. But if you want me to tell him to go away, I will. No questions asked."

Eliza glanced in the direction her stepfather was pointing and then looked across the field to where Isaiah and Peter's kites, like Samuel's, had also dropped from the sky. It appeared they were trying to unsnarl a web of strings on the ground. *I suppose talking to Jonas might be a* little *easier than trying to help the* buwe *untangle their kites*, she thought. Sighing, she said, "I'll be back in a few minutes."

When she rounded the stand of trees near the parking area, she spotted Jonas's buggy before she spotted him. He was leaning against a split-rail fence about twenty yards away, his head bowed and his hands clasped across his stomach. Was he praying? He couldn't possibly be *crying,* could he?

As she neared him, he lifted his head and Eliza immediately noticed how pale he appeared. Even the green of his eyes seemed to have faded. Her concern for his physical well-being momentarily overshadowed her anger and she blurted out, "What's wrong? Are you sick?"

"Jah." He straightened his posture and came toward her, his mouth flattened into a tight, grim line. "I'm sick about the way I treated you, Eliza. I'm so sorry I accused you of flirting with Willis. I know you're not interested in him."

Now that she knew he wasn't actually physically ill, Eliza took a step backward and crossed her arms over her chest. She wasn't ready to forgive him. "What made you change your mind all of a sudden?"

Jonas licked his lips before answering. Either he was very nervous or very thirsty. Maybe both. "Honor asked me to thank you for encouraging Willis to ask her to walk out with him."

Inwardly, Eliza smiled, in spite of herself. *That means she accepted him as her suitor*, she thought, pleased on her friend's behalf. But outwardly, she was frowning. Since Honor had apparently let the cat out of the bag already about her courtship, Eliza explained, "*Jah*, that's what Willis and I were talking about at the *blohbier* festival. He was giving me a note to pass to her." She sighed and then admitted, "I suppose it probably did look like we were holding hands, though, so I understand why you may have been suspicious. But it hurt my feelings that you didn't believe me when I specifically told you I wasn't interested in Willis. I was angry that you didn't trust me more than that."

Jonas nodded. "You're right, I should have believed you. But my lack of trust wasn't a reflection on *your* character. It was a reflection on mine." Jonas removed his hat and fanned himself before putting it back on his head. He asked if Eliza minded moving out of the sun, and he seemed so shaky that she followed him farther down the fence to a shady spot beneath the tall pines. They both leaned against the rail and looked toward the trees instead of at each other.

After a long pause, Jonas said, "I've been betrayed in two courtships. One of the *weibsleit* only courted me to make someone else jealous. The other one…well, she didn't really have any genuine interest in me as a suitor—she just didn't want to be single. Both times I was crushed to find out that—that I'd been used." Jonas rubbed his jaw and shifted to face Eliza. "After the second breakup, I felt like I just couldn't trust *weibsleit* anymore. In retrospect, I realize how much unforgiveness I've been harboring in my heart and how unfair my attitude toward *weibsmensch* has been…especially toward you. And I'm very sorry."

Although she appreciated what Jonas had shared about his past and she could see how it had contributed to his recent behavior, Eliza still needed to have her say before she could accept his apology. "I understand why your previous experiences as a suitor may have affected your outlook on courting. And I can see why you might have thought you were protecting your *bruder.* But for the record, I've never strung any suitor along just for the sport of it. And that includes Petrus, regardless of whatever he may have told you. In fact, I've always made it clear to every suitor I've ever had that I only wanted to start with a friendship."

Out of the corner of her eye, she could see Jonas's head moving up and down. "I remember you saying that same thing to me, too. You were very straightforward. I'm the one who was untrustworthy and deceptive for entering into a courtship with you, knowing full well I wanted to remain single for the rest of my life."

Eliza inhaled sharply at Jonas's words. It was as if she'd just looked into a mirror of her own behavior and was appalled by what was reflected there. She swiveled her head to meet his eyes and confessed to herself as much as to him, "I've entered courtships under false pretenses, too."

Jonas furrowed his brow. "What?"

"The only reason I ever walked out with anyone was because Uri had been pressuring me to have a suitor, not because I was interested in a courtship. And not because I ever wanted to get married." The words seemed to fly from Eliza's mouth as she blinked back tears of shame and regret. "I thought that because I was so careful to tell my suitors that there was no guarantee we'd have a romantic relationship, then I wasn't being dishonest. But I was really being every bit as deceptive as—" She stopped herself in midsentence.

Jonas finished it for her. "As *I* was?" His face turned red and he snorted. "*Ha.* You were a lot *more* deceptive than I ever was."

Eliza could understand how angry and disappointed he must have felt to discover she'd only pretended to be interested in having a suitor when he'd first asked her to walk out with him. But she didn't think it was fair for Jonas to heap more blame on her when she was trying to apologize. Especially in light of his own transgressions. "What makes you think my behavior was any worse than yours?" she demanded.

"Because you held my hand. You kissed me!" he said in a loud voice.

"You held *my* hand and you kissed *me,* too!" she echoed, equally loud.

"*Jah,* but by that time, I sincerely liked you. By that time, I had reconsidered staying single for the rest of my life." Jonas snickered in disgust. "I never would have kissed you otherwise."

"Well, by that time *I* really liked you, too!" Eliza realized she was actually shouting, so she lowered her volume and crossed her arms against her chest. "And for your information, you're the only suitor I've ever kissed. The only suitor I ever held hands with, for that matter. Because you're the only suitor I ever developed any romantic feelings for."

"Oh."

"*Jah.* Oh," Eliza said as she sullenly mimicked him. She turned to face straight forward again, absently watching a chipmunk scampering beneath the trees as she reflected on what she and Jonas had just admitted to each other.

After a few moments of shared silence, he sidled closer to her and brushed her prayer *kapp* string over her shoulder, causing her to shiver. "Do you *still* have romantic feelings for me?" he whispered into her ear.

"Not at the moment, *neh*," she claimed, shaking her head, but she was only teasing. However, her tone grew serious when she asked, "Do you forgive me for deceiving you?"

"*Jah.*" Jonas's voice was solemn, too. "Do you forgive me?"

"*Jah.*"

Eliza was silent again for another minute, as the sweetness of their reconciliation washed over her. Then Jonas nuzzled her ear once more. "*Now* do you have romantic feelings for me?"

After stealing a look around to be sure no one else was in the area, she turned her head toward him, and when she nodded, their noses bumped.

You're not just the only mann *I've ever kissed*, Eliza thought as their lips met. *You're the only* mann *I ever want to kiss...*

Epilogue

"Look at this," Samuel said to Jonas, pointing to the ragged green leaves. After courting for over a year, Eliza and Jonas were getting married in two weeks. Since Jonas's extended family and several of his friends were coming from Kansas to attend the ceremony, Eliza wanted to be sure they had plenty of the leafy green vegetable for their wedding meal. So she, Lior and Uri had cultivated a celery patch that was almost as large as the rest of their garden. But rabbits had been snacking on the celery, much to Samuel's dismay. "Do you know what kind of rabbit ate these leaves?" he asked.

"Cottontails? Or snowshoe hares?" Jonas mused. When the child shook his head, Jonas asked, "Then what kind of rabbit do you think it was?"

"The *hungerich* kind!" Samuel exclaimed, making Jonas laugh as hard as he'd laughed the first time the child had made the same joke about the birds eating blueberries at the farm.

"Speaking of *hungerich*, your *breider* are in the *haus* eating pumpkin *kuchen* with your *daed* and *mamm*,"

Eliza said. "You should go join them before all the treats are gone."

"Okay. 'Bye, Jonas. 'Bye, Eliza." Samuel skittered into the *haus* and Eliza and Jonas climbed into his buggy. As soon as they were seated next to each other, he took her fingers in his.

"Remember that day we ate *kuche* and whipped cream without forks in your buggy in the rain?" Eliza asked, reminiscing. "On the way home, you held my hand for the first time. I was so distracted by your touch I could hardly concentrate on anything you were saying."

"You think *you* were distracted—imagine how I felt. I had to hold your hand, talk and guide the horse all at the same time. It's amazing we didn't end up in a ditch."

"It still makes my heart skip a beat every time you take my hand."

"And it still nearly makes me go off the road," Jonas said, turning his head to smile at her.

When they arrived at the Hiltys' property a few minutes later, Mary, Freeman, Honor and Willis were already there, donning life vests by the water's edge.

"Let's race to Pine Island," Freeman suggested. "My fiancée and I will take this canoe."

"My *husband* and I will take the other one," Honor said. Because Willis had already been married, he wasn't required to wait until the fall wedding season to wed, so he'd married Honor the previous April. During the past six months of marriage, he'd lost over thirty pounds. Almost everyone in the district credited Honor's cooking for his weight loss, but Honor had boasted to her friends that Willis claimed he was too happy to overeat any longer.

"Uh-oh. We don't stand much of a chance in the rowboat," Jonas remarked to Eliza as she settled onto the seat, facing him. Sure enough, within sixty seconds of pulling away from shore, the other two teams had paddled so far ahead that there was no catching up to them. Jonas didn't just give up trying; he actually dragged his oars through the water.

"Why are you coming to a stop?" Eliza asked.

"Because I'd rather talk than race. It's more romantic."

"I agree." She nudged his knee with hers. "What would you like to talk about?"

"About how much I really and truly, genuinely love you," Jonas answered, grinning slyly.

"Neh." Eliza playfully shook her head. "I want to talk about how much *I* really and truly, genuinely love *you.*"

"Hmm." He scratched his jaw, pretending to think it over. "How about if we compromise and don't talk after all? Let's do this, instead."

Leaning forward, Jonas cupped Eliza's cheeks with both of his hands and pressed his lips to hers for a long, sweet kiss.

And then another. And another. And one more after that…

* * * * *

Get 3 FREE REWARDS!

We'll send you 2 FREE Books plus a FREE Mystery Gift.

FREE
Value Over
$20

Both the **Love Inspired**® and **Love Inspired**® Suspense series feature compelling novels filled with inspirational romance, faith, forgiveness and hope.

YES! Please send me 2 FREE novels from the Love Inspired or Love Inspired Suspense series and my FREE gift (gift is worth about $10 retail). After receiving them, if I don't wish to receive any more books, I can return the shipping statement marked "cancel." If I don't cancel, I will receive 6 brand-new Love Inspired Larger-Print books or Love Inspired Suspense Larger-Print books every month and be billed just $6.49 each in the U.S. or $6.74 each in Canada. That is a savings of at least 16% off the cover price. It's quite a bargain! Shipping and handling is just 50¢ per book in the U.S. and $1.25 per book in Canada.* I understand that accepting the 2 free books and gift places me under no obligation to buy anything. I can always return a shipment and cancel at any time by calling the number below. The free books and gift are mine to keep no matter what I decide.

Choose one: ☐ **Love Inspired Larger-Print**
(122/322 BPA GRPA)

☐ **Love Inspired Suspense Larger-Print**
(107/307 BPA GRPA)

☐ **Or Try Both!**
(122/322 & 107/307 BPA GRRP)

Name (please print)

Address   Apt. #

City   State/Province   Zip/Postal Code

Email: Please check this box ☐ if you would like to receive newsletters and promotional emails from Harlequin Enterprises ULC and its affiliates. You can unsubscribe anytime.

> Mail to the **Harlequin Reader Service:**
> **IN U.S.A.:** P.O. Box 1341, Buffalo, NY 14240-8531
> **IN CANADA:** P.O. Box 603, Fort Erie, Ontario L2A 5X3

Want to try 2 free books from another series! Call 1-800-873-8635 or visit www.ReaderService.com.

---

*Terms and prices subject to change without notice. Prices do not include sales taxes, which will be charged (if applicable) based on your state or country of residence. Canadian residents will be charged applicable taxes. Offer not valid in Quebec. This offer is limited to one order per household. Books received may not be as shown. Not valid for current subscribers to the Love Inspired or Love Inspired Suspense series. All orders subject to approval. Credit or debit balances in a customer's account(s) may be offset by any other outstanding balance owed by or to the customer. Please allow 4 to 6 weeks for delivery. Offer available while quantities last.

Your Privacy—Your information is being collected by Harlequin Enterprises ULC, operating as Harlequin Reader Service. For a complete summary of the information we collect, how we use this information and to whom it is disclosed, please visit our privacy notice located at corporate.harlequin.com/privacy-notice. From time to time we may also exchange your personal information with reputable third parties. If you wish to opt out of this sharing of your personal information, please visit readerservice.com/consumerschoice or call 1-800-873-8635. **Notice to California Residents**—Under California law, you have specific rights to control and access your data. For more information on these rights and how to exercise them, visit corporate.harlequin.com/california-privacy.

LIRLIS23

Get 3 FREE REWARDS!

We'll send you 2 FREE Books plus a FREE Mystery Gift.

FREE Value Over **$20**

Both the **Harlequin® Special Edition** and **Harlequin® Heartwarming™** series feature compelling novels filled with stories of love and strength where the bonds of friendship, family and community unite.

YES! Please send me 2 FREE novels from the Harlequin Special Edition or Harlequin Heartwarming series and my FREE Gift (gift is worth about $10 retail). After receiving them, if I don't wish to receive any more books, I can return the shipping statement marked "cancel." If I don't cancel, I will receive 6 brand-new Harlequin Special Edition books every month and be billed just $5.49 each in the U.S. or $6.24 each in Canada, a savings of at least 12% off the cover price, or 4 brand-new Harlequin Heartwarming Larger-Print books every month and be billed just $6.24 each in the U.S. or $6.74 each in Canada, a savings of at least 19% off the cover price. It's quite a bargain! Shipping and handling is just 50¢ per book in the U.S. and $1.25 per book in Canada.* I understand that accepting the 2 free books and gift places me under no obligation to buy anything. I can always return a shipment and cancel at any time by calling the number below. The free books and gift are mine to keep no matter what I decide.

Choose one: ☐ **Harlequin Special Edition** (235/335 BPA GRMK)   ☐ **Harlequin Heartwarming Larger-Print** (161/361 BPA GRMK)   ☐ **Or Try Both!** (235/335 & 161/361 BPA GRPZ)

Name (please print)

Address   Apt. #

City   State/Province   Zip/Postal Code

Email: Please check this box ☐ if you would like to receive newsletters and promotional emails from Harlequin Enterprises ULC and its affiliates. You can unsubscribe anytime.

Mail to the Harlequin Reader Service:
IN U.S.A.: P.O. Box 1341, Buffalo, NY 14240-8531
IN CANADA: P.O. Box 603, Fort Erie, Ontario L2A 5X3

Want to try 2 free books from another series! Call 1-800-873-8635 or visit www.ReaderService.com.
